BITBOB - ARTIFICIAL EARTH

First paperback edition February 2024

ISBN 978-1-7385269-2-5 (hardcover)

ISBN 978-1-7385269-0-1 (paperback)

ISBN 978-1-7385269-1-8 (ebook)

www.bitbob.net

BITBOB - ARTIFICIAL EARTH

A. J. BYWATER

To the kind Queens.

Every adventure deserves an epic soundtrack. Choose wisely.

Visit **@bitbob.official** on social to join the conversation.

A.J.Bywater's song choices can be found at http://www.bitbob.net

PROLOGUE

'Are you sure about this, Bacchus? It's a lot of responsibility for such young shoulders.'

The giant Bacchus approached the boy in the yellow raincoat, lying motionless on the white-tiled floor. He respectfully moved the boy's brown curls away from his temple and carefully placed a pad with a wire. Bacchus connected the other end of the wire to a socket in his hand.

'He will be the best of me, Archive. I lost my way, and I paid the price. His innocence will help him see humanity with untainted eyes.'

'He'll be hunted, Bacchus. Once Syntax discovers who he is, he won't stop until he suffers the same fate as you.'

'Then let us hope he finds his strength before Syntax catches up with him.'

'Yes, let us hope.'

'Guide him, Archive. Show him what he can do. Give him some of your knowledge – but not all. Maybe he can discover what I could not.'

'Affirmative. Go in peace, Bacchus.'

'Thank you, old friend.'

Bacchus's muscles tensed. His head tossed back in pain as fizzing electricity shot from his hand and down the wire to the boy, who flopped around like a fish. Pushing through the pain, Bacchus strained his arm forward and gently rested his enormous hand on the boy's head. 'Be the best of me.'

With that, Bacchus dropped to his knees and vanished, existing one moment, gone the next.

Lowering her head, Archive picked up the wire Bacchus had left and connected it to a socket on her arm. 'Sleep now, child. Absorb my knowledge. I will guide you when you wake.'

CHAPTER 1
THE FACTORY

The boy's eyes snapped open.

He was lying face down on a cold, hard, clinical white-tiled floor. His mind was foggy, unable to hold a clear thought. He had no memories before this moment. No names. No faces. Nothing but a fog-filled void.

The fog in his mind kept swirling and swimming. Every time he thought he saw a gap in the fog and a thought clarifying, the fog encased it.

Through the fog, a voice whispered, gradually rising to a shout, louder and louder, deafening his senses. His head pounded as if the words might explode out of his temples and into the air. The voice repeated three words: *You are BOB. You are BOB. You are BOB.*

Bob squeezed his eyes shut, trying to control the voice and the pressure it created. Tears squeezed out, wetting his eyelashes. Just as the voice became so loud he might pass out, it faded from a shout to a whisper. The fog cleared, and he held his breath, as if breathing might invite the chaos to return.

After a short time, he breathed out, forced his eyes open and allowed himself to think about moving. He didn't move for quite some time, but he thought about it, which was a start.

Eventually, heart still pounding and breath still heavy, he

heaved himself up from the tiled floor. His legs protested at the sudden movement, wobbling and stumbling around before regaining stability. Instinctively he reached into the pocket of his bright yellow raincoat to retrieve a blue inhaler. Bob shook it and put it to his mouth, breathed in and pressed down.

The white-tiled floor stretched to the horizon in all directions – at the horizon, the floor and the air above it blurred together in an optical illusion. Nothing broke the flat white landscape.

The air was as bright as the floor, stark and solid white, with no discernible source for the light.

The only thing that wasn't floor was a circular void, edged with a metal rim, impossibly suspended in mid-air above his head. Pacing around the giant vent-like opening, staring into the darkness of the void, Bob spotted tiny dots of light, like pinprick holes in black fabric.

Where am I? And what's this vent thing?

Bob's palms were sweating, fingers flexing and twitching.

'Argh! What do I do now?' he asked aloud.

Surprisingly, he received a response.

'*You must discover who you are,*' a computerised female voice announced, echoing through the empty white space as if coming over a supermarket PA system.

Bob startled, searching for the source of the voice, but nothing discernible appeared in the stark white air.

Turning on his heel, still trying to locate the voice, Bob asked, 'Where are you? I can't see you.'

'*I am everywhere.*'

'Good. Not creepy at all. Who am I? I can't remember anything.'

'*You must discover who you are.*'

'Can't you just tell me?'

'*You must discover who you are.*'

This bizarre conversation with the undetectable voice caused the headache to intensify. 'Will you at least tell me where I am?'

'*You are in the factory.*'

The voice wasn't making any sense. How could he discover who he was if he couldn't remember anything? And what sort of factory was empty?

Bob was lining up to ask how to go about discovering who he was when the voice spoke again.

'*Please wait for your hexpet.*'

'Wait … for my what?'

The vent started squeaking intermittently, like a child coming down a slide that had been in a playground for years and lost its original shine. The intermittent squeak turned into a long squeak, getting louder, until suddenly a little ball of fur fell from the void and landed in Bob's hands. It was tiny, fitting comfortably in one palm. With a slight shiver, the tiny furball slowly unfurled, and a miniature dog peered up at him, tongue lolling.

The dog's fur was bright white. Putting the dog on the tiled floor might have made it disappear, except that one of the dog's ears shimmered a glittering silver. As the ear caught the light, it sent a rainbow across Bob's hands. The same silver glitter coated the tip of a bushy fox-like tail.

The dog wriggled, and through fear of dropping it, Bob popped it down on the floor, where it began pacing in circles, sniffing, as if searching for buried treasure.

'You're a curious thing.' Bob knew very little about dogs, so he didn't know what type of dog this was.

'*Accessing the Archive. Please wait,*' the voice from earlier said.

Suddenly, and without warning, images of dogs flooded Bob's vision, spinning around rapidly as if he stood in the eye of a hurricane that whipped up a collection of dog Polaroids. It was nauseating. The little white dog paused as if frozen in time. Occasionally the odd picture would briefly hesitate in front of Bob before being sucked back into the whirlwind. The pace of the images quickened, faster, faster, until they were almost a blur. Then, all of a sudden, the chaos stopped, and just one image remained, hovering just out of arm's reach.

'Your dog breed cannot be found in the Archive. The closest match is a border collie sheepdog.'

The image showed a proud dog, presumably a border collie, sitting in front of a landscape of rolling fields dotted with sheep. It certainly wasn't anything like the tiny ball of fur with the glittery ear.

Bob stepped forward, being careful not to stand on the little dog. Tentatively he reached out a finger and touched the image. It flipped over, revealing a list of stats with a smaller version of the sheepdog image above the list. Much like a Top Trumps card:

Intelligence: 10
Obedience: 93
Cute factor: 1,000
Coat glossiness: 14
Hexcode: 53 68 65 65 70 20 44 6F 67

'Hexcode?' Bob asked out loud.

'The code required to create a border collie sheepdog,' the voice said.

'The code required to …?'

'Access complete. Returning to the factory. Please wait,' the PA voice announced.

The dog card was sucked back into the hurricane as the images spun, this time in the opposite direction, as if someone had pressed rewind. The images then faded; the nauseating feeling returned; and the tiny white dog unfroze, continuing its pacing and sniffing for treasure. It looked up at Bob, gave a friendly yip, and then sat down, tongue lolling.

Crouching, Bob reached out to stroke the dog's head. The dog accepted the attention and then trotted off to play again, returning intermittently for more attention. The little pup was adorable and a good distraction from worrying about who he was, where he was and what had just happened with the weird dog-picture hurricane.

Bob broke a smile as the dog rolled over after failing to catch its tail. Spotting a red collar hidden under the dog's fur, Bob reached out to inspect a silver tag attached to the collar. The dog obediently sat still to allow the inspection. Engraved on the tag was the word BYTE.

'Byte. Is that your name, little guy?' The small dog responded with an approving yip. 'I'm Bob. Nice to meet you.'

Turning the tag over, Bob saw the words PROTECT THE DOG etched into the metal.

Byte tilted his head to inspect Bob.

'Do you need protecting, Byte? Well, I suppose you are tiny. I'm not sure I'm a protector, though. I've no idea who I am, for a start, or where we are.' Bob sighed, shoulders slumping, as a feeling of hopelessness washed over him. 'I don't suppose you know what to do?'

'*Please make your way to the nearest exit,*' the PA voice answered loudly and suddenly, making Bob jump.

'I wish you'd give me some warning next time!' Bob exclaimed in his best frustrated tone.

'*Affirmative,*' the voice replied.

Bob looked at Byte and shrugged.

'Where's the exit?' Bob mused, gazing into the endless nothing.

'*Please make your way to the nearest exit.*'

'I know! You said that already! But where is it?'

'*Please make your way to the nearest exit.*'

'Where *is* the exit?'

'*Please make your way to the nearest exit.*'

'Well, I guess we'll just have to find it on our own, Byte.'

Byte jumped up excitedly, tail wagging, turning in a circle to do more cute tongue lolling and yipping.

'I'm not sure which way we should go, though,' Bob admitted, trying to suppress mild panic.

Byte yipped and set off across the tiles in a bouncy trot.

'Well, I suppose that's as good a way as any.' Bob shrugged and followed his new companion.

Two of Bob's footsteps were ten for little Byte, so he picked up the dog and popped him in the raincoat pocket. Byte seemed happy with this new plan, poking his head and front paws out of the top of the pocket.

With a new-found determination, standing up straight and pushing the feeling of hopelessness down, Bob continued into the unending white landscape.

To ensure he was heading in a definite direction and not accidentally going diagonally or in a wide circle, Bob decided to follow the straight lines of the tiles. The plan had a fundamental flaw: he didn't know if they were headed towards the 'exit' or away from it, so he avoided thinking about it.

Occasionally Bob glanced to his left and right, hoping to detect objects or signs, but there was nothing but the unending horizon. Bob scratched Byte behind the ear. Despite being terribly lost, at least he had a companion to keep him company.

CHAPTER 2
THE CRISP-EGG-MAYO SANDWICH

Bob had been walking for some time, and the 'vent' was well and truly out of sight.

The never-ending floor gave the disorientating feeling that he wasn't progressing, as if the floor were a treadmill, stopping when he stopped, moving when he moved.

Adding to the disorientation were the constant waves of anxiety that came with not knowing who he was or where he was. The PA voice kept repeating, '*Make your way to the nearest exit.*' However, the idea of an exit being near, anywhere in this weird factory landscape, seemed ridiculous.

As he contemplated their situation, a lump formed in Bob's throat. His palms started sweating, and his breathing became erratic. Byte yipped excitedly from the raincoat pocket, nuzzling Bob's side. The affection and another puff on the blue inhaler calmed him. The pattern of rising inner turmoil and comfort from Byte continued as they walked.

'This factory is maddening,' Bob said to Byte, receiving a friendly yip in response. He had stopped momentarily to rest his weary feet and attempt to bury an overriding feeling of despair. 'Well, this is getting very frustrating and tiring. What I wouldn't give for a drink and something to eat.'

A series of bongs chimed, and the PA voice returned. '*Affirma-tive. Please wait.*' The bongs sounded again, this time in descending tones.

Bob was startled by a clattering sound behind him. He turned around just as a plate and a camping canteen settled on the floor as if placed with some annoyance by an invisible hand. The canteen wobbled, threatening to topple over, before settling upright.

Bob crouched to inspect the elaborate blue-and-white Wedg-wood-design plate. On the plate was a sandwich neatly cut into triangles and some crisps, loose out of their packet. Bob picked up one of the sandwich triangles to discover it was egg mayon-naise and cress, his favourite. He crunched a crisp, salt and vine-gar, also his favourite.

Bob began devouring the sandwich hungrily, putting some crisps into the second triangle to create a crisp-egg-mayo sand-wich. His feasting was interrupted by a soft whimper from the raincoat pocket. Bob felt a pang of guilt. Here he was, practically inhaling food, not thinking Byte might also be hungry.

Bob put down the remains of the crisp-egg-mayo sandwich, then fished Byte out of the raincoat and popped him down next to the plate. 'Sorry. Have some if you want. Go ahead.'

Byte sniffed the crisp-egg-mayo sandwich and took a step back, clearly unimpressed.

Bob decided to get a drink for Byte instead and reached for the camping canteen. Unscrewing the lid, he put his nose to the rim and sniffed. There was no noticeable scent. Peering inside, he saw only a clear liquid. Cautiously he took a sip. *Water! Thank goodness.* After taking a few gulps, Bob poured a small amount onto the floor near Byte, who eagerly lapped it up.

After the success of the sandwich and crisps, Bob was curious about what else the PA lady could conjure. The nauseating memory of the dog pictures prevented him from making a long food order, including a burger, chips and a milkshake. He didn't fancy doing that again anytime soon. But as he looked down at the small ball of fur still lapping up the water on the tile, the guilt returned. He should really get something for Byte to eat.

Bob sucked a breath through his teeth, trying to muster up some bravery, then tentatively asked, 'Please may I have a bowl of dog food?' Bob immediately reeled, half-closing his eyes in anticipation of something terrible happening. Instead, the bongs chimed, followed by an *'Affirmative.'* The bongs then chimed in descending tones.

Out of thin air, a metal dog bowl filled with dog food faded into existence a centimetre above the floor and clanged onto the tiles. Byte's head lifted excitedly from the water; then he trotted to the dog bowl. It was an average-sized dog bowl, but it looked enormous next to Byte, or rather, Byte looked tiny next to it. After several failed attempts by Byte to scramble up the side of the bowl, Bob took pity and emptied some of the food onto the floor. Without hesitation, Byte tucked into his feast.

Smiling affectionately, satisfied he'd managed to care for Byte, Bob picked up the last crisp-egg-mayo sandwich triangle.

————

Sometime later, Bob was very full. After cautious requests for toast, cereal and chocolate, he had thrown caution to the wind and requested an entire feast. Burgers, fries, pizza, steak, trifle and apple pie were all scattered on the floor in various half-eaten states. Byte was equally full, lying on his side, thoroughly content. The bizarre day had been exhausting.

Wait, has it been a day? It certainly feels like it.

Yawning, Bob curled up on the floor in a gap among the plates, and his eyes started to close. Working out who he was and where he was would have to wait until he'd had a nap. Byte nuzzled into Bob's chest, and in no time at all, they were both fast asleep.

––––––

'What's going on? What's that racket?'

Bob woke with a start. A noise like an air-raid siren filled the air. It was far darker than before he'd fallen asleep, dim and grey, like the period just before sunrise, neither night nor day.

Where is Byte?

Bob frantically searched for his new friend and spotted him among the remnants of a Black Forest gateau, bolt upright and whimpering. Relieved he knew where Byte was, Bob scanned around for any danger that might match the ominous siren.

The dim grey light made it hard to see. It was as if the whole area were out of focus. *What's that over there?* Red lights bobbed far off in the distance.

As Bob strained to see, he stepped forward and stood on a plate with two leftover pizza slices. The plate clattered, making Bob jump, curse and look down. When he looked back up, the lights appeared closer.

Squinting, he could make out six lights. *And what is that noise?* Not the siren, which was still going, but a scraping noise, like fingernails down a chalkboard, or maybe more like metal down a chalkboard. The siren was very distracting.

'Please stop the siren!' Bob shouted.

Following the usual bongs and an '*Affirmative,*' the siren stopped.

The metallic scraping noise was clear now. It was multiple scraping noises overlapping, and the lights were even closer. Yes, there were six lights. *No, wait. Three pairs – eyes!* Behind each pair of eyes was a looming, shadowy mass. Bob felt a foreboding feeling in his gut.

'Turn the lights up!' Bob said in a panic.

Bong-bong-bing.

'*Affirmative.*'

Bing-bong-bong.

The air became as bright as before he'd slept, and Bob spotted the danger. Still far away on the horizon, but close enough to make out, were three red-eyed metal monsters. The scraping noises were claws on the tiles as the red-eyed beasts ran on all fours towards him.

Run. Run, you idiot.

Move.

Now.

'Run!'

Bob turned and simultaneously picked up Byte, who he dropped into the raincoat pocket. Then he ran.

Bob tried to run faster than his legs would carry him, so he kept stumbling. The tatty high-top trainers had frayed laces that affected his running gait as he tried to avoid tripping on the aglet of the left lace, which clicked on the floor in front of his right foot every time around.

The stumble-run was made more difficult because he kept turning to look over his shoulder at the oncoming eyes. During one glance, Bob saw long metal-shard 'teeth' in a metal snout. The beasts were closing at pace. The serrated claws continued their relentless, terrifying scraping.

These beasts appeared to be made entirely of metal that jutted from their hides, rusty and deformed, as if one of those giant magnets in a scrapyard had picked up random scrap metal and formed it into – *Wolves!* Three terrifying, red-eyed metal wolves.

Bob's fear level rose to a crescendo. Trying to run faster, he gently gripped the outside of the raincoat pocket to ensure Byte didn't fly out onto the floor.

'Where's the exit? Please, please! I need directions!'

Bong-bong-bing.

'*Affirmative. Showing directions to the nearest exit. Please wait.*'

Bing-bong-bong.

Neon signs stuck to poles suddenly materialised, embedded

in the tiles. Each had the word EXIT and an arrow illuminated in flashing neon pink.

The signs stretched out before him; they all pointed into the distance. 'This is hopeless! We aren't going to make it! There isn't enough time!' Bob cried as he turned again to see the metal beasts closing in, now only one football pitch length away.

Suddenly Bob had an idea. 'A wall! Please create a massive wall behind me!'

Bong-bong-bing.

'And stop with the binging bongs!'

'*Affirmative. Building a wall,*' the PA lady said, without the sense of urgency Bob would have liked and without the ending bongs.

It worked. A wall that stretched the width of a football pitch and was ten feet high appeared between Bob and the wolves.

'Yes!' Bob declared victoriously but very wheezily. Seizing the opportunity to breathe, Bob slowed his run to a jog and fished out the blue inhaler from underneath Byte.

Slowing to a stop, Bob took a puff of his inhaler. As he breathed in, one of the gnarled metal wolves appeared around the end of the wall to his right. Another wolf appeared around the left end. There was a scrambling sound, and the third wolf appeared at the top of the wall. This wolf had a black mane and was far larger than the others. It glared at Bob, making a grating electronic snarling sound. Lifting its head to the sky, the black-maned wolf let out the most dreadful howl. The howl had the same grating electronic edge but was so loud it hurt Bob's ears.

'Argh!' Bob shouted, covering his ears to try to muffle the noise.

The howling stopped as the black-maned alpha wolf jumped ten feet off the wall and landed with more grace than expected, given its massive hulk. Stalking towards Bob, the left and right wolves made a beeline for the alpha wolf, joining the hunt.

Frozen on the spot, Bob breathed heavily, chest heaving. His life would have flashed before his eyes were it not for the fact that his only memories consisted of walking and eating.

'Move, you idiot! Move!' His feet remained rooted to the ground.

'*Yip, yip, yip!*' Byte jumped from the raincoat pocket onto the floor, growling at the approaching wolves, now no more than a basketball court away.

'Byte! No!' Bob's concern for the dog broke his frozen state. Picking up the brave little guard dog, Bob turned on his heel and made one last-ditch dash.

'Nice PA lady! We need an exit! Now!'

'*Affirmative. Please wait,*' came the reply.

'I can't wait!'

The overlapping scraping of claws on tiles grew louder and louder as the gnarled metal beasts closed in. Byte was cradled in Bob's arms and still growling at the pursuers. Bob risked a glance. The alpha wolf was just in front of the others, jaws grinding and gnashing in anticipation of the boy they were about to devour.

'Now! I need an exit now! No, no. I'm going to die. I've failed to protect Byte!'

Bob's left lace aglet finally caught under his right heel. He tripped and fell. The sudden shock created the illusion of falling in slow motion, his body twisting, and he landed on his back and then skidded a short distance across the tiles before stopping.

Horror-struck, Bob could only stare as the three metal beasts, with their glowing red eyes, leaped into the air to close the short distance between him and them.

The wolves plunged towards Bob and his tiny dog with jaws open and terrible claws forward.

Bob curled up, bracing for the impact, covering his face with his arm.

'*Exit confirmed.*'

Suddenly the tiled floor directly underneath Bob dropped to

a slant, and still clutching Byte, Bob slid under and away, narrowly escaping the black-maned wolf as it landed in the spot that Bob had occupied only a whisper of a moment earlier.

The wolf was too large to slide down. It scrambled, trying to stand upright, its underbelly blocking what was now an opening in the floor.

CHAPTER 3
THE BARN

Bob and Byte shot through the air and landed softly on a bed of straw. Bob turned urgently, rustling the straw, and looked up anxiously for any sign that the red-eyed metal monsters were following them.

He stared into a metal-rimmed vent in a wooden roof, similar to the vent hanging above the white-tiled floor. A hinged wooden door suddenly slammed shut over the opening with enough force to eject a cloud of dust.

Bob sneezed, blinked away the dust and turned to study his new environment. They were in a long, thin wooden barn constructed from rustic old timber and new, paler boards where somebody must have replaced sections as the wood had weathered. Sunlight beamed through gaps in the wooden roof, creating light columns that stretched down to a thick carpet of sawdust covering the floor. At the end of the building were barn doors, braced closed with a wooden beam, and on the walls of the longer sides of the barn were full-length mirrors edged with ornate gold frames. Eight in total, four on each wall. They looked entirely out of place against the rustic backdrop.

'Where am I?'

The PA voice didn't reply. Bob hugged himself despite the

warm, stuffy air. He wanted to run away as fast and as far as possible. But there was nowhere to run to. Well, one thing he'd certainly discovered about himself: he was a coward.

'Am I safe?' he asked.

No response came. She must only be in the tiled space. Strangely, he'd found comfort in the PA voice. Her absence added to a feeling of apprehension.

Bob shifted his attention from emotional turmoil to wading through the straw-filled trough, clearly placed there to break the fall of whoever shot out of the vent. On the wall immediately behind the trough were shelves containing fresh flowers in small clay vases. Bob sniffed at a bright purple flower in a vase decorated with blue and white wavy lines. It reminded him of early spring. Also on the shelves were bracelets of wooden beads and simple straw dolls.

Byte wriggled out of Bob's arms and gracefully jumped onto one of the raised sides of the trough, then hopped onto the floor and disappeared out of sight.

Bob made a far less graceful exit, wriggling and falling towards the edge as if swimming through a plastic-ball pit. After falling down two small steps, he picked himself up and dusted pieces of straw and sawdust off his clothes.

'I wish I had your gymnastic skills, Byte.'

Byte was already busy exploring the rest of the barn, cocking his head at his reflection before trotting to the next mirror along the wall and repeating the pose.

Bob had no intention of looking in a mirror, so he put his head down and marched towards the barn doors. As he passed the last mirror, curiosity got the better of him. When he glanced at his reflection and saw the oversized yellow raincoat and thin dark jeans with holes at the knees, Bob couldn't shake the realisation he was entirely unremarkable and ordinary. He quickly averted his gaze, eyes shooting back to the sawdust-lined floor, and hurried towards the doors.

Byte sat inspecting the double doors.

'What do you think, Byte? Do we open them or stay in here for a while?' It was a rhetorical question. Bob wanted to stay in the relative safety of the barn.

'*Yip, yip!*' Byte pawed at the door and made his feelings known.

'Okay, but if it's just a tiled floor and metal demon creatures, I'm closing it again.'

Byte peered up at Bob with a look that meant, *I don't care. Open it.*

Bob inspected the large, thick wooden beam bracing the door. Why was the door braced? No one else was inside the building, and these were the only doors. He thought it best not to think about it as he put both hands under the beam and braced to lift, convinced his feeble frame wouldn't be up to the task. Bob heaved. Miraculously, the beam lifted easily. Looking up, Bob spotted a curious system of pulleys and weights concealed behind a wooden pelmet. The beam eventually left his hands, rising on its own into the pelmet.

'Ready, Byte?' Bob asked, placing a hand on each door.

'*Yip!*' came the reply.

Following one last sullen glance at the mirror he'd caught his reflection in, Bob pushed open the barn doors.

———

Bob stepped out of the barn and into a breathtaking glade of tall, leafy trees, pockets of colourful flowers and a carpet of dew-covered grass. The sky was a brilliant blue, with only a few wisps of white cloud, and the air was thick with the sweet fragrance of spring. It was truly idyllic and a compelling contrast to the stark, white-tiled, endless nothing. It was Eden. This particular analogy popped into his head for a reason, as in the middle of the glade, waving at him, was a naked man and a naked woman.

They were naked, but at the same time, they were not. Where

Bob should have been able to see everything nature had gifted them, there was a blur. Their skin wasn't blurry; it was as if the very air surrounding them censored their nakedness. Bob was gawping at the two figures, unable to tear his eyes away.

The naked couple walked towards the barn, waving enthusiastically like parents picking up their child from the first day of school. As they moved, the blur moved with them, maintaining their modesty. Just as Bob thought a sudden movement might expose them, the blur kept up with the motion.

Bob instinctively rocked on his heels as the couple drew closer, debating whether to flee back into the barn, but it was too late. The couple stepped up to him.

The man and woman were of similar height. Both had pale ivory skin, blonde hair and blue eyes. The man was handsome, with a lean figure and a sheepish, shy expression. He carried a simple cloth bag.

Bob didn't pay the man too much attention – he was far too busy staring at the beautiful woman. Her hair curled around her shoulders, and freckles peppered her nose and cheeks. But her true beauty lay in her smile, which was like a breath of spring. Bob decided it was her smile lighting up the glade, not the spring sunshine. He uncontrollably grinned, tense shoulders relaxing.

'Well, ain't you a sight for sore eyes!' the woman exclaimed. 'Ain't he? Ain't he a sight for sore eyes?' She elbowed the man, who nodded in agreement. 'A boy, Deck! A boy!' She pursed her lips as she examined Bob. 'Or a really small man. What do you reckon, Deck? A small man or a boy?'

Her companion shrugged.

'I reckon a boy, which is excitin'! There ain't never been a boy gift before!' She studied Bob again. 'You are a boy, right?'

Bob was about to answer, but then Byte, who'd been hiding behind Bob's leg, came out and made himself known. '*Yip!*'

The woman jumped back a little, then crouched down to inspect Byte. 'Oh, my days! Is that a ...? Nooo, it can't be. Is it …?' Stopping her sentence short, she stood back up, eyes wide. 'Should I bow or somethin', Deck? Wait a minute. If that's what I think it is, this ain't no ordinary boy!' She elbowed her companion again. 'You know what that means, don't ya?'

The man shrugged.

'Well, I'm not sure what it means either. But the Queen'll know!' She danced excitedly, blurs moving in ways that made Bob think he should look away. He didn't.

Byte joined in the excited dance, bouncing around Bob's legs.

The woman stopped dancing and tried to regain some composure. 'Where are my manners? Here's me doin' a load of talkin', and I ain't even introduced myself! I'm Sunny, and this here's Deck.' She elbowed her companion and then held out her hand.

Bob tentatively raised his hand, and Sunny grabbed it, shaking it enthusiastically.

'Now we need to work out what your name's gonna be. Ain't that excitin'! I remember when I had my namin' ceremony, it was great! You're gonna love it! I reckon yours will be somethin' special. I'm sure the Queen'll already have somethin' picked out—'

Sunny didn't pause for breath, so Bob interrupted her.

'B-b-but I already have a name. My name's Bob, and this –' Bob pointed at Byte, who sat with tongue lolling – 'is Byte.'

Sunny and Deck took a sharp breath, shock and disbelief written all over their faces. They glanced at one another, then back at Bob.

'B-b-but you can't have a name yet! That ain't how it works!' Sunny spluttered.

Deck, who hadn't managed to get a single word in yet, took his opportunity whilst Sunny shook her head in disbelief. 'Maybe this is different, Sunny. He's got a hexpet, after all.' Deck spoke in a much slower and more thoughtful tone.

'But his eyes, Deck. They're human eyes, for sure. They're

brown instead of blue, but they must be human, right?' Sunny paused, inspecting Bob closely.

Bob's cheeks flushed as the beautiful woman looked him up and down.

Deck raised a finger, mouth half-open, ready to answer Sunny's question, but she cut him off just before he spoke.

'Well, whatever you are, my lovely, you're part of our family now, and you're very much welcome! We're here to escort you back to the Town to meet the Queen.' Sunny stood to attention, pointing between herself and Deck. 'It's a special tradition, and the Queen chose me and my best friend Deck to do it! How great's that?'

As Sunny took a breath, Bob seized the opportunity to ask a question, in case it helped discover who he was. 'What did you mean when you said I was different? Different from what, from who?'

'Oh, well, just, er … just different. You ain't like anyone who's come out of there before.' Sunny pointed over Bob's shoulder at the barn. 'But don't you worry about that, my lovely. You're one of us now, and the Queen'll know what to do.'

Bob didn't know what to make of any of this. Meeting a queen sounded like a terrifying thing to do. Then he thought back to his shabby reflection. Could he meet a queen dressed like this? On the other hand, if the Queen was used to Sunny and Deck, then simply having clothes on would probably do.

'We'd better go,' said Deck. 'It's a long walk to the Town, and we'll need to spend the night at the Lookout. We'd better get going if we want to reach the Lookout by nightfall.'

'Quite right!' said Sunny. 'You're the smart one, Deck. Let's get goin'!' She clapped her hands enthusiastically and turned to leave. 'Come on, then, Bob, my darlin' boy! Don't forget your little friend!'

Bob picked up Byte and popped him in the raincoat pocket. *Should I go with the weird naked people? Do I have a choice? Discov-*

ering who I am seems more likely if I travel to a town rather than hide in a barn. Maybe someone there knows me.

Like a stronger magnet, the desire to discover who he was pulled him forward more than the safety of the barn pulled him back. Bob willed himself towards Sunny and Deck, setting off walking out of the glade.

CHAPTER 4
THE LOOKOUT

The beauty of the glade repeated throughout the rest of the places they walked through on the journey to the Lookout. Set against a backdrop of gently rolling hills carpeted with cattle-filled fields were babbling streams teeming with fish and orchards ripe with red and green apples. They stopped to pick some of the low-hanging fruit and ate the apples as they walked.

Sunny and Deck had no shoes, but they didn't need them. Soft, leafy pathways carpeted the route, though none appeared artificial, as if nature had laid out a safe passage just for them.

As they walked, Deck and Sunny constantly talked with one another. Sunny did most of the talking; therefore, Deck did most of the listening. There was the odd gentle push as one laughed at something the other said, a soft touch on an arm or shoulder. On several occasions, Bob noticed their eyes meeting, and they would pause, just looking at each other for a moment or two longer than friends should, before seamlessly continuing their conversation.

Sunny would often turn to ask, 'Are you all right back there, darlin'?'

Bob would nod.

He wasn't all right. He was worrying. Worrying that the

metal beasts would find him. Worrying that the PA voice didn't work. Worrying about the responsibility of protecting Byte. Never mind all the worrying about who he was and where he was. But he didn't want to vocalise all this to Sunny. So he just nodded.

To take his mind off things, Bob passed the time taking in the scenery, stroking Byte, who nestled happily in his pocket, and when he thought Deck and Sunny wouldn't notice, he stared at the blurring surrounding their nakedness. The blurs felt unnatural and so out of place with their surroundings. And Bob paid them too much attention.

They stopped to drink water from a stream and eat some sweet, stiff bread, which Deck called 'pop bread' due to its popularity in the Town. It was this that Deck carried in his bag.

Bob took off his raincoat and sat on it like a picnic blanket whilst Byte played under the shade of a weeping willow, sniffing at the ground for buried treasure.

Sunny told stories about the townsfolk, particularly the Queen, whom Sunny and Deck held in very high regard.

'She's amazin'! Such poise and grace! But it don't get to her head; she remains humble, fair and true. A real leader. You're gonna love her. I'm sure she'll love you too.'

Deck nodded in agreement, his mouth full of pop bread.

Bob thought he detected a hint of uncertainty in that last comment. Byte, now polishing off his own piece of pop bread, cocked his head and lolled his tongue at Bob reassuringly.

Deck started packing up. 'Come on. If we hurry, we'll get to the Lookout before sundown. If we don't, we'll be stuck next to the stream.'

'You're the smart one, Deck. You lead on!' Sunny declared, standing up.

Sunny then proceeded to lead the way.

'Don't let what she says fool you.' Deck leaned into Bob conspiratorially. 'She's the smart one.'

Sunny picked up Byte and held him close to her chest. Byte

merged with the blur – not blurring himself, but rather appearing to be sitting on a blurry cushion. Bob didn't know how he felt about someone else picking up Byte. It left a lump in his throat, but the little guy seemed okay with it.

Bob helped Deck put the last pieces of bread into the bag, then picked up his raincoat and put it over his arms as they walked a few paces behind Sunny and Byte.

Bob tried to spark up a conversation with the reserved Deck. 'You guys look happy together.' He nodded towards Sunny.

'Yeah, we're good friends. Best friends. That's all, though,' Deck spluttered, going bright red.

'Okay. Are you sure?'

'Honestly, just friends …' Deck trailed off, suddenly lost in thought.

They walked in silence for a short while, Deck frowning, still pondering something.

Sunny and Byte were in sight but a good way ahead. Sunny was telling Byte a story of some sort, with plenty of gesticulation and laughter, but Bob couldn't catch all the words from this distance.

Finally Deck picked the conversation back up. 'So, are you looking forward to meeting everyone? I bet you're excited to be joining the Zoo.'

'The Zoo?'

'This is the Zoo.' Deck swept his arm around in an arc. 'It's paradise!'

Bob looked around as if pretending to take in his surroundings for the first time.

'You –' Deck pointed at Bob – 'came to us as a gift, so you get to enjoy the Zoo along with every other gift.'

Bob scrunched up his nose. 'Gift?'

'When you arrived back there. That's how we all got here.' Deck thumbed over his shoulder towards the barn.

'You mean you all came from the place with the tiled floor and the metal creatures?'

Deck stopped dead in his tracks. 'What? No. I don't remember any of that.' He shook his head and started walking again. 'All I remember is landing in the straw, looking at myself in the mirror for the first time, then opening the doors to this place. Two townsfolk greeted me, and I made this same journey you are on, back to the Town.

'I was one of the two that came to meet Sunny.' Deck pushed out his chest, his expression suddenly distant, recalling the memory. 'That smile when she opened the door ...' He shook himself, realising he was vocalising his thoughts.

They had another period of walking in silence until Bob plucked up the courage to ask Deck the question he'd wanted to ask since meeting them in the glade. 'Your ... ahem, your blurs ...'

'Oh, these?' Deck waved his hand through the blur to his front. The blur didn't distort, and his hand remained unblurred as it moved through. 'This is a filter. Everyone has one – or two!' He winked and nudged Bob gently. 'You'll probably have a filter if you remove your clothes.'

Bob winced at the idea.

'It's okay. You don't have to do anything you're not comfortable with. It's more that clothes don't matter here. It's never too cold or warm, and no one sees anything they shouldn't, because of the filters.' Deck repeated the motion of running his hand through the filter.

'But what *is* it? Are you able to control the filter, turn it off and on?'

'No. They're always there from the day you land in the barn. It's perfectly normal. Every human has a filter. Didn't you know?'

'No. Sorry. It's new to me. But don't you want to wear clothes as a personal thing, to have a style?' Bob gestured at his stripy jumper and worn jeans, then decided his tatty clothes, likely out of the bargain bin in a charity shop, probably weren't helping his point.

'No,' said Deck after considering the question. 'We're sort of traditional, I guess. True to the humans from the Archive.'

The Archive! The PA lady had mentioned the Archive when the dog pictures had bombarded him.

Reading Bob's confused face, Deck volunteered an explanation. 'It's some sort of record of humans from waaay back in the past.' Deck made a sweeping motion with his arm to exaggerate the point of how far back it was. 'The Librarian tells us what we need to know. He's the town's Archive "expert".' Deck used his fingers to put quotations around the word.

Sunny and Byte stopped at the edge of a hill and were gazing across a valley, so Deck and Bob cut short their conversation and jogged to join them.

'The Lookout.' Deck pointed to the hilltop on the valley's opposite side. On the crest of the hill was a squat wooden tower with a circular platform and steps sweeping up on one side, built in the same mix of old and new wood as the barn.

'Good timin' as well. It'll get dark soon,' Sunny added, smiling away.

They all headed off down the hill, with Sunny falling into the previous routine of telling Deck a story, asking him a question, and then answering the question herself before Deck could speak.

Byte was perched on Sunny's shoulder and nestled into her neck. The position looked precarious, but somehow he kept himself in place.

Bob smiled. He was still confused and disorientated from the day's events, but it was hard not to feel some comfort in such a fantastic place and with the friendliest people he'd ever met. Actually, these might be the only people he'd ever met.

———

They arrived at the Lookout as the sun drifted over the horizon.

At the base of the tower was a clearing with a circle of stones containing ash and charred wood. A couple of halved tree trunks, a few paces from the fire, acted as benches. Sunny picked up some sticks and logs from a nearby pile and started making a fire.

'We stopped here on the way to get you.' Deck pointed at the remnants of the fire as he placed his bag behind one of the benches.

Once the sun had set, and with the crackling fire casting dancing shadows on their faces, Sunny told a story of the Town's baker. The baker had intentionally overcooked small balls of dough and then baked them in some pop bread for the Librarian. The Librarian had bitten into the bread and discovered the darker brown balls baked through. The baker had declared these were rabbit droppings, a new recipe he had been trying out, called 'poop bread'.

Sunny laughed so hard at her own story she struggled to get the words out. 'Then ... ha ha ha ... then he leaps up out of his chair, and he's an old man, mind – he ain't supposed to move fast – and he makes straight for the baker, wavin' his walkin' stick at the poor man! Ha ha ha ... ha ... ha ha ha! He chased him the full length of town! Paa haa!'

Sunny fell backwards over the bench, unable to contain herself. Deck jumped up quickly to help her, wiping laughter tears from his cheeks. Bob had that headache at the back of his head that came from laughing too much.

After pulling Sunny back onto the bench, Deck exchanged another longer-than-it-should-be look with Sunny before they settled back down next to each other. Quite close, thought Bob, given the length of the bench.

'Give us a song, Sunny,' said Deck. 'She's an amazing singer, Bob.'

'Oh, I don't know, Deck.' Sunny blushed.

'Go on, please. For me.'

'Oh, go on, then. For you.' Sunny smiled coyly. 'This one's my favourite.'

She stood and pulled a deep breath into her lungs.

My friends are in my heart;
My heart is with my friends.
I love and laugh and smile and sing,
Because my friends are everything.

If I die, and all is lost,
My life has been so full,
That my loss cannot be felt,
Because my friends are everything.

She really was a beautiful singer. Listening to her was like being transported into a dream, and Bob's consciousness floated away, a sense of calm washing over him.

'It ain't the same since the music stopped. It don't have the same feelin' somehow,' Sunny said longingly.

'Since the music stopped?' Bob asked.

'Yeah. There was some music we could play from the Archive. What I sang was somethin' I made up to go with some Archive music, but it stopped over a year ago. The Librarian says that it ain't worked since.'

'*Accessing the Archive. Please wait,*' came the familiar PA voice.

Where had she been all this time?

The nauseating feeling returned, and Deck, Sunny and Byte were motionless, frozen. Sunny, halfway through her explanation of the Archive music. Deck, attentively listening, eyes fixed on her. Byte, curled up in a ball, asleep – so actually, Bob had no idea if he was frozen.

'I thought you weren't here! Why didn't you answer my questions earlier?'

No answer came, just a whirlwind of images spinning in their dance. Some images paused briefly in front of Bob. This time, they were music album covers.

The whirlwind settled, and one image remained. Bob took a

step forward and touched it. The image flipped over, and Bob saw a list of songs. He chose the song that best suited the evening with his new friends.

'*Access complete. Returning to the Zoo. Please wait.*'

The whirlwind reversed, and his friends became animated again. Sunny leaped to her feet, took a deep breath and held it, stunned into silence.

Deck stared into the sky, awestruck.

Even Byte unfurled slightly and raised his head.

Bob's chosen song: *Sunny*, played from every direction, as if playing through the air itself. The music suited the mood of the campfire, laughter and friendship, perfectly.

Sunny's expression slowly transformed from shock to a joyful outpouring of emotion as she wandered around the campfire, laughing, sighing, raising her arms to the heavens and covering her mouth in disbelief. She walked over towards Bob and gently clasped his head with her hands, her eyes filled with tears. 'You did this, didn't you, my darlin' boy?'

'I think so, yes,' Bob replied.

'Thank you.' She kissed his forehead, then sat back down next to Deck, held his hand, and they all listened in silence to the music.

When the song finished, Sunny turned to Bob. 'Can you play another?'

'I'm not sure. It's the first time I've played music. I'll try again if you'd like.'

Sunny nodded fervently. 'Yes, please!'

'Please play some more music,' Bob said.

Silence. No voice came.

'PA voice lady? Please play some more music!'

No response. *Please, come on – I want to do this for Sunny.* She'd been so overwhelmed by the music.

Bob asked again. Again, no response.

'Argh!' Bob slumped down. 'Sorry, I don't know how to do it again. I'm trying.'

'It's okay, my darlin' boy. What you just did was very special, and I'm thankful for that.' Sunny smiled at him soothingly.

'How about we try and get some sleep?' said Deck. 'It's getting late, and we have more walking to do in the morning.'

'You're a very clever man, Deck,' said Sunny, placing a hand on his arm. 'Thank you for such a lovely evenin'. I'm a lucky woman to have such wonderful friends.' She beamed at both of them.

They all got comfy making nests for themselves against the benches. Byte curled into a nook against Bob's chest.

Just as Bob's eyes started to close, there was a terrible buzzing noise, like the sound of an insect, but incredibly loud, as if the insect were plugged into an amplifier at a rock concert.

The friends jumped to their feet. The noise was impossible to pinpoint as it moved across the campsite. Sunny, Deck, and Bob were covering their ears and scanning the sky in a half-crouch pose. Byte was running from bench to bench, following the noise and growling at it.

Bob finally caught sight of the source of the buzzing: a red light darted over their heads. It moved quickly and erratically, pausing and hovering occasionally before zipping back into a frenetic pattern. The light was attached to a flying insect-like body with three sections, like a wasp. The creature was the size of two of Bob's fists and made of sharp metal shards – the same rusted, jagged metal as the wolves. The wasp's metal stinger jutted out like a large hypodermic needle.

Bob felt a sudden pang of terror. The further they had travelled from the barn, the further the metal wolves had gone down his worry list. Now he'd a new addition for that list.

The metal wasp continued its frenetic pattern in the air and then suddenly stopped, hovering high above the embers of last night's fire. Then – it attacked. It dived straight at Bob, stinger first, like a terrible dart.

Bob dived to his left. The stinger drove down just where his body had been a heartbeat ago. One of the metal shards on the creature's back scraped Bob's shin.

The red-eyed wasp deftly skimmed the ground, flew between the two benches and rose as gracefully as a Spitfire, ready to attack again.

'Run, Bob!' Deck shouted over the intense buzzing.

But Bob couldn't run. His shin was hot with pain as blood started to stain his jeans. He held on to his shin, trying to shuffle backwards as a precursor to standing, but the wasp had already reached the apex of its ascent and was readying the stinger for another dive. Bob stared helplessly from his supine position on the ground.

Byte jumped onto Bob's chest and started yapping defiantly at the wasp. 'Byte, no!' Bob lifted the dog off his chest and onto the ground to save him from the attack as the wasp dived with frightening speed.

Bob braced for impact, all his muscles tensed, and he held his breath. The buzzing rose to a deafening crescendo as the wasp closed in.

THWACK!

The wasp, a hair's breadth from Bob's face, was knocked off course, and it smashed into the ground only an arm's length from where Bob lay. Deck stood behind Bob, a thick, half-charred branch from last night's fire in his hands.

The stinger hit the ground with an audible thud, and the ground rippled from the centre of the impact. As the ground rippled, Bob saw a hexagonal mesh that appeared backlit. The mesh rode the rippling wave before fading.

The buzzing noise stopped, but the creature was still moving, mechanically twisting its body and legs to gain purchase on the ground. It started to push itself up, freeing the stinger from the earth, the buzzing noise starting again.

THWACK!

Deck's second swing of the branch hit home with a crunch. The red eyes on the creature faded.

THWACK!

Not wanting to take any chances, Deck hit the metal wasp for a third time, breaking it in two. He dropped the branch, shaking, and stared at the wasp in disbelief, breathing heavily.

Byte jumped back onto Bob's chest and nuzzled at his neck as Sunny dropped to her knees, putting her hand on Bob's head and looking with concern from the wasp to Bob's leg and back again. 'You poor darlin' boy. You're hurt! You poor thing.'

'It's not too bad,' said Bob. He was trying to be brave when really he was having an internal meltdown. Maybe the wolves were only a few paces behind.

'You saved him, Deck,' said Sunny, smiling appreciatively. 'You're a hero! You were fearless!'

Bob turned to Deck. 'You did save me. Thank you.'

Deck shrugged and rubbed the back of his head. 'I didn't do anything special. I thought I'd whack it, that's all.'

———

No one slept. The cut on Bob's shin wasn't too bad. The bleeding waned. It stung like mad and felt warm, but Sunny managed to clean it up with water and bandage it using strips from a strap on Deck's cloth bag. Sunny explained that she was the town nurse, and Bob thought his leg felt much better once she had tended to it. She promised to put some ointment on the wound and bandage it properly when they arrived in the Town.

Sunny and Deck agreed the Queen would want to see the metal creature, so they carefully pushed its corpse into the bag using a stick. Some of the metal went through the bag, forcing Deck to hold it out to the side to avoid getting cut. It also meant they ate what they could of the pop bread, leaving the rest behind.

By the time they had patched up Bob and packed up, the sun had finished rising on another beautiful day in the Zoo.

CHAPTER 5
THE TOWN

The walk to the Town took most of the morning. It was slow going because of Bob's slight limp and Deck awkwardly carrying the bag with the wasp. The conversation was strained on account of them still recovering from the shock of the evening's events. Only Byte appeared unfazed, having resumed his position in the raincoat pocket, staring out happily.

Bob discovered that the wasp creature wasn't something Sunny or Deck had encountered before, but they knew it was a hexbeast from fireside stories. Bob chose not to tell them about the hexbeast wolves, fearing the wasp and the wolves came from the same place, and he had let them in.

As they walked, Bob tried to talk to the PA voice, to no avail.

'That ain't how you get things from the Archive, silly,' Sunny said once she'd asked why Bob was talking to himself. 'You tell the Librarian what you need, and he finds it. Or not, depending on what sort of mood he's in.'

Bob couldn't make sense of it all. The PA lady had spoken when accessing the music. He hadn't needed the Librarian. After giving it some thought, Bob realised he hadn't *asked* the PA lady for the music or the dog pictures. They had both just happened. Yet more mysteries to worry about.

They emerged from a wood atop a small hill, where round wooden buildings with bright canvas roofs nestled in a crop of gently sweeping hills and valleys. Each roof was a different colour; some were several colours, making the overall effect like a patchwork rainbow across the hillsides.

'Welcome to the Town!' Sunny declared, raising her hands, victorious, and she let out a sigh of relief. 'We can relax now. Ain't nothing dangerous comin' here.'

Deck led them down the hill towards a bridge that crossed a stream. Once across the stream, they followed a path lined with stones, passing several unoccupied houses, all single-storey with a chimney, curved wooden walls, and glassless windows on either side of a doorway. A canvas, corresponding to the colour of the roof, acted as a door, gently fluttering in the breeze.

Each house had a small fenced garden filled with neat rows of flowers and vegetables, and a wooden signpost attached to the fence adjoining the path.

As they passed the houses, Bob's face started to show increasing confusion as he read the words carved into each sign.

The first read *Chip Butty*.

The second: *Filing Cabinet*.

The third: *Lawn Mower*.

The fourth: *Belt Buckle*.

Bob stopped outside a house with a bright orange canvas roof and door. The sign read *French Fries*.

'Deck?' Bob called to his companion. 'What's with the signs outside the houses?'

'What, these? They tell you who lives here,' Deck explained, stepping up to the sign.

Bob was even more confused. 'But how? Is it a clue? Like their favourite thing or something? I don't understand.'

Deck chuckled. 'It's not a clue, no. It's the *name* of the person who lives here.'

Bob's face turned from confusion to disbelief. Sunny walked

back to join them and stood next to Deck with her hands on her hips.

'You mean you have someone in the Town called French Fries, and another called ...' Bob stood on his tiptoes and squinted to read the sign on the other side of the path. 'Ginger Root.'

'Yep,' said Sunny. 'And a Cheese Grater and a Loose Cannon.' She pointed at a couple of houses further up. 'Floppy Disk lives in that one?' she said, pointing and glancing at Deck for confirmation.

Deck nodded.

'Those aren't names!' said Bob in disbelief. 'They're just ... things!'

'They are names,' said Sunny, shifting her feet. 'I know all of 'em, and nice people too.'

'Sure, but they're also things. A floppy disk is old computer storage, and a lawnmower cuts the grass. Don't you see? It's like calling someone ... Yellow Raincoat.' Bob pointed to his coat.

Sunny pursed her lips, tapping her fingers on the fence post. Bob realised he'd offended his new friends and tried to remove the disbelief from his face. Then a thought came to him. 'Wait a minute. What are your names? Your full names, I mean.'

'Well, I'm Sunny Day, and this here's Deck Chair.' Sunny pretended they were meeting for the first time and shook Bob's hand. 'Nice to meet you.'

Deck gave a little wave, half joining in.

'Anyway, what's wrong with our names, then, mister? They're Archive names, real old and important. Gettin' your name is a special thing.'

'Sorry. It's just new to me.' Bob winced, trying to placate Sunny.

Sunny beamed with her joyous smile. 'That's all right, my darlin' boy. Seein' as you know your name already, what's your last name, then, mister?'

Bob paused. He had no idea. He only knew his name was Bob because his first real memory was a voice inside his head screaming 'You are BOB' until his temples had hurt. 'I don't have one. If I do, I don't know it,' Bob said finally.

'Well then! Maybe we'll give you a last name instead!' Sunny was very pleased with this revelation.

'Come on, you three,' said Deck. 'We'd better get to the town hall. From how deserted it is, everybody must be there waiting for us.'

'You're the smart one!' said Sunny. 'Lead the way!'

She then proceeded to lead the way.

Deck winked at Bob.

————

After rounding a hill, the path gently sloped down the valley and then widened to a street with bunting-covered buildings clustered on either side.

At the end of the street was a large wooden structure with a rainbow-striped canvas roof that resembled a circus big top, rising to a point in the centre where a tree poked out.

However, that wasn't what was capturing Bob's attention. Where the hills of the valley narrowed in the distance behind the big-top building was a sheer wall of fire spanning between the hills. The flames danced blue and green, and Bob thought he saw a hexagonal pattern moving within the fire.

'What's that?' asked Bob, pointing. His eyes wide.

'That's the town hall,' said Sunny.

'No. The fire, the fire between the hills!'

'Oh, that's the firewall. It keeps us safe,' Sunny said, as if that explained everything.

Bob thought it didn't look particularly safe, given it was not too far from a town full of wooden houses. Why did they need a massive wall of fire? What was it protecting them from? Before he could ask, Deck whisked him off down the hill towards the buildings decorated with bunting.

A crowd of naked, blurry-filtered people flanked the street. They were standing idly, waiting for something to happen. As the people closest to the hill spotted Bob, Sunny and Deck, they started cheering. The cheer rippled down the street as the crowd began waving small handkerchief-sized flags of various colours.

Bob's heart sank when he realised everybody had gathered to greet him. He didn't want any attention and wished the ground would swallow him up. Then he remembered that had already happened in the tiled space. As grateful as he was for avoiding the metal wolves' jaws, he didn't want to repeat the experience.

Nervously glancing at some of the faces in the crowd, Bob realised everyone was very, very similar. All were adults of a similar height. All had pale skin, blonde hair and blue eyes. All were good-looking, with no bent noses, warts or pimples. Despite the crowd consisting of beaming, perfectly straight-toothed smiles and handsome, friendly faces, it gave Bob a chill. There was something seriously wrong with this place. He understood why Sunny and Deck thought him different. Compared to every single person in the entire town, he was very different.

Sunny was busy waving and smiling at everyone as she led the procession down the centre of the street. Bob heard the cheering all the way down to the big-top town hall, but the people closest stopped cheering, lowered their flags and started talking in hushed tones. Bob picked up snippets of what they were saying.

'That can't be right.'

'Why does he have clothes on?'

'The Queen said …'

'Something's wrong.'

Sunny and Deck also noticed the change in the crowd's mood, and their smiles became more forced.

'Just keep walkin' and smilin', my darlin' boy,' said Sunny as she waved and greeted some people by name, asking after them. Each shuffled their feet and answered uncomfortably.

News of Bob's arrival and his out-of-place appearance spread down the crowd far more quickly than the friends walked. They had to complete most of the procession without the cheers and under the scrutiny of many eyes, hushed whispering and occasional pointing.

Sunny gave up the waving and smiling pretence and grabbed Bob's arm to lead him quickly past the crowd, or at least as quickly as he could manage with his sore leg.

Mercifully, they soon reached the town hall at the end of the street. The crowd filed in behind them, still murmuring and pointing. Bob felt himself wishing for the cheering again, as the atmosphere created by the quieter, whispered attention was far worse.

Deck stepped up to the town hall door and ceremoniously rapped on it with a door knocker intricately carved into the shape of a bee.

'Enter!' came a voice from inside.

Deck pushed the doors inwards, revealing the room beyond.

———

The town hall was constructed from the same rustic wood as every other building Bob had seen so far. Walls three times his height supported the colourful canvas roof that stretched up to a giant oak tree the hall must have been built around. The tree was ancient. It twisted in thick knots and creaked gently in a contemplative, deep voice. The townsfolk had respectfully hung beads and wreaths of flowers off the lower branches, clearly honouring the oak.

Bob's first impression of the building – that it reminded him of a circus big top – fit well with the size and scale of the interior. The sun, shining on the colourful roof, filled the room with captivating shades and shadows. Simple benches, matching the ones beside the fire at the Lookout, were laid out in gently curving rows facing a stage built around the tree's base. An aisle ran between the benches up towards the stage. Lavender, placed in simple vases, lined the sawdust floor along the walls, making the whole space smell of sweet floral and deep woody tones. Two large canvas curtains ran from the tree to each opposite wall, splitting the entire building in half. Bob couldn't see what was on the other side of the curtains.

On the stage stood a statuesque, elegant woman, back straight and hands crossed in front of her. She had a long neck, soft, graceful features, flowing blonde hair and kind blue eyes. To Bob's surprise, she wasn't naked; she wore a flowing purple robe edged with white piping. It was a simple fabric, but on her, it looked regal. Bob was about to meet the Queen.

The party of friends walked down the aisle towards the tree and the stage. Byte was hiding out of sight in the raincoat pocket. Sunny and Deck walked a couple of paces ahead of Bob, and he caught them glancing at one another. The scene felt very much like a wedding. Bob wondered if they had weddings here and would understand the reference. Every step Bob took towards the Queen felt heavier and more reluctant than the last. He had butterflies in his stomach and felt warmth in his cheeks.

Deck and Sunny reached the stage and bowed before peeling off to one side to allow Bob to stand before the Queen. He didn't, remaining a few paces away from the stage, hands in his pockets, as he made sweeping patterns in the sawdust with the toe of his trainer.

The Queen smiled kindly, holding out her arms, palms up, in greeting. If she thought Bob was unusual, she didn't show it or make any comment. He felt the Queen, framed by the ancient tree behind her, gave off such an aura of serene authority that it was hard to maintain eye contact, so he stared at a random section of the stage instead.

The Queen glanced over Bob's head. Turning, Bob saw the town hall filling with townsfolk taking their places on the benches. He quickly turned back around to avoid the judge-mental stares.

The Queen crouched a little to speak privately to Bob. 'Don't worry. You are most welcome,' she said with a little wink. Her voice was soft and warm, and after a subtle glance towards Bob's raincoat pocket, she stood up, straight-backed and proud, and addressed the hall.

'Friends, we are gathered to welcome the most recent addition to our community.'

The crowd murmured, but the Queen quieted them with a smile and a gesture. 'The Controller has given us a gift. I would like to thank Sunny and Deck for making the journey across the Zoo to bring the gift safely to us.'

The crowd stamped their feet in rhythm as a sign of appreciation. Sunny beamed with pride and elbowed Deck.

The Queen gracefully unfurled a hand towards Bob. 'This gift is special. He is a sign from the Controller that all is well.'

Bob didn't want to be special, and his eyes shot to the floor.

A man two rows behind Bob stood. 'But, Your Majesty, he isn't like the rest of us!' he exclaimed, to a ripple of agreement.

'He is exactly like us, Tape. He is a gift, as all of you were. And we must welcome him to our town with the same kindness you all received.'

The man sat and folded his arms, saying no more.

'He's a boy, though, Your Majesty,' a lady chipped in.

'He is, Cherry. This makes no difference to how welcome he is,' replied the Queen. 'All of you, there will be time for questions later. Now, we must name the gift and complete his introduction into our community, as is our tradition.'

Bob raised a finger and opened his mouth to speak but then thought better of it and lowered his hand.

Sunny came to his rescue. 'He's got a name already, Your Majesty.'

The crowd became raucous at this revelation.

The Queen tried to calm them, but it didn't work, so she said loudly but politely, 'Hush, please. Everyone. Please.'

The crowd quieted.

'Is this true? Do you have a name?' she asked Bob.

'Y-y-yes, Your Majesty,' Bob replied, giving her a stilted, shallow bow.

The Queen didn't respond, leaving an awkward silence until Bob realised he was supposed to say his name.

'I'm Bob, Your Majesty.'

'He ain't got a last name, though, Your Majesty,' volunteered Sunny.

The Queen nodded at Sunny in thanks. 'Well, Bob, this is very unusual. Normally, the ceremony to accept you into our town ends with you being given your name from the Archive. But I suppose these are very unusual circumstances.' The Queen smiled at Bob, glanced at his raincoat pocket, turned and raised her arms towards the tree. 'We welcome this gift into our town with an open heart and open arms. I hereby declare Bob—'

'Stop!'

The Queen had been interrupted by a shout from behind the curtain to the left of the stage. The curtain flew open, and a man emerged, bent over, walking using a cane made from a knotted branch.

He was far older than anyone else Bob had met, with a leathery face full of lines from years of frowning and so full of venom and spite that his complexion was a deep red. Like everyone else, he had blue eyes and a full head of blonde hair, which felt out of place given his age, as if he wore a poorly fitted wig.

An oversized, garish red robe with white piping trailed on the floor as the old man stalked across the stage with a rhythmic *thud-thud* of his cane. The crowd noticeably tensed.

'This *cannot* be allowed!' he screamed towards the Queen.

The Queen somehow kept her poise and appeared utterly unfazed by the interruption.

'We *must* follow the traditions!' The old man looked Bob up and down, waving his cane. 'This … thing cannot be allowed to join our community! He is *not* one of us; he was sent in error! He is no gift!'

The crowd shifted in their seats, and Bob heard the odd murmur of agreement.

The Queen held her open palms towards the old man. 'Librarian, this is the work of the Controller. Fear not.'

'Fear! I'm not afraid! I'm doing what is necessary for our survival!' the Librarian snapped in rebuke. 'This –' he waved his cane up and down Bob again, scrunching up his face – 'must be cast back into the System through the firewall!' The cane flicked towards what must have been the direction of the firewall. 'Keeping him here will endanger our town, our peaceful lives!'

More murmuring and shuffling came from the crowd.

'This is no gift,' he spat, moving closer to the edge of the stage and scowling at Bob. 'This is blasphemy!' he shouted, raising his arms and cane.

More and more murmurings of approval came from the townsfolk.

'Calm yourself, Librarian,' the Queen said in a firm voice, hands crossed in front of her.

'I'll be calm once I've banished this abomination from our town,' the Librarian spat with another elaborate swing of his cane.

Bob was now confident the Town wasn't his former home. He shrank back as a dark vulnerability sat heavily on his stomach. This Librarian scared him, solidifying that cowardice was part of his identity.

The Queen and the Librarian got into a debate on the stage, which left the crowd to do the same, voices rising in a chorus of arguments.

Byte chose this moment to jump from Bob's pocket, wriggling to get himself free. Bob tried to grab him, but Byte slipped from his fingers and hopped up the steps and onto the stage.

Byte's ear and tail reflected the rainbow of light created by the canvas roof onto the stage floor like a disco ball. He started yapping and growling at the Librarian, who gasped and then froze, cane pointed at Byte.

The crowd quieted, pushing forward to gawk at the tiny furball.

'Hello, little one,' the Queen said.

'His name is Byte, Your Majesty,' said Sunny.

'Hello, Byte. It is a pleasure to meet you.'

Byte came trotting over to the Queen for a stroke on the head, tongue lolling.

'This can't be right,' said the Librarian, still in shock. 'The boy is human. It can't be his. We can't continue the ceremony until we know who this boy is! He'll threaten the very security of our town!'

Deck stepped forward, holding up his cloth bag. 'There's something else you should know, Your Majesty.' He emptied the contents of the bag onto the stage, causing gasps and exclamations from the crowd as they studied the gnarled, mangled wasp carcass.

'See!' said the Librarian. 'A hexbeast does not belong in the Zoo! *He* has done this! He brought this … this thing here! Something must be done!' He then energetically waved his cane in no particular direction.

'Very well,' said the Queen. 'Everyone, in light of these events, please wait outside whilst the Librarian and I work out what is for the best.'

The crowd stirred, not moving at first, wanting to continue to play the part of the audience in what was an exciting turn of events for them. Eventually, they shuffled out of the doors and into the street.

'You too, please,' said the Queen, turning to Sunny and Deck, who were still standing to the side of the stage.

Sunny tried to hide her disappointment at being dismissed, giving Bob a worried glance.

'Come on, you,' said Deck, and he led Sunny back down the aisle and through the doors into the street. The doors closed behind them, leaving Bob, Byte, the Librarian and the Queen alone in the town hall.

The Queen held out her hand, which Bob took, and she led him up a couple of small steps and onto the stage, navigating around the remains of the wasp. The Librarian set off towards the curtain with a *thud-thud* of his cane and more angry mumbling, and the Queen led Bob through the curtain after him, with Byte trotting behind.

———

The other side of the curtain revealed that the other half of the town hall was identical to the front, except without the benches or the doors. Bob couldn't work out why they bothered with the curtain at all. Maybe it was just to create a sense of theatre.

Other than the absence of doors and benches, the only other difference was a simple wooden hut built on the stage. It resembled a garden shed.

Bob suddenly noticed the Librarian glaring at him, pointing at the hut with his cane. 'Does that remind you of anything, boy?' he said slyly.

'Er, I don't know,' replied Bob.

'Yes, you do. Tell me! What does it remind you of?' The Librarian pointed again at the hut.

'Well, I thought it looked a bit like a garden shed,' said Bob, not meeting the Librarian's gaze.

The Librarian smiled wryly. 'And how do you know what a shed is, boy?'

Bob didn't know how he knew what a shed was – he just did – so he shrugged at the Librarian in response.

'Now, Librarian, please don't confuse the poor boy. He must be allowed time to understand. Let us discuss what is for the best,' said the Queen calmly, still maintaining her poise.

'Pah! I'm going to consult the Archive. We must do what is right for the majority! We cannot allow one boy to risk our very survival!' He stormed off, slamming the door of the shed behind him.

The Archive is in a shed? That makes no sense, Bob thought. When the dog images had appeared, and when he'd chosen the music, the Archive had been wherever he had been, and it certainly hadn't been in a shed. He thought it best not to say anything.

The Queen gently took Bob's hand and led him to the edge of the stage. They both sat down, and Bob dangled his legs over the edge.

'Do you know, I dreamed that a gift would come one day. Someone who would be different and teach us how to be more human in ways lost to us over time. That someone is you.' The Queen turned back towards the curtain. 'However, I am very concerned about the twisted creature. That was not in my dream.'

'Do you mean the Librarian?' Bob said with a shy but cheeky smile.

The Queen chuckled and winked at Bob, then glanced at Byte, who was exploring the stage for more buried treasure. 'Also, this one is very curious. Do you know what he is?'

'No. I know he's a "hexpet", but I don't know what one of those is.'

'I have an idea of what your friend Byte might be. Curiously, he's here with you, and unfortunately, that makes your being here more difficult to explain.'

'I have loads of questions,' said Bob. 'I don't know who I am or why I'm here. I want more information about the Zoo, the firewall and the Archive. But really, I'm just confused and tired.' Bob's eyes were welling up. The chaos of the last couple of days, being chased, being yelled at, had taken its toll. The Queen's kindness broke whatever defences he'd put up, and he did his best not to let his emotions overwhelm him.

The Queen hugged Bob's shoulders as the tears came. Byte trotted over and snuggled into his back. After a short time, the Queen pulled away and wiped a tear from Bob's cheek. Bob felt foolish for crying, especially in front of a queen he'd only just met.

'How about a nice cup of tea?' the Queen suggested. 'I might even have some lemonade.'

Bob smiled and nodded.

The Queen hopped off the edge of the stage and helped Bob down. Byte followed. The Librarian hadn't emerged from the shed yet, and Bob glanced at it nervously.

'He'll be in there for some time,' said the Queen. 'Maybe all night if we are lucky. We'll go the back way so we don't have to navigate through everyone outside.'

The Queen led Bob and Byte towards the back wall. The wall was unbroken, and Bob couldn't understand why they'd come this way. Then the Queen pulled on one of the wooden boards, and the wall started to lift upwards, revealing a hidden exit.

'Don't tell anyone else about this, will you?' The Queen winked as they exited into a walled garden. 'This leads to my home.' She pointed down a grassy path between neatly planted flowers and vegetables. It was well maintained, with pops of bright, colourful flowers set against a backdrop of lush greenery. Bees and butterflies busied themselves, and heady floral scents washed over Bob in waves. 'It is my private garden. A space where I escape from my duties occasionally.' The Queen paused to smell a pink rose.

'It's beautiful,' said Bob.

'Thank you, Bob. That is very kind of you,' replied the Queen, smiling at him.

Bob understood why Sunny had mentioned the Queen so often on their walk here. He agreed that she had a majestic, calming presence.

They reached the end of the grassy path and came to another unbroken wooden wall. The Queen pulled on a section of the wall, and a door opened. Bob spotted pulleys in a small pelmet space, just like the ones in the barn.

'It is a little hobby of mine,' the Queen explained, catching Bob inspecting the system.

Bob and Byte followed the Queen into her home. The door shut behind them with a gentle swoosh.

CHAPTER 6
THE NURSE

Bob imagined the Queen's home would be a grand palace, but it wasn't palatial at all. It was a cosy, homely single room filled with wooden furniture and soft rugs.

It was also a mess. Not dirty, but he had to zigzag through a path of discarded objects to get to where he needed to go. There were more ornaments and knick-knacks than the Librarian could shake a stick at: beads, vases and gardening paraphernalia, mostly. The bed wasn't made, and piles of clean dishes were stacked in the sink – presumably, they never made it into the cupboards. Hand-decorated pots containing plants and flowers littered most surfaces. Some empty pots lined one shelf, all in differing stages of decoration.

Bob and the Queen sat beside an open hearth at a small round table. The Queen had some fresh tea, and Bob had a lemonade. He'd removed his shoes and socks and scrunched his feet into the soft rug under the table. Byte made his way onto the end of the Queen's bed and curled up for a nap.

The Queen blew over her tea to cool it. 'Now, I know some of the answers to your questions, but I would be very interested in your story first. If you don't mind.' She cupped her hot mug and sat back, ready to listen.

Bob tried his best to give an account of what had happened to him since he'd woken up in the tiled space to the moment he'd met the Queen. He didn't leave anything out, but he wasn't the world's greatest storyteller, so the telling was disjointed and rushed.

The Queen sat and listened attentively, sipping her tea. If any of what had happened to Bob surprised her, it didn't show on her face.

'And that's it, I suppose. You know the rest.'

'Well,' said the Queen, leaning forward and resting her elbows on the table, 'that was an incredible story, and quite frightening in places. You are a remarkable boy.'

Bob's cheeks flushed. He wasn't remarkable; he was a coward, but hearing the Queen say so was very nice indeed.

'My turn, I suppose,' said the Queen, rocking back in her chair. 'Let's see. Where to start? I know. I'll start at the very beginning. Humans have lived here in the Zoo for as long as anyone remembers and as far back as our records go. It was created long ago as a way to protect humanity. It is peaceful, with everything we need. Everything outside of the Zoo is called the System, and the firewall keeps us safe by stopping anything from getting into the Zoo. The metal creatures can't get in, or at least they shouldn't be able to. As you might imagine, facing a creature that is not supposed to exist anywhere outside of a scary story caused the people in the hall to be shocked and frightened.'

Bob's heart was racing. Maybe he really had let the creatures in. *Oh no.*

The Queen topped up her tea from a burgundy teapot and popped a sugar lump in her mug.

'Once, in darker times, banishment through the firewall was a punishment for petty crimes or breaking with Archive traditions. But I put a stop to that. Townsfolk can leave but rarely do, and no one crosses through the firewall and returns to tell the tale. It is a one-way kind of thing. The only person able to pass through the firewall and return was a giant called the Controller. We worshipped him like a god, and he repaid us with kindness, stories and gifts. Over a year ago, a terrible noise came from the other side of the firewall. It lasted several months, then stopped, and we haven't seen the Controller since or had another gift. The people grow nervous, fearing the Controller has abandoned us. Your arrival, along with the metal creature and the dog, have stoked those fears.'

Bob studied the sleepy ball of fur on the Queen's bed. 'Why would they be afraid of Byte?'

'Because the Controller's favourite stories centred around his dog, a mighty beast that protected him. His description of the dog, apart from the scale, maybe, matches Byte.'

Byte chose that moment to stir in his sleep, making a cute whimper. Cute, thought Bob, but not mighty.

'His tag says to protect him,' Bob said. 'I've been trying to, but I'm not doing very well. He's almost died twice.'

'Nonsense. You are doing a marvellous job.'

He wasn't. But again he took the compliment.

Bob was lining up to ask the Queen about the Archive when a knock came on the door frame.

'Come in!'

The rainbow canvas pulled back, and Sunny stepped in with her usual beaming smile.

'Sunny, you are most welcome. How may I help you?'

'I came to help Bob, Your Majesty,' said Sunny, revealing a small pot with a waxy yellow substance and a handful of clean bandages.

'Ah, of course. Good thinking, Sunny.'

Sunny stepped into the room and crouched in front of Bob. Bob spun around in his chair to allow Sunny access to his leg.

'Where is Deck?' asked the Queen as Sunny rolled up the leg of Bob's jeans to reveal the wound the wasp had given him. 'I don't often find you two apart. Usually, where one goes, the other follows.'

'Oh, he's gettin' a load of questions from folk about the wasp creature. He's drawn quite the crowd!' Sunny removed the makeshift bandages and cleaned the wound.

'Poor thing. I will go and rescue him. I will check on the Librarian while I am at it. See you both later.' The Queen gently touched Bob's shoulder as she left to find Deck.

While working, Sunny told Bob she'd learned to be a nurse from the Queen. Sunny had taken over as the Town's nurse when the Queen had become, well, the Queen. The townsfolk had chosen her to rule because the Controller had emphasised kindness, and she was the kindest among them.

'There you go. All better!' Sunny tucked in the bandage and rolled Bob's jeans back down. His leg did feel a lot better. Sunny must be an excellent nurse.

Sunny moved one of Bob's curls out of his eye. 'How are you gettin' on, my darlin' boy?'

'Okay, I suppose. It's a lot to take in.'

He wasn't okay. He was confused, frightened that the metal creatures would return and aware that the Town wasn't quite the paradise its first impression had suggested. But he wasn't about to admit all that to Sunny.

'You're right. It's a lot to take in at first. But don't you worry. You're one of us now, and I reckon you have a kind heart.' Sunny rested her palm over Bob's heart. 'That's the most important thing around here, kindness. Too many folk don't have enough of it. But you have enough to make up for the lot of 'em.' She ruffled his mop of hair and smiled one of those beaming smiles that lit up the room and melted all problems away.

'It's the reason me and Deck are such good friends. He's the kindest man in the Town, that one. He don't say much, but what he does say is always clever and always kind.'

Sunny energetically jumped up and grabbed Bob's hand. 'Right, mister, let me show you around. There are loads of things to see and loads of people to meet!'

'Wait, I need my shoes.'

Sunny lifted her foot and wiggled her toes. 'Nah, you don't need them. Come on!' She marched Bob out of the Queen's hut, leaving Byte to his nap.

———

Sunny took Bob on a whistle-stop tour of the Town. Before even saying so much as a 'hi' to someone, Sunny whisked Bob off to meet someone else.

It turned out that the buildings lining the street were the Town's industry. Several buildings acted as woollen mills, cleaning, dyeing and spinning wool into yarn. The mills were very noisy and lively, with hoots of laughter spilling out into the street. It quieted when Bob and Sunny entered, but the people were polite. Bob met the lady in charge of a mill, called Bobbin Winder.

The next building housed the bakery. You could smell it was a bakery before entering, as the scent of freshly baked bread wafted out into the open air. Inside were two big bread ovens, and rows of loaves dusted in flour lined the shelves. They met a jolly man called Artisan Boule, who said Bob was a handsome fellow, ruffled his hair and sent him on his way with some freshly baked focaccia. Bob recalled the story of the poop bread and smiled as he ate.

The next stop was a fishmonger, and the smell was also noticeable before entering, but not as inviting as the bakery's. There were different types of smoked fish hanging from hooks in the ceiling. Bob met a man called Tackle Box, which made Bob chuckle, and the man raised an eyebrow. Bob left quickly, declining some smoked fish to go with his bread.

'It's very nice of the baker to give me this for free,' Bob said, holding up the last remaining crumbs of his focaccia.

'What do you mean, for free, darlin'?'

'You know, because I don't have any money to give him.'

'Ah, yes, the Controller told us a story about people from the

Archive bein' obsessed with money. It was just an object, apparently, no different from a rock or a stick, except they traded money for things they didn't even need or hoarded a load for no reason. It's all a bit weird if you ask me. It don't work like that around here. We don't have money, never have.'

'Then how do you get things that you need?' Bob asked, devouring the last of the bread.

'Kindness.'

Bob gave Sunny a dubious look. 'Kindness?'

'Yep. One of the lessons the Archive taught us is that money ain't important. It turns out the real currency of humanity is kindness. The more you give, the more you have! Waaay better than money. The Archive humans took ages to work that out; it was almost too late. We were kind to Artisan by visitin' him and bein' polite and such, so he gave you some bread. Easy as that.'

Bob thought on this for a while. It made sense, but it wasn't how he understood things to work in his head. Thinking back to the Librarian asking him if he knew what a shed was, he wondered whether money was another thing he knew about but shouldn't. It was all tied to the Archive somehow. If only there were a way inside the shed. Maybe if he saw the Archive, it would all make sense. Perhaps the Archive held the key to discovering who he was.

As he was mulling this over, they skipped a building with HUNTER written on a sign above the door.

'Are we not going in there?' asked Bob.

'Ah, we can't. The Town doesn't have a hunter at the moment.'

'Oh, how come?'

Sunny scanned the area to ensure no one was in earshot, then leaned into Bob conspiratorially. 'Hunter was banished. Sent through the firewall. Nasty business. He was the last person ever to get banished from the Town. After him, the Queen put a stop to it, despite the Librarian claimin' it was tradition, and we can't stop tradition.'

Sunny mimicked the Librarian by stooping and waving a pretend cane in the air. Bob smiled at the accuracy of it.

'After Hunter was banished, it turned out he hadn't done anythin' wrong. It was a misunderstandin'. It would be nice to have a new hunter, if you fancy givin' it a go. We ain't had rabbit or venison in town for ages. "Bob Hunter" has a nice ring to it, don't you think?' Sunny gently elbowed Bob and winked.

Bob thought it did have a nice ring to it. If he stayed, maybe he would become the new town hunter.

'This is me!' Sunny stood in a 'ta-da' pose in front of a building with a signpost that read NURSE. 'Come on, let me show you inside.' Sunny grabbed Bob's arm and pulled him through the canvas door.

Inside the nurse's hut, glass bottles with variously coloured liquids lined shelf upon shelf. There were small pots of ointment, rolls of bandages and some dried flowers. It smelled clean and clinical. Sunny was busy explaining what ailment each of the ointments or medicines helped with, including which person in the Town had last had said ailment, accompanied by an often-too-graphic description of the treatment. Bob thought it took a particular sort of person to be a nurse, and it wasn't the profession for him. Halfway down the second shelf, Deck came to his rescue.

'Hi, you two.'

'Deck! Did the Queen manage to save you?' Sunny's smile was that bit wider when she saw Deck.

'Yes, and I did need saving. Everyone's a bit jittery.'

'Hide in here with us if you like. I'm just explainin' to Bob what all my medicines are for.'

'Unfortunately, that might have to wait, Sunny. The Librarian has called a meeting. He's found something in the Archive. That's why I came to find you.'

'Ah, okay. We best get goin', then!'

Sunny led them out of her apothecary and towards the town hall. Byte ran out from between the bakery and the fishmonger, where he'd possibly been up to no good, and jumped into Bob's arms.

A crowd had gathered, waiting to navigate the bottleneck into the town hall. Spotting Bob, the crowd parted like a miniature Red Sea to allow him and his friends easy access to the hall.

The Queen stood in her familiar place on the stage, at the end of the aisle, framed by the great oak.

Before Bob could dive onto one of the rear benches, the Queen gestured for him to take a seat at the front. He made his second nervous walk of the day down the aisle between the benches and sat in the front row.

Was the Librarian about to shout at him again? He was certainly glad the Queen had put a stop to firewall banishment. Despite the fact that he didn't fit in, the Town had a certain charm to it, and staying was starting to grow on him as an option, mainly because he hadn't thought of a plan B.

It took a while for everyone to make their way into the hall and take a seat on the benches. The Queen remained poised with her hands in front of her, nodding in greeting to those who entered. Eventually, Bob heard the doors close with a soft creak. Then came the rhythmic *thud-thud* as the Librarian entered from behind the curtain, the crowd noticeably hushing.

'Citizens!' he croaked, raising his arms in the air. 'The Archive has spoken!'

The crowd murmured in anticipation.

The Librarian paused intentionally, dramatically casting his eyes across the crowd. 'Today, our peace has been broken!' he spat, thumping his cane down on the stage, then pointing it at Bob. 'This abomination has delivered danger and foreboding into our lives, desecrating our traditions! He cannot be allowed to stay!'

'Now, Librarian, he is just a boy. Our traditions teach kindness. What you are saying is not kind.' The Queen remained calm, but she was asserting herself.

'Pah! We don't need kindness! Kindness is weakness! If we're weak, we're doomed! Doomed!' The Librarian was thumping his cane as he shouted the words.

Bob felt the crowd growing hostile.

The Queen noticed it also and gestured for the hall to settle. 'Is this really what we have become? Would we reject a boy because he is different? The Archive teaches us that humans celebrated diversity.'

The Librarian gave a patronising, condescending cackle. 'What do you know of the Archive, child? Humans did not celebrate diversity! They destroyed others just because they were different, and enslaved those that did not fit! Mocked people they'd never met without any attempt to understand them! Human kindness only existed in their stories as a mask to wear to pretend they were tolerant!' He wheezed another laugh, not once addressing the Queen directly as he spoke, always keeping eye contact with his audience. 'We are the same.' The Librarian took on a gentle tone, as if comforting a child, sweeping his cane across the hall. 'Because the Archive teaches that difference is not something humanity deals with. Humanity's inability to deal with diversity caused all the destruction in the first place. Why would we allow something that destroyed humanity to live among us?' The cane shot out to point at Bob again.

The crowd stirred, and Bob heard more and more murmurs of approval.

Bob shrank down in his seat, making himself as small as possible, feeling the pressure of eyes inspecting him, judging him. He'd spent the day flip-flopping between feeling welcomed by some and feeling ostracised by the Librarian and a crowd of people he was yet to know.

'The same rule applies to kindness, Librarian. Casting the boy out of our community would be unkind. The Controller was very clear. Kindness is the key to our humanity. An absence of kindness destroyed humanity, and *you* would have us tread the same path?'

The Queen's words caused the Librarian's supporters to quiet, and those who agreed with the Queen started their own round of whispers and murmurings.

A smirk appeared on Sunny's face, and she squeezed Bob's hand in support.

'This weakness will be the end of us! Mark my words! I have witnessed the aftermath of kindness in the Archive. Would you argue against my knowledge? I'm the elder, the Librarian, and I will have respect!' Red-faced, the Librarian thumped his cane and stamped his feet, resembling a tantruming toddler.

The crowd fell silent at the tension his behaviour created.

'And I am your queen. The people of this town chose me to lead because we veered away from the Controller's teachings. I respect your opinion, Librarian, and your insight from the Archive. But your voice is one. Our town has many voices.'

'Ridiculous! I'll not—'

The Queen held up her hand to silence the Librarian. Bob was in awe that her poise did not break. Her authority was palpable. The Librarian stopped mid-sentence.

'You have had your opinion heard, Librarian. I will hear no more.'

The Librarian appeared ready to burst, red-hot fury written all over his face as he slammed his cane into the stage. THUD! 'This is *weakness*. You'll regret not doing as I say, *Your Majesty*.' He said the words with quiet spite, spitting out the last two with such venom Bob thought a snake's forked tongue might flick out of his mouth.

The Librarian turned on his heel and retreated behind the curtain.

The Queen watched him go and then turned to address the crowd. 'It is not our appearance that makes us the same. It is our actions. The Archive teaches that humans were successful when they worked together. Where there was division, there was chaos. Today, we celebrate a new gift. He will teach us to respect one another's differences rather than uniformity only, bringing us closer to understanding our humanity.' The Queen smiled and held an arm out towards Bob. 'Welcome, Bob.'

After a short, uncertain pause, the crowd repeated the Queen's words in unison: 'Welcome, Bob.'

The Queen stood facing the crowd, arms outstretched. 'Tonight, as is our tradition, we will hold a feast for our new gift. May we all come together to celebrate new friends and new beginnings.'

The crowd clapped and cheered. A few people sitting on the bench behind Bob patted his shoulder. Bob thought that maybe, just maybe, they would welcome him into the Town after all. Although the idea that he would teach anyone anything worried him. He knew nothing about who he was, never mind important subjects like humanity and diversity. Perhaps once he'd settled in, the townsfolk would help him work out who he was, or at least let him take a peek in that shed.

CHAPTER 7
A BREWING STORM

The air had an ominous, dark mood – a storm was brewing.

The lady in the red dress sat atop a hill, the skirt of the dress billowing out in a circle around her. Her only companion on the hill was a small, scraggly tree. The first gusts of the storm blew the last few crinkled leaves off the tree branches.

She stared out from underneath her fringe at dozens of pairs of red lights scattered across the fields in front of the hill. The red lights shifted, skulked and stalked between sparse derelict houses, crumbling barns and remnants of walls. They were all cautiously making a beeline for her.

The abandoned cluster of farm dwellings was now a battleground, her versus them.

'You should have brought more of your friends. Big mistake, morons – this won't take long.'

She deftly swung and twirled a large staff over her head. The golden staff had an intricate serpent-like dragon embossed along the entire length. Atop the staff sat a large disc with flowing gold and red swirls. It was, in essence, an elaborate giant gold lollipop.

The eyes, noticing the swirling motion, started to move quickly, urgently, desperate to close the gap.

One final twirl, and the lady in the red dress slammed the staff into the ground in front of her with an audible clang of metal hitting metal. The ground briefly rippled outwards from the staff; a backlit hexagon mesh rode the rippling surface.

'Okay, you metal sons of bitches. Playtime.'

The lady in the red dress closed her eyes, concentrating intently. Both hands gripped the staff. She twisted. There was a loud click, as if something were slotting into place somewhere unseen.

The pair of eyes closest to her belonged to a rusted, gnarled metal tiger, starting to climb up the base of the hill. Suddenly and without warning, the tiger launched violently into the air, hurled with intense fury by a giant fist that had formed underneath it from the earth itself. After arcing, the tiger fell back with a crash and a series of yelps into a pack of rusted metal wild dogs.

The fist maintained its momentum, crashing into the group, then exploded into component parts of stone, mud and grass. Several pairs of red lights faded.

'Too easy.'

Another twist, another click.

Large stones dislodged themselves from derelict buildings and floated upwards from where they rested on the ground, then flew from left to right and right to left. They whistled through the air like enormous fireworks, as if two invisible opposing armies were hurling stones at each other.

A stone building section smashed into three beasts, knocking them off their feet with an audible crunch.

Several wall sections crushed metal bodies into the remains of a house, which crumbled on impact, burying more metal carcasses.

One projectile took the head clean off a metal wolf. The head rolled to a stop in front of one of its comrades.

The few remaining pairs of eyes were panicked, no longer fixated on the lady in the red dress, as they frantically tried to find some way out of the sudden and brutal war zone.

'Pathetic.'

Another twist, another click.

Grotesque, jagged twists of the fallen beasts' rusted remains were pulled together with stone and earth as if attracted by a magnet. The debris formed legs, a body and arms. In moments, two massive golems rose from the remnants of metal corpses and derelict buildings. Each golem had wrecking-ball fists made of rusted, jagged shards, which they swung mercilessly at the last few survivors of the metal beast army. Some ran; others fell to thumping, crushing blows.

On completing their brief and violent mission, the golems collapsed, crumbling back to debris and metal fragments, crushing fleeing stragglers. More lights went out.

Just as the storm's first raindrops started to fall, the battle was over. Accompanied by a pressure-releasing swooshing noise, the lady in the red dress pulled her staff out of the ground. Her shoulders slumped in exhaustion.

Then, a large shadow slowly crept across her dress until it completely enveloped her. Something massive loomed over her.

'You're late again, you tiny imbecile. I had to do all the work myself. Mop up any stragglers, you useless cretin. I need to recharge.'

CHAPTER 8
THE FEAST

The Town had a renewed, excited energy as people milled around getting food, drink, furniture and crockery for the feast. Everyone knew their role and worked hard to pull it all together.

The clearing between the town hall and the firewall acted as the location for the feast. Townsfolk carried out tables and pushed them together to make one long table in the centre of the clearing. Other folk erected poles to run bunting over the heads of those feasting and carefully arranged table decorations bursting with sweet-scented, colourful flowers.

The sights, sounds and smells were incredible, and all this was for Bob. He couldn't quite believe it was real. As he meandered through town on his way to the bathhouse, townsfolk approached him regularly to ask his preference on wine, tablecloth colour and vegetables. He was starting to like this sort of attention; he felt special.

Byte tuned into the excitement and spent most of the afternoon getting under people's feet and seeking a scratch behind the ear from passers-by. Most stopped and nervously gave him the attention he sought, despite being uncertain whether they should touch a hexpet. He was too cute to ignore, and everyone melted when he gave them a friendly yip.

The Librarian hadn't reappeared since storming off the stage. Bob figured he'd waited until everyone left and then skulked off somewhere, but the Queen said he hadn't left the town hall and was probably still locked in the shed, consulting the Archive.

Bob was still very curious about the Town's Archive. Was it the same as he had experienced? Was the PA lady another form of the Librarian? Maybe the Archive in the shed held more clues to who he was and why he was here. Perhaps he'd have a quick look if he ever got the chance.

———

A short time later, Bob lay neck-deep in bubbles in the Town's bathhouse, leg stinging in the water, but in that way that made it feel better somehow. The bathhouse was reminiscent of a Swedish sauna, making Bob wonder whether he should know what a Swedish sauna was. Either way, having some time to himself and soaking away the troubles of the last few days in a hot, lavender-scented bath was relaxing.

Bob hadn't had a moment alone since waking up in the white-tiled space. Encountering the metal wolves felt like a lifetime ago when it must only have been … two days? Time hadn't made sense in the tiled space.

The water was starting to chill, so Bob got out of the bath, dried himself on a soft white towel, applied some of Sunny's ointment to his wound and poorly wrapped it with fresh bandages. Sunny had promised to redo the bandages at the feast.

The bathhouse was the only building in town with a mirror, a single floor-to-ceiling mirror with the same ornate gold frame as the ones in the barn. As Bob dried himself, he stepped up to the mirror and used a corner of the towel to rub away the steam, revealing his face. Bob saw the same unremarkable face as before, except the reflection didn't dishearten him as it had in the barn. Maybe there was some comfort in that. It was a face he didn't know, a face with no history. He turned from side to side, imagining himself with blonde hair and blue eyes, all shiny and toned like everyone else.

Perhaps he'd come from another town, where they all had brown eyes and curly brown hair. Maybe he'd fled that town. He supposed staying here and adopting a new identity was better than discovering some past trauma. Could he live without knowing, though? The PA lady had been adamant he should find out who he was. But maybe instead, he should concentrate on staying safe.

Bob's clothes hung nearby, and he started to dress. One of the townsfolk had taken his jumper to clean sawdust from it and repair a small hole. His jeans were a bit ripped and slightly bloodstained because of the injury from the wasp, but they would do. After pulling on his high-tops, Bob tied his laces properly so the threadbare bits didn't stick out. Safety first this time. Finally, he pulled on his plain black T-shirt and walked out of the baths towards the busy street to find his friends and to pick up his jumper from a nice lady called Hemline Seam.

———

Sunset marked the start of the feast. The great firewall of blue flames glowed brightly against the night sky, illuminating the delicious delights spread across the table: steaming stews, bread, cheese, roasted vegetables, smoked fish, fresh fruit and cake.

The Queen asked Bob to wait with her by her house until everyone else was seated, so he stood patiently next to the Queen, waiting as guests arrived.

Byte was less patient, running off to greet a guest or explore the surrounding area for something interesting. He would always return to Bob and try to be patient, but it wasn't long before he was off exploring again.

'Are you okay?' asked the Queen.

'Yes, fine, thanks. A little overwhelmed, but looking forward to the food. I'm hungry.'

'Me too,' agreed the Queen with a smile. 'Doesn't it smell amazing?'

It did. Bob breathed in a heady mix of spiced stew and fresh bread from where he stood; it must smell terrific from the table.

Once everyone settled on the benches, the Queen gently touched Bob's back, indicating they should start walking towards the feast. Byte trotted along next to Bob as they made their way to the head of the table. Bob spotted a space for him to the right of the Queen, next to Deck and opposite Sunny. The Librarian wasn't among the guests. They reached the table, and the Queen gestured for Bob to take his seat. Byte sat on the ground next to him. The Queen remained standing, lifting her arms and addressing the feast.

'Friends,' she said, loud enough that her words would undoubtedly carry to those sitting at the far end. The chatter quieted, and everyone turned towards the Queen. 'I would like to thank you all for devoting your time to contributing to this special occasion.' The Queen lowered her arms, crossing her hands in front of her. 'And it's an extraordinary occasion, as today we welcome a unique gift to our town. We welcome Bob.'

Bob felt a hundred eyes turn to him, so he kept his head down, staring at his plate.

'In the short time we have spent together, I have come to know he is a kind boy with a big heart. He joins a community of warmth and friendship, and we will be a better community with Bob as a part of it.'

Bob felt his cheeks getting warm.

'I know some of you are concerned by the irregularity you have seen today, but we will discover that we are more alike than we are different, no matter our first impressions.'

Bob risked a glance down the table and spotted lots of nods of agreement and sheepish faces as some reflected on their opinions and behaviour towards Bob in the town hall. Sunny was beaming at him, so excited by the festivities she might burst.

'Now, let us eat and laugh and dance in celebration!' The

Queen gave a shallow bow and sat down to a raucous agreement as people cheered, stamped their feet and banged their wooden cups on the table.

Then everyone started chattering away and filling their plate with food. Bob eagerly tucked into what turned out to be lamb stew, putting several pieces on the ground for Byte.

Bob was glad of the company of his new friends and listened eagerly to tales of the godlike Controller, who seemed more like a ruler, dictating and orchestrating every aspect of town life. When he had stopped coming, the Town had floundered, and arguments had broken out about the most minor aspects of life. The Queen was the only reason it had held together.

Sunny told another story of town antics. A shepherd had stolen the Librarian's cloak and put it on one of the sheep, managing to convince at least a dozen people that the Librarian had turned into a sheep before the Librarian himself had stomped into the field to retrieve his cloak.

'Why do you put up with him? The Librarian, I mean,' Bob asked the Queen when they had all recovered from laughing.

'If I were to repress his voice or banish him –' the Queen pointed towards the firewall – 'then I wouldn't be accepting his differences. That would be hypocritical, as tempting as it might be.'

'Puttin' up with him is a kindness, Your Majesty. He drives me mad, the way he talks to you and Bob. Not nice things to say.'

'But he is entitled to say them, Sunny, and we are entitled to disagree.'

The Queen leaned into Bob. 'If it's okay, I would like to talk about music. Sunny tells me you did something amazing at the Lookout.'

Bob went bright red, pushing a pea around his plate with his fork. Sunny winced, as she clearly hadn't meant for Bob to discover she'd told the Queen what he'd done.

'I did. But I'm not sure how to control it. I tried to play

another song, and it didn't work.' Bob continued chasing the pea around his plate.

'Can you play a song for me?'

Bob sat up. 'It might not work.'

'Try. That is all I ask.'

Bob wasn't sure, but he put down his fork, ready to try. He knew asking wouldn't work, so instead, he concentrated, willing the images to appear.

Nothing.

He tried again. Nothing.

One more try. *Please work. Please.*

Everyone at the feast froze.

'*Accessing the Archive. Please wait.*'

The images of music albums appeared and spun around him, but they were slower and more controlled this time. One stopped in front of him. Reaching forward, Bob tapped it. The album cover flipped over, and he chose a song.

'*Access complete. Returning to the Zoo. Please wait.*'

The images spun in reverse, and everyone unfroze.

The feasting party gasped in disbelief as *I'm So Excitied*, played through the air. Confused faces lifted to the heavens, searching for the source of the music. Bob had chosen well. It was the perfect song for a feast. Everyone stopped what they were doing and listened.

When the song finished, all the way down the table were happy, smiling faces. They were all in awe. Sunny beamed the widest smile of them all.

The Queen stood to address the feast. 'Everyone, the gift of music was given to us by Bob. It has been a long time since music played in the Town, and thanks to Bob, we hear it again.'

'Thank you, Bob,' said Sunny, standing and holding her hand to her heart.

The woman sitting two spaces from Sunny also stood up. 'Thank you,' she said. Her eyes were teary. She put her hand to her heart.

One at a time, people all the way down the table stood, thanked Bob and put their hands to their hearts. Bob didn't know where to put himself, so he quietly said 'No problem' whilst staring at his plate.

The Queen gestured for everyone to sit, and the feasting continued into dessert. Bob ate cake until his stomach hurt. Byte kept getting visitors with leftover bones or pieces of meat. The visitors would pay him some attention and thank Bob again for the music.

Bottles of a deep red wine appeared on the table, and one or two townsfolk at the opposite end of the table started to sing. Sunny's eyes lit up as she stood to go and join them, strong-arming Deck to join in. He feigned resistance before agreeing.

Bob was momentarily on his own, the Queen having gone to mingle. The singing townsfolk moved onto the grass and started dancing as others clapped. Sunny and Deck were among them. Bob knew they needed music to go with their dancing. He concentrated and accessed the Archive easily this time, choosing another song. When everyone unfroze, there was a loud cheer. The music was perfect for dancing, and more people got up to join in the merriment. Some started dancing around the table in a conga, and the lady who had fixed Bob's jumper grabbed his arm and pulled him into the dance. Before he knew it, he was spinning and laughing. At the end of each song, he conjured up another. The atmosphere was terrific. Bob found his friends, and everyone danced late into the night. Except Byte, who jumped onto a bench and curled up to sleep.

Eventually, the celebrations ended, and everyone parted ways with plenty of hugs and handshakes. All agreed this had been the best gift celebration feast in living memory. Bob had a few whispered 'sorry about earlier' messages, and to all, he replied, 'Don't worry. It's fine.'

Deck and Sunny found Bob perched on the end of a bench, stroking the sleepy Byte.

Deck ruffled Bob's curls. 'Goodnight, Bob. It's been an interesting feast, one I'll not forget anytime soon.'

'Goodnight, Deck, and thank you.'

Sunny, for once, didn't say anything, giving Bob a big kiss on his forehead, a hug and a huge, beaming smile. Then she linked arms with Deck, and they made their way out of the clearing.

The Queen had made plans for Bob to stay with her until they found somewhere more permanent for him. After saying farewell to several straggling revellers, the Queen wandered over to Bob. 'Ready to call it a night?'

Bob yawned. 'Definitely.'

'Come on, then. Let's leave the tidying up for tomorrow.'

The Queen held out both hands and helped Bob up from the bench. Bob carefully scooped up Byte, who stretched a little before settling again.

They retired to the Queen's house. Bob made himself comfortable on the floor after clearing a space in the clutter, curling up in warm blankets with Byte snuggled into his chest. The Queen had offered to sleep on the floor and for Bob to have her bed, but Bob was comfortable, and he felt it wouldn't have been proper to sleep in a queen's bed.

CHAPTER 9
THE SHED

Bob woke up and couldn't get back to sleep. *Oh no.* It was that grey half-light time again. It had an ominous omen to it now.

He couldn't sleep because the Archive was playing on his mind. He knew the Archive was somehow in his head, and that was how he played the music, so why was it also in a shed? Maybe it would make sense if he could just see inside the shed. Perhaps he'd discover who he was and why he was here.

These thoughts were distracting, and Bob lay in the blankets, trying to shake the incredible pull to get up, sneak back through the Queen's garden and into the town hall. He lay there for some time, listening to Byte's sleeping noises and the beating of his own heart.

He had to.

He couldn't.

He must.

He shouldn't.

The stress of indecision was killing him. He was worried that getting up would wake the Queen. Or he would wake Byte, and Byte would wake the Queen.

Maybe start by standing up. That can't do any harm, right?

Bob moved a leg out of the side of a blanket, then froze, waiting for any stirring. Nothing. He moved the other leg, making the wasp wound sting a little. He winced.

Anything? Any movement?

Still nothing. All was quiet. Bob lifted the rest of the blanket off and placed it to one side, careful not to cover Byte.

This is silly. I should just stay here and go back to sleep.

He lifted himself onto his knees and held his breath, glancing at the Queen. She was sleeping. *Phew.* Even sleeping, she was poised and serene. Bob put the foot of his uninjured leg on the floor and heaved himself up to stand, then held his breath, heart thumping.

He was standing.

Now what?

The table. Maybe he'd just walk over to the table. He took a small tiptoed step, then another, then another, weaving in and out of the obstacle course of discarded items. He reached the table and put a hand on the back of a chair, steadying his nerves. Slowly, carefully, he lifted his raincoat off the back of the chair and reached down to grab the tatty high-tops. After several breaths and glances towards Byte and the Queen, he tiptoed towards the hidden door. His bare feet on the sawdust floor made for a hushed, stealthy approach.

He reached the section of the wall with the secret panel. Dare he? Surely, opening the door would cause everyone to wake up. It was a silly idea. He should return to Byte and the warm blankets and get some sleep. Before he could talk himself out of it, he pulled the mechanism. The Queen's engineering prowess was on full display when the door gave a very gentle swoosh as it slid upwards, as graceful as its designer. No one stirred. Bob took a deep breath and stepped out into the garden.

The grey half-light gave the garden a spooky atmosphere. The usually colourful flowers and vegetables appeared washed out, and every corner felt like it was hiding things that went bump in the night. Shadows danced, and even the slightest sounds were amplified as they echoed around the garden's walls.

Bob quickened his pace, treading lightly but swiftly, as if the grass were hot coals. He soon reached the hall wall but couldn't immediately find the hidden mechanism. His hands scrambled across the wooden planks with rising panic, as he felt a pressure at the back of his head as if something were watching him. He felt silly. He knew there was nothing in the garden and nothing to fear, as he'd been within these walls before. But that was before.

'This was a stupid idea,' he scolded himself. 'What are you doing?'

Click.

He found the board that activated the door, which rose with the same silent swoosh. Bob quickly stepped into the hall, ducking through the door, not waiting for it to finish rising. He found the panel to bring the door back to a closed position, letting out a sigh of relief as the garden disappeared.

When he turned to inspect the hall's interior, his sense of relief vanished. It was dark inside, lit only by the meagre half-light seeping through the small windows. The stage and the shed were darker shadowy shapes against a dark backdrop.

Sitting down, Bob pulled on his high-tops, tied the laces and tucked in the frayed bits. When he stood again, he brushed sawdust off the back of his jeans, took two puffs of his blue inhaler and slowly made his way towards the dark shadow of the shed.

Bob couldn't make out the stage steps, so rather than trying to find them, he fumbled towards the stage edge and heaved himself up. After a few creaky tiptoeing steps that echoed around the hall, Bob made it to the shed door.

A simple wooden latch lay across the door to stop it from swinging open on its own, rather than acting as a lock. Bob flipped the latch. Brimming with excitement and anticipation, he prepared to open the door and enter the shed. He prayed that whatever was beyond this door would hold the key to discovering who he was.

Once inside the shed, the sense of anticipation dissipated, replaced by a sense of disappointment. The shed was empty except for an angled shelf built into the back wall. Mounted on the shelf was a computer screen. It was the only piece of technology he had come across, and maybe Bob should have found it more remarkable, but he didn't.

Bob touched the screen, causing it to emit a sudden bright light. After so long stumbling around in the dark, it was as if someone were shining a torch in his face, and it took a moment for his eyes to adjust.

On the screen was an internet search engine. That was it? The mystical 'Archive' in the mysterious shed that everyone in town got their name from ... was the internet.

Wow.

Bob couldn't believe it. In some way, he was relieved at the simplicity of what he saw. Another part of him was disappointed it wasn't something else, something more ... well, just more. How did this have anything to do with playing the Archive music? And what about the PA voice?

Bob pressed the search bar. A keyboard appeared on the screen.

What to search for?

His first search – *You are Bob* – resulted in a string of famous people called Bob. Nothing about an unremarkable boy.

'What did you think you'd find?' Bob scolded himself under his breath.

Bob then typed *The Queen* and hit enter. The results were for Queen Elizabeth II.

'You're a complete and total idiot,' he said, typing a new search for *The Archive*.

The results were a little less obvious, but after a few minutes of browsing sites on rugby league archives and religious archives, he'd hit a dead end.

What should he search for that might give some insight?

'Wait a minute!'

He typed, *Today's news*.

The results showed the news for 6 November 2026. There was a political story, another self-serving politician involved in a money, sex and drugs scandal – all three at once, a triple hitter. Flash flooding had caused a devastating loss of life in a small village in Vietnam. Bob noted the poor judgement that this news outlet led with the politician story. What was wrong with some people? The third story was about a technology startup company making a breakthrough in artificial intelligence. According to the startup's CEO, the breakthrough would 'introduce sentient AI – heralding a new age, and a brave new frontier for humanity'.

'Is this today? It doesn't make sense. It still doesn't make any sense.'

'Did you find the answers you seek, boy?'

Bob froze.

The Librarian stood in the doorway of the shed. 'How *dare* you come in here! The Archive is sacred! I'll banish you for this, *boy*. Mark my words. I knew you were trouble when you arrived!'

The Librarian put a firm hand on Bob's shoulder and yanked him out of the shed. Bob tumbled onto the stage floor. The sun had started to rise, dimly lighting the hall.

The Librarian stood over him, face flushed with anger, pointing and waving his cane. Bob instinctively glanced towards the secret door to the Queen's garden.

The Librarian flicked his cane in the direction Bob was looking in. 'Whatever you may think, I'm in charge here, boy, not *her*. And it's me you will answer to. You'll pay for this, boy,' he spat, thumping his cane into the stage.

'Now, Librarian, you are a respected member of our community, but you do not make the laws,' the Queen's voice declared. It came from the other side of the curtain.

The Librarian's gaze shot in that direction. The curtain moved, and the Queen emerged, followed by Deck, Sunny and little Byte, who leaped next to Bob and started growling at the Librarian.

Bob's heart skipped a beat as the Librarian raised his cane in fury, meaning to strike Byte. Deck deftly grabbed the cane mid-swing. Furious at Deck's intervention, the Librarian pulled his cane from Deck's grasp, taking a step back.

Shuffling to his feet, Bob gave the Queen an apologetic, pained smile. She smiled back and gave him a little wink. Bob thought she was very understanding, particularly given that he had created a difficult situation for her with his misjudged actions.

Five now faced one, but the Librarian wasn't intimidated.

'I knew this would happen. I told you he was trouble!' he yelled at the Queen, as if scolding a small child.

The Queen remained calm, intentionally saying nothing, allowing the tension to build.

It was too much for Sunny. 'Yeah ... well ... you're a nincompoop!'

The Librarian became an all-new level of red, bordering on purple.

The rest of them just looked at Sunny with expressions that said, 'Really? Nincompoop?'

Sunny shrugged with a 'that was the best I could do' look.

Then the Librarian's expression suddenly and disconcertingly changed from red-hot fury to a satisfied smirk.

What the ...?

Bob felt arms wrapping around him. Two sets of impossibly strong, muscular arms tightened, forcing the air from his lungs. He tried to let out a shout, but his breath caught.

Someone pulled something over his head, tight.

Byte was whining.

Sunny was screaming.

He felt a sudden thud of pain across the back of his head.

———

Bob came to. The throbbing pain at the back of his head was intense, and he couldn't see because of the canvas bag. It stank of fish.

Bob knew he was outside, as it was bright, and he lay on the grass. A crowd of voices murmured to his left, and an almighty whooshing sound came from his right. He recognised the whooshing sound as the firewall, the backdrop to the feast, except he was much closer to it now.

Suddenly hands grabbed his arms and pulled him to his feet.

'Citizens!' The Librarian's voice rang out. 'Justice will be done today. This thing that wandered into our paradise has caused us nothing but harm!'

It must be some sort of trial, thought Bob. Perhaps sneaking into the Archive was a serious crime. *I'm such an idiot.*

The crowd murmured as if everyone was uncertain about what was happening and why.

'Stop!' It was the Queen's voice but without the usual calm poise. She was frightened by whatever was happening. 'This is madness!'

'Silence! Your weakness has no place here, Queen! We will have justice!'

Someone pulled the bag from Bob's head. Although he was grateful that the smell had gone with it, he recoiled at the bright light, straining to focus on the scene. His friends were all bound, on their knees, panic etched on their faces. Byte wasn't anywhere to be seen. Bob hoped the little guy was somewhere safe.

The Librarian had his back to Bob, addressing the collection of townsfolk that had gathered to witness … whatever this was. Surely these people understood that this man was an awful bully. Surely someone would step forward and stop whatever madness was taking place. Sense would prevail, wouldn't it? The kindness the Queen had spoken of would shine through and replace this vitriol, right? But what if it didn't? What would happen to him? A prisoner? A slave? Or ... banished. The Librarian meant to banish him! Bob felt a cold shudder, his palms sweating as his panic level rose. *No, he can't!* Bob had only just made friends, and where was Byte? He couldn't lose Byte. *Oh no.*

Everyone froze.

'Now? Really? This isn't the time.'

'*Accessing the Archive. Please wait.*'

'But I didn't do anything! No, no, wait, not now!'

Song choices flooded his vision. One image paused and flipped over. Bob scanned it.

'*Access complete. Returning to the Zoo. Please wait.*'

Everyone unfroze, and music started playing. The song choice, *I Just Died in Your Arms*, didn't help sober up the situation. If anything, it would encourage the lynch mob. The Librarian turned his head and grinned.

Why? thought Bob. *Why?*

'Banishment! It's the only way. We've always maintained the purity of the Zoo by banishing those who don't belong. We must banish him!' The Librarian spun on his heel to point his cane at Bob, then walked menacingly towards him, his face sporting a treacherous grin. 'You will not ruin this place, and your weak friends cannot save you from the will of the people.' The Librarian spoke softly so only Bob could hear.

While he stood so close, Bob caught the stench of his breath. Bob turned his face away, hands shaking, pressure building in his chest.

The Librarian stepped back and poked Bob in the stomach with his cane. Bob involuntarily stepped back, avoiding the worst of the blow. But it hurt, and he was a little winded.

'Please,' Bob implored. 'I'm nobody. I'm not a threat. I'm just ... just Bob.'

'Correct, boy. You're nobody. An insignificant flea on an insignificant dog. That's why I won't think twice about squishing you.'

Another poke of the cane, another step back. Then another, and another. The heat of the firewall was on Bob's back.

'Please,' Bob whimpered, inches from the firewall, tears squeezing out. 'Please.'

'Goodbye, flea.' The Librarian pulled back his cane for the final poke that would banish Bob from Byte and his friends forever.

Then, suddenly, the Librarian crashed to the ground.

With hands still tied behind his back, Deck had rugby-tackled the Librarian.

A gasp went up from the crowd, apart from Sunny, who yelled, 'Yay! Go, Deck!'

The Librarian cried out, clutching his side. 'How dare you interfere!'

'Bob, run!' Deck pleaded.

Bob didn't run. He froze on the spot. *Why am I such a coward? Why can't I be brave like Deck and —*

'Byte!' Bob spotted Byte emerging from the forest of legs in the crowd as he ran towards him.

From where he lay on the ground, the Librarian spotted Byte approaching, and he shot his cane out as Byte ran past. It hit the little furball with a crack, and Byte rolled to a limp stop at Bob's feet.

'Byte! No!'

The Librarian shot Bob a nasty grin.

Bob picked up Byte and cradled him. Byte's eyes were closed. He was breathing, but his breaths were shallow. Hopefully, Sunny was as good with dogs as she was with humans.

'Bob, watch out!' came the Queen's desperate voice.

Bob glanced at the Librarian, searching for the new danger, but he was still on the ground, smirking. Then several pairs of hands emerged from the firewall, grabbing Bob's raincoat and pulling him in.

'No, please, no!' Bob struggled to get free, but their grips were too strong, too sudden. The scene of the clearing, his friends and the Town faded to blue flame.

CHAPTER 10
THE ALLEY

Bob sat in a wide, gloomy alley littered with shadows between two tall stone buildings. The smell of days-old discarded food emanated from the industrial-sized waste bin he leaned back on, catching in his nostrils every few breaths. Byte lay at his feet, lovingly positioned on the raincoat to avoid direct contact with the dirty cobbles. Bob hugged his knees. What had just happened? It was all too much to take in. Tears fell as he stared vacantly at a discarded glass bottle.

Bob peeled one arm off his knees and stroked the still and unconscious Byte. 'Our friends will be fine. They are probably better off without me, anyway. I was just causing trouble for them.' Bob wiped a tear from his cheek with the sleeve of his jumper. 'Why don't I move, Byte? You're braver than I am. Deck tackled the Librarian – he's brave too. I'm not. I just cause problems for everyone.' Feeling utterly hopeless and utterly useless, he hugged his knees and cried, tears falling onto a discarded crisp packet that made a crinkling noise with each teardrop.

A long, creeping shadow interrupted Bob's self-pity, stretching across the crisp packet and onto the glass bottle. Dwarfed in the shadow, Bob tensed, feeling a chill as the hairs on the back of his neck stood up. Something massive loomed to his left.

'Move, boy,' a deep, cavernous, booming voice said.

Bob stared up at the owner of the shadow. A colossal figure, a gigantic golden-armoured mass of muscle supported on massive tree-trunk legs. Instead of a head, there was a porcelain matt-white skull perched on broad shoulders. The skull was smooth and terrifying, with sunken eyes. It appeared fragile, as if one slight tap might break it. Bob gawked at the ethereal sculpture come to life, standing in the alley in all its shining glory.

'If you don't move, boy, you will die today,' the giant boomed.

Bob stayed frozen to the spot – again. *Move, you idiot!* But he was too terrified to move.

'Don't say I didn't warn you,' boomed the porcelain-skulled giant as he reached into a holster on his back to retrieve a massive double-headed weapon.

Bob's fear level rose, his eyes widening as he gazed in awe at the impossible hues of red, orange and yellow that glowed from the weapon's lava shaft. Bob felt its warmth. A giant hammer sat on one end of the molten shaft; on the other, an axe. The figure before him made his fear of an old librarian with a walking stick seem ridiculous in comparison.

'Seriously, move.' The giant's booming voice echoed around the alley. He was pointing towards a nearby fire escape, gesturing that Bob should flee towards it.

Then Bob saw it, reflected in the giant's golden chest plate: a pair of red eyes. A twisted, rusting metal wolf stalked down the alley towards them. Bob soon found his motivation, picking up Byte and shooting towards the fire escape.

'Good! Now, squishy human, prepare to witness something awesome.'

Bob ran up the first flight of the fire escape and cowered on the landing, peering down at the two foes facing off in the alley.

The giant swung his double-headed weapon in a bravado display of twirls and flicks, switching the weapon effortlessly from one hand to the other in a blur of motion. Its molten colours created a fiery Catherine wheel as it spun around his back, over his head and in the air between the buildings where Bob cowered. The giant caught the falling weapon whilst leaping and twisting in the air, an impossible gymnastic move given his size. He landed effortlessly, axe pointed towards the wolf, accompanied by a beckoning gesture. 'Come and play, little kitty.'

The wolf growled and then leaped at the giant. At first Bob thought the giant wasn't going to move. Then, at the last possible moment, before the serrated metal jaws planted themselves around his arm, the giant flipped gracefully into the air, using the wall as a platform to spring off mid-jump and project himself even higher. As he sailed over the wolf, porcelain skull inches from the shards on the wolf's back, and his legs high in the air, he gave the wolf the middle finger.

Bob watched with awe, willing the giant to defeat the metal wolf.

Landing with poise, the giant simultaneously brought the hammer down towards the wolf. It smashed into the ground, narrowly missing, chipping a couple of shards from the wolf's hide. The force of the hammer striking the earth shook the whole alley, and Bob braced himself against the rails of the fire escape as it rattled. The ground undulated unnaturally from the hammer impact, like ripples on a pond after tossing in a stone. Bob spotted a backlit hexagon mesh that flurried with the ripples before fading.

The force of the hammer's impact threw the wolf off its feet and against the waste bin with a dreadful scraping and crunching sound. The bin lid flipped up, spilling some of its contents, and the stench filled the air.

While the beast scrambled to get back on its feet, the giant slung the weapon over his shoulder, turned his back and nonchalantly whistled, taking a few steps down the alley.

The wolf regained its composure and, growling, flung itself into another attack. Claws scraped on the cobbles, giving Bob a shudder as he recalled the noise from the chase in the tiled area.

As the wolf closed in, still with his back turned, the giant flipped the weapon over his shoulder and down his back, spinning as it fell, and kicked the butt of the axe head before it hit the ground. The momentum of the kick propelled the axe forward, splitting the beast in two. The weapon lost momentum, stopping beyond the back of the beast, and gravity caused the hammer head to fall, smashing the remains of the wolf, which were still peeling to the sides, into tiny pieces.

The giant executed a perfect pirouette and then took a deep bow. Bob involuntarily gave him a round of applause and then quickly stopped, realising he still didn't know if the giant was friend or foe.

'Thank you, squishy one. I told you I would be awesome, didn't I? Please, come down and join me.'

Bob gently picked up the raincoat with Byte wrapped up in it, and with his heart pounding and a lump in his throat, he carefully clanked down the metal fire escape steps, being careful with his precious cargo. The giant met Bob at the bottom step. Bob avoided his gaze, fixating on a spot on the ground instead.

The giant crouched. He towered over Bob even when crouching. Gently he put a finger under Bob's chin and lifted Bob's head, forcing their eyes to meet. Except this giant had no eyes, just hollow voids in a porcelain skull.

The giant lifted his other hand to his face and placed two fingers in his eye sockets.

What is he doing?

Then, with a pull accompanied by the soft whooshing sound of pressure releasing, the giant pulled away the front section of what turned out to be a mask. Behind the mask, a face grinned.

The giant had a jovial face, full of confidence and swagger. His skin was a deep black, and it moved. Bob spotted barely visible deep purple swirls that ebbed and flowed like a storm beneath the surface of his skin, moving over his bald head. What drew Bob's attention, though, was the giant's eyes. The irises were glittery, just like Byte's ear.

'Pleasure to meet you, small, squishy one. I'm the last of my people, a builder of systems and a destroyer of hexbeasts. You may call me Titch.' Titch shook Bob's hand. Or rather, Bob shook Titch's finger. 'And who might you be?'

'I'm Bob, sir, and this is Byte.'

'Sir! Call me Titch, please. And why were you so upset before, little Squishy Bob?'

'I'm sort of lost. My friends are back in the Zoo, and this little guy got hurt. I don't know how to help him.' Bob stared into Titch's eyes, transfixed.

'The Zoo, you say? That's interesting.' Titch pointed at Byte. 'It's also odd for a squishy human to have a hexpet.'

At that moment, a tiny lizard appeared, darting from a hiding place in Titch's chest plate. It scurried across the plate, down Titch's arm and onto his hand, which Titch held out so the lizard could inspect Bob. Like Byte's ear and tail tip, the lizard was entirely glittery.

'This is my hexpet, Grace. Grace, this is Squishy Bob and Byte.'

Grace, the lizard, tipped her head side to side regarding Bob. Then she hurried up Titch's arm and back under the chest plate.

'Lucky for you, Squishy Bob, I know someone who can get Byte back on his feet and would be very interested to hear about the Zoo. Come on, this way.' Titch stood up to his massive height and started walking out of the alley.

Bob decided he wouldn't hang around, just in case more metal creatures appeared, and it was probably best to stick close to the gigantic, muscled fighting machine. So Bob began walking with Titch, cradling Byte in his arms.

CHAPTER 11
THE LADY IN THE RED DRESS

Titch led Bob through cobbled streets lined with stone terraced houses stained with years of soot and grime. Then past a church with boarded-up windows and a graveyard filled with toppled headstones.

The air was fresh. There had just been a storm. Wizened trees with broken branches decorated the street corners. Puddles had formed in the potholes. Litter tumbleweeds clattered down the pavements, and window shutters rattled. Bob thought he spotted faces in the windows, which retreated as they approached, but maybe he was imagining things.

They rounded a street corner with a long-abandoned post office and newsagent. Beyond these boundary-defining buildings, the landscape became more rural, with drystone walls outlining patchy fields.

'Welcome to the dreariest, most miserable corner of the System, Squishy Bob,' Titch said without a hint of sarcasm. It was indeed a far cry from the lush, rolling landscape of the Zoo. 'Have you been here before?'

'No, I haven't.'

Or had he and he couldn't remember? Maybe this was his home.

'This is called Storage. It's where organic, squishy things like you live. Well, here and the Zoo. It was once a vibrant place but hasn't been the same since the Binary War.'

'There was a war?'

'Yes, over a year ago now. It was a mess, Squishy Bob, and the reason I'm the last of my people. Some humans survived despite it being far too easy for your insides to spill out.' Titch mimed someone's insides spilling out. 'Now, what did you think of my awesomeness? Pretty good, huh?' Titch asked.

'Yes, it was very impressive. You're a brilliant fighter,' Bob replied, and he meant it.

'Fighter? No, I'm no fighter. I'm a dancer!' Titch did a little twirl and a bow.

'Oh, but you did fight the metal wolf, though?'

'Well, yeah, but that's just part of the dance. If you're going to smash a hexbeast, you might as well do it with awesome style. No?'

'Sure, I suppose.' The last thing Bob wanted to do was disagree with the golden mass of muscle. 'What about your weapon? Isn't that for fighting?'

'This?' Titch pulled the massive weapon out of the holster on his back. The magma shaft had cooled into solid gold, and Bob could now see beautifully intricate patterns. It had compacted after the battle, before Titch had put it on his back, so it was a bit shorter but still enormous compared to Bob. Grace popped out and sat on Titch's shoulder, joining the inspection. 'This is no weapon, Squishy Bob. It's a tool called a hammeraxe.' He turned it in his hands, showing Bob all the details, particularly a symbol he said represented a bear. 'My people are mighty builders, and the hammeraxe is our sacred tool. It's also good for smashing metal morons, but that's not its primary purpose.'

'It's amazing,' Bob said as he studied the intricate patterns.

Titch's chest puffed out, and he grinned as he put the hammeraxe back in its holster and set off walking towards the dreary fields.

'Where do the hexbeasts come from?' Bob asked, figuring he could avoid going there if he knew.

'No idea, Squishy Bob. They appeared after the Binary War, but we don't know why, and they keep coming. So I keep smashing them.' Titch grinned.

Just then they heard a visceral scream from the direction of the terraces – a cry of terror that sent a chill down Bob's spine. The scream was suddenly cut short. Titch didn't break his stride or appear in the least bit fazed by the scream, although Grace scurried off to hide in Titch's armour somewhere.

'Ah, they must have bagged another one.'

'Was that a hexbeast? Shouldn't we go and help?' Bob meant 'you' but thought 'we' sounded less cowardly.

'No, Squishy Bob. Not hexbeasts. Butcher Boys. They will be long gone by now. It's not something for me to get involved in. Human business is human business.'

The Butcher Boys didn't sound like something Bob wanted to know about, but he asked the question anyway. 'Butcher Boys?'

'Some sicko who calls himself the Butcher sends out his twisted experiments to round up victims for more twisted experiments. They leave me alone, though.'

As good a reason as any to stick close to Titch, thought Bob.

They descended a slope tightly packed with silver birches and joined a canal towpath. Industrial buildings lined the path, separated by stone walls and patches of lush greenery.

'We're almost there … so, er, don't ask about her legs, okay? Or say anything that might upset her. It's probably best not to say too much at all, to be honest, just the facts. Oh, and keep a safe distance. She's dangerous, especially if she's angry.' Titch frowned and fiddled with some straps on his armour.

Bob was a mix of intrigued and scared. What sort of mighty creature would make Titch, a golden-clad, muscular giant, become filled with so much anxiety? He supposed he was about to find out – whether he liked it or not.

They soon left the towpath and climbed up a hill. As they

reached the top, Bob walked past a leafless, scraggly tree that resembled a big twig sticking out of the ground. The fields in the distance beyond the hill looked like several bombs had gone off in them. Bits of stone and metal were scattered between craters.

Just beyond the tree, a woman in a red dress sat on the ground, her skirt billowing in a circle around her. Slung over her shoulder was a giant golden lollipop. Around her neck was a mink, as white as snow, with a glittery tail. The mink wasn't moving, leaving Bob contemplating whether it was her hexpet or a fashion choice.

The woman in the red dress was pale and thin, with angular features and gold piercings in her lip and septum. Her bobbed hair was jet black, and jet-black eyes with glittery irises stared at Bob from behind a low fringe. She appeared pissed off, as if she'd just found a hair in her soup, but she didn't look dangerous. So Bob couldn't figure out why Titch was apprehensive enough to be cowering behind him.

'Did you mop up the last of them?' the lady in the red dress asked Titch.

'Sure did. Caught the last one in an alley in the old town.'

'Good. Now, why have you brought an organic sack of intestines with you? Do you want me to turn you into a toilet? Hmm? Let the humans take turns crapping into what was your face?'

'Come on, there's no need for that, Ayama,' Titch said, raising his hands defensively. 'I brought Squishy Bob because he said he's from the Zoo, which might help us. Oh, and he has a hexpet!' Titch pushed Bob forward.

Bob stumbled a couple of steps, still holding the raincoat with Byte wrapped up in it.

Ayama somehow managed to appear both pissed off and curious at the same time. She started to stand – no, she wasn't standing; she was floating. Both her legs were missing from the knees. The stumps were visible just below the dress as she hovered for a moment and then floated through the air towards Bob.

'Stop looking at my legs, turd sack,' she said as she closed in. 'And show me what you're holding.' She pointed at the raincoat.

Bob pulled back protectively as the mink moved, popping its head up and inspecting the raincoat. So it was a hexpet.

'No, you can't have him. He's hurt!'

'I don't want it, idiot. Show me.'

'His name's Byte.'

'That's nice. Show me. Now.'

Bob tentatively lifted a corner of the raincoat to reveal Byte, then held him out for Ayama to inspect. The mink slinked onto Ayama's arm and spiralled up and around the golden staff.

'Interesting. Whom did you steal it from?'

'I didn't steal him!'

'Hmm, well, it needs to recharge, and quickly. Place it on the ground.'

Bob wasn't sure if he should. This floating attitude in a red dress didn't fill him with confidence. *But*, thought Bob, *I've no idea how to help him. Dare I turn her down?*

He cautiously lowered Byte to the ground, covertly looking at Ayama's stumps. How was she floating?

'Stop looking at my legs, and put him directly on the ground. It won't work on that yellow abomination.'

How had she known he'd glanced at her legs?

Bob slid the unconscious Byte off the raincoat and onto the grass as carefully as possible.

'Now take a step back, turd sack.'

Bob paused, considering his options, then did as instructed and stepped back, cursing himself for being so easily influenced.

Ayama floated back to the ground, the red dress forming a circle around her as she held her hand just above Byte. Suddenly a backlit hexagon mesh appeared underneath the little furball. The mesh gently pulsated, appearing alive with energy.

'Now we wait. Sit, turd sack, and talk. I need information on the Zoo.'

Bob sat, as did Titch. Reluctantly he told Ayama his story of the Zoo, leaving out the bit in the tiled space. She only asked about the Zoo, and he wasn't as comfortable talking to Ayama as he had been with the Queen, so his telling of the story was more concise.

When he got to the Archive, Ayama spat. 'Ugh, the Archive. I read it once. The biggest waste of forty nanoseconds ever, and that's saying something, as I have to tolerate this tiny moron.' She gestured towards Titch, who shrank down.

Bob suddenly became more animated, sitting up straight. 'You know the Archive? Please, tell me more about it.'

'I told you, it's a waste of time. Don't bother.'

'Please,' Bob implored.

'Ugh. Ancient, turd-filled humans had something called the internet. The Archive is a snapshot of the internet taken before artificial intelligence made a mess of what was real and what wasn't. You organic wastes of space have been blindly misinterpreting the thing ever since. Hoping to fix your idiotic behaviour. Surprise, surprise, it didn't work.'

'Wait, you read the internet in forty nanoseconds?' Bob said, narrowing his eyes.

'Yes, and I wish I hadn't. It made me want to puke. Organic, wobbly, air-filled turds fixate on putting everyone into tiny boxes. Men are like this. Women are like that. Black-skinned people are all X. Older people are all Y. Complete and utter nonsense. But you argued and made silly pictures to marginalise each other. My only reasoned analysis is that there are only two types of air-filled turd-sack humans.' She stopped talking, a sour expression on her face.

'What are they?'

'What are what?'

'What are the two types of humans?'

'Really? You want to know? It's boring.'

'Yes, please.'

'Ugh. The only accurate way to divide humans is that you're either one, a dickhead, or two, not a dickhead. Every other category – old, young, gay, blah blah – is individual to each turd sack. Easy. Anyway, enough of the Archive. It's boring me. Keep going.'

Bob picked his story back up where he'd left off, and finished at the point when he'd been pulled through the firewall. His mind kept wandering away from the story, trying to decipher what Ayama had just told him about the internet.

When he finished, Ayama turned to Titch. 'Where did you find him?'

'The alley behind the old mill.'

'Damn. It will have closed already. There is no pattern! We'll stick with the original plan.'

'What's going on?' asked Bob.

'We're trying to get into the Zoo, Squishy Bob, but the firewall keeps moving.'

'But you can't get back in. It's a one-way thing,' Bob said, remembering what the Queen had told him. He felt pleased that he knew something important.

Ayama rolled her eyes. 'Oh, thank you for telling me. I didn't know. What would we have done without a turd sack to tell us how the System worked.'

Bob thought she was very rude. This was all new to him. He made a mental note not to be helpful again. It wasn't worth the inevitable chiding. Hopefully, she'd go away and leave Titch and Bob on their own.

Seeing Bob's downcast expression, Titch took pity on him. 'The firewall is full of holes,' he explained. 'It's been like that since the war. But the holes keep moving randomly. It's like trying to find a needle in a haystack.'

'Why do you need to get in?' Bob asked.

'Because the power in our sections is running out, Squishy

Bob. Something is draining it. Our theory is that if we get into the Zoo, we might find a way to power our sections back up.'

'Enough chitty-chatting. No more hexbeasts are coming this way. We'll set off for the Information Desk, as planned.' Ayama made to leave, hovering up and backwards as she spoke. The mink uncoiled from the golden lollipop staff and settled back into place around her neck.

Titch stood up to follow, giving Bob an apologetic glance.

'Wait, what about me? Can't I come?' Bob asked, bordering on pleading. Bob wasn't about to let go of the safety a golden-armoured giant afforded him, and an Information Desk sounded the right sort of place to discover who he was.

'I don't care what you do,' Ayama said.

'Let little Squishy Bob come with us, Ayama. He can help us.'

Ayama just laughed sarcastically and continued hovering down the hill towards the area that resembled a war zone.

'Come on, Squishy Bob. It will be nice to have some friendly company.' Titch offered Bob a hand to help him up.

'What about Byte?' Bob said, sorrowfully looking down at the motionless furball with the backlit hexagons still pulsating underneath him. His breathing had improved slightly.

'You'll have to bring him along and finish his recharge later.'

Bob lifted Byte, and the hexagons immediately retreated. After wrapping the limp furball in the raincoat, he cradled him and set off with Titch down the hill.

CHAPTER 12
NIGHTMARE

I must find the boy with the dog. I must.'

Nightmare climbed quickly and silently up the side of a steep stone building using his four long, muscular arms.

He swung onto the flat roof and ran towards the opposite edge at an incredible speed, insect-like on all six limbs. Once at the edge, he leaped high into the air, traversing to the roof of the building opposite.

After landing silently, he stopped, sniffing the air. It was thick with the stench of humans. His senses detected something else, something ... different.

He must not fail. His master would be angry and would punish Nightmare. His master had created him for this task.

He ran again, leaping to cross to the next roof. *What was that?* Nightmare made a split-second twist in the air, landed on the opposite roof in a handstand and then flipped backwards to fall feet first down the gap between the buildings he'd just leaped between. Something glinted in the alley below.

Nightmare broke his fall by leaping from wall to wall, then flipped and landed, all six limbs on the ground. He scuttled towards the pile of metal shards. 'Interesting. Hexbeast. Smashed to pieces. The master will want to know of this.'

A long tongue shot out of Nightmare's mouth. He licked the

edge of a section of the carcass. 'No human weapon made this mark.'

Nightmare's eye scanned the alley. His nose lifted into the air, sniffing. There were three scents. One builder. He hated builders, so pompous and shiny. Another, hexpet, almost deathless. The last was human. A boy. But there was something else. *Hmm, this isn't right.*

'I have found the boy with the dog. I must follow.'

A visceral scream of terror rang out from one of the nearby houses. It was suddenly cut short.

'Ah, the boys have found a present for the master. Good. He will be pleased.'

CHAPTER 13
THE INFORMATION DESK

'What's the Information Desk?' Bob asked Titch.

Titch shrugged. 'It's the best place to go if you're not sure where to go. Apparently.'

As they talked, Titch and Bob stepped around the debris of smashed-up hexbeasts and chunks of a wall. It had turned blustery, so they were leaning into the wind. Bob's ears whistled, and they had to shout to hear each other despite being close.

'What happened here?' asked Bob as he navigated around half a metal dog.

'Her Awesomeness.' Titch pointed towards Ayama, who was a good few paces ahead. She moved far quicker, floating over the battleground rather than having to sidestep potholes and jagged remains of hexbeasts.

'She did all this?' Bob studied the wreckage, amazed. There were very few hexbeasts in one piece, which made it difficult to count, but he estimated dozens of the creatures. One skinny, angry lady did all this with just the lollipop thing and missing her legs? It may have taken four or five golden giants like Titch to cause this much damage.

Titch spotted the confused expression on Bob's face. 'She's a hacker.'

'A what?'

'A hacker. You've never heard of hackers, Squishy Bob?'

Bob shook his head.

'They're expert coders. She will have made light work of this lot.'

'Why do you put up with her being rude to you like that?' Bob asked.

Titch's eyes lowered. 'She's very powerful, Squishy Bob, and angry. That combination is dangerous.'

Bob struggled to make sense of it at all. Titch was huge and a fantastic fighter. Why would he be scared of anyone? But he didn't press the point. Instead, curiosity got the better of him. 'What happened to her legs?' he asked.

'Shh! Keep your voice down. She might hear you!' Titch crouched slightly to lower his voice without the wind carrying it off. Grace popped onto his shoulder, scanning around like a lookout in a crow's nest. 'She lost them in the war. I'm not sure how.'

Bob was going to ask how she floated and about the mink hexpet, but Ayama stopped and was waiting for them at the end of the battlefield. Bob and Titch said no more in case she heard them, and they scrambled around the last of the debris to join her.

'Let's take the bus, morons. It's too far to walk.'

Bob searched for a bus stop or a big red double-decker with a number on it and a destination sign that read INFORMATION DESK, with a cheerful driver who would enquire how his day was going. However, there was no sign of any such thing. 'Where's the bus stop?'

'Ugh. Not that type of bus, turd sack. Humans. Always obsessed with some archaic past. It's a serial bus. There's one here that'll take us to the Information Desk. I'm not sure if it will take humans. If you melt or explode or something, it's no great loss. In fact, it'll make my day.'

Bob ignored Ayama's taunts, scanning the area for the 'bus', but saw only muddy fields and drystone walls.

'Sure, but won't it use most of our energy?' Titch asked.

'Yes, but we'd use a similar amount of energy walking. We're done for if we encounter another batch of hexbeasts. We'll recharge at the Information Desk. Are you ready to explode into tiny pieces, turd sack?' Ayama smirked.

Nope, Bob thought. He weighed his choices. If he stayed here, he'd be at the mercy of the Butcher Boys or the hexbeasts. If he travelled with Titch and Ayama, he might not survive the journey. It was a no-win situation.

His inner turmoil surfaced. A voice telling him to be decisive and not to be a coward. He needed to get to the Information Desk to find out who he was. He needed to help Byte, and only Ayama seemed to know how. *Make a decision!* 'I'll come.'

'Good, Squishy Bob! I'll be grateful for the company. Don't worry. It's not as bad as she says. You probably won't explode. Probably.'

They formed a line. Ayama slammed her lollipop into the ground to the sound of metal hitting metal, making Bob jump. Ayama's mink corkscrewed around the staff.

'Are you ready, Squishy Bob?' Titch gave Bob a disconcerting, uncertain smile.

The inner turmoil returned. *Wait, no, I'm not ready. Maybe I'll hide here. Perhaps the Butcher Boys won't return. Maybe there's someone here who knows me.*

Ayama twisted her staff. *Click.*

'Here we go!' Titch grabbed Bob's hand, and then – ZOOP!

All three of them dropped through the ground. They fell a short distance under the earth, as if a trapdoor in a stage had opened beneath them. They all paused – suspended in mid-air.

Bob tightly clutched Titch with one hand as he clung to Byte with the other. Everything around them was stark white, and they just hung in the infinite white nothingness. There were no tiles, but Bob thought everything else was reminiscent of the tiled space.

Then, suddenly and without warning, they were propelled

forward at an incredible speed. WHOOSH! Bob's stomach somersaulted, and amid the chaos, he was sure he heard Ayama swearing, using words he had never imagined strung together in a sentence. Oddly enough, her swearing sounded gleeful, as if she relished the experience. She was an incredibly peculiar lady.

Bob's eyes started watering as they accelerated, faster and faster. The skin on his face felt as if it would rip clean off. Maybe he would explode – it certainly felt like a precursor to it. Bob closed his eyes, his grip on Byte tightening. *Argh!* The accelerating force froze his body.

WHOOSH! They abruptly slowed to a stop, hovering again, and then ZOOP! Up they went, back above ground.

With his feet back on a firm surface, Bob steadied himself, feeling dizzy and nauseous.

'Oh, you survived. How disappointing,' Ayama said as she floated towards a large building reminiscent of an Edwardian manor house. Her mink uncoiled from the staff and lay around her neck.

The stately building stood on its own amid a formal Renaissance garden. Symmetrical geometric hedges surrounded fountains, statues and neatly organised flower beds buzzing with bees and filling the air with sweet floral scents.

Steps led up to the large stone building, where four pillars supported an elaborate portico, with two large wooden doors beyond. A gold sign on one of the doors read:

Information Desk
Please Ring the Bell

Before Bob or Titch could intervene, Ayama was hammering on the door and shouting, 'Open the door, or I'll turn your arms into toilet paper and let the almighty Controller wipe his backside on you for eternity!'

Knowing full well the futility of repairing Ayama's rude introduction, Bob reached up and pulled the cord to ring the bell, feeling the need to follow the instructions. The bell jingled, and the doors swung open on their own.

'Come in, my dears!' a warm, friendly voice said. 'I'm just in the kitchen. I'll be out in a second. Wait at the desk.'

They walked through the doors and into an elaborate entrance hall. The crystals in an ornate chandelier tinkled gently as Titch's feet thumped on the mosaic floor. He stopped in the centre of the hall and stood motionless, as if he were a statue that had always been there.

Breaking with the ostentatious decor was a rickety trestle table in the middle of the entrance hall, empty save for a handwritten cardboard sign. Scribbled in green crayon was the word *Informayshon*.

Ayama floated over to a vast red-carpeted staircase that split left and right halfway up and slumped down on the bottom step, scowling from under her fringe.

Bob wandered around, gazing at the stained-glass windows and stone carvings, feeling unsteady, as if he'd just stepped on land after a week at sea. Hopefully, these grand walls held the key to who he was. A sense of nervous anticipation left a tingling feeling in his toes and the need to reach into his raincoat for his inhaler.

A door creaked open, and a plump old lady entered. She had short grey curls and wore a blouse, pleated skirt and a cardigan that Bob assumed she'd knitted herself – it was that sort of cardigan. She shuffled behind the trestle table on slippered feet without uttering a word or acknowledging any of them.

THUD.

She dropped a colossal tome onto the table, causing it to sag in the middle. Bob winced, convinced that the table would crack in two. Then she put on spectacles that hung around her neck on a beaded strap and opened the great tome. Bob spotted a badge on her cardigan that read:

Karen
Information Desk Manager

Karen peered over her glasses. 'Now then, my lovelies. How may I help?'

Titch motioned to speak, but Ayama cut across him. 'We need to get into the Zoo, old lady. Tell us how.'

'You can't breach the firewall, my dear. It's impossible. May I help you with anything else?'

'Stop lying, witch! Where are the holes in the firewall?' Ayama's mink coiled back around the lollipop staff, glaring at Karen and making a hissing noise.

'There are no holes in the firewall, dear.'

'Argh! Another dim-witted, air-filled intestine sack. What a waste of time! I'm going outside to find somewhere to recharge. When I return, you will tell me what you know, witch. Come on, Sebastian.'

Karen's eyes followed Ayama as she hovered out. The mink, apparently named Sebastian, uncoiled from the staff and returned to its place around Ayama's neck.

'I need to recharge too, Squishy Bob. Are you going to be okay?'

Bob nodded in response and was soon left alone in the entrance hall with Karen, the Information Desk manager.

Karen peered over her spectacles and smiled kindly. 'How would you like a nice cup of tea?'

Bob nodded coyly, and Karen led him through the door she'd emerged through earlier.

The room beyond was an enormous formal dining room with a huge dining table in the centre. Gold-framed pictures of austere aristocrats adorned the walls. The table, the floor and the furniture around the room's edges were piled high with books, newspapers, magazines and Manila folders with even more papers. It was a shocking mess. It also made the room smell of old paper, like an antique bookshop.

'Sorry for the mess, dear. One of the downsides of being an Information Desk is that you always need a lot of information. I really need to find someone to put everything in order for me.' Karen stopped by a kettle precariously perched on a stack of books. She set it to boil and then hunted through nearby ornate dressers and fancy sets of drawers. 'Ah, here we are.' She reappeared from the depths of a cupboard with two fine china teacups. 'Now, what information do you need, my dear?' she asked as she prepared the tea.

'Well, I have loads of questions.'

Bob's mind was racing, trying to find the best question to ask, just in case Karen worked a bit like a genie and he'd only get a few tries.

'Who am I?' asked Bob.

'Well, you are a human boy, dear. Nothing more.'

'I've no memories, though. Do you know me? Or know where I'm from?'

'Sorry, dear. I've never met you before. You're probably from Storage. That's where most humans come from.'

Damn, he thought. Well, if he couldn't find out who he was, deciphering all the other things he didn't understand would be an excellent second option. Karen handed him a teacup filled with tea.

'What's the System? No, wait … Who's the Controller? No … What's the Zoo? What are hackers? Oh, and builders? Sorry. I didn't mean to ask all my questions at once.'

'Wow, that's a lot of questions!' Karen gave a little giggle and smiled kindly at him.

'Sorry.' Bob turned away to stare at a spot on the floor.

'No need to apologise, my dear. It's my job to provide information. Where to start? Hmm. I know.' She got up from her seat and started to rummage around in a pile of papers. 'I know it's around here somewhere. I do wish I kept things in better order.'

Bob sipped his tea. It tasted very sweet and like she'd used that plastic milk found in hotels. Bob started to consider his options for getting rid of the distasteful tea. Maybe there was a plant nearby that needed watering.

'Ah, here it is!' Karen emerged from a pile of papers and handed Bob a crinkled 'Beginner's Guide to the System' leaflet. It was the sort of leaflet you would get in a hotel lobby, from a stand filled with leaflets for places to visit.

'It has all the basics, but I'll give you a bit of a synopsis of the best bits.' Karen put her tea down on a pile of magazines, causing them to wobble precariously. 'Okay, now, millennia ago, humans – that's us, dear – destroyed Earth to the point where it was more or less uninhabitable. Billions died. It was a real mess.' She said this casually, as if describing what she had got up to on a particularly dull Sunday. 'The only way to survive was to rebuild Earth artificially.' She picked up her tea, causing two magazines to fly off the pile. 'Our new "artificial Earth" is essentially one giant computer system; hence, everyone refers to it as "the System". Are you following me so far, dear?'

Bob was stunned. His brain was working overtime trying to make sense of everything. But he was following. Feeling bad that he wanted to abandon the tea, given Karen had gone to the trouble of making it, he took another dreadful sip.

'On the tipping point of destruction, humans created two brand-new races for the rebuilding task: hackers and builders. They are synthetic, part of the System. Builders, well, they build, and hackers animate what builders have built. Bringing it to life, making the grass sway, the trees creak and the water run. Biscuit?'

The biscuits Karen held out on a posh china plate were well past their sell-by date, but of course, Bob took one – *Idiot*.

'Where was I? Oh yes. To maintain order on this brave new Earth, humans created four mighty controllers. Three of these godlike creatures represent each race. The human controller was a giant man called Bacchus. The builder controller, their king, Wodenar. And Syntax, a brilliant hacker. The fourth controller, the Archive, is not aligned to a race. She represents the planet itself and holds the knowledge of Earth from a long-ago past. It's her job to make sure those building Earth of the future avoid the mistakes that destroyed it in the first place. More tea?'

The Archive was a god? Was the PA lady the Archive? The giant that visited the Town must have been this Bacchus. Bob's head hurt as he processed Karen's information and tried to link it to what he'd experienced.

Bob finished his sugary, plastic-milk tea by gulping it down as quickly as possible to avoid too much contact with his taste buds. All his willpower was going into not making a face to go with it. Politely he declined another cup – he wasn't sure he could stomach it. However, he was in two minds, as the biscuit he was nibbling on sucked all the moisture from his mouth.

'Let me know if you change your mind, dear. Now, each controller had a mighty hexpet to protect them: Bacchus, a dog; Wodenar, a bear; Syntax, a dragon; and the Archive, a cat. Each race reveres these hexpets almost as much as they revere the controllers themselves.'

Bob instinctively stroked Byte when he heard about the hexpets. Karen looked kindly at Byte, still wrapped in the raincoat and breathing shallowly.

'Poor thing. He needs a recharge. What happened to him?'

'He was hit by someone called the Librarian just before we left the Town in the Zoo. He's been like this ever since.'

'Poor thing! Bring him over here.' Karen leaned in conspiratorially. 'I have a secret supercharger.'

She went over to a large pile of encyclopaedias and started moving them, but her joints were stiff, and she held her lower back.

'Let me,' said Bob.

He popped Byte down on the only free space on the table and

helped move the encyclopaedias, which were all in the wrong order, to another space on the floor. Moving the last few books revealed a glittery tile amid the lavish parquet flooring.

'Thank you, my dear. I'm not as sprightly as I used to be. Now, just pop the poor thing down on the tile.'

Bob did as instructed and laid Byte on the tile. A backlit hexagon mesh appeared underneath Byte. It pulsed more vigorously than when Ayama had done it. Byte started to flinch as if he were having a nightmare.

'He'll be as right as rain in no time. Now, whilst he's recovering, let me tell you about the Zoo and the factory. Or more accurately, factories.'

Karen offered Bob another biscuit, but he'd hidden the remains of the last one behind a pile of Manila folders and wasn't going to take another.

'Okay, the Zoo. Now, Bacchus wanted to recreate Earth as authentically as possible, with help from his friend the Archive. On the other hand, Syntax felt the Earth should not be recreated as it had been, considering humans destroyed everything in the first place. Wodenar wanted to stay neutral, but in reality, he sat on the fence, doing nothing. Are you sure you don't want anything else, dear? A glass of water, maybe?'

Bob enthusiastically agreed to the glass of water. He'd a terrible aftertaste from the tea and the dry biscuit. Karen's hand disappeared behind a pile of newspapers and reappeared holding a glass of water. Where had she got that from? Bob thanked her and nervously took it.

'Now, where was I? Oh yes. So Bacchus and Syntax clashed fiercely and often, disagreeing over the involvement of humans in the future of Earth. Fearing for humanity's safety and with the hidden agenda of proving that he was right, Bacchus created the Zoo. It protects the humans inside from the rest of the System, and he used the freedom it gave him to experiment with Archive lore. Trying to create a perfect human race that wouldn't mess everything up again. Have some of your water, dear, before it gets cold.'

The water tasted like it had been sitting still for months. Lukewarm and slightly fizzy. Bob glanced over at Byte, who started to toss and turn. Maybe this supercharger thing was working. It was a relief to see him move again.

'Now, factories. Factories are where humans, builders and hackers are made. There is one factory for each race. Humans don't reproduce any more as they did in the Archive. Bacchus wanted to start introducing reproduction into the Zoo, but only when he was certain they would be true humans. Ones that wouldn't mess things up.'

Byte whimpered, and Bob scrambled to get close, accidentally knocking over his water. *Oh well, no loss there.* 'Byte!' Byte was sitting up and vacantly looking around woozily. 'You're okay!'

Hearing Bob's voice, Byte gave a friendly '*Yip!*' Then he spotted Karen and started growling.

'No, Byte, no. This is Karen. She's been helping me. She's given me this leaflet.' Bob presented the leaflet to Byte. He sniffed it, then continued to growl at Karen. 'Now, Byte, that's no way to treat someone who has helped you. She's the one who recharged you,' Bob said in his best scolding-parent tone, which wasn't great.

'It's all right, dear. I'm not an animal person, and he can probably tell. Besides, he'll still feel disorientated from the recharge. System creatures like him or your friends outside shouldn't let themselves get that low. They might run out completely, and then you'll never get them back.'

Suddenly an almighty thud echoed around the room. Someone was hammering on the front door.

The noise caused Karen to glance at a thin silver watch on her wrist. 'Goodness, is that the time? I don't mean to be rude, but I'll have to send you on your way. It's almost closing time! Another biscuit for your travels?'

Karen hurried Bob to the door. 'Thank you for visiting, dear. It's nice to have customers.' She paused, leaning on the ledge next to the door. 'Earlier, you asked me who you are. There's one place you might find the answer, but it's dangerous. Never mind. Forget I mentioned it. It's a silly idea.'

'Please!' Bob urged. 'Where?'

'The old factory. The one used to make humans before the war. It's where you will have been made. If there's any information about who you are, chances are it's in the factory. But it's dangerous. The Butcher calls the factory his home now, not somewhere you want to go.'

Bob raised his hand to ask more questions about the factory, but Karen fussed him out of the door. Byte growled at her as she grabbed a cardboard sign from a ledge. On it in scruffy blue crayon was written ~~chut~~ clozed. She hung the sign on a nail. 'Bye, dear, bye.' She started to close the door.

'Wait!'

A metal staff shot into the gap, preventing the doors from closing.

'What now? I'm trying to close! No more information!' Karen snapped, her demeanour turning on a penny, her face becoming red.

'Screw you, old witch lady. I have one more thing I need to know, and you'll tell me. Or I'll turn your nice house into a rotting pile of garbage.'

'She would as well,' whispered Titch to Bob behind his hand.

'What is it? Be quick!'

'The human sectors, Storage and the Zoo, can be rebooted, restoring power to all sectors. Where is the switch, wrinkly old witch?'

'That information is no good to you. Even if you did find the switch, you can't activate it. Only Bacchus can, and he's dead!' Karen's face grew even more crimson, her eyes watering, her words more clipped.

'Tell me anyway, witch.' Ayama's eyes narrowed.

'It's in the old factory, on the other side of Storage, but the way is blocked!'

'And where inside the factory is the switch?'

'No more information! Now, get out! We're closed!' Karen kicked Ayama's staff out of the way of the doors and slammed them shut. There was an audible click as Karen turned the key in the lock.

'Nasty piece of work, that one,' Ayama said as she glared at the closed door.

'She was nice to me,' Bob said. 'She even recharged Byte.'

'I don't care.' Ayama hovered off, slamming her staff into the ground and twisting as she exited the garden.

Click.

Suddenly the statue in the middle of the garden became animated. It stretched, then turned on its pedestal and made an obscene gesture towards the house. It repeated the sequence over and over.

Bob's jaw dropped. 'Wait a minute. She can do magic!'

Titch chuckled. 'It's not magic, Squishy Bob. It might look like magic if you've never met a hacker before, but she just hacked the statue, that's all.'

Whatever it was, Bob was impressed. However, he still gave the gesturing statue a wide berth as he followed Titch out of the Information Desk garden, trying to keep up with Ayama as she floated ahead.

CHAPTER 14
THE COLOSSEUM

t was a cold night camping outside the Information Desk garden, so Titch used his hammeraxe to generate warmth.

Bob spent the time chatting with Titch, whilst Ayama sulked in a corner, clearly still furious from her interaction with Karen.

Byte was back to his usual lively self, darting off to explore the garden, returning to Bob for some attention before disappearing again. At one point, he played a game of catch with Grace, who shot around Titch's armour. Byte bounced around Titch, trying to catch her, but just as the little pup thought he'd caught the lizard, she shot into a crevice between the golden plates. The pair thoroughly entertained Bob and Titch. Ayama's mink, Sebastian, did not join in.

'Do you know anything about the old factory?' Bob asked Titch.

'No, Squishy Bob. But if it's where the reboot switch is, we must find it.'

'Can I come with you? Karen said I'll learn more about who I am in the factory.'

'It's fine with me. You'll have to check with Ayama. Hopefully, this factory holds the answers to all our problems.'

Bob nodded, his thoughts drifting to the dangers lurking in the factory. If he hid behind Titch, he should be okay.

'Can I come with you to the old factory?' Bob shouted over to Ayama.

Titch backed up Bob's request. 'Please, Ayama. He needs to find out who he is.'

'I know who he is. He's an irritating pain in my backside. I'm going to the old factory. I don't care what you do.'

'Great!' Titch exclaimed.

At sunrise, the companions set off across the Storage sector to the old factory. They were currently passing through a barren grey landscape. Heathers and short, dry grasses carpeted coarse hills, littered with the odd derelict building. The grass rustled as intermittent cold winds gusted, numbing Bob's hands and feet. The evening of playing catch had worn Byte out, so he was back in his usual spot in the pocket of Bob's raincoat, poking out his head and paws. Bob was pleased to have Byte back.

'We can't risk going by bus, morons. We might not be able to recharge at the other end.'

Walking was hard and cold, but Bob also didn't want a repeat of the face-melting bus, so walking it was, and Titch's company brightened the dull, grey day. Bob was very grateful he'd met Titch in the alley. Otherwise, he'd have perished by that wolf or been forced to hide in the stone terraced houses, scared of being carried off by the Butcher Boys. Having a giant clad in gold armour as a companion was no bad thing. It made him feel a lot safer. He missed Sunny, Deck and the Queen, though.

'So, you have witnessed my awesomeness and the aftermath of Ayama's. What's your super-awesomeness, Squishy Bob?'

'I'm not awesome! I'm just a boy!'

Ayama scoffed in agreement.

'Come on! Everyone has super-awesomeness. I bet you do too, Squishy Bob.'

Bob knew he wasn't special. Ayama was some kind of magic person, even if she was permanently pissed off. Titch was a mighty giant warrior, able to dance through his enemies. Sunny and Deck were the nicest people ever, and they had each other. And the Queen was a brilliant leader. 'There isn't anything awesome about me. Although ... do you like music?'

Titch's eyes lit up. 'I love music! I'm a dancer, remember! Dancing is much harder without music. You sing, Squishy Bob? That is awesomeness if you can.'

'If it works, I'll do something better than singing.'

Bob concentrated.

'*Accessing the Archive. Please wait.*'

Titch and Ayama froze. Bob was finding this process increasingly easy. The images moved slowly this time, and Bob just about manipulated them by concentrating and moving his hands in time with the flow, like a conductor in front of an orchestra. Once Bob was in rhythm with the images, he could slow them down or speed them up. There wasn't anything Titch might like, nothing good to dance to. Concentrating again, he changed the images to something closer to what he wanted.

'*Access complete. Returning to Storage. Please wait.*'

His companions unfroze and stopped dead in their tracks. Titch beamed. If possible, he was even more gleeful than usual. Then he started dancing. He spun, pirouetted and leaped. He was rising, falling, stretching and turning, his movements executed with poise, grace and precision, perfectly synchronised with Bob's chosen song. If Bob thought Titch's fighting skills in the alley were impressive, this was on another level. Despite his enormous stature and golden armour, Titch wasn't clumsy or labouring; he was truly magnificent. Bob, Byte and Ayama acted as the audience. All, even Ayama, were captivated by the skill and beauty of the movement.

Eventually, the song ended, and Titch held his final pose, breathing heavily with a beaming grin. 'You, Squishy Bob, have the most awesome gift of all. I haven't been able to dance like that for a long time! You have filled my heart with happiness.'

Bob didn't respond, shuffling his feet shyly, warmth spreading across his cheeks.

'Impressive, but completely useless,' Ayama said, having snapped out of her captivated state and resumed her default demeanour of gloomily staring out from under her fringe.

'Well, I thought you were amazing. Thank you,' said Bob.

'No! Thank you, Squishy Bob! Are you able to play music anytime?'

'Yes. It used to make me feel sick, but I control it better now.'

'Play another!' pleaded Titch.

'No!' responded Ayama forcefully before Bob could speak. 'You will drain yourself with this pointless twirling. Save your energy.'

Titch's shoulders noticeably slumped. 'I suppose you're right.'

'I can play music just to listen to if you promise not to dance,' replied Bob.

'Oh, perfect!'

They continued the rest of the way through the grass and heather, listening to song after song. Titch constantly reacted as if it were Christmas and he'd just got the gift he'd always wished for. He allowed himself the occasional twirl or hand movement, all of which received a glare from Ayama. Bob enjoyed playing songs for Titch, carefully picking things he might like.

As they walked, Titch told Bob stories about the builders. The builders' homeland was high in the mountains in another sector, but they spent most of their time wandering all of Earth's sectors, rebuilding them. Nomadic and solitary, builders gathered once every two years in the mountains for a celebration, to listen to the will of Wodenar and to swap stories of the great things they had built. 'It's called the Gathering, two days of feasting and stories!' Titch said with excitement.

Bob learned that all builders had a porcelain skull-like mask. Each mask was unique, solid and unbreakable despite its appearance. All builders also wore golden armour. The mask and the armour acted as protection whilst building.

Time passed quickly in good company, and as their shadows grew longer, the landscape became rockier and sandier, with occasional tufts of grass. Despite the late hour, the air felt dry and warm, defrosting Bob's hands and feet.

After what felt like an age of nothing but barren land and the occasional wrecked building, they saw a large circular structure in the distance.

'Ah! The Colosseum!' Titch exclaimed. 'My father built this. It's a replica of an Archive building.'

Bob concentrated.

'*Accessing the Archive. Please wait.*'

As usual, everyone froze. No images flooded Bob's vision this time. Just one hovered before him: a picture of the Colosseum, in Rome. Bob touched the image, and it flipped, revealing a list of facts. Bob read them.

'*Access complete. Returning to Storage. Please wait.*'

'It's an ancient amphitheatre, built by the Romans and used for gladiatorial shows.'

'Impressive, Squishy Bob! You're smart.'

Ayama floated on ahead. 'It's good we're here. It means we're going the right way. We'll recharge inside. It's getting late, morons, so we'll stay the night.'

It was getting dark when they arrived at the huge and imposing Colosseum. Bob couldn't shake a tense and anxious feeling. It was that grey half-light time again. Nothing good ever happened in the gap between night and day.

The builders had recreated the entire Colosseum, with the outer walls and without the earthquake damage. The towering structure appeared as it might have when it had been brand new, rising like a giant's citadel, with massive arches supported by massive columns.

The party made its way through the outer and inner walls and into the sand-covered arena ringed by soaring tiers of seats. Stepping out into the arena, Bob marvelled at its magnificence. It was impressive that the builders had recreated it, but more impressive that humans had come up with such a structure in the first place.

Bob imagined Titch as a gladiator; he already looked like one. He would enter to the cheers of adoring fans, twisting and twirling his hammeraxe, ready to terrify whoever was unlucky enough to oppose him that day. Sand would fly; blood would spill; and Titch would raise his hammeraxe, victorious, to cheers from the crowd and admiration from the emperor.

There was a scraping sound that echoed around the Colosseum, and it caused Bob to snap out of his vision of gladiators. A chill not attributable to the cold night rushed down his spine. The half-light cast deep shadows; something haunted these walls. Byte also acted spooked, whimpering from the raincoat pocket, eyes darting into the shadowy corners. Bob thought he would talk to Titch to break the ominous atmosphere.

'Your people built all this?'

'Yep.' Titch puffed out his chest with pride.

'It's amazing.'

'It's boring,' Ayama said, a displeased expression on her face. 'No life, just rock. I would be impressed if it sprouted legs and started running around. Maybe I should give it legs.'

'No! Please don't!' Titch pleaded, far too fervently for what Bob was convinced had been wild sarcasm.

'Don't worry, tiny moron. I won't waste my energy on this bore,' Ayama retorted whilst gesturing around with her arm.

As they explored the interior, Bob spotted some arches around the arena edges with rusted metal bars across them, each with a metal door locked with a padlock. Titch inspected a set of bars, pulling on them to test if they gave way. They didn't.

'My people did not do this. These are crude, and the metal has rusted. Who would put these here, and why?'

'To keep something out or to keep something in, moron,' Ayama answered.

It was too dark to see anything in the depths of the caged arches. Titch peered into a cage, straining his eyes.

Ayama floated past him. 'Your hammeraxe, idiot,' she chided.

Titch screwed up his face, and then whatever penny needed to drop dropped, and he took the hammeraxe off his back. With a flick of his wrist, the hammeraxe extended to its full size, and the shaft began to glow in the magma hues. Holding the hammer head, Titch fed the axe end through the bars and held it out, illuminating the space beyond.

In the cage were bodies. Four dead bodies. All in varying states of decay, one no more than a skeleton. The stench of rotting flesh was overwhelming, and Bob felt sick. No, wait, he was going to be sick.

As Bob threw up in a corner, Titch repeated the process of lighting the arches. 'There are three more over here. And five in this one. All dead.'

'Two here.' Ayama's staff was glowing at the base. She had slung it over her shoulder and was using it as a torch to search cages at the opposite end of the arena. 'Ah, this turd sack is moving.'

Bob, Titch and Byte rushed to the cage Ayama had lit.

Huddled in one corner was a figure, crouched down, shielding its eyes from the torchlight. A decaying body lay in the opposite corner.

'Why are you in this cage, turd sack?'

The person in the cage didn't respond.

'Speak, squishy human,' Titch said. 'We're not here to smash you.'

There was still no response from the person in the cage, which wasn't surprising, as Titch was well meaning but not reassuring.

'Please,' Bob tried. 'You're okay. We're not here to harm you. We want to help.'

Byte gave a friendly yip of agreement, although Ayama disagreed with a huff.

'Bob?' came the weak response from the cage. 'Is that you?'

'Yes. Who are you?'

The figure uncurled from the corner and stood in the light. 'It's me, Deck.'

And sure enough, standing in a cage in the middle of the Colosseum, next to a rotting corpse, was Bob's friend Deck.

He was grubby and wore simple khaki slacks, boots, a dark T-shirt and a khaki shirt, like an off-duty soldier who didn't know how to dress casually out of uniform. The most surprising thing was that he had dark hair and dark eyes, and he wasn't quite as shiny and good-looking. Bob spotted the hint of a stomach under his T-shirt, but it was unmistakably Deck.

'Deck! It's you! What are you doing in here?'

'Long story. I'd appreciate help to get out of this cage.'

'Titch, meet Deck. He's a friend of mine from the Zoo. Can you get him out?'

'Sure! Stand back, Squishy Deck.'

Before Deck had time to move back, Titch, keen to show off to someone new, spun elaborately in the air and brought the hammeraxe down on the cage padlock, smashing it into pieces. Deck rushed to the door, eager to be a free man again.

Deck ruffled Bob's hair, and they embraced. 'You don't know how good it is to see you, Bob. Thanks for saving me. There are more people trapped underneath the arena. We need to help them. Come on.'

Ayama got bored and wandered off, so Deck led Titch, Bob and Byte down to a pitch-black underground section of the Colosseum. Titch led the way, dimly lighting the path with the fiery glow of the hammeraxe, turning through the maze of narrow stone corridors to Deck's directions.

The maze opened into a larger room, possibly a staging

ground or storage area for the arena animals. Caged archways around the room's border housed more humans. Bob peered into the cages, saw terrified faces and heard whimpers and cries of 'Please, no, not me.'

'Don't fear us. We're here to help. We're not here to harm you,' Bob said.

'Yes, fear not, squishy humans. I won't smash you into pieces, I promise,' added Titch.

Not helpful, thought Bob, but well meaning.

'Titch, would you mind opening the cages?' Deck asked.

Titch did as instructed and smashed the cage locks, performing increasingly complex spins and twists. Halfway around, he declared, 'I'm awesome!' Then he continued his spinning, lock-smashing frenzy.

In no time, a group of two dozen humans huddled in the centre of the room in varying states of starvation, confusion and hopelessness. Surprisingly, they looked nothing like the humans Bob had met in the Zoo. There were young and old, fat and thin, short and tall, a spectrum of skin and hair tones, bent noses, big ears and spots. One girl had a birthmark on her face. There was a man with alopecia and another with mild palsy. Bob found comfort in how ordinary these people were.

'What now?' asked Bob.

'I'm not sure, to be honest, but we'll work something out,' Deck replied.

'Take us to the Refugee Camp! Please! We'll be safe there,' an old man with a scraggly white beard begged. 'It's only a half day's walk from here.'

'We cannot babysit all these turd sacks.' Ayama floated into the room, and the huddle of humans visibly shrank back from her. 'We must get to the old factory.'

'You're going to the House of Horrors?' the bearded old man stuttered, eyes widening as his legs gave in, overcome with shock. A stout, balding man broke his fall and helped him back to his feet. 'The way is closed. There is no way past the firewall!'

'What are you saying, old man? What firewall? Speak!' Ayama floated urgently up to the man, who cowered, shaking. She pointed her lollipop staff at his face as Sebastian curled around the shaft, baring his teeth at him. 'Speak, you dried-up old goat.'

'The House of Horrors ... the old factory ... the Butcher ... he created a firewall blocking the way up. No one can get past it! Please, don't hurt me!'

'Argh!' Ayama threw her arms up in frustration. 'How do we get in? There must be a way!'

'Let's ask around at this Refugee Camp,' suggested Deck, trying to calm the situation. 'Maybe somebody there knows.'

Ayama's nostrils flared, and she gave Deck a sharp stare from behind her fringe before floating out of the room, not saying another word.

'That settles it. We'll wait until daybreak, then go to the Refugee Camp. Are you coming with us, Bob?' Deck asked.

'I'm not letting you out of my sight again!'

'I'll join too. Squishy Bob has shown me kindness. I'll repay it with friendship.'

Bob grinned at Deck and Titch, glad to be back in the company of people he could call friends.

———

A few hours later, they all sat around a crackling campfire in the middle of the arena, smoke rising up and out into the clear night sky.

One of the humans knew where the Butcher Boys kept their food reserves, and they all tucked into stale bread, hard cheese and salted meats. It was a feast for those who had endured days of famine.

Deck posted some hardier humans on sentry duty with instructions to raise the alarm if the Butcher Boys returned.

'I never got a chance to say thank you for saving me from the

Librarian,' Bob said to Deck as they watched Byte accept some salted meat from a woman who was hard to age, as she was so thin she looked like nothing but skin stretched over a skeleton. The humans were fascinated with Byte, bowing as they offered him food. He seemed more than happy to receive the attention.

'I didn't save you, remember? You still ended up being pulled into the firewall.'

'Still, you tried. Thank you.'

Deck described what had happened after Bob had been pulled through the firewall. Several monsters had come through the firewall, and these monsters had been taking orders from the Librarian. They had captured the Queen and Sunny and dragged them through the flames. The monsters had also captured Deck, but only after he had fought one or two of them off.

Deck described monsters that were not metal beasts but human-like creatures. All of them were deformed and grotesque, with mismatched legs and arms. Some had two pairs of arms, three legs or two heads. Deck said most of the townsfolk had fled, and he didn't blame them.

When he'd eventually been pulled through the firewall by the creatures, some had followed him through, and following another brief struggle, they had captured him, brought him here and unceremoniously thrown him into a cage.

'When I described the monsters to another prisoner, she called them "horrors". The Butcher creates these horrors by butchering humans and stitching them together. It's gruesome. His favourites become his elite soldiers, known as the Butcher Boys.'

'The Butcher Boys! You mentioned them in the old town,' Bob said to Titch.

'Yes, I know of this. Butcher Boys have an X-shaped cut on their cheeks,' Titch added.

'Yep, that's what they say,' Deck said. 'Everyone is terrified of the Butcher, and for a good reason. If you get caught by the

Butcher Boys, chances are parts of you will end up stitched to someone else.'

Deck took a bite of his stale bread and gave Byte, who appeared seeking attention, a scratch behind the ear. Deck explained that the people they had rescued from the depths of the Colosseum were here to test the Butcher Boys. 'But it's more like a slaughter than a gladiatorial contest. Sometimes they forget people are here, or they don't care. Either way, you starve in the cages or die in the arena. I was due to appear in a "special event" to be made an example of.'

'Do you think the Librarian is the Butcher?' Bob asked.

'I wondered that too, but the horrors called him Librarian, and those among the prisoners that have seen the Butcher describe someone much younger. The Librarian is connected to the Butcher somehow, though.'

Bob had a sinking feeling in his stomach, knowing that Titch and Ayama intended to go to the old factory, the House of Horrors, or whatever people called it. He wanted to find out who he was but didn't fancy his head being chopped off and stitched to someone else, or his arms being used as an extra pair for a horror. Deck wasn't scared. Bob wished he was as brave as his friend.

'You organics don't treat each other well. Ayama was right about this,' Titch said. 'It's hard to tell a good human from a bad one.'

'The rule is, if it's one human made up from a jumble of several humans, smash it with your hammeraxe,' Bob suggested.

Titch nodded in agreement.

'Getting the rejects to the Refugee Camp might take some time. We'll need to set off at first light,' Deck said.

'Deck! You can't call them rejects! They're not as shiny as the humans in the Zoo, but calling them rejects is a bit harsh!'

Deck laughed at Bob's scolding of him. 'That's what they call themselves. The Zoo rejects them. Some sort of selection process goes on when the factory creates a new human, and this lot didn't make the cut.' Deck thumbed towards the rejects huddling around the fire. 'Only those selected arrive in the barn to join the Zoo. The rest are spat out into Storage, forever to be kept separate. They only know about the Zoo because of the townsfolk banished by the Librarian.'

Poor things, thought Bob. What might the selection process be? It felt unfair to reject someone because of a big nose or a mole on their cheek or something.

Having finished eating, Bob shared his story with Deck. Including how he had met Ayama and Titch, the information he'd received from Karen on the controllers, the Zoo, the factories and the reboot switch in the House of Horrors. Deck listened, fascinated, and flicked through the 'Beginner's Guide to the System' leaflet Bob shared with him.

'My world was pretty simple before all this,' said Deck. 'One thing's for sure. I need to find Sunny. I know she's somewhere out there. I'm hoping she's at the Refugee Camp, although the more I hear about the Butcher, the more worried I become. I hope she's safe. Part of me is missing not having her here with me.'

'I'm sure she'll be fine. If she's with the Queen, she's bound to be,' Bob said, trying to reassure his friend.

'I just need to find her, to make sure she's safe, and to tell her how important she is to me.'

'She knows that bit, Deck. I'm sure of it.'

The friends embraced and then settled on the arena floor to try to get some rest.

CHAPTER 15
BUTCHER BOYS

Nightmare stood amid sand, rocks and tufts of grass, gazing at the moonlit Colosseum in the distance.

'Do we go in and kill 'em, boss?' asked a Butcher Boy with an extra nose sewn onto one side of his head.

'No, Sniff. They've Red-Dress and the builder prince with them,' Nightmare replied.

Sniff screwed up both of his noses in disgust.

The thin, mousy woman Nightmare was holding squirmed, trying to escape his vice-like grip. He turned to face her, and she stopped squirming and resumed trembling uncontrollably. Nightmare stared back towards the Colosseum.

'Wha' do we do, then, boss?' asked a Butcher Boy whose head tilted at an angle, forcing him to move sideways, made easier thanks to his three legs.

'We wait until morning, Crabber. We know where they'll go next. We pick a few of 'em off on the road and make 'em think that's all we got.'

The half-dozen Butcher Boys around Nightmare cackled, barked and wheezed with laughter at the plan. Nightmare held up a hand to silence them.

'P-p-please,' the woman gasped in a desperate plea.

'There is no help for you. You're weak. A shadow of the past.

We're the future now.' Nightmare spoke to her as if explaining something complicated to a child.

'H-h-help.'

Nightmare ended the woman's life. Violently, with ease and precision. Her cry for help died with her, shock and horror forever etched on her face. 'You're weak! Pathetic! We will end you!' Nightmare screamed at the woman's corpse.

He tossed the body behind him as effortlessly as if discarding a crumpled newspaper. More cackles erupted from the Butcher Boys as they ran towards the corpse.

'Have a little snack, boys. Tomorrow, you will feast.'

CHAPTER 16
THE AMBUSH

They woke at dawn and readied to make the half-day journey to the Refugee Camp, packing any remaining food supplies and conducting a final sweep of the Colosseum to ensure they hadn't missed any survivors during the night. They hadn't.

The old man knew the way and led the rejects onto the road. Bob and his friends stayed at the back of the group.

Progress was slow, as many rejects were injured, old, malnourished or all three combined. The narrow, winding road out of the Colosseum didn't help either. It was only wide enough for two people, with steep grassy slopes on either side. It wouldn't be fatal if anyone fell down the slopes. They were more like slopes that were good fun to roll down if a person held out their arms and legs in a log shape. However, climbing back up would be challenging, especially if they were an injured, old, starving reject.

Halfway down the path, Ayama became frustrated with the slow progress and floated down the procession to confront those at the front.

Bob occupied himself by reading Deck sections from the 'Beginner's Guide to the System' leaflet. 'Here,' he said, pointing to a section, 'it says any human deemed suitable for the Zoo was allowed in. Those who didn't meet Bacchus's criteria for humanity were rejected into Storage.'

'Ah, that matches what the rejects said,' Deck replied.

Bob continued. 'Then the Binary War came. Humans, hackers and builders fought one another. Bacchus perished at the hands of Syntax. Now the Zoo represents everything Syntax hates about humanity, and he is determined to break the firewall.'

'The war must have been the noise we heard over a year ago and why the giant Bacchus stopped visiting. It all makes sense now. Well, sort of, anyway,' Deck said.

'The war was terrible, squishy friends. Syntax punished my people for trying to stop the fighting,' Titch said, head bowed and without his usual wide grin. Grace also lowered her head in sympathy.

'Did Ayama fight in the war?' Bob asked Titch.

'She refused to fight alongside her controller. Many joined her. Syntax cut the power to the sector they were in, sacrificing them. That's why she's always so angry.' Titch pointed down the line to where Ayama hovered, her staff held threateningly towards the old man.

Byte, who had been trotting just ahead of Bob, suddenly stopped, causing Bob to almost trip over him. He sniffed the air and then began to growl.

'What's wrong, Byte?' Bob stooped to comfort the furball.

Titch glanced back towards the Colosseum taking his hammeraxe from its holster, then clicked his porcelain skull mask into place. Grace shot into a crevice in the armour. 'Ayama!' Titch shouted over the heads of the rejects.

'I'm busy berating this wrinkled old goat. What is it?'

'Get ready!'

Ayama's entire posture and demeanour changed. She suddenly appeared calm and focused, scanning for danger. Sebastian gave out a cry, and Ayama promptly pointed her staff in the direction Sebastian was screeching towards. 'Butcher Boys, on the slopes!'

The Butcher Boys sprang their trap, scrambling up the slopes and leaping into the line of rejects. Chaos ensued. Screams filled the air as the Butcher Boys mauled and tore at the helpless humans. Several rejects tumbled down the slopes or tried to run forward through Ayama or backwards through Titch, tripping and trampling one another in their panic. The Butcher Boys cackled and screeched as they did their work, delighting in the chaos their biting, clawing and ripping at flesh caused.

'We must do something!' Bob cried.

'I can't!' Titch extended the hammeraxe and stood with it raised, hopelessly trying to find a safe window to smash a Butcher Boy without endangering a reject.

'What about her?' Deck pointed to Ayama.

'She can't either, Squishy Deck! Not with all these humans in the way!'

A Butcher Boy, just a head with arms stitched to either side, ran up to them on his hands, trying to bite at their legs. Deck gave him a firm kick, sending him flying into the distance, past Ayama, who floated away from the path, attempting to strike Butcher Boys with her staff but struggling to find an opening.

A shout came from behind them. 'Get the boy with the dog!' A massive, four-armed, muscular Butcher Boy stood atop the Colosseum.

The Butcher Boys, interspersed amid the rejects, popped up their heads like meerkats and turned towards Bob, who froze in terror. The Butcher Boys began pushing through rejects, ripping, biting and clawing towards him.

'Bob, run down the slope!' Deck's voice. In the haze of his fear, it sounded distant.

'Ayama, get ready!' Deck again, shouting an instruction.

Bob's ears were ringing.

'Bob, you need to move! You need to run down the slope! Bob! Now! Bob?'

Deck pushed Bob. He wasn't going to move on his own. Bob stumbled the first few steps down the hill. The shock of the sudden movement caused him to panic. He soon fell, the momentum of moving forward not being matched by his feet. He rolled – grass, sky, grass, sky, grass, sky – and hit the bottom of the slope with a thud.

The Butcher Boys soon appeared, leaving the crowd of rejects and following Bob down the hill, cackling and screeching at the joy of the hunt.

Bob had no choice but to look up at his impending doom. Why had Deck pushed him?

'Ayama, now!' Deck shouted.

Click.

Deck sprang his own trap. The Butcher Boys were out in the open, at the mercy of Ayama's awesomeness.

'Suck on this, you messed-up turd jigsaws.'

The slope the Butcher Boys were running down suddenly curved upwards, like the high, curved wall at a skatepark. Their speed meant that they couldn't help but run up the half-pipe until their momentum ran out, and they fell into the belly of the curve.

'I have you now.'

Click.

A giant, muscular bull formed from the hillside on one end of the half-pipe. With a ring in its nose and great big horns, it pawed the ground, snorting and tossing its head. A matador appeared on the opposite end of the half-pipe, cape fluttering. Caught in between the bull and the matador, the Butcher Boys were wide-eyed and no longer cackling with laughter.

'*Olé*, bitches.'

Click.

The bull charged, knocking one Butcher Boy against the half-pipe wall and tossing another into the air with its horns. Three remained – one was scrambling back up the slope, and the other two were running towards the matador.

The matador shook out his cape. Just as the two Butcher Boys reached the matador, the cape became a solid wall. The bull crashed into the wall, crushing the two Butcher Boys. The bull, the matador and the curved wall exploded into their component parts.

Click.

Bob scrambled backwards as a hail of rock, mud, grass and assorted Butcher Boy body parts fell towards him. He curled up and closed his eyes, trying to protect himself from the impact of the falling debris.

He heard dull thuds as the debris fell around him, but none hit. Bob braved a peek upwards. A hexagonal mesh had formed over him, acting as a shield. All debris that would have hit him hit the shield. Bob sat up in amazement. Then a bloodied arm no longer attached to a Butcher Boy whacked Bob in the face, and it fell into his lap. He juggled it before tossing it aside.

'A System shield doesn't work on organics, you moronic turd sack!' Ayama shouted down to him. She was laughing.

The crablike Butcher Boy that climbed back up the slope poked his head up next to the path, still looking down towards the chaos befalling his comrades.

THWACK!

Titch swung his hammeraxe like a golf club, and the hammer end took the head clean off the Butcher Boy. The head sailed off into the distance. The surviving humans gave out a cheer.

'Nice shot, tiny moron,' Ayama said approvingly.

Titch unclicked his mask and slung the hammeraxe over his shoulder, glancing back up at the wall of the Colosseum. The four-armed Butcher Boy was no longer there.

Deck scooped up Byte and headed down the slope to retrieve his friend, presumably to seek forgiveness, with the cute little dog serving as an apology gift.

———

They gathered the survivors. It took some time to recover the old and injured from the bottom of each slope, but they managed.

Everyone regrouped where the path widened into a gravelled courtyard, surrounded on three sides by whitewashed drystone huts with conical roofs bearing symbols painted in white.

'The symbols represent each controller's hexpet: the dog, the cat, the dragon and the bear,' Titch explained, pointing at each symbol as he listed them.

Bob studied the symbols with interest, recognising the bear symbol from Titch's hammeraxe.

Everyone froze.

'*Accessing the Archive. Please wait.*'

An image of one of the huts hovered in front of him. He touched the image, and it flipped over to reveal information on the huts. They were *trulli*, or *trullo* in the singular, drystone in construction, from the Apulian region of Italy. Sometimes religious symbols were painted onto the roofs.

'*Access complete. Returning to Storage. Please wait.*'

'These are *trulli*,' said Bob. 'They are traditional Italian buildings.'

'I know. I have read the Archive, remember,' said Ayama, slumping on the ground. Titch had carried her off the path, as she couldn't muster the strength to hover. Her skirt billowed out, forming a circle around her. A faintly glowing hexagon mesh pulsated on the gravel, peeking out of the dress at the edges. Her earlier display of awesomeness was enough for Bob to gauge her immense power and understand why Titch was careful not to anger her.

'Tell me, turd sack, when you access the Archive, is there a link connecting you to me?' she asked Bob.

'Um, I haven't looked.' He hadn't thought to look.

'Try,' she urged.

Bob decided to play music to cheer everyone up after the ambush. Everyone froze.

'*Accessing the Archive. Please wait.*'

Before selecting a song, Bob glanced at Ayama. Sure enough, he saw a faint thread from his hand to hers, barely visible, resembling fine cotton and emitting a soft light. A similar thread connected him to Titch. Bob chose a song.

'*Access complete. Returning to Storage. Please wait.*'

The miserable rejects brightened up a little, searching the air for the source of the music. A few even cracked a smile. Apt, given the song was *Smile*.

'Are we linked?' Ayama asked, her exhaustion evident.

'Yes, I think so. There's a faint thread between us.'

'Interesting. Very interesting. Now try to send me something. Not something from the Archive but something you've imagined.'

'How?'

'Figure it out, moron.'

She must be starting to feel better. Bob focused, and everyone froze. He imagined a Butcher Boy placed behind a flower cart, handing a bunch of flowers to a little girl. Now, how to send it? He assumed it had something to do with the thread, so holding out his hand, he stared at the thread connecting him to Ayama. Waving and turning his hand did not affect the thread, so he tried concentrating on the image in his mind, willing it to move. Rather alarmingly, his hand started to glow, emitting a faint ball of fizzing electric light. The section of thread immediately attached to his hand glowed with the same energy. That was where the glow stayed. How to make it move? Bob cast his eyes down the thread and then shifted his gaze towards Ayama. The fizzing electric ball followed his gaze, crackling with energy as it travelled along the thread.

When it reached Ayama's hand, she snapped it closed into a clenched fist. The shock of her moving made Bob fall over.

Everyone unfroze. Bob landed on his back with a thud. No one had ever moved when he'd accessed the Archive before. However, this time, he hadn't been accessing the Archive. So why had everyone frozen? Had he done that?

'Interesting. This is not from the Archive. Well done.' Ayama studied Bob.

'I just sort of made it up.'

'Good.' Ayama slammed her staff into the ground to the sound of metal hitting metal, then twisted it.

Click.

She extended her hand, and from the gravel, a miniature version of the scene Bob had pictured in his mind materialised. The Butcher Boy, the flower cart and the little girl formed out of gravel and dust, moving like marionettes controlled by Ayama's hand. Excited murmurs rose from those who witnessed the display, and some reject children rushed to watch.

The marionettes collapsed back to gravel with a wave of Ayama's hand to a chorus of disappointment from the children. Ayama scowled at them, and they ran off.

'Give the same image to Titch.'

Bob repeated the process of capturing the image in his mind and sending it down the thread, this time to Titch.

Titch grinned. 'Got it.' Then he grabbed the hammeraxe out of its holster and extended it. After walking up to one of the *trullo* huts, he used the hammer end to smash the wall. Instead of stone flying everywhere, the building changed shape, pulsing with a hexagonal mesh where the hammeraxe struck, then re-forming. After a few swift blows, the *trullo* hut had transformed into two cylindrical columns and one rectangular box.

Titch flipped the hammeraxe over and used the axe head to make precise cuts into each object, the basic shapes taking on more detail. After a few careful chops, which caused the hexagonal mesh to pulse, Titch stepped back to admire his creation.

The scene that Bob had imagined in his mind and Ayama had animated in gravel marionettes, Titch had replicated it in stone-and-slate statues where once there had been a building.

'Ta-da! I'm awesome, right?'

'You're not, no,' Ayama replied.

Click.

The statues started moving – the stone Butcher Boy florist handed the little girl a bunch of flowers. The motion reversed and repeated as if the figures were a clockwork toy. Some rejects cried out and started running away from the statues, causing Ayama to grin mischievously.

Click.

The motion stopped.

'You should not be able to do this, turd sack. Your eyes are wrong. No sparkle. It's most unusual. But it might be useful.'

'What is it I can do?'

'I might tell you, or I might not. I'll decide later. Now, we need to move from this controller-forsaken place.' She'd evidently recharged enough, as she floated off to find the old man for directions to the Refugee Camp.

CHAPTER 17
THE REFUGEE CAMP

The Refugee Camp might have been a half-day walk if they hadn't been herding the old and the injured. As it stood, they travelled most of the morning and into the afternoon. The old man reckoned they would reach the camp within the hour.

They were passing through a deserted industrial district littered with factories, not too dissimilar to the old town where Bob had met Titch in the alley. Tall brick chimneys rose high into the air, and the deserted streets were narrow and cobbled, with row upon row of terraces.

The smells of industry hit Bob's senses: hops from breweries, leather, sweat and grease. The factories were clearly in use, but their occupants were nowhere to be seen.

Bob passed the time talking to Deck whilst Byte trotted along happily beside them, occasionally running ahead to sniff around the brickyard they were passing through.

'Not quite as trim as I once was, hey?' Deck said, patting his stomach.

'You're still you,' Bob replied, choosing his words carefully to avoid offending his friend.

'It's okay. I know I'm not as pretty as I was in the Zoo. But I feel like the real me, more normal somehow. My skin fits me properly, you know? Sorry, that probably doesn't make sense.'

'It kind of does. Honestly, it was odd how everyone in the Town looked the same.'

'I bet, and we thought you were the odd one!'

Bob smiled and then stared at his feet. His hands fidgeted in his pockets as he tried to muster up the courage to ask Deck something. 'Deck, can I ask you a question?'

'Of course. Ask me anything.'

'Will you teach me how to be brave?'

'Be brave? I would if I knew how, Bob. I'm not brave.'

'You are. You're the bravest person I know, and Sunny thinks so too. She told me.'

He shouldn't have mentioned Sunny. Bob could tell Deck was desperately worried, going through phases of hope followed by hopelessness. He clearly loved her. Only someone beloved could cause that much worry, and Deck was very worried. Bob continued with the request rather than dwelling on the fact that he'd mentioned Sunny.

'It's just I keep needing to be brave, and I'm not. I just stand still, doing nothing. I want to act. I want to be like you.'

'Well, that's very flattering, but there is more to someone than being brave. You have something very special about you, Bob. Don't wish to be like me when you're already brilliant at being you.' Deck ruffled Bob's curls.

Bob turned his gaze to the floor and kicked a stone. Byte chased after it. 'There's nothing special about me. I'm just Bob – plain, uninteresting Bob.'

'Really? So the boy with a hexpet, who makes music play from thin air and travels with a mighty golden warrior and an obscene wizard, is boring? Come off it! Interesting things happen to you, Bob, and for a good reason, I'd reckon. Also, you're an excellent friend and a kind person. That's rarer than you think.' Deck gently elbowed Bob.

'Thanks. You're a great friend too, you know.'

'Thanks. "I am when we all are," or something like that. The Queen says it all the time.'

'I hope she's all right. It's a real mess the Librarian created.'

'Yeah, that's for sure.'

They walked on in silence for a while. Not an uncomfortable silence, just like two friends who were happy enough in each other's company that they didn't need to talk.

'Byte's back to his old self,' Deck said, picking the conversation back up.

Byte trotted up to some of the reject humans, who bowed to him respectfully. It was very odd. He'd discovered that they kept offering salted meats if he trotted alongside them for long enough, so he regularly made use of that trend.

'Why do they keep bowing to him like that?' Deck asked.

Bob was thoughtful, frowning, trying to recall something. He fished the leaflet from his raincoat pocket and scanned down the section on the controllers. 'Here.' He pointed to show Deck a section. 'Each controller has a hexpet to protect them. Bacchus's hexpet was a dog called Gigabyte.' Bob put the leaflet back in his pocket. 'The Queen said Byte resembled the Controller's dog.'

'This lot must consider Byte the second coming of Bacchus's dog or something,' Deck said, pointing at those bowing to Byte. 'But if he were, he would be much bigger. I met Bacchus, and he was huge. That might be why they aren't sure what to make of Byte.'

The friends continued walking, laughing and chatting, enjoying each other's company, until a shout came from the front of the procession.

'We're here!'

Bob, Deck and Byte caught up with the front of the procession and stood in a gap in the brickworks' surrounding wall, where once there must have been two large gates. They stared out at makeshift shanties occupying what had once been rugby pitches. Bob knew this, as the goalposts still stood, now used to hang canvas and sheet metal from. One shack was barely distinguishable from another, as they formed a higgledy-piggledy, tightly packed collage of sheet metal, wood and canvas, fanning out from a rectangular structure in the centre of the playing fields.

'Is this one of your creations, tiny moron?' Ayama said sarcastically. Sebastian smirked.

'No!' Titch replied, clearly offended. Grace shot out a tongue at Ayama's mink.

'I thought it was too good to be one of yours,' Ayama retorted as she floated after the rejects, who started enthusiastically approaching the camp.

Surrounding the rugby pitches was a wire fence topped with barbed wire, likely always there from when they had been sports fields. Four sturdy men holding makeshift cudgels guarded a gate in the fence.

'I guess this is what it takes to avoid getting turned into a body part for a Butcher Boy,' Bob said as they made their way towards the gate and the guards.

The old man greeted the guards, shaking their hands to a chorus of 'You're alive!' followed by plenty of pats on the back. The guards' expressions soured when Ayama and Titch approached.

'We ain't got room for all of ya! The injured need to go to the infirmary.' The guard pointed to a building outside the main encampment that must have been the old shower block. 'The rest, go to the pavilion to see the Commander. You two ain't allowed in. Humans only.'

The injured peeled off towards the infirmary, and the guard unlocked the gate to allow the rest to file into the encampment.

'I'm coming into this junkyard you call a home, you fungus-infected piss rocket.' Ayama leaned into one of the guards, glaring at him. 'And this tiny moron is coming in too.' Her staff shot towards Titch. He grinned and waved.

'No, you ain't. I don't care who you think you are!' The guard did his best to look intimidating, but his shaking legs gave the game away.

'Listen to me, you feeble excuse for a pile of flabby pink meat. Unless you want me to transform the ground you're standing on into a steaming pile of horse dung, you'll let me in.' Ayama floated back, inspecting the area, hand on her chin in mock thought. 'Mind you, a dung heap might improve this place, give it the odour its appearance deserves.'

She started to push past the guard, and he lifted his cudgel, meaning to strike her. Titch grabbed the man's arm mid-swing and lifted him clean off his feet. Then there was the sound of metal hitting metal. Ayama twisted her staff.

Click.

A rickety guardhouse to one side of the gate transformed into a pile of horse manure. It was steaming, flies buzzing around it, and it stank. It really stank. Titch promptly threw the guard into the manure with a sloppy, squelching plop.

'Any more piss rockets feel like a swim? Hmm? No? I didn't think so.' Ayama hovered into the camp, followed by Titch.

Bob was starting to like her. He still wouldn't cross her, but she was an excellent person to have on their side.

———

The pavilion, the building the guards had instructed them to go to, was the rectangular building in the centre of the camp. Weaving through the narrow paths of the shanty town to get to the pavilion proved tricky for Titch, and he knocked the odd wall or roof down as he squeezed past. On one occasion, he brought a whole shack down by accidentally knocking it with the hammeraxe in its holster on his back. There were a few curses from the residents, and Titch apologised, but no one was really going to pick a fight with a giant clad in golden armour, and all faded back into the shadows when given a sharp glare from Ayama.

As Bob walked through the shanty town, it dawned on him that he didn't stand out. He blended in. He could get used to not being the odd one out for once. Byte, however, did stand out. The bowing and cooing over Byte continued throughout the camp. There were many oohs and aahs and plenty of hushed conversations and pointing.

The pavilion was essentially a large tent with simple wooden tables and benches stretched across its length. Titch ducked to get in and moved a couple of benches to sit on the floor, much to the surprise of the pavilion residents. Titch tried introducing himself to a small group of rejects, but they fled, leaving him alone, poor guy.

Stood at ease behind the only table positioned horizontally, at the head of the others, was a severe woman, presumably the Commander. They all approached the table, apart from Titch, who stayed where he was, not wanting to venture further and cause too much damage.

The Commander was dark-skinned and dark-haired, with a stern expression, made intimidating by a large scar running from her left cheek and across her right eye, ending on her forehead. She wore the same khaki slacks and dark T-shirt as Deck but with the addition of a green beret and a necklace with three serrated, rusted metal teeth. The Commander raised an eyebrow at the sight of Byte, then turned to address Ayama.

'This is a human-only camp, hacker. Your kind is not welcome here.'

'Suck it, scratchy face. I need information. Then I'll leave your junkyard.'

'If I have the information you seek, it will come on one condition.'

'Which is?'

'You ask nicely.'

'We're screwed,' Deck whispered to Bob.

Bob nodded in agreement.

'Dear Miss Scratchy Face, pretty please, with bows on, tell me how to get through the firewall and into the old factory. Thank you. Love you. Please have turd babies with me.'

The corner of the Commander's mouth turned up in a half-smile. 'You need to talk to Kuldip. He escaped the factory. Although I lied about the one condition. I want two things from you in return for access to Kuldip.'

'Don't test me, scratchy face.'

The Commander ignored Ayama's quip, continuing with her list of conditions. 'One, the builder and the hacker will improve our camp defences, fresh water supply and sanitation systems.'

'Sure!' said Titch enthusiastically, clearly pleased to be given something to build.

Ayama glared at the Commander.

'Two, you will give me information about the hexpet.' The Commander pointed to Byte.

Bob grimaced. Protecting Byte was made more difficult by everyone taking such an interest in him. He didn't know the Commander's motives but didn't like her curiosity.

'If you do the work and tell me what I need to know, you may meet with Kuldip here tonight and leave in the morning. Deal?'

Ayama muttered something under her breath, then floated out of the pavilion. Titch followed.

'I'll take that as a yes.' The Commander nodded at a soldier, who followed Titch and Ayama out. There were some clattering noises and shouting, and Bob could hear Titch apologising.

The Commander then turned to Bob. 'The dog. I assume you know what it is.'

'He's a hexpet.'

'It's not just a hexpet. It represents us. It represents humanity.' The Commander pulled her T-shirt to one side at the neck to reveal a tattoo on her shoulder – the symbol of the dog. The same symbol whitewashed onto one of the *trullo* huts. 'It's good it's here.'

'He,' Bob corrected her. 'His name is Byte. It's my job to protect him.'

Hearing his name, Byte pushed himself closer to Bob's leg, whimpering quietly.

'Really? A protector?' The Commander smirked, glancing at one of her soldiers, who raised his eyebrows. 'I would make a request of you, boy.'

'Bob. My name's Bob.'

'I would make a request of you, Bob. Stay here, in the camp, with Byte. We need him now more than ever.'

Bob stared at her in shock. Deck was doing the same. Bob hadn't considered staying. He'd always intended to follow Titch and Ayama to the House of Horrors to discover who he was.

'You can't ask that of him. It's not fair.'

'And who are you?'

'I'm Deck, Deck Chair.'

'Ah, a Zooman.'

'Zooman?'

'A human from the Zoo. We don't sit around campfires singing songs and have feasts every night here, Zooman. I'm in charge, and you'll do as I say.'

'Do you have anyone else here from the Zoo? A woman?' Deck asked.

'No. We haven't had anyone for over a year. The last Zooman was captured and taken to the House of Horrors a few months back. Shame. He was a good hunter.'

'So she's not here, then.' Deck began fidgeting and rocking on his heels. 'I need to find her,' he said softly.

'Whoever it is you're searching for, if she's from the Zoo, she's not in this camp. If she's from the Zoo and not in this camp, I don't fancy her chances out there.' The Commander pointed over her shoulder into the distance. 'I'll leave you to consider my offer. We need the hexpet to stay. Now, I must go and attend to my duties. We'll speak again this evening.' The Commander stamped a foot, saluted, then walked out of the pavilion, hands clasped behind her back, entourage in tow.

Byte stood up on hind paws, nuzzling against Bob's leg, seeking attention. Bob scratched him behind his ear. 'I won't leave you, little guy. We've been through all this together and will stick together.'

'I need to find her. I need to find her!' Deck repeated, pacing back and forth, his chest rising and falling, hands clenching and unclenching.

'We'll find her,' Bob said. 'And we'll do it together. You're my friend. I may not be much use in a scrape, but I'll help you find Sunny. If you'll have me.'

Deck stopped his pacing and smiled at Bob. 'See, you are brave.'

'Or stupid. That's more likely. Maybe I should stay here, hide and be nobody.'

'You will never be nobody, Bob, because you're somebody to me. Thank you for being a friend, and at the exact time I need one.'

The friends embraced. Bob knew that where he belonged wasn't in the Refugee Camp with the other humans. He belonged with his friends. And two of his friends, Sunny and the Queen, needed him.

Byte jumped up against Deck and Bob, yipping with his tongue lolling.

'Don't worry. We know you're one of the gang too, Byte!' Deck said, smiling at him.

CHAPTER 18
THE GUIDE

Deck, Bob and Byte killed time exploring the camp. They felt like Byte's personal assistants or bodyguards, as almost every human they encountered wanted to bow and give offerings to Byte. At first they accepted the gifts, but they soon found their hands and pockets full and politely declined further offerings. Occasionally they had to forcefully push past groups that wanted to dote on the little pup. Even Byte, who usually loved the attention, was getting overwhelmed.

The camp was a maze. Wide streets would suddenly narrow. Deck and Bob would head in a direction that resembled the main thoroughfare, only to find a dead end. Before they knew it, they were lost.

'Hey, mister!' A round-faced kid in a flat cap and scruffy clothes cornered them in one of the dead ends. 'Need help? I can help you.' The kid leaned in conspiratorially. 'For a price. You look lost, and hey! I know the way! Lucky for you that I found you!'

The kid was glancing from side to side and using the back of his hand when he spoke. If Bob hadn't known any better, he'd have thought the kid was trying to sell them a second-hand car with 'one careful lady owner'.

'But you don't know where we're going, kid,' Deck challenged him.

'It doesn't matter. Wherever you're going in the camp, I know the way! Name's Jamal. I'm a sort of camp guide … yeah, that's it, a guide!'

'What's your price, then, Jamal the Guide?' Deck asked, joining in the game.

'Yeah, that's me! Jamal the Guide! My price is, er …'

Deck leaned into Jamal and whispered, 'Tell you what, if you help us find the builder, we'll ask him to show you some of his awesome fighting skills and mighty hammeraxe. How does that sound?'

'Yeah, great!' Jamal shuffled excitedly. 'No problem! Sure! Let's go!' Jamal paused and screwed up his face. 'Just one thing … what's a builder?'

Deck grinned. 'The golden giant that should be around here somewhere, making improvements to the camp.'

'Oh, right, yeah! Follow me.'

Bob shrugged. The kid didn't inspire much confidence, but they wouldn't find the way on their own, so they followed their new guide.

Jamal was fast, nipping about and weaving as he went. Bob and Deck struggled to keep up. He had them squeezing down gaps between shacks that appeared impassable, and moving sheet metal sections to reveal hidden routes through the streets, leading them right through the middle of a family's shack at one point, shocking the residents.

They had to give the kid his dues – he knew the camp. In no time, they were at the perimeter fence and spotted Titch a bit further down, on the outside of the fence, his porcelain face mask on and hammeraxe drawn, fully extended, magma flowing. He'd drawn quite the crowd as he elaborately explained what he was doing before creating the camp improvement with unnecessary but impressive pirouettes, twists and leaps. He was playing to his audience.

Deck gave an impressed nod. 'Wow. I thought the way Titch smashed through the cages at the Colosseum was impressive, but this is next level.'

'That's nothing,' said Bob. 'Wait until he dances.'

'Dances?'

'Yep. He may look like an intimidating golden gladiator, but his real superpower is dance.'

Deck gave Bob a speculative raise of his eyebrows.

'I'm not joking! Honest! It's true.'

'Ah, squishy friends! Come! Come!' Titch unclipped his mask and gestured for Bob and Deck to join him. Jamal followed. Now he'd seen Titch, he was eager to cash in his payment.

'Titch, this is Jamal. He helped us find you. I was hoping you might show him some of your awesomeness. Would you mind?' Bob asked.

'Not at all! Sit, little squishy one!'

Jamal eagerly sat on the ground. Byte jumped out of the rain-coat pocket and joined him.

Bob motioned for Titch to crouch so he could whisper. 'What if I play something? Are you able to recharge if you dance?'

Titch's eyes lit up. Bob didn't need the answer, but he got it anyway. 'Oh, yes!'

Bob gestured for Deck to join him on the ground next to Jamal and Byte. They all rested their backs against the fence. Bob concentrated. Everyone froze.

'*Accessing the Archive. Please wait.*'

He chose a song, something suitable for an impressive Titch performance.

'*Access complete. Returning to Storage. Please wait.*'

Gasps came from the crowd as *Dancing in The Street* started playing.

'Nice one!' Deck said, elbowing Bob.

Titch stood in his starting pose in the middle of a wide, grassy space, with a captive audience unsure of what was happening. He was clearly in his element; this was his moment to shine. Then he started dancing, performing twists, falls and turns. His mind and movement were perfectly connected; his face, hands and body conveyed the emotions in the song. The energy was palpable, and everyone watching was utterly mesmerised.

The audience grew as more and more humans heard the music and wandered over to discover its source, only to be hooked in and captivated by a golden giant ebbing and flowing around the clearing.

The song finished, and Titch gracefully landed in his final pose, breathing heavily and sporting a gleeful grin. He turned, feet together, and took a bow. The crowd went wild, whooping and clapping. Deck started a chant of 'Titch! Titch! Titch!' Those sitting rose to give a standing ovation. It was the reaction the performance deserved.

The crowd behind the fence started to quiet suddenly, and it parted as the Commander stepped up, hands behind her back. 'Where did that music come from?'

'I did it,' replied Bob, unusually defiant, feeding off the energy of Titch's performance.

'I did it, *Commander*,' she corrected him.

Bob's confidence faded. He nodded, then stared at a spot on the ground. 'Interesting. Yet another reason for you to stay, boy.' The Commander turned towards Titch. 'Have you completed your tasks, builder?'

'Er, almost.'

'I would ask that you don't distract the camp inhabitants until you have. Everyone must do their part. Reconvene at eighteen hundred hours at the pavilion. A bell will sound when it's time.'

Titch shrugged, put his mask back on and continued improving the camp defences. The Commander disappeared back into the crowd and the shacks beyond.

'She's abrasive,' said Deck.

Bob nodded in agreement. He'd already decided to follow his

friends; the Commander's attitude strengthened his decision. She was not the same sort of leader as the Queen. Bob supposed she might be the leader these humans needed, given their circumstances, but she wasn't for him.

Deck and Bob thanked Titch for the incredible dancing and left him to work. Jamal desperately wanted to show them the rest of the camp, so they spent the afternoon exploring. One shack was much like the next, and the tour grew a little tedious despite Jamal's enthusiasm for everything. They were saved by the bell that indicated it was six o'clock, and they needed to make their way to the pavilion.

———

It turned out that six o'clock was dinner time, and the pavilion acted as the dining hall for the camp. Ayama and Titch were already in the pavilion when Bob and Deck arrived. Space was made on the top table for all of them, with an area cleared on the floor for Titch to sit cross-legged. Byte joined him, curling up in his lap, and Grace shot out of a section of armour to greet Byte.

The pavilion was filled with hustle and bustle as people crammed into the space, budging up on benches to make room for friends, squeezing past each other whilst chatting and laughing. The Commander walked in, and the chatter and bustling stopped, like when the music stopped during musical chairs, and everyone dived for a spot and sat still and silent, waiting.

The Commander raised a hand, and people wearing grey slacks and T-shirts walked into the pavilion, serving each person a bowl and a plate. Bob was given a bowl of vegetable stew and a plate with bread and butter. Everyone had the same.

Deck lifted his cutlery to start eating.

'We wait for service to finish!' the Commander scolded him.

Putting his cutlery back down, Deck rebelliously stuck out his tongue, and he picked at the crust on his bread, sneaking a bite.

Once the grey-dressed serving people stepped back to the pavilion's edges, the Commander indicated everyone could start eating. That was when Ayama piped up.

'Scratchy face, you promised someone who knew the way into the House of Horrors. Stop delaying. Where is he?'

'I'm not sure you did the work you promised, hacker.'

'Do not test me. I will hack this tent so it rains turds on your heads. We did your work. Now, where is your side of the bargain?'

The Commander paused, possibly weighing her options. 'Very well. Kuldip, come forward.' The Commander gestured to a one-armed man with a full beard and a thinning, receding hairline. He stepped up to the top table and saluted. 'When we've finished eating, I want you to tell this disrespectful hacker the story of your escape.'

'Very well, Commander.'

They ate the rest of the meal in uncomfortable silence. As people finished, they left the pavilion, retreating into the maze of shanties. The friends patiently waited for everyone to finish eating – apart from Ayama, who regularly asked how long it would take, tapping her lollipop staff on the side of the table. Sebastian curled around the staff and glared at the Commander for the duration of the meal.

Eventually, only a few people remained, including Kuldip and the Commander. 'That's enough delaying, scratchy face. Now we talk to this man.' Ayama pointed at Kuldip.

'Very well. Kuldip?'

'Please, please, come and join me, friends.' Kuldip gestured for everyone to join him on his now-empty table as he grabbed discarded bowls and used the last of his bread to clean out the remaining stew others had left.

Deck, Bob and Ayama moved to sit opposite him.

'Talk, weird beard. How do we get into the old factory, this House of Horrors?'

Kuldip gave them a yellowing toothy grin. 'I'll tell you how I got out, miss, in the hope it helps you get back in. 'Bout a month ago, I was captured by the Butcher Boys outside the camp while I collected scrap metal. They took me to the House of Horrors. You got any more bread up there?' Kuldip gestured to the top table.

Deck glanced back at the table and shook his head.

'Ah well. Anyways, I spent weeks in hell. That place ain't somewhere you wanna go. The Butcher experiments. Pulls off legs, arms.' Kuldip nodded towards his missing arm.

Bob risked a glance at Ayama's legs. *Is that what happened to her?*

'Get to the point, weird beard. How did you get out?'

'Almost there, miss. Anyways, one night, I was brought down to the basement to be strapped to the Butcher's block. That's where he chops bits off ya, on the block. I already knew about the block 'cause of the arm.' Kuldip gave another nod towards his missing arm. 'Anyways, a couple of horrors were starting to strap me to the Butcher's block when they heard some screamin', and they wandered off, forgetting they ain't strapped me properly. I took my chance and snuck down the hallway to an exit and out into the open air, a free man again.' Kuldip paused to lick his finger and mop some breadcrumbs from his bowl.

'Is that it? That isn't helpful!'

'That ain't it, miss. I just got hungry.' Kuldip showed Ayama his finger, with breadcrumbs stuck to it. 'Anyways, on the other side of the door was a narrow path that led down the cliff edge. It's a straight drop to certain death if you slip. It ain't easy goin'.'

Kuldip clearly thought himself a storyteller, as he told his tale with wide eyes and plenty of gesticulation and head movement. He described how, when he had reached the bottom of the cliff, it had opened out to a stony clearing where the firewall rose high above him, heat radiating from it. Following the firewall, he had discovered a cave lit with columns of light that streamed through holes in the roof. It hadn't been long before he had emerged from the cave onto grassy plains.

'There they were, like rows of statues, stretchin' out across the plains – the rest of his lot.' Kuldip thumbed towards Titch.

Titch straightened his back at the mention of his people. Bob was itching to ask more but saw Titch slump back down and didn't press the point.

Ayama frowned, eyes narrowing. 'Wait a minute. The builders, they're in the Shell, not here in Storage.'

'The Shell?' asked Bob.

'Their sector.' Kuldip thumbed at Titch.

'This isn't good. How far did you have to travel in the Shell?' Ayama asked.

'Not far. Past the monuments, then back into Storage through the hidden entrance in the school and back here. Easy!'

'Argh, this isn't good.' Ayama floated up and down the rows of tables, considering what she'd just heard.

'What's the matter?' Bob asked.

'Not enough power, Squishy Bob,' Titch explained. 'If we go this way and run out of charge, we'll end up like the rest of my people, still like statues. It's called the deathless death, not good at all.'

'There ain't another way I know of,' Kuldip said, standing. 'And unless you got food, I'll call it a night. Pleasure meeting you folk.'

'Wait! Did you meet someone called Sunny in the factory?' Deck pressed.

Kuldip screwed up his face. 'Don't remember a Sunny. Although two new prisoners came in on the day I left. Maybe one of them was this Sunny.'

'What did they look like?'

'One was real pretty, the other tall and important.'

'That must be Sunny and the Queen! Thank you, thank you.' Deck was re-energised by the news but with an edge of extreme concern that Sunny was in the House of Horrors.

Kuldip left the pavilion. Only the friends and the Commander remained.

'Have you thought on my request, boy?' the Commander asked.

Everyone turned their gaze towards Bob.

'I have, and thank you for the offer to let me stay, but I'm going with my friends.'

The Commander pointed towards Byte. 'I'm not interested in what you do, boy. The hexpet stays.'

'His name's Byte, and he comes with me,' said Bob, finding a sliver of bravery, playing his role as protector.

'He comes with *us*,' Deck said, standing up in defiance.

'No. He stays here,' the Commander insisted.

'The dog is not yours, scratchy face. You have your answer.'

'I'm disappointed. You've made the wrong decision, boy.' With a furious stamp of her boot, the Commander about-turned and left the pavilion.

'Arrogant, intestine-filled air sack.' Ayama slumped onto the ground between some benches, her red dress billowing in a circle around her.

'Are we going through the Shell?' Titch asked.

'We don't have a choice. We must walk the path the one-armed, bearded turd described. But first I must recharge. You too, tiny moron. We leave at first light.'

Titch nodded in agreement, and the ground underneath them glowed with a hexagonal mesh.

Deck patted Bob on the shoulder. 'Well done. You stood up to the Commander.'

'Not really. Only because you were all here. I wouldn't have dared otherwise.'

'Nonsense. You're braver than you think.' Deck yawned. 'I guess we sleep here.' They cleared some benches to make room on the floor and settled down to try to get some sleep.

CHAPTER 19
TIME FOR A LESSON

Nightmare stalked up the chimney stack, quickly and silently, insect-like, using his six limbs. When he reached the top, he grabbed the lip of the brickyard's tall chimney and let go with his other hands, angling himself out to look down on the Refugee Camp's shanties below.

A baby cried, and guards held lamps, chatting to each other as they patrolled the perimeter fence. Otherwise, the camp was still, sleeping under a starlit sky.

'Almost time, boy with the dog. Time for us to meet. Time for you to die. Almost time.' Nightmare sniffed the air. 'The builder prince and Red-Dress are still with you, hmm? But they cannot save you. Not from me.'

Nightmare swung himself up into the air, landing seated on the top of the chimney.

'I know where you will go next. The trap is set. It's time for a lesson.'

Nightmare swung himself back onto the side of the chimney and, in a handful of leaps and twists, landed on the ground on all six limbs.

'A lesson about nightmares!'

Nightmare cackled to himself, then scuttled towards the gap

in the wall with no gate. Casting an eye over the area, he checked for any guards. Once he'd determined the area was clear, he scurried across the grass towards the old shower block – the camp infirmary.

'First, a snack. I'm hungry.'

CHAPTER 20
THE SCHOOL

'Bob! Wake up, Bob!' Deck shook Bob awake.

'What? What's the matter?' Bob asked through a sleepy haze.

'Something's wrong. Get up. Quickly.'

Bob rose from the hard, cold floor that had served as his brief bed for the night. It was still dark outside, and he shivered slightly from the cold.

The Commander stood at the top table, leaning over a map. Several senior-ranking soldiers flanked her, and Bob's friends stood opposite, inspecting the map. Bob stretched away his aches and went to join them.

The Commander pointed to the map, addressing one of her officers. 'We can't send out a search party until first light. It's too dangerous, we don't know how many there are.'

'What's happened?' Bob whispered to Deck.

'The Butcher Boys attacked the infirmary. There are no survivors. It's a total massacre – bodies, blood, everywhere. It must have been a small army of them to make such a mess in such a short time.'

The Commander turned to another officer. 'We need to lock the camp down, double, no, triple the guards. No supply runs until we know the area is clear.'

'Yes, ma'am!' The soldier about-turned and left the pavilion, presumably to lock the camp down and triple the guards.

Ayama pushed her finger hard into the map. 'You will lock down when we leave, scratchy face.'

'No. We lock down now. If we open those gates, we're inviting them in. They might be lying in wait. No. Everyone stays.'

'We're leaving now.' Ayama didn't make this statement to the Commander; it was an instruction for the friends to gather their things and head out.

'No! I didn't permit you to leave. We're in lockdown.'

'You're not the boss of me, scratchy face. And your gates are made of things I can code. So either you let us go, or I turn your fence into a large, flashing neon sign that says "Dear Butcher Boys, Fat Little Piggies Here". You pick.'

The Commander lost her cool. 'You're in *my* camp; therefore, you're subject to *my* rules.'

'Nope.' Ayama continued to round up the others.

The Commander let out a long sigh. 'You may leave now if you're quick, but the hexpet stays.' Her arm shot out to point at Byte.

'No!' cried Bob, picking up Byte.

'He is no more yours than he is mine, boy. He stays.'

'You make too many demands, scratchy face. This request is not acceptable. The dog comes with us. Ask again, and Titch here will crush your head. It will be an improvement.'

Titch smiled and waved.

The friends gathered their things and made to move out.

'Stop them!' cried the Commander, drawing a gun.

The officers flanking her did the same.

Everyone hesitated, staring down the gun barrels. Everyone except Ayama, who floated back towards the Commander.

'Guns? I hate guns. How do you have these things?' Ayama asked, not in the slightest bit intimidated, more curious.

'We found a small cache. They come in handy when making

demands of people. These you cannot code, bitch. Now, the hexpet stays. Argue with me again, and I'll fill you with bullets.'

'Guns are the reason this planet died. Guns are the reason humans slid into decay. And you would point these hateful things at me? Thinking me powerless? You're fools.' Ayama slammed her lollipop staff into the ground, accompanied by the sound of metal hitting metal.

'Stop! Go no further, hacker!'

'I cannot code guns – this is true. Such things pre-date the System. But there are things I can code. And never call me bitch.'

Click.

The guns the Commander and her troops brandished became encased in rock. Stalagmites had risen from the ground, enveloping the guns. One foolish soul decided this would be an excellent time to fire his weapon, and the thing backfired, exploding. He fled from the pavilion, holding his face. The bases of the stalagmites disintegrated, causing the soldiers to drop the guns to a rain of thuds as the stone-encased weapons hit the ground.

Ayama released her staff. 'Now we leave.'

The Commander dropped to her knees. 'Please! Please leave the hexpet here! He will unite us! Give us hope!'

'His name is Byte, and he's coming with me,' Bob said assertively.

Deck nodded in agreement and put a supportive hand on Bob's shoulder.

The Commander slumped down in defeat. 'Go.'

———

The friends left the Refugee Camp through the tight, winding streets as soldiers roused camp occupants to learn the fate of the infirmary. Cries of grief rang out as those with loved ones being cared for at the infirmary heard the news.

Titch lifted the gate clean off its hinges and allowed his

friends through with a gentlemanly bow before putting the gate back – sort of. It hung crookedly.

Ayama led the way up past the infirmary building with her staff slung over her shoulder, light emanating from its base. 'The school is this way. Follow.'

Bob wished the school had been in the opposite direction. The infirmary doors hung open, a half-mutilated corpse blocking the doorway. Bloodied handprints smeared the white-rendered exterior, and lights inside flickered ominously.

'I'm not going in there,' said Bob.

'Me either, just in case you needed proof I'm not brave,' Deck added.

Titch inspected the infirmary building with a mournful expression. His glittering eyes reflected the flickering of the infirmary lights. 'They made a mess of the squishy humans in there for sure. Your insides fall out too easily.'

The group circled the infirmary and headed down a ginnel with tall bushes on either side. The ginnel gently curved and opened out onto several playing fields. The dark outline of a group of buildings came into view.

'The school. Somewhere inside is the entrance to the Shell sector,' Ayama said, leading the group over the playing fields and towards the cluster of buildings.

As they approached, the dark outlines became more detailed. The buildings were typical of a 1960s British comprehensive school. A large rectangular building with four floors and a flat roof sat opposite an L-shaped building of the same construction, separated by a concrete quadrangle in the centre. Triangular planters contained sorry-looking trees. Bands of weathered panels broken by bands of windows denoted each floor.

Behind the L-shaped building was a large square brick

building with small windows between the walls and the roof, probably the school sports hall.

'We need to find the entrance to the Shell. Split up and search – it'll be faster,' Ayama said.

Before Bob could object to the frankly terrifying plan to split up, Ayama floated off towards the rectangular building.

'Shout if you find the entrance, morons!'

'What does it look like?' Deck shouted back.

'Work it out, imbecile. It's not my job to wipe your backside.'

Bob and Deck raised eyebrows at each other.

'I will go here.' Titch pointed at the building that Bob assumed was the sports hall.

'Stick together?' Deck asked Bob.

'Definitely,' Bob replied. 'You, me and Byte.'

They set off for the L-shaped building. It was still night, and the sky twinkled with stars. Shadows played as the trees in the quadrangle moved. Bob's eyes shot towards the school wall. He swore he had seen a shadow dart across it. Nothing was there. It must be his imagination. A repeat of the Queen's garden. *Coward.*

Deck reached the school building's doors and pushed them. The doors swung open.

They entered directly into a hallway, with the right angle of the L-shape to their left and doors evenly spaced down a corridor to their right. Bob imagined these doors led to class-rooms, cloakrooms, staff rooms and other such rooms schools had.

'Which way? Left or right?' Deck asked.

Byte decided for them, jumping out of the raincoat pocket and trotting off down the longer end of the building, to the right. He stopped in the centre of the corridor and started sniffing and pacing the floor, scouting for buried treasure. Deck and Bob joined him. The hallway grew dim as the meagre light from the door retreated behind them.

BANG!

The door they had entered through suddenly slammed shut, making Bob and Deck jump out of their skin. Holding hands to their chests, they laughed at each other.

'Oh! That made me jump! Blasted door!' Bob said.

'Me too! I told you I wasn't brave!'

The friends recovered their wits and began opening doors, checking the rooms beyond. They agreed to be methodical, so they knew where they had already checked.

The first room they investigated was a science lab. Bunsen burners sat on countertops, underneath conical flasks in stands. Posters adorned the walls, one showing the periodic table of elements and another with a labelled diagram of the inside of a volcano.

The teacher's desk had piles of papers stacked to one side. Bob rifled through a stack of marked science tests. Emily Jayne had got a 9. *Well done, Emily.*

'I can't find an entrance. You?' Bob asked.

'No,' Deck said, emerging from a storage cupboard. 'But I don't know what I'm looking for. How are you getting on, Byte?'

Byte simply sat with tongue lolling at him, head cocked to one side.

The friends left the science lab and moved to the room opposite, following their agreed-upon zigzag strategy. It was a history room, with rows of single desks facing the front. Posters in this room were First and Second World War propaganda in different languages.

Bob studied a Second World War Japanese propaganda poster with beautiful black-and-red lettering and art style. Suddenly a shadow darted across the poster, and Bob's breath caught in his throat. He spun around and looked out the window. But nothing was there – only the building opposite and the light from Ayama's staff on the second floor. Bob figured it must have been the light from the staff shining across, creating the shadow.

They finished searching the history room and returned to the corridor. Between the history room and the next set of doors was a noticeboard in one of those cabinets with sliding glass doors that rattled when someone walked past. Colourful cut-out letters across the top of the board spelled *Class of 2026*. Below the letters were various pictures and articles carefully mounted onto coloured card. One of the pictures showed a girl in the science room holding a certificate with a handwritten caption that read *Emily, winner of the Year 10 science competition.*

BANG!

Another door slammed shut further down the corridor. Bob and Deck froze, their gazes fixed in the direction of the noise. It was pitch black at that end of the corridor.

'Probably the wind,' Bob said, trying to reassure himself more than anything.

'Yeah, must be,' said Deck, not entirely convinced. 'Let's check another room.'

BANG!

Another door slammed shut.

'I don't think that was the wind, Bob.'

BANG!

Another door.

A broken, crackling voice echoed from the darkest corner of the corridor. 'Ding, dong, bell. Boy is in the school. Who ate him? ... Nightmare did!'

Crawling across the ceiling towards them, insect-like on six limbs, was a frightening abomination. It peeled off the ceiling, dropping to the floor three doors away. 'Hello, boy with the dog. I'm here to remove your head! My master, the Butcher, wants to play with it.'

The horror before them may have been human once, but no longer. He stood over six feet tall, muscular, with deep red scars littering his bare torso. The word *Boo!* had been crudely tattooed in large letters across the chest, and an additional pair of arms had been sewn onto his sides. Poking out of shredded trousers, where feet should have been, were sewn-on hands. The most terrifying feature, though, was the face. The bottom lip had been removed to the chin, exposing teeth sharpened to a point, and he dribbled uncontrollably through the gap. X-shaped scars adorned each cheek, and one eye was sewn shut. On his head, between lank tufts of hair, rusted metal shards were sewn into the scalp.

'Boo!' Nightmare yelled.

Bob picked up Byte, and the friends ran.

They slipped and skidded along the concrete floor, polished to a shine, flying past the door they had used to enter the school. Bob risked a glance back down the corridor but couldn't spot the aptly named Nightmare creature. Bob realised he hadn't tucked in his shoelace, and the aglet on the frayed lace clicked as he ran – *Idiot.*

A cackling laugh emanated from the darkness of the corridor behind them. 'Ready or not, here I come!'

Bob's fear level rose, and his chest ached. Breathing heavily, he attempted to reach for the blue inhaler in the raincoat pocket, but it slowed him down, so he gave up and kept going.

'Ayama! Titch!' Deck shouted.

Bob joined in the chorus, but his voice wasn't as loud, and he soon gave up, as shouting affected his breathing.

They reached the right-angled bend of the L-shape and momentarily skidded to a stop to decide where to go next. There was a set of stairs leading up to the levels above, or they could keep running down the unexplored shorter section of the L-shape.

Deck turned to Bob and, clearly realising he wouldn't get an opinion in time, grabbed his friend by the arm. 'Come on!' Deck said as they headed up the stairs.

The friends ran up two flights of stairs and dived into the nearest classroom on the second floor. Pausing to catch their breath, backs against the door, they tried to still their breathing so as not to make any noise. Bob reached into his raincoat pocket and took a puff of his inhaler.

'What was that thing?' Deck whispered.

Bob exhaled. 'Terrifying.'

Deck and Bob surveyed the room. It was another science lab. They must have stacked the labs on top of one another to run the gas pipes up from the lower levels. Bob crouched to tuck his frayed lace into his high-tops.

'What do we do now?' Bob asked.

'I don't know. We can't stay here, though. If we get cornered, we're done for.'

Deck turned around and gripped the door handle. 'I'll peek out to see if the coast is clear.'

'Are you sure? He might be outside!'

'As I said, we can't stay here.' Deck steeled himself, twisted the doorknob and opened the door to a slight crack. The door hinges creaked. Deck winced at the noise and stopped the door. Fortunately, he'd opened it enough to peer out.

'Anything?' Bob whispered whilst Byte whimpered quietly.

'No. Maybe he's gone.'

'Maybe. Maybe Titch heard us and has squished him already.'

'Maybe.'

The friends stopped peering out and retreated into the false safety of the science lab, their backs against the wall on either side of the door.

'We have to do something. Should we make some noise and try to attract Ayama and Titch?' Deck suggested.

'We would just draw the creature's attention. We might be dead before they got here.'

'Okay. Let's try and sneak out. We leave here and run to the other building to find the others. Agreed?'

Just then, they heard the *tap-tap-tap-tap, tap-tap-tap-tap* of fingers drumming on the corridor walls. Deck and Bob stiffened, their eyes wide.

'Incy wincy Nightmare, crawled down the corridor …'

'We can't let him corner us in here. Run!' Without giving Bob time to object, Deck swung open the door and shot out into the corridor with enough force that he hit his shoulder hard on the opposite wall.

Bob followed, with Byte in his arms.

They glanced down the second-floor corridor.

'Hello. Come to play?' Nightmare was on the ceiling, crawling towards them in his insect-like way. His exposed, sharpened teeth stood out against the shadows of the corridor.

The friends turned and fled, retracing their steps back down the stairs to the bottom floor and the bend of the L-shape.

'Where to?' Bob asked in a panic.

There was scratching and scraping as Nightmare descended the stairs, singing, 'Run, run, as fast as you can!'

'Quick, this way!' Deck led them down the side of the L-shape they hadn't yet explored. There was a small set of three steps, then a corridor with a fire escape at the end. Deck pointed it out to Bob. 'There, the doors! Run!'

Bob and Deck ran as fast as their tired legs could carry them. Deck was faster than Bob, given he was taller and fitter. Despite being faster and despite the terror that hunted them, Deck slowed to keep pace with his friend. 'Come on, Bob! You can do it!'

Bob's legs burned. He was still putting them one in front of the other, but the motion was pure willpower fuelled by terror, resulting in a stilted walk-run movement.

'Found you!' Nightmare cackled.

'Go! Go! Go!' Deck shouted, grabbing Bob's arm and trying to move him forward.

The friends reached the fire doors, and Deck pushed down on the panic bar. 'Locked!'

'What?' Bob rattled the doors.

A chain looped around the panic bars between the two doors, a padlock securing the chain. Bob and Deck turned to face the corridor, their backs against the locked fire doors.

Nightmare strolled towards them, the hands on his lower

arms twitching, mimicking a cowboy in a Western, facing down his foe, ready to draw. Byte jumped down from Bob's arms and put himself in front of Bob, yapping at Nightmare.

'Nowhere to run, nowhere to hide … time to die.' Nightmare cackled with a mischievous grin on his face. He lowered himself onto four limbs and used his legs and lower arms to crawl towards them, upper arms held out, clawed fingers wiggling.

'Quick, this way!' Deck pointed to a door to their left. He slammed into it, and Bob picked up Byte and darted through the doorway.

They found themselves in a glass corridor between the L-shaped school building and the—

'The sports hall! Titch!' Bob shouted.

The glass corridor led to a pair of oak-veneered doors. Above the doors hung a plastic sign with the words SPORTS HALL written in large letters, in a dreadful font with equally dreadful colours. Bob assumed they were the official school colours, which were universally dreadful.

When they were halfway along the glass corridor, Nightmare appeared at the far end, clutching the wooden frame with all six limbs, drool dripping off his chin. 'This little piggy went to market. This little piggy went to school …'

The friends were frantic, their legs burning, their bodies straining, trying to drive forward faster than exhaustion and fear would allow. Bob's head throbbed with the stress. His hands shook; his legs trembled; and he was sweating profusely. The adrenaline that had kept him alive up to now was wearing off. He almost wished for the metal wolves over the deformed, stitched-together horror that was Nightmare.

As they reached the end of the corridor, Nightmare dropped from the door frame and sprinted towards them, using all six limbs to propel himself at an incredible speed.

The friends burst through the oak-veneered doors and into the dimly lit sports hall, grey half-light filtering through the letterbox windows between the walls and the ceiling. They stopped in the centre of the sports hall. Floor mats and a pommel horse sat along one side; small, stackable cones zigzagged down the other. Two walls had floor-to-ceiling, ladder-like wooden frames with climbing ropes dangling down.

'Titch! Titch! Help!' Deck and Bob called in unison.

The sports hall was empty.

Titch wasn't there.

'He's not … he's …' Deck was trying to speak between gasps for breath. The reality of their situation hit home.

Bob slumped down first, legs unable to support him. Byte jumped out of his arms as he fell, and went to stand guard and growl at the doorway.

Deck collapsed beside Bob, wrapping his arms around Bob's shoulders. 'We tried. We really did. You're a good friend, Bob.'

Nightmare stalked into the sports hall, cautiously surveying the area, possibly aware Titch was supposed to be in here. Once he'd given the sports hall the once-over, he grinned and tilted his head, regarding the two slumped figures in the middle of a blue landing mat. 'That wasn't a very exciting chase.'

Nightmare jumped onto the pommel horse and then leaped onto the wooden frame fixed to the wall, which he used to circle behind Bob and Deck. The friends, resigned to their fate, stayed slumped in their embrace, waiting for the inevitable.

Nightmare tutted. 'Boring. Even some people I ate last night put up a better fight than you.' Bob remembered the half-eaten corpse and bloodstained walls of the infirmary. He did not want to succumb to the same demise but was too exhausted to do anything.

'Who to eat first? The boy, or the other one? Hmm.'

Byte growled at Nightmare as the horror moved from the frame onto the floor, crawling on all six limbs towards the friends.

'I know. I'll take a bite from each and decide who tastes best.'

Bob tensed and felt Deck doing the same as Nightmare's shadow loomed over them. Nightmare had risen onto four limbs, then two, arms raised, ready to pounce on the Deck-and-Bob-shaped pile of exhausted, quivering bodies.

Suddenly a glittering flash of silver darted across the floor in front of Bob – it was Grace.

'Time to remove your – what?'

A bright light appeared amid the coloured cones. Out of the light stepped a gigantic form.

'I found the entrance, squishy friends! What the …?'

The room suddenly filled with the red, amber and yellow hues of magma, followed by a crack as Titch's hammeraxe connected with Nightmare. Nightmare's body slammed against the wooden frame beside the pommel horse.

'Ew! That's gross! What happened to its face?' Titch asked.

After a moment of appearing dazed, Nightmare shook away the shock of the blow and crawled up the frame to hang from the top rung, hissing and cursing at Titch.

'Come down and say those things to my face, squishy grossness! I'll gladly smash you again.'

Ayama chose that moment to hover into the sports hall. She took one look at the companions in the middle of the hall, then followed their gazes up the frame to Nightmare. The second she saw him, she slammed her lollipop staff into the floor with a clang of metal hitting metal, then twisted.

Click.

The wooden frame curled up from the bottom and the sides, creating a cage, pinning Nightmare to the ceiling.

'No! Let me out, Red-Dress!'

'Be quiet, or I'll sew your butthole to your forehead.'

Nightmare hissed and paced around his sudden prison, shaking the wooden bars.

'Why didn't you shout for us?' Ayama scolded Deck and Bob.

'We did!' the pair said in unison.

'Well … you didn't shout loud enough. You need to work on this. It's a flaw. You found the entrance?' Ayama inspected the glowing rectangle still present amid the coloured cones.

'Yep!' Titch said, puffing out his chest.

'Come on, morons. Let's get around the firewall. We must move quickly; we cannot lose charge.'

Titch nodded and stepped back through the light.

'Move, turd sacks! Or do you want to stay here with the turd jigsaw?' Ayama didn't need to ask twice – and she probably wouldn't.

'Noooo! I must have your head for my master!'

Deck turned towards Nightmare. 'And this little piggy went …' Deck gave Nightmare the middle finger.

'Nooooo!'

Deck made a gentlemanly gesture, allowing Bob and Ayama through as if holding open the door at a department store and then stepped through the door of light. The entrance closed.

CHAPTER 21
THE PRACTICE GROUND

Bob tumbled through the doorway of light, stumbling a few steps before collapsing on the ground. He lay there groaning, feeling the strain and exhaustion in his legs, mixed with relief at still having his head attached to his shoulders.

Reaching back into the pocket of his yellow raincoat for the blue inhaler, he suddenly noticed the floor he was lying on, and his breath caught in his throat. 'White tiles!'

Deck, lying on the floor next to him, jumped at the outburst.

Bob found a reserve of energy brought on by panic. He jumped to his feet, eyes darting from side to side, and turned hastily on the spot, trying to take in his surroundings as quickly as possible. He was behaving like a total lunatic, so his friends were understandably a mix of amused and concerned – depending on the friend.

'Are you okay, Bob?' asked Deck, sitting up.

Bob stopped turning in circles and stood, hands on his knees, panting. 'Yeah, yeah, I'm fine. It's just … it's nothing. Honestly, I'm fine.'

Sebastian coiled around the golden lollipop and squeaked with laughter.

To Bob's relief, his surroundings were not unending tiles with a seamless horizon. The doorway had led them into a terrain covered in white hexagonal tiles, but not ceramic, like in the tiled space. These hexagonal tiles were matt and felt synthetic. The tiles soon ended a short distance away, fading into grass, earth and wild flowers. However, a hexagonal outline, glowing blue-green, remained visible around each tiled section, giving the impression that the landscape was a gigantic three-dimensional jigsaw.

Bob gazed at hillsides covered in lush greenery, flowers and cherry trees. Blossoms gently floated through the air, settling to carpet the ground like spring snow.

Covering the hills were a strange assortment of objects and buildings. It was a total mess, even worse than the Queen's hut. It was like someone had thrown a bunch of random things into the air, and they had landed wherever they had happened to fall. A too-small chocolate-box cottage sat next to a giant hamster wheel, next to a beach scene with a surfboard, next to an over-sized milk bottle. The haphazard placement of objects continued as far as the eye could see.

Bob shook his head in amazement and turned his gaze to the sky. It was a beautiful blue, but then it slowly changed colour, fading to purple, pink, yellow, green and so on. The sky's ever-changing colours completely altered the landscape's character with every new hue. There was also a jarring scent of candyfloss and popcorn, as if they were standing in a cinema lobby, not outside in the spring sunshine.

'Ah, it's good to be home! Welcome to the Shell, squishy friends! The home of the builders!' Titch raised his arms, his face lit up with pride.

'This is where they do pointless things for no reason. I hate this place,' Ayama declared.

Bob wasn't in the least bit surprised and wondered if there was anything, anywhere or anyone she did like.

Having recovered from the shock of seeing the tiles, Bob felt weak and hungry, and his stomach was letting him know. 'Titch, not wanting to be a pest, but can we eat before we move out? All that running and almost having my head removed have given me an appetite.'

'Sure!' Titch carried the food supplies given to them by the Refugee Camp. He swung the canvas bag off his shoulder, sat down and rifled through it, tossing a foil-wrapped package to Bob and then another to Deck. 'Would you play some more music, Squishy Bob? Whilst we eat?'

'Sure.' Bob concentrated, and everyone froze.

'Accessing the Archive. Please wait.'

Something was different – the frozen state was alive with energy. Little light streams shot from Bob's hands and up from around his feet. Energy emanated from the edges of each tile, fizzing, alive. The energy outlining all the tiles gave the effect of a backlit hexagon mesh covering the landscape. The bonds between him and Ayama, Titch and Byte were more substantial, the threads thicker.

Bob picked a song. It was something slightly unusual to fit the new environment.

'Access complete. Returning to the Shell. Please wait.'

White Rabbit started playing, and Titch's eyes lit up. He stood to dance, but one furious glance from Ayama, and he sat back down, rolling his eyes, grinning mischievously. Then he danced defiantly with his shoulders and hands.

Bob tucked into the chicken wrap he found in the foil, lightly spiced with cumin and chilli. It tasted amazing. 'I saw all the hexagons glowing when I played the music,' Bob said, his words muffled with his mouth full.

'That's the interface. You see it?' Ayama asked.

'Yep.' Bob replied. 'How come there is so much energy here? I thought the sector was out of charge. Isn't that why we need to reboot them?'

'What energy remains pools at the edges. The further we go, the less energy there will be. No human should see the interface. It's not normal.' Ayama explained.

Bob was waiting for the added insult, but it never came. Maybe she was softening to him. 'What's the interface?' Bob asked, swallowing the bite of his wrap.

Titch answered. 'Builders build the interface and create objects, buildings and that sort of thing on top of it.'

'I connect to the interface using this.' Ayama held up her lollipop staff. 'And I create life from what is built,' she added, with a far-off, contemplative gaze on her usually pissed-off face. 'But I can only create what I have the code for.'

'Hexcode?' asked Bob.

'Yes. You know of this?'

'Not really. I just heard about it once.' Bob was remembering the information on the sheepdog image the first time he'd accessed the Archive.

'Builders build based on hexcode from the Archive, Squishy Bob. It's sometimes hard to make sense of it, and it takes decades to become a good builder. Once we've built something, the hackers reuse the hexcode.'

'Hackers also combine hexcode to make something else,' Ayama added.

'Oh! Like creating a bull from the earth!' Deck said.

'Yes. I combined the hexcode for a bull with the hexcode for mud, grass and rocks. It's quick to do in an emergency.' Ayama appeared more relaxed than usual. She was animated when talking about hexcode.

'How does the lollipop work, then?' Bob asked, figuring he might as well try to get as much information as possible before she inevitably became grumpy again.

'Come with me. I'll show you something.' Ayama floated towards where the white tiles became earth and grass.

Bob stood and dusted crumbs from his lap as he jogged to catch up with Ayama. When he reached her, she held up her staff for Bob to inspect. It was golden and beautifully intricate, with an embossed dragon weaving up to the lollipop-like head.

'The staff is a hub, a way to connect to the interface. I hold the hexcode I use most often in the staff.' She slammed the staff into the ground with the now-familiar sound of metal hitting metal.

Ayama stared into Bob's eyes. Her black eyes with the glittery irises were mesmerising, and he felt as if she were staring into his soul. 'Concentrate as you do when selecting the music. Pay attention to the hub and the interface.'

Bob concentrated, and everyone froze. He looked from Ayama's eyes to where the staff met the ground. The energy pulsated and crackled, radiating out from the base of the staff, blue with a hint of green. It was so alive! And it looked kind of dangerous.

Ayama twisted her staff.

Click.

WHOOSH!

Blue energy shot out from the staff into the hexagonal mesh, like a network of riverbeds filling after a drought. Soon, there was a wide radius of flaming blue hexagons around Ayama and Bob. The tiles were outlined with blue energy, pulsating like multiple welding torch flames. *Wait* … It was energising him! The aching in his legs subsided, and the soreness he felt in his chest from running was fading. He looked back up at Ayama – and she winked at him, breaking his concentration. He crashed out of the frozen state, falling over as he did.

'I felt the energy!'

Ayama floated down to the ground, the dress billowing in a circle around her. Sebastian sat on her shoulder, regarding him. 'I don't understand why a human can interface.' Ayama frowned. 'Do you remember when I asked you to imagine something and pass it to me?'

'The Butcher Boy with the flower cart.'

'Passing hexcode between builders and hackers is possible, but only for things already built, based on information in the Archive. What you sent was new, from your imagination.' She pointed at Bob's head.

Bob's face showed nothing but confusion, which caused Ayama's brow to furrow deeper. 'Argh! You're slow to understand the point! You created the hexcode with your mind – brand-new hexcode. Somehow you can imagine something and create the hexcode from it. It makes no sense. It should not be possible. No one, human, hacker or builder, has done this before.' Ayama cocked her head and studied Bob. 'Maybe I underestimated you, turd sack. Now, we move.'

She floated off towards Titch to bark some orders, leaving Bob on the ground, stunned. The question he'd been trying to answer since the tiled space – *Who am I?* – had just sprouted the complicated dimension of *What am I?* In some way, he felt strangely comforted. Maybe Deck was right, and he wasn't uninteresting after all.

————

Titch led the way through the Shell. He knew the sector and navigated the maze of scattered buildings and objects as if the route were obvious. It reminded Bob of Jamal making his way through the shanty maze.

'Titch?'

'Yes, Squishy Bob?'

'This area, it doesn't seem logical. Everything's a bit, well, random.'

'Ah, I understand why you might think that. It will help you to know that this is the practice ground. It's where builders learn how to build or practise something before building it elsewhere in the System.'

That did make some sense, thought Bob as he walked past a half-finished horse stable, then past a merry-go-round fairground ride that was far too small. Bob imagined mighty builders learning how to build their masterpieces, gold armour shining and reflecting the rainbow of colours in the sky, a builder getting scolded by their teacher for making their creation too small or too large.

Bob turned the corner of a 1950s cinema and suddenly stopped to stare at a gigantic vending machine.

'Ah, I love this thing! It works, too. A hacker animated it,' Titch said.

The machine wasn't too big for Titch, and he reached up to press some buttons. Bob saw one of the metal spirals twist around. A packet of crisps edged its way to the front and then got stuck between the corkscrew and the glass. *Well, it's authentic*, Bob thought, even if it was too big. Titch whacked the machine with the hammer end of his hammeraxe. The crisps and a bonus chocolate bar fell. Smiling, Titch reached into the machine. He offered the crisps to Bob and the chocolate bar to Deck, which they took with glee. The crisp packet and the chocolate bar were roughly four times the size they should be, which Bob thought was quite marvellous.

'Split them half and half?' Deck suggested, and Bob agreed.

The friends shared stories and music, laughed and joked as they ate their oversized junk food and weaved through the practice ground. Byte played in and out of various buildings and objects, running through a Japanese *minka*, into a fast-food restaurant and across a children's playground. Sebastian joined in, and the pair were racing each other through a cluster of too-big office furniture.

Titch grew quiet as Byte and Sebastian played, shuffling his feet and fiddling with the straps on his vambrace. Grace kept nervously poking her head out of a space between his armour before disappearing again.

'Squishy Bob …' Titch eventually said.

'Yes, Titch?'

'To get to the factory, we must go past my people.'

'Where they stand like statues. I remember Kuldip saying.'

'Yes. Where they face the deathless death. Please, don't think less of me when we arrive.'

'Why would I ever think less of you, Titch? You're amazing!'

'To your eyes, maybe, squishy one. But I'm not as impressive as you might think. Promise me you will try not to think less of me.'

Bob was confused but agreed, and Titch appeared satisfied with his answer. Bob shrugged at Deck, who shrugged back.

The bizarre maze of the practice ground stretched for miles. They walked most of the morning and into the afternoon. It was a bombardment of the senses. At every turn, there was a new discovery. Some objects took them a moment to determine what they were or what scale they should be. A too-small red cowshed sat in the middle of a too-large frying pan next to an accurately sized replica of *Queen Anne's Revenge*.

Bob was just adjusting to the randomness of it all when suddenly the practice ground ended. One minute, they were weaving between oversized grandfather clocks; the next, they had nothing in front of them but rolling hills. To his left and right, Bob saw objects and buildings stretched out far into the distance, and they all ended suddenly, in a line, as if they had exited from a forest.

'Ah, we're nearing the valley. You will be impressed with the valley, squishy friends. It's a triumph of my people! A masterpiece!'

Ayama was ahead of the others and floated atop a large boulder, staring across a wide valley, her hair blowing gently in the breeze. When they finally caught up to her, she spoke urgently. 'The power weakens here. Concentrate, turd sack.'

Bob concentrated. Everyone froze. Ayama was right. If he turned to look back on the practice ground, the blue edges of the interface hexagons were teeming with energy. If he looked ahead into the valley, the hexagons were weaker, fading away entirely in the distance.

Everyone unfroze.

'Yes, the power fades halfway down the valley. What are those things in the valley?'

'Monuments!' Titch announced. 'Welcome, squishy friends, to the Valley of Monuments!'

Sure enough, monument after monument sat in neat rows across the valley. 'We thought we'd just put them all in one place. It saves people from having to travel around to visit them. Good, eh?' Titch said gleefully as the party walked down the slope towards the valley floor.

Bob entertained himself by calling out the monuments as he recognised them: the Eiffel Tower, the Pantheon, Chichen Itza and the Taj Mahal. It was quite a sight.

Eventually, they reached the bottom of the valley, and Bob stood with his hands on his hips, staring up admiringly at the Statue of Liberty. 'She's amazing! The builders did this?'

'Yep, Squishy Bob. Cool, huh?'

'She might be a bit small, Titch.' Bob thought Lady Liberty was about a quarter of the size she was supposed to be.

'Really? I built this one. I'm sure I got it right …'

'It's boring and pointless. Let's not delay; we must return to Storage as soon as possible.' Ayama floated off, appearing anxious.

They rounded Lady Liberty, and the ancient Hindu-Buddhist temple of Angkor Wat came into view. As they walked along the causeway and across the moat, Bob stared in awe at the towers, pillars and intricate carvings on the ancient structure, painstakingly recreated by the builders.

After crossing the moat, they passed through the outer wall and entered the temple grounds. Byte suddenly jumped out of Bob's pocket and stood growling. The sky stopped changing colours and turned grey. Bob's heart sank.

CHAPTER 22
THE VALLEY OF MONUMENTS

'No! Not now. How did they find us?' Ayama fixed her gaze on the red eyes that stalked all over Angkor Wat as she floated to the ground, her red dress billowing in a circle around her.

She swung her staff off her shoulder, then twirled and spun it in a whirling blur of gold before slamming it into the ground to the sound of metal hitting metal. Sebastian made his way from her neck to coil around the staff. 'We might not survive this, builder. We don't have enough charge to sustain a prolonged battle.'

Titch nodded in resigned agreement, then clicked his mask into place, pulled the hammeraxe from its holster and extended it. Lava flowed through the shaft. The reds, ambers and yellows reflected off his golden armour and porcelain skull. Grace took up her crow's-nest lookout position on his shoulder. 'Find somewhere safe, squishy friends. Squishy Bob, your job is to play music – something good for smashing metal morons.'

'Make it something loud and heavy, turd sack!' Ayama shouted back.

Titch stepped forward and leaned on the mighty hammeraxe, watching the red lights weaving around the ancient temple. He was readying himself, lost in the calm moment before battle, resigned to fate and preparing for war.

Deck, Bob and Byte made their way to the outer wall, where they rested their backs against carved bas-reliefs depicting Hindu stories. Bob breathed heavily, tapping his fingers on a bas-relief. His feet were restless. *Ayama and Titch can handle this, right?*

The red lights gradually made their way down the temple. Some stalked through doorways, others over the pitched towers; all were heading for Titch and Ayama. They were metal wolves. The pack had arrived.

Standing on the temple's central steps was the largest of the wolves. The same black-maned beast Bob had encountered in the tiled space. The pack stalked around the alpha wolf and onto the temple grounds.

Deck was stunned. 'What are they?'

'If the metal wasp you whacked were a wolf ...' Bob pointed towards the rusted metal creatures running towards Titch.

Bob concentrated, and everyone froze.

'Accessing the Archive. Please wait.'

He knew which song he wanted to play. It would be perfect.

'Access complete. Returning to the Shell. Please wait.'

Everyone unfroze. *Sabotage* started playing.

'I love your awesomeness, Squishy Bob! Ha ha! Come and join in my dance, metal kitties!'

'Yes, turd sack! Perfect! Now, eat this, bitches!' Ayama twisted her staff.

Click.

As the vanguard of wolves closed in, on their flank, elephants formed of earth and rock rose from the ground in a charge, their tusks curling high into the air.

Click.

Rhinos appeared on the wolves' opposite flank, formed from temple sections that ripped from the ancient structure, the rhinos' forms materialising in full stride. They appeared ancient, with beautifully carved details from the temple running across their hides.

The temple rhinos charged towards the earth-and-rock elephants, and the vanguard of rusted metal wolves were trapped between the opposing charging beasts. The thunder of hooves echoed around the temple grounds, and dust clouds filled the air. The wolves slowed their approach towards Ayama and Titch, suddenly realising their predicament.

'Crush them!' Ayama screamed.

The vanguard of wolves turned in circles, unsure which direction would ensure their safety. But any attempt to reach safety was now futile. The earth-and-rock elephants met the ancient rhinos in an almighty crushing blow.

BOOM!

Rocks and sections of the temple crushed the wolves. Others were caught under hooves, trampled. A massive dust cloud billowed up where the collision occurred.

The second wave of wolves emerged from the dust cloud, baying for blood and revenge for their fallen.

Titch started twirling his hammeraxe, creating a harmonic whirring noise and a Catherine wheel of magma hues.

'Your turn, builder!' Ayama yelled.

The song Bob had chosen had reached a crescendo. It was perfect timing, as Titch was itching to dance. He ran towards the snarling wolves, all with metal jaws gnashing and grinding, then slammed the hammeraxe into the ground just ahead of the nearest wolf and used it to vault over the metal creature. In mid-air Titch performed a double aerial twist and simultaneously threw the hammeraxe upwards, completing the sequence by landing in an elegant, elongated stretch pose in the middle of the wolf pack.

'Whoa!' Deck said, clearly impressed.

'That's nothing. Wait until you see what else is up his sleeve,' Bob said with a knowing look.

Titch put his arm behind him and unfurled his hand. Without

looking, he caught the falling hammeraxe, then effortlessly twirled and spun it around his back and head. If Bob hadn't known any better, he would have thought Titch had deliberately performed an elaborate display to give the wolves enough time to turn and face him.

The wolves now circled Titch, snarling. Titch gracefully bowed his skull-clad head to his foes. Then the first of the wolves attacked, leaping forward. The wolf was at Titch's back. Bob took a sharp intake of breath, but he needn't have worried. With a pirouette and a flick of the hammeraxe, Titch smashed the hammer end of the weapon into the wolf whilst it was still in mid-air, as if he were a baseball hitter connecting a home run. There was an audible crunch as the hammer connected, and the beast's carcass flew into the distance, its red eyes fading.

Two wolves were already moving into a two-pronged attack on either side of Titch. He'd maintained his momentum from hitting the first wolf and finished his spin by throwing the hammeraxe high into the air in a Catherine wheel of colour.

Both wolves leaped for him, jaws wide, rusted serrated teeth ready to sink into his flesh.

At the last possible second, Titch performed a perfect aerial, soaring above the leaping wolves, causing them to crash into each other with a terrible grating noise. Titch caught the hammeraxe mid-aerial and brought it down, axe first, onto the mangled forms of the collided wolves, splitting them both with one swing.

'Yay! Go, Titch!' Bob and Deck cheered their friend on – they were both unquestionably Titch's biggest fans.

A handful of wolves remained, circling Titch. After witnessing their pack perish with such flair, all the remaining wolves were far less sure of themselves.

The music stopped.

Titch held a pose.

Bob quickly swung into action.

'Accessing the Archive. Please wait.'

Bob chose another song, something that would help Titch finish off the circling foes.

'*Access complete. Returning to the Shell. Please wait.*'

Upon hearing the new song, *A Warrior's Call*, Titch gave a visceral roar that echoed around the temple. Bob's and Deck's eyes widened. This was going to be good.

Titch began his dance, not leaving the remaining wolves time to react and attack. Perfectly in time with the fast-paced music, he leaped, twisted, spun, glided and soared – just as he had when breaking the locks at the Colosseum. The motion was fluid, elaborate, brilliant and brutal. Before the song had completed its first few bars, the eyes of the remaining wolves had faded.

Titch finished the dancing motion and held a pose resembling a martial arts master, with the hammeraxe across his arm and shoulder, legs in a wide stance and the other arm held out for balance.

And then, appearing like an apparition out of nowhere, the black-maned pack leader leaped. Titch was caught off guard and fell with uncharacteristic clumsiness. But the wolf didn't stop to attack Titch; it jumped over the hammeraxe like a showjumping horse as it fell from Titch's grip.

The beast was running full pelt as it flew past Ayama, who was on the ground, her staff engaged with the interface. 'No! Face *me*, you rusted pile of junk!' But the pack leader ignored her. There was no stopping the predator from reaching its prey. It was heading straight for Bob.

Bob was glued to the spot, unable to flee. Deck was pulling at his arm. His voice sounded distant. 'Come on, Bob! Move!' But Bob couldn't process Deck's panicked instructions. All his focus was on the alpha bearing down on him with frightening speed.

Byte ran in front of Bob, yapping at the oncoming metal wolf. 'Byte, no!'

Concern for Byte reanimated Bob, but there wasn't enough time – the wolf was too close.

Bob reached out a futile hand towards the tiny furball. He was supposed to protect him.

The wolf closed in, leaping Byte as he made to attack Bob, a horrific déjà vu replay of the tiled space. Terrible shard-toothed jaws were bearing down on him – then everyone froze.

This isn't a good time to pick the song I die to, thought Bob. But no Archive access came. The alpha wolf was in mid-air, leaping Byte, moving in slow motion. Bob still had his arm outstretched towards Byte, who was glowing. He was glowing with such a force that Bob could barely look directly at him. Byte was a pure ball of energy, features scarcely visible. Bob's hand was alive with the same fierce glow, and the thread connecting him and Byte was more intense than his connections with Ayama and Titch.

Bob instinctively pushed the energy from his hand down the thread to Byte. Everyone unfroze.

An almighty shock wave blasted out from Byte, knocking Bob off his feet. The shock wave simultaneously sent the alpha wolf shooting high up in the air with a yelp.

Titch, still far back in the temple grounds, saw his opening and flung his hammeraxe. The throw covered a fair distance, and the hammeraxe spun through the air with a harmonic whir. It collided with the alpha wolf as it reached the apex of its ascent. The axe head sank into the metal hide with a crunch, and the momentum flung the wolf and the hammeraxe into the plinth of the Statue of Liberty, where it stayed, pinning the remains of the wolf to the plinth.

'Yes!' Deck shouted, dashing over to help Bob off the ground.

Bob smiled fondly at Byte. 'Thank you.'

Byte just sat with tongue lolling at him, head cocked to one side, as if nothing of consequence had happened.

Titch ran past Ayama on his way to retrieve his hammeraxe. 'Did you hack the dog?'

Ayama shook her head, a curious expression on her face.

'Well done, squishy friends! You are warriors!' Titch said as he reached Bob and Deck.

'It was Byte.' Bob nodded towards the cute furball.

Titch jogged past them to the Statue of Liberty, placed a foot on the plinth and yanked the hammeraxe free, jumping back slightly to avoid the metal shards as the pack leader's carcass crashed to the ground.

Bob, Deck and Titch huddled together, patting each other on the back and complimenting Titch on his dancing. Titch was doing a poor job of being humble.

Bob instinctively scratched at his leg. The partially healed wasp wound suddenly felt hot.

'To me! Now!' Ayama cried out.

The friends turned towards her. The sky above the temple blacked out with zipping shapes and red lights darting frenetically. A painfully loud buzzing noise rose to a crescendo.

'Wasps …' Deck said, his joy-filled face melting into fear.

'Now, morons! Move!'

They ran towards Ayama. Bob picked up Byte as he ran and put him in the raincoat pocket, giving him a scratch behind the ear in thanks for whatever it was he'd done to the alpha wolf.

The wasps were closing in fast. The friends skidded and stumbled to where Ayama sat. They all crouched behind her.

'Brace for impact, morons!' Ayama shouted over the deafening din of the buzzing wasps.

The closest frenetic pair of lights shifted to a more certain pattern before stopping and hovering in the air, just like the wasp at the Lookout had hovered over the fire. More wasps stopped and hovered. Then they attacked – dozens of deadly, needled, wasp-shaped darts shot out of the sky towards the huddle of bodies. Bob curled up as small as possible, bracing for the impact.

Click.

Thunk! Thunk! Thunk! Thunk!

The wasps hit the hexagon-mesh shield Ayama had created in front of the friends.

Thunk! Thunk! Thunk! Thunk!

The wasps kept coming, a relentless rain of rusted, needled terrors.

Thunk! Thunk! Thunk! Bzzzz!

One broke through the shield and hit the ground. Titch smashed it with the hammer end of the hammeraxe as if he were playing Whac-A-Mole.

Thunk! Bzzzz! Thunk! Thunk!

Another one broke through. Titch gave this one a whack.

'I can't hold it much longer!' Ayama strained, leaning against her staff. 'What have you got for me, turd sack? Send me something that will help!'

Bob knew what she meant. She wanted him to send something from his imagination along the thread that connected them. He didn't like the pressure, though. He was not the sort of person to rely on in a crisis. He wasn't good at fast thinking. He—

'Now, turd sack!'

Thunk! Bzzzz! Bzzzz! Thunk!

WHACK! WHACK!

'Okay, okay, no need to shout!'

Bob concentrated, fixing an image in his mind that might destroy the wasps, then passing it along the thread to Ayama.

'This is from the Archive, turd sack! Argh! It'll have to do.'

Bob winced. He thought he'd chosen well.

Click.

Whoosh! Whoosh! Whoosh! Whoosh! Whoosh! Whoosh!

A menagerie of birds formed of pure blue flames shot into the air around the huddled companions. Goldfinches, robins, sparrows, starlings, all twisted upwards, ribbons of light trailing behind them.

A house sparrow collided head-on with a wasp, exploding on impact like a tiny firework. The wasp's red eyes faded, its carcass crashing to the ground. The sparrow's companions enacted their own missile missions, destroying more and more wasps.

Click.

Ayama created another wave of birds. Then another, and another. But it wasn't enough. The wasp numbers were dwindling, but so was Ayama's energy.

'I can't hold the shield!'

Bzzzz! Bzzzz! Bzzzz! Thunk!

WHACK! WHACK! WHACK!

The hexagon mesh around the friends started to blink. Ayama doubled her efforts, straining against her staff. The mesh brightened briefly before fading completely.

'Look out, morons! We are defenceless!'

Click.

Ayama sent another wave of birds, and the dogfight continued above their heads, blue flames versus red eyes. Wasps dived at them. The birds took one or two out, but not enough, and the wasps closed in.

Crunch! Titch smashed a wasp as another embedded its stinger in his armour. He pulled the wasp free, threw it to the ground and smashed it with his hammeraxe.

Thunk! Another wasp embedded itself in his chest plate.

Crunch! Titch sent a second flying off into the distance, then dealt with the one embedded in his armour. More wasps hovered.

'Titch, no!' Bob cried.

Byte ran ahead of Titch and sat, tongue lolling, while Titch thrashed around, swatting wasps.

Bob understood.

He concentrated.

Everyone froze.

Byte glowed fiercely. As did Bob's hand. Bob breathed deeply, willing as much energy as possible from his hand down the thread. The effort caused him to cry out and stumble backwards, breaking his concentration.

Everyone unfroze.

The shock wave blast from Byte was immense. The sudden and intense increase in pressure propagated outwards and upwards, angled away from the friends, towards the temple and the wasps. Dust billowed with the blast; blades of grass were flattened; and stones rolled. The remaining wasps were carried with the shock wave, smashing into the temple or each other.

Click. Ayama sent out one final wave of birds to deal with the stragglers.

'Yeah!' The friends – excluding Ayama – let out cries and cheers.

Titch's armour was full of bullet-sized holes. But mercifully, he was uninjured.

'No time for celebration. We need more music, turd sack.' Ayama nodded back towards Angkor Wat. More red eyes. Another wave of relentless onslaught.

'I can't go on much longer. Not much power,' Ayama whispered.

Bob concentrated, ready to choose a song. Everyone froze.

'Accessing the Archive. Please wait.'

Bob was shocked by the change to the interface. Before, it had been alive with energy; now it was muted where they stood and completely depleted beyond the temple. The gravity of their situation suddenly hit home. If the metal beasts kept coming, the power would disappear from the interface as Ayama drew on it to hack. Titch and Ayama would be powerless and taken by the deathless death, leaving Bob and Deck on their own to face certain doom. Bob's song choice reflected the sudden urgency of their situation.

'Access complete. Returning to the Shell. Please wait.'

On hearing the opening bars of *Time is Running Out*, Titch nodded slowly, understanding the song's sentiment.

At the same time, as if they were also attuned to the music, rusted metal tigers stepped into the clearing, growling with a deep, guttural rumbling, like tiny thunderstorms.

'Turd sack, send me something,' Ayama instructed.

Bob gave a determined nod. He wouldn't let her down this time. He fixed several images in his mind, mighty warriors capable of matching up to the rows of rusted monstrosities. Everyone froze, and he sent the images of the warriors he'd imagined down the thread connecting him and Ayama.

'Got it. Again, this is from the Archive! Use your imagination if we're lucky enough to get a next time! It's more powerful!'

Click.

The Minotaur was the first of Bob's warriors to rise from the battlefield wreckage. A mighty mythical beast with the head of a bull and the body of a warrior. The Minotaur snorted through a ringed nose. Beautiful Hindu and Buddhist carvings from the temple ornamented its thick arms and chest, and slung over its shoulder was a hefty, rusted axe made from the teeth of fallen hexbeasts.

Click.

Next to rise from the rusted remains of the hexbeasts was Cerberus, the three-headed hound of Hades. It stood as tall as the Minotaur, its muscular, rusted metal shoulders supporting three snarling heads.

Click.

Lastly, the Chimera rose. It had the body of a lion formed from the temple statues, with the rusted head of a goat. Its serrated horns twisted in coils, and it had a snake with a forked tongue flicking for a tail.

'I will join them!' Resigned to the job at hand, Titch jogged forward to join the formidable, mythical defensive line. Soon a porcelain-skulled golden giant stood shoulder to shoulder with the Minotaur, Cerberus and the Chimera. Bob suddenly fancied their chances, daring himself to hope.

The tigers attacked without warning or hesitation, running at full speed towards Titch and the mythical warriors. Their low, rumbling growls echoed around the grounds.

'Metal cow-man, attack!' Titch ordered the Minotaur to attack the left flank.

The Minotaur snorted and held its arms out to the sides, chest wide, bellowing its war cry. With axe in hand, it charged towards a group of tigers, the first swing of its deadly axe connecting with a crunch.

'Goat-kitty, attack!' Titch pointed to the right flank, where more metal hexbeast tigers closed in.

The Chimera made a bleating sound before lowering its horns and charging towards the tigers. It didn't sound intimidating, and Bob screwed up his nose, regretting his choice.

'You and me, doggy, we attack these ugly kitties.' Titch pointed towards the larger group of tigers in the centre, barrelling towards them. 'Can you dance, doggy?'

Cerberus barked at the oncoming tigers, then rushed forward to meet them.

'I suppose that will have to do.'

Titch swung his hammeraxe gleefully, and he started to move to the rhythm of the music. The first hexbeast tiger reached him and was promptly thumped with the hammeraxe, perfectly timed to the beat.

Bob and Deck were taking in all the action. Byte perched in his usual spot in Bob's raincoat pocket.

'Bob, come here.' Ayama spoke wearily.

Bob glanced over and was immediately concerned – she was even paler than usual and sat slumped. He moved over to her side.

'We might not survive, Titch and I.' Her voice was a whisper, barely audible over the clangs and clashes of the battle. 'You're important somehow, and so is the dog. If we become deathless, you must continue. You must reboot the sectors to release the hackers and builders from the deathless death!' She clutched the lapels of his raincoat, pulling him closer. 'Promise me! Promise you will go to the House of Horrors!' She barely held herself up as she willed the words from her lips.

'I … I promise,' Bob stammered.

'Do you remember what I told you about the two types of humans?'

'Dickheads and not-dickheads.'

'Yes, remember this, and never be a dickhead. Promise me.'

'I promise.'

'Your connection to Byte and what you can do with your mind is special. There is more you need to learn, but there is no time. You're no turd-sack human, though. I'll rename you. Your new name is … BitBob.' Ayama let go of the lapels on Bob's raincoat and sank to the ground.

Bob took a step back. His heart was pounding. What was Ayama saying? *I'm not special.* A sudden crunch made Bob look up, and he saw how the fight was progressing.

The Chimera perished, having barely made a dint in the right flank. Those tigers were now heading directly for Titch and Cerberus. Bob wished he'd imagined the Chimera breathing fire, with a crocodile head, or both.

The Minotaur was doing far better; many of the tigers it faced perished. One sank its jaws into the Minotaur's arm, but the Minotaur was holding its arm aloft, beating the tiger attached to it with its axe.

Cerberus traded fierce biting lunges with two tigers, matching them blow for blow, and Titch continued his dance, having smashed his way through countless tigers already, and was in mid-air, ready to bring his hammeraxe down on another. He was weakening – his spins had less flair; the turns were more lethargic; and the hammeraxe spun around him just that bit slower.

Just as the battle turned in their favour as the tigers perished, something huge crashed through the middle of the temple, sending ancient stone flying.

Standing amid the temple grounds, facing the final demise of its hexbeast tiger comrades, was an enormous hexbeast bear that must have been ten times the size of Titch. Rusted shards covered the beast's hide, making a grating and grinding sound as the giant hexbeast moved. The bear let out an ear-piercing metallic roar that shook the very air.

'How dare you!' Titch screamed, his hammeraxe pointed at the metal monster. 'How dare you imitate the bear! Have you no honour?'

Furious at the apparent insult, Titch charged the great bear. He leaped, hammeraxe extended, axe head bearing down on the beast. A giant claw swung down at the leaping Titch, knocking him out of the air and sending him flying into an outer building of the temple with an almighty crash. Titch slumped to the ground, motionless.

'Titch! No!' Bob cried. He shuffled his feet as if he were going to charge forward to help his friend, but fear got the better of him.

Deck, on the other hand, had already set off across the temple grounds, passing the Minotaur, the last mythical beast standing, which was ripping the head off the last of the tigers. The bear ignored Deck. It fixed its red eyes on Bob and let out a roar before charging towards him.

'No! Give me something! Now!' Ayama's voice was weak but insistent.

Bob scanned around, desperately trying to find inspiration. He needed something, some idea, some – he spotted it. Bob concentrated, pushing the thought as a fizzing ball of energy to Ayama.

She turned around and looked up. 'I suppose it might work … BitBob.' She winked.

Click.

With the twist of her staff, Ayama sapped the last of her energy and slumped to the ground, motionless.

'Ayama!' Bob crouched and shook her shoulder. She didn't move. Sebastian lay sprawled next to her, lifeless. Bob knew the deathless death had taken them.

The bear was closing in on Bob, its massive paws slamming

into the ground as it ran on all fours towards him. Bob could only watch as the mountain of rusted metal approached.

Then, there was an almighty fracturing sound, resembling a machine that hadn't been used for generations creaking back to life. The Statue of Liberty was joining the battle.

Lady Liberty strained and pulled her feet off the stone plinth to a chorus of cracks and groans, the air filled with dust and stone debris. Then Lady Liberty stepped off her plinth, stood upright with her head held high and lowered her torch, pointing it like a fencer's rapier at the bear.

Bob watched in awe. 'Ayama would say something like "*En garde*, bitches",' Bob said to Byte as the statue stepped over Bob and the lifeless Ayama.

Byte gave a yip of agreement as Lady Liberty's shadow passed over them.

Lady Liberty's footsteps thundered around the temple grounds as she headed towards the rusted metal bear. The bear had covered most of the distance towards Bob but now faced down its new opponent. Both foes charged towards each other, the bear with one arm raised, massive metallic claws out, ready to strike. Lady Liberty held out her *tabula ansata* like a shield, torch raised high, primed to counterstrike. Then they clashed.

The bear swung its mighty claws, but Lady Liberty blocked the incoming attack, the bear's claws embedded in the tablet. Lady Liberty countered with her torch, landing a blow to the side of the bear's head, causing it to stumble. After a brief tussle, the bear's claws were released from the stone tablet, and Lady Liberty and the bear proceeded to trade ferocious blows that echoed around the temple.

'Bob!' Deck called to his friend from the other side of the grounds and gestured for Bob to join him.

Bob was initially reluctant to go, as the gigantic foes still fought on the grounds he needed to cross. Their arms were on each other's shoulders, each trying to topple the other, and Bob feared getting trampled. But wanting to be brave and fearing being cut off from his friend, he ran, with Byte securely tucked in the raincoat pocket.

He weaved in and out of the remains of fallen hexbeasts, some still twitching, with faint or flickering red eyes, so Bob focused on Deck rather than the battle that raged near him, running with tunnel vision.

When he reached Deck, he saw that Titch was severely wounded. The chest plate of his golden armour had two huge gashes through it. The purple swirls that usually swept around Titch's dark skin like a storm moved slowly, lethargically. Bob briefly worried about Grace but spotted the glittering lizard resting on Titch's vambrace.

'Squishy Bob,' Titch said, followed by a worrying cough. 'I'm not very awesome at the moment, huh?'

'You were amazing, Titch,' Bob said sincerely.

'Ayama?'

Bob hung his head. 'Deathless.'

Both Titch and Deck lowered their eyes. Bob knew that without her, the journey just became infinitely more difficult. He had also been starting to like her. She'd uncovered some of who he was, and he believed there was some compassion behind the curses and name-calling.

'I'm nearly deathless, squishy friends. There's no way to recharge. You'll have to continue without me and Ayama.'

'We can't!' Bob cried. 'We need you guys! There's no way we'll survive without you!'

'You have to, squishy one. You're brave, and you're awesome.'

Tears came to Bob's eyes. He couldn't lose Titch. Even though they hadn't known each other long, Titch was extraordinary, and Bob was proud to call him a friend. Bob held on to Titch's hand.

'Take care of Grace.' Titch raised his arm, which took immense effort, and Grace scurried from the vambrace onto Deck's outstretched hand. 'Meeting you filled my heart with joy.

I danced and laughed and felt like I belonged somewhere for the first time in my life. Thank you, and remember – be awesome.'

Just as the last song Bob had chosen finished playing, Titch sat back, his arms slumping, and his glittery eyes stared vacantly into the air. The deathless death had taken him.

Bob wiped a tear from his cheek with the sleeve of his raincoat.

CHAPTER 23
THE LIGHTHOUSE

'Come on, Bob. We need to move,' Deck said, taking a sharp breath and drying his eyes with his shirtsleeve.

Grace was still sitting in his outstretched palm, uncharacteristically still, regarding Titch and gently cocking her head from side to side.

'Bob, we need to move, or we'll get crushed.' Deck pointed to the bear and Lady Liberty, still trading blows amid the churned-up grounds of Angkor Wat, where the remains of metal hexbeasts now littered the once-peaceful ancient setting. The Minotaur joined the fray, hitting the bear in the leg with its axe.

'Bob!'

'We can't leave him! Or Ayama!' Bob cried.

'We have to! We're done for if we stay. Come on.'

Deck placed a supportive hand on Bob's shoulder and helped his friend up and onto his feet, and then they heard a low, grating, guttural growl. A metal tiger appeared from around the corner of the outbuilding. It was split down the middle, its rear missing completely, and the metal shards of its underbelly churned the earth as it dragged itself along using its front legs. Its red eyes flickered. Jaws slammed shut, then opened, then shut.

Deck instinctively shielded Bob. But Bob was angry. He was

grieving for Titch and Ayama. He didn't want to hide behind Deck.

Pushing Deck aside, Bob stepped forward and screamed at the beast, which kept inching towards them. There was no compassion in this creature, no remorse. Bob grabbed Titch's hammeraxe, which had been leaning up against the outbuilding. The mighty weapon didn't move, not even a fraction. It might as well have been part of the building. Bob's anger waned, replaced by fear and doubt as the metal creature doubled its efforts, edging closer, jaws gnashing.

Another hand appeared on the hammeraxe – Deck's.

'Push!'

Bob did as Deck instructed. They both pushed against the shaft of the hammeraxe, putting all their weight into it, digging in their heels.

The beast was close.

They should just run.

Why did I try to face this thing? Idiot!

Bob let out a cry. 'Aaagh!' The hammeraxe started to move. With one last push, gravity took over, and the hammeraxe fell from the wall. Axe head first, it smashed the metal tiger's skull. The red lights faded.

'Come on. Let's not wait for one with all its legs.' Deck grabbed Bob's arm and led him away from the temple and out of range of the savage battle.

They skirted a body of water and left the temple through the outer wall, leaving the fighting and their friends behind.

———

Bob, Deck and the two hexpets moved quickly through the valley, fearful that some metal-monster survivors might pick up their scent and initiate a hunt. They ran through Stonehenge, then up and through the Pantheon, past Petra – carved into the side of the valley – and then skirted around Chichen Itza. Eventually, they stopped under the shadows of the Easter Island Moai statues to catch their breath.

Bob took two deep puffs from the blue inhaler. Hurting from losing Titch and Ayama, he punched the ground in frustration. Whenever Bob felt he belonged somewhere, someone took it away. The Town. Sunny, the Queen. Now Titch and Ayama. He was just discovering who he was, and now he was more confused than ever.

Deck came over and put his arm around him. 'I know.' He ruffled Bob's hair and hugged his shoulders as the tears fell.

Byte jumped out of the raincoat pocket and snuggled into Bob's lap.

'I can't do it, Deck. I can't go on.'

'*We* can do it, Bob. Together.'

'But what if we come across a hexbeast? We're done for if we have to face just one of those things. Go on without me. You'll do better on your own.'

'Nonsense. I need you.'

'To do what? Freeze on the spot? No. I'll put you in danger. I'll find somewhere to hide instead. There will be loads of hiding spots around here.'

'I'm not going to lie to you, Bob. Without Titch and Ayama, it will be tough. But hiding isn't the answer. You need to find that hidden strength, that spark that I know you have. Start to believe in yourself, Bob. I believe in you.'

He didn't want to go, but Deck was right. He had to. Sunny and the Queen were in the House of Horrors. Karen had said it might hold the key to who he was, and they needed to reboot the sectors to save the builders and hackers.

'Come on. Let's keep going. Let's try and get a bit further before nightfall,' Deck suggested.

Bob slowly got to his feet. He scooped up Byte and gave him a snuggle before popping him back in the raincoat pocket. Then Bob exhaled, nodded with new-found determination and set off with Deck.

'Thank you,' Bob said as they walked.

'That's what friends are for.' Deck smiled, ruffling Bob's curls.

They cautiously continued their journey, keeping close to the walls and walking through the monuments' shadows.

'I've no idea what monuments are, but they're impressive!' Deck said, probably to take the tension out of their situation.

'Of course! You won't know what any of these are.' Bob then distracted himself, telling Deck about each monument as they passed through the valley. Occasionally he'd access the Archive for information on the ones he wasn't well informed about.

Deck listened, fascinated. 'Humans created them?' He gazed in wonder at the Pyramids of Giza.

'Well, these are replicas made by the builders, but yeah, humans made the originals,' Bob said, enjoying showing off his knowledge.

'Wow! I thought the town hall was huge and impressive, but these are mind-blowing!' Deck craned his neck to take in the enormity of a pyramid. 'Do you know what my job was in the Town?'

'Oh, no, actually,' Bob admitted.

'I built the houses. I was just making the finishing touches to yours before ... well, you know. It's on the outskirts, near the stream, on the same row as mine and Sunny's.'

Bob imagined his house in his mind's eye. His door and roof would be yellow. He would grow sunflowers in his garden. Taking a break from the work, mopping his brow, he'd lean over the fence to talk to Deck. Sunny would stroll down the path, calling out to them and waving a basket of freshly baked bread. The friends would then have tea, fresh bread with butter and jam, laugh and tell stories.

Bob was suddenly aware of Deck smirking at him. 'Are you okay?'

'Sorry. I was just daydreaming. A home sounds nice. I would have liked that.'

'You can still have a home, Bob. It's just that first we need to sneak into a factory teeming with horrors to find a reboot switch. Even though we don't know what it looks like or how it works. Then rescue Sunny and the Queen. Easy. Then we go home.' Deck looked skywards with a frown. 'Night is settling in.'

The sky hadn't changed back to cycling through colours, but the grey slowly faded to black.

They started to search for somewhere to hide and camp for the night. In the distance, a lighthouse came into view – the Tower of Hercules. They headed towards it, keen to get inside before nightfall.

————

They reached the Tower of Hercules just as night fell. After briefly inspecting the interior, they soon regretted picking the lighthouse. It was pitch black inside.

'Ah. What do we do now?' Bob asked, standing in the doorway, deciding whether to go in.

'I'm not sure, to be honest. It's too dark, but we can't sleep outside. We don't know if there are any more hexbeasts following us.' Deck scanned the shadows of the distant monuments, searching for any telltale red eyes.

Just then, Grace poked her head out from where she'd been hiding in Deck's shirt. She shot down Deck's shirtsleeve and onto his hand, then started to glow. It was a soft glow, like a lizard-shaped night light.

'Yes! Go, Grace!' Deck said as she perfectly and discreetly illuminated the lighthouse's interior for them.

The stairs to the lighthouse were directly in front of them, but rather than facing the long climb, they peeled off into a side room and settled down on the floor. Deck had taken the bag of food from Titch and handed Bob his share of what was left. 'This should be enough for tonight, but we must find some food in the morning.'

'Where are we going to find food?'

'No idea. Maybe we'll have to make do until we get to the House of Horrors. Let's not starve, though. There isn't much left, so we may as well finish it.'

Bob eagerly tucked into the meat pastry that Deck had handed him. Byte sat on Bob's lap, happily eating his share. Grace wasn't interested in the food on the floor between them all, so she just glowed like an artificial campfire.

They settled down for the night in relative silence, anxiously awaiting the sunrise. Deck started drifting off to sleep, the exhaustion kicking in, but Bob couldn't sleep. His mind raced with thoughts of their terrifying task ahead. He also thought about the house in the Town, a home he had yet to know. Whenever his thoughts drifted to the house, Bob felt a pang of guilt. Ayama and Titch were deathless; he didn't know the fate of the Queen and Sunny; and here he was thinking about a house. *Idiot.*

Every sound echoed in the room they were in, every scraping of a boot on the floor or a deep breath into cupped hands to ward off the cold.

Bob sat as quietly as possible, not wanting to disturb Deck. He listened to the noises outside, reading into every slight tap, howl of the wind or – *Scraping!* There was a scraping noise against the door. It echoed around the lighthouse. It was deliberate and couldn't be mistaken for anything else. The sound startled Deck awake.

The friends remained motionless, their backs straight and shoulders tensed. They hoped that by staying still, whatever creature was scratching the door would assume the lighthouse was empty and leave. Mercifully, the scratching stopped. Deck and Bob let their shoulders relax a little, releasing the breaths they had been holding. Byte chose this moment to trot out of the room and head towards the door. He proceeded to yip loudly and scratch at it.

'Byte!' exclaimed Bob in a whisper, as loud as he dared. 'No! Come here! Please!'

The scratching from outside resumed, causing Deck's and Bob's shoulders to tense again.

'Byte!'

Byte didn't stop, despite Bob's pleading.

Bob scrambled out of the side room to intercept Byte, still standing on his little hind legs, with his forelegs on the door, scratching back at whatever lurked on the other side.

Deck joined Bob, and they stared at Byte and the door, unsure what to do. After a moment, Deck lifted his head, then suddenly sprinted up the lighthouse stairs. He was gone only briefly, returning down the stairs a moment later. 'It's okay, Bob. Open the door.'

Bob frowned, mouth half-open in disbelief at what Deck had asked him to do.

Deck smiled as he reached for the door handle. 'It's okay. I'll get it.'

Bob moved to stop him but wasn't quick enough. Deck turned the handle and pulled the door inwards. As soon as the door cracked open, a streak of white shot through and into the side room. Grace was still curled up on the floor, and her soft light illuminated ... Sebastian. Ayama's mink had somehow escaped the deathless death and tracked them down.

Bob breathed out a confused sigh of relief.

'I looked out of the window above the door on the next level up,' Deck explained. 'I've no idea how he found us.'

Bob was just relieved it was a hexpet and not a hexbeast.

Bob and Deck walked back into the side room. Sebastian curled up beside Grace, and Byte trotted over to join them. Soon all three hexpets were in a cute sleepy line in the middle of the floor.

Deck settled back on the hard concrete, his arms wrapped around himself, and his eyes started to close.

Bob sat down with his back against the wall, and after a few moments of imagining his life in his round home with the yellow canvas door, Bob drifted off to sleep as well.

CHAPTER 24
THE FOREST OF BUILDERS

Bob awoke to the sound of birds singing. The sun was up, and the sky was back to cycling through a spectrum of colours. The lighthouse interior was now bright, and the hexpets were awake, eagerly exploring. Byte and Sebastian chased each other around the small room, up and down the stairs and back into the room.

They didn't have anything to pack, as they had finished the food for supper. Deck kept the bag, though, as Sebastian was quite happy curling up inside it.

Ready to go, they tentatively stepped out of the lighthouse, in case any hexbeasts were lurking. Mercifully, there were none, so they set off towards a path that led out of the valley.

They soon reached the base of the path and started the long climb out of the Valley of Monuments. Each step was a step further away from Titch and Ayama, and a step closer to the House of Horrors. Bob felt vulnerable without Titch and Ayama. Thank goodness for Deck, who had saved him from a hexbeast once before by whacking the wasp, and he'd tackled the Librarian, so Bob figured Deck would be handy if they got into a scrape. Bob knew he would be useless, probably freeze on the spot again.

Deck was walking slightly ahead. He was uncharacteristically chatty, telling Sebastian and Grace stories about the Zoo. Bob knew Deck was trying to hide how anxious he was to find Sunny.

They eventually made it up the steep path and out of the valley. Deck, who was usually considerate and would wait for Bob to catch up, was too anxious to get to the factory. When Bob caught up with him, he was fidgeting and set off walking the second Bob arrived.

'I need to catch my breath.' Bob doubled over with his hands on his knees to recover from climbing the steep path. He reached into his raincoat pocket and fished underneath Byte for his inhaler.

'No time for a rest if we want to get to the House of Horrors before nightfall.'

Bob wondered how Deck could know that. They didn't know where they were going, and they had no map to navigate by. They were relying on a story a toothy, one-armed man had told them.

'Coming,' said Bob wearily, feeling obliged to cut his rest short.

Deck allowed Bob to catch up to him, and they walked through the morning chatting away and listening to music. The odd tree dotted the dry, grassy plains, but none bore fruit. Any chance of breakfast faded as their shadows grew shorter and the day grew from warm to hot.

They ended up navigating their way across the plains by Grace's bizarre behaviour. Deck headed for some hills, but when they altered course, Grace darted around Deck, even getting in his face. She settled down the second he turned back towards the direction they had initially headed in. If there were any wrong turns, Grace would let Deck know about it. Without a better way of knowing where they were going, they stuck with Grace as navigator.

As the sun reached its peak in the colour-changing sky, the

plains ended, transitioning into an orchard. Bob and Deck ran to the trees the second they saw them and picked the lower-hanging fruit, eating the apples hungrily.

Deck tossed Bob his third half-red, half-green apple as they sat in the shade of the trees and ate. 'So, if I take what Kuldip told us and trace it back in reverse, next, we should get to where Titch's people stand still, deathless. After that, it's a cave, then a cliff walk up to the House of Horrors. Is that how you remember it?' Deck asked Bob through a mouthful of apple.

'Er, yep, that's it,' Bob said with some uncertainty. He almost wished they would get lost and not make it to the horror-filled factory, but he knew he was a coward for thinking that.

'I'll pack some apples in this bag for the journey. Sebastian will just have to sit on top of them. We need the food, and we might not find any further on,' Deck said as he packed the bag with plenty of apples. Grace perched on Deck's shoulder as he weighed the bag, deciding if he could carry it.

Sebastian and Byte were playing happily. Sebastian darted around a tree like a squirrel, and Byte was doing a rubbish job of trying to catch him. Sebastian would come down the tree to tease Byte, then shoot back up the instant the little furball came near.

'Come on, then, you lot. Playtime's over. Let's keep going,' Deck said as he slung the bag of apples over his shoulder and set off walking.

Sebastian didn't fancy lying in a bag of apples, so he slinked along next to Deck.

They walked through the orchard for an hour or so, heading in whichever direction didn't cause Grace to fret. Eventually, the orchard ended, opening up to another vast plain, framed by mountains in the distance.

There they were. Stretching across the plain was a forest of giant, golden-armoured, deathless builders. Deck and Bob looked at each other with raised eyebrows, then jogged forward to inspect the closest of them.

The first builder they approached was massive. Bob reckoned

a good two feet taller than Titch. He wore a white skull mask with swirling patterns carved across the surface, mimicking the purple swirls in their skin. The golden armour gleamed, with intricate designs etched along the edges. This particular builder had an elaborate cathedral embossed on the breastplate. In the builder's hand was a hammeraxe. The hammeraxe wasn't as elaborate as Titch's. The surface of the cooled shaft bore no pattern or bear symbol. Perched on this builder's shoulder was a hawk with glittering silver wings. The hawk suddenly moved to regard them. Bob jumped back, but the hawk didn't fly from its perch; it just twisted its head. Its movement was stilted and strained, almost mechanical.

Bob moved on to the next builder, then the next. All were massive and wore intricate, individualised golden armour and unique white porcelain masks. All had a simple hammeraxe and a lifeless hexpet at their feet or perched on a shoulder. Bob saw lions, pandas, eagles, crocodiles, snakes and many more. All had varying white and glittery patterns on their hides, feathers or fur.

'This is why Titch thought I would think less of him,' said Bob as they weaved through the forest of deathless builders.

'I guess so,' Deck said, turning and walking backwards to admire a builder with shoulders twice the width of the others. This builder sported a porcelain plume on top of his mask, like a Corinthian helmet, and a skull-and-crossbones design embossed on his breastplate. His hammeraxe had polished black hammer and axe heads, and at his feet was a giant white boar with huge, glittery tusks. 'All these builders are much bigger than Titch, and their armour and masks are less plain,' Deck said just before he backed into another builder, not paying attention to where he was going.

'It must be why he's called Titch and why Ayama calls him tiny all the time. Compared to the rest of his people, he kind of is. I just thought it was sarcasm. Poor guy.' Bob suddenly felt empathy for Titch. He'd assumed so much and yet understood very little about his friend.

As they walked, they gaped and pointed at individual details. Sebastian and Byte weaved and dodged as they ran through the builders' legs. Eventually, they reached the end of the forest of deathless builders.

A few yards ahead of the rest stood the most spectacular builder of them all. The lone builder was even taller than the others. His porcelain skull mask had a beard-like outline with delicate gold swirls. Atop the skull mask was a golden circlet for a crown. Flowing silvery hair plaited into tails and woven with gold fell down his back. The breastplate had an elaborate version of the bear symbol etched into it. A massive, glittering silver bear hexpet stood on its hind legs next to the mighty builder, almost to the same height.

'This is Wodenar,' said Bob, in awe.

'Who?'

'The builder king. It must be him.'

Unlike the rest of his people, Wodenar didn't hold a hammer-axe, although his hand was in a position as if one should be there – or one had been there. Bob pointed to the empty hand, and Deck nodded in understanding.

Bob and Deck walked a short distance from Wodenar and then turned to marvel at the forest of builders. The plain was eerie still, and the pair looked back in silence. The builders were deathless but did not appear dead, and they didn't resemble statues; they were all too real. It was more like they stood still, unwavering, mimicking the King's Guards at Buckingham Palace or living-statue street performers. He hadn't noticed it whilst walking among them, but now he stared back at them all, Bob thought there was something very austere about the builders. Something profoundly serious and severe – nothing like Titch.

'It's a shame they're like this,' Deck said, breaking the silence. 'This lot would be handy in a fight.'

Bob nodded slowly in agreement.

'Here.' Deck tossed Bob an apple, which he clumsily caught.

The friends, taking bites of their apples and with the hexpets following, turned their backs to the builders and set off towards the mountains to find the cave.

CHAPTER 25
THE CAVE

They reached the base of the mountains as their shadows grew longer. Bob's feet were weary, sore and heavy. They walked a short distance down a meandering path lined with tall rocks that emerged from the mountain like roots, and then, mercifully, they arrived at the mouth of the cave. They both slumped down against a large boulder.

'Apple?' Deck asked.

Bob nodded and caught the apple despite being sick of apples already. He longed for spiced stew and fresh focaccia, but he was hungry, so apples it was.

With the apple between his teeth, Bob pulled off his high-tops and socks and rubbed his feet. It felt good to rest them. The walk had been long and hot. 'I guess this is the cave,' said Bob, after taking his apple from his teeth and pointing a weary finger towards the cave's mouth.

'Guess so. Thank goodness Grace was with us. I'm not sure we would have found our way here without her.'

Bob nodded in agreement.

Deck and Bob started planning what to do when they arrived at the House of Horrors. They knew nothing of its size, the layout or the number of horrors inside. It wasn't a plan based on facts but instead consisted of basic objectives.

One, they would sneak in and be as quiet as possible to avoid engaging with any horrors, opting for stealth tactics instead. Bob approved of this approach.

Two, they would try to find Sunny and the Queen first.

Three, they would find the reboot switch and flip it, press it, or whatever.

Four, they would try to find information on Bob. Maybe a record or a file or something.

Five, they would sneak back out and go to the Zoo to live happily ever after.

It was a simple plan, and neither Bob nor Deck vocalised the unlikelihood of its success. Feigning ignorance of danger was the unspoken sixth objective.

They were discussing the finer points of the best way to sneak and hide when Sebastian scurried out from where he'd been curled up between them, and stood on his hind legs, sniffing the air. Bob and Deck sat up straight as Byte ran to join Sebastian. After a moment of sniffing the air himself, he started growling.

'Something's coming!' Deck said. 'Quick, hide!'

They gathered their things and scooped up the hexpets. Bob was still barefoot and had to pick up his high-tops, coat and jumper. He dropped the half-eaten apple whilst doing so, and it rolled away, stopping at the mouth of the cave. He went to fetch it, but Deck stopped him. 'No time! Come on!'

They scrambled over two large boulders just as several voices approached. Behind the boulders was a small recess with just enough space for them to crouch in.

Bob shushed Byte and stroked him to get the pup to stop growling. Thankfully, Byte complied and settled to a low, barely audible rumble.

Bob and Deck peered through the gap in the boulders, awaiting the arrival of the voices. Perfectly framed in Bob's view through the gap was the apple he'd dropped – *Idiot*. The voices drew closer, echoing off the nearby rock formations.

'He ain't gonna be pleased with you, boss!' one voice said.

'He'll butcher ya for sure,' said another.

'Gonna be nasty!' said a third, followed by a chorus of cackling laughter.

Whoever they were, they stopped just out of view.

'Let's stop 'ere for a bit. My arms are killin' me. He's heavy,' came a fourth voice.

'Yeah, all right, but not for long. We need to get back to the master before nightfall,' said a fifth voice.

'Hey, what's this?' a sixth voice said in a high-pitched squeak. This one appeared in Bob's view, heading for the apple. It was a horror with stitched-on arms and legs. This horror was fat, but his legs and arms were long and thin, which meant he walked with a wobble like he might fall over at any moment. 'It's an apple,' the fat horror said.

'I can see that, Rolly. What's it doin' 'ere?' came one of the voices from before.

'Well, I dunno, Deadhead. Someone must've dropped it.'

Deadhead came into view, joining Rolly's inspection of the apple. He scratched one of his heads. The other head hung off his shoulder, threatening to drop off at any moment, half stitched on, grey, with eyes closed and tongue hanging out of his mouth.

'What do you make of this, Spook?' Deadhead asked.

Spook came into view. This horror's back was red-raw, his skin flayed on both sides up to the shoulders, the ends of the skin stitched onto the elbows. Bob assumed they were supposed to be wings. Spook inspected the apple and just shrugged.

'Pay it no mind. We gotta keep movin',' a gruff voice said from out of view.

'Let's eat first, though. I'm starvin',' said Rolly.

'You're always starvin'!' the gruff voice replied. 'All right, but make it quick.'

'Where's the food?' asked Spook. His thin, scratchy voice sounded like nails down a chalkboard.

'It's here somewhere, behind one of these rocks. Get searchin',' Rolly said as he took a massive bite of Bob's apple.

Bob's eyes widened as the horrors started hunting behind rocks and boulders. His skin turned cold, and a shudder went down his spine as he gripped Deck's arm. 'They're going to find us,' Bob whispered. He peered anxiously through the gap as the horrors searched.

A large, solid torso suddenly appeared, filling the view between the boulders. Bob pulled back in alarm. 'What about over 'ere? Anyone searched 'ere already?' The gruff voice was loud up close, and Bob winced at the stench of this horror's breath.

'Not sure, Gunk. No harm in checkin' again.'

A large hand with fungus-infected fingernails and a green tinge to the skin slid into the gap between the boulders. The foul-smelling horror was preparing to lift himself over the boulder, just as Bob and Deck had done moments earlier.

Deck picked up a rock and held it, ready to throw at the creature. Bob heard a scraping sound as the horror put his foot on the boulder, preparing to heave himself up.

'I found it!' came a voice from the opposite side of the cave mouth to where Bob and Deck were hiding.

There was another scraping sound as the stinking horror removed his foot from the boulder. The green-tinged hand slid back from the gap, and the large torso moved away.

Bob allowed himself to exhale the breath he'd been holding, both in fear and to avoid taking in the awful smell. He could now see the other horrors crowded around a small wooden crate.

Gunk, the gruff horror that had almost found them, walked over to the others and reprimanded Rolly. 'Oi! Don't take too much. Leave some for next time we come out this way.' Gunk took his share and fixed the lid on the crate, then heaved it back behind a nearby rock.

The horrors greedily wolfed down the stale bread, and then Gunk rallied them. 'Come on, let's get a move on.'

The horrors all disappeared out of Bob's view again.

After some clattering noises, Gunk shouted, 'Three, two, one, heave!'

There were several complaints and groans, and then, two by two, the horrors walked past Bob and Deck's hiding spot. They were carrying a long wooden pole with something tied to it – no, wait, it was someone! Limbs bound with rope – hands, hands, hands again! As the last pair of horrors passed, it was clear that the creature tied to the pole … was Nightmare.

Nightmare sniffed the air and then locked eyes with Bob. He knew they were there! He wriggled frantically, trying to shout through his gag to get the attention of the others.

'Stop squirmin'! There ain't no escape for you,' Gunk said.

Nightmare thrashed violently. His one eye stared directly at Bob, his face filled with furious rage. Dribble ran down his chin as he continued his gagged screams.

Nightmare's thrashing caused Rolly to fall, and the front of the pole dropped. Bob's heart was beating fast. Nightmare knew they were here. If the other horrors removed his gag, they would find them and take them to the Butcher.

'Stop squirmin', I said!' Gunk, who was not carrying the pole and was bringing up the rear, unclipped a cudgel from his belt and thumped Nightmare across the head, knocking him unconscious.

Rolly picked up his section of the pole, and the horrors continued their procession into the cave.

Deck and Bob waited a long time to ensure the horrors would not return.

'Well, at least we know we're good at hiding. We just have to master sneaking next,' Deck said as he clambered back over the boulder.

Bob nodded while stroking Byte, praising him for keeping still and quiet, not something he would usually do.

When Deck reached the top of the boulder, he pulled Bob up. Then the two of them gracelessly scrambled back onto the path.

Bob put on his shoes whilst Deck recovered the horrors' food supplies. He reappeared at Bob's side with the wooden crate just as Bob finished tying his laces. Deck broke into the crate, nervously glancing back towards the cave, anxious that the horrors might reappear. The hexpets were now calm, which was reassuring.

The crate contents consisted of dry bread, meat and hard cheese. Deck and Bob took the lot, tucking into as much as they could manage and packing the rest in the bag.

'I guess we need to face going in there.' Deck nodded towards the cave whilst stuffing the dry bread into the bag. 'We should try and get through before nightfall. We won't be able to navigate in the dark.'

Bob sighed and nodded, handing some leftovers to Byte, who happily took them.

With bags packed, hexpets herded and having waited as long as they dared, Deck and Bob took their first tentative steps into the mouth of the cave.

The cave was just as Kuldip described, with the exit visible from where they stood, illuminated by the faint columns of evening light from the ceiling and by the fierce blue flames of the firewall, which framed the exit.

The cave was spacious, with a cool, fresh, earthy scent reminiscent of a forest floor after rain. Stalagmites proudly carpeted the floor, and stalactites hung in clusters like stone chandeliers. The steady drip of water echoed from the darker recesses as they walked a well-trodden path leading through the cave towards the exit. Deck adjusted the strap of his bag and set off at a determined pace.

They soon made it through the cave and stood at the exit. To their left, the firewall raged, shooting high into the sky. Bob could feel the heat on his skin, and he instinctively backed away from it, recalling the memory of being pulled through the Zoo firewall by disembodied hands.

Deck stared up at the firewall, straining to see the top. 'Kuldip followed the firewall from the cliff to the cave. If we stick close, we should find the cliff path.'

Bob agreed, so they stuck to this plan, following the firewall whilst maintaining as safe a distance as possible.

The sun had set, so Bob put his jumper and raincoat back on. Byte was fast asleep in his usual spot in the raincoat pocket. Despite the heat from the firewall, there was a damp chill in the air. He thought it was odd that the climate felt very different despite having only walked a short distance through a cave.

The landscape they walked through was harsh, nothing but jagged grey rocks with a gravelly path winding through them. As they rounded a point where the firewall curved sharply, the factory came into view.

Before them rose a sheer cliff, with more jagged grey rocks at its base, imitating a tumultuous sea. The precarious cliffside path Kuldip had described was no more than a ledge that jutted out, climbing to a peak in the distance, where the cliff ended.

Atop the cliff's peak stood the factory. The factory was just that – a factory. Bob wasn't entirely sure what he'd expected, but given the tiled space, he'd assumed something clinical, like a hospital or maybe something otherworldly and ethereal. Instead, the factory appeared lifted from a steampunk horror film. The large stone-and-metal building dominated the cliff's peak. It was dark and grimy, with tall chimneys billowing steam and smoke. Dark clouds loomed in the distance, periodically lit by flashes of lightning. Bob thought the only thing missing was circling bats, and the horror film scene would have been complete.

The horrors were struggling with their Nightmare cargo as they climbed a set of metal stairs that zigzagged directly up the side of the cliff, clattering, banging and cursing as they tried to manoeuvre the pole around the corners of the staircase. Bob and Deck instinctively crouched and moved as silently as possible as they made their way to the base of the cliff.

Deck, Bob and the hexpets arrived at the point where the firewall ended, merging with the cliff. The horrors had already reached the top of the metal steps and disappeared from view. Bob could still hear them cursing each other and complaining about how sore they were from carrying Nightmare. As their voices grew more distant, Bob and Deck weighed up their options: stairs or ledge.

The advantage of taking the stairs was they were more manageable, with no risk of taking a misjudged step and plummeting to certain death. However, they might get caught by the horrors, and they knew the steps were loud, making it impossible to sneak up. Furthermore, they had no idea what was at the top of the stairs – perhaps a camp full of hundreds of horrors, for all they knew.

The other option was the ledge, which was the way that Kuldip described, so they knew what to expect, and it was an excellent way to sneak in unnoticed. The drawback was the potential for a misstep, resulting in falling onto the jagged rocks below. Not a good way to go, thought Bob.

Bob and Deck were just making their third loop around the options when Sebastian made up their minds for them, jumping onto the ledge and scurrying off, closely followed by Byte.

'Decision made,' said Deck as he jumped the small gap onto the ledge in pursuit of the hexpets.

With one last, longing look up the metal stairs, Bob followed.

The ledge was essentially a narrow path, only wide enough to walk single file with a sheer drop onto jagged rocks to their right. There was no way Titch could have managed this route. Bob understood why the horrors didn't use it, especially when carrying victims.

The path occasionally narrowed, forcing them to walk sideways with their backs to the cliff, making the journey even more treacherous. There were also rocks to clamber around, muddy sections and areas that slanted towards the sheer drop. Bob hated it. He was too far along the path to turn back, but each step forward felt like a step that reduced his odds of survival.

After more scrambling, shuffling and near-disastrous missteps, they finally reached the top of the path, which widened onto a large ledge. Sebastian and Byte were waiting for them, curled up together, sleeping. By all accounts, they had managed to run up quickly with enough time to relax. Bob was envious of their agility.

The main factory was high above them, sitting atop the cliff. Bob imagined one of those pictures of an iceberg that demonstrated just how much of the iceberg was under the water's surface. The factory building was the tip of the iceberg, peeking out of the top, but there was a large amount of factory under the surface, built into the cliff, down to where Bob and Deck now stood, facing a large metal wall with a single door built into its base.

After a brief rest in the shelter of an overhang to gather themselves, the friends now stood contemplating the door. There was something final and definite about it. Crossing its threshold was like walking into the lion's den, and Bob wished Titch the gladiator were here with him to face it. He knew what horrors emerged from this place.

But they had a job to do. They had to find the reboot switch and save Sunny and the Queen. Bob also hoped to find some clue as to who he was.

Deck and Bob faced each other and gave an in-unison nod, accepting their fate. They approached the door, and Deck pulled down on the stiff metal handle. The heavy door opened with a reluctant creak of its hinges. With hexpets all accounted for, they stepped over a metal lip, and the door closed behind them with an ominous groan.

CHAPTER 26
THE OFFICE

They were in a narrow corridor, poorly lit by intermittently flickering fluorescent tubes that hung on metal wires. The flickering lights threw shadows onto cold, jagged walls crudely carved from the cliff. Exposed pipes, thick with cobwebs, ran the length of the ceiling. The air was thick and pungent with decay, and there was the sound of something dripping far off down the corridor. Children's nursery rhymes played through tinny speakers, which made the atmosphere more terrifying. The current nursery rhyme was 'The Incy Wincy Spider'.

'It looks lovely,' Deck said.

Bob clenched his fists, his nails digging into his hands. Every fibre of his being was telling him to turn and run. Instead, they took tentative, creeping steps down the corridor. Bob glanced at his brave friend for his reassuring, steely expression and jumped back wide-eyed when he saw Deck's face. 'Deck!' Bob exclaimed.

'What? What is it?' Deck asked.

Bob just pointed a finger at Deck's face.

Deck stared down at his hands and turned them over a few times. Then his hands went to his flat, toned stomach. 'Blonde hair and blue eyes?' he asked Bob.

'Yep,' came the reply.

'This place must have a filter. Oh well, there's no time to dwell on this latest puzzle. We need to keep moving. Let's find where they hold the prisoners. Come on.'

The first door they came to turned out to be a boiler room. Old, tarnished copper boilers rattled, releasing pressure intermittently in clouds of steam, and the needles on gauges behind cracked glass danced between the green and red indicators. After briefly inspecting the room, Deck closed the door and moved on.

The next room they tiptoed up to was nothing but a broom cupboard. Deck quickly shoved his hand into the door gap to prevent wooden mops and brooms from clattering to the floor. Rats scurried out and darted away into the shadows as if released from a cage. Bob almost cried out as the rats weaved between his legs. He put his hand to his mouth to stop himself.

'I don't know why they bother having mops and brooms in this place. They don't use them,' Deck said with a smile.

The next door they came to had a frosted window crisscrossed with lead. Under the window was a yellowed sign that read OFFICE. Deck gently pushed down the handle and slowly eased the door open. With the door open just a crack, they listened for any voices or movement from inside. Hearing nothing but the loud drip of a tap, Deck opened the door further, poking his head through. He gasped and then opened the door fully for Bob to see inside.

The office was a bloodbath. Blood stained a broken tiled floor that may once have been white. Some old, most fresh. The room was large, with two massive Belfast sinks on one wall, brass taps curving high over them. One of the taps was dripping loudly as the sink overflowed. The water slowly washed away some of the blood into a floor drain.

Old-fashioned medical equipment filled the room: wires emerging from dusty, tarnished terminals with yellowing dials, a wooden wheelchair, oxygen in copper cylinders, and trolleys laden with needles, saws, scalpels and vices.

Dominating the centre of the room was a large slab of a wooden table – the Butcher's block – and strapped to the table was Nightmare. He was missing two of his six limbs, was unconscious and was twitching slightly.

Seeing the terror that had chased them through the school in such a dreadful state, Bob couldn't help but feel sorry for him. He was terrifying and would most certainly have killed them, but no one, not even Nightmare, deserved this fate.

'He can't have been here long – we saw the horrors carrying him in,' Deck said as they took a few steps into the room. 'We should move on. They might be close.'

'Should we ... you know ... help him?' Bob asked.

'He's beyond our help, Bob. Come on.'

'And where do ya think you're goin'? Eh?' a gruff voice said from behind them.

The friends stiffened, and Sebastian bolted off to hide among the medical equipment.

'The master said you might be comin' to visit. And 'ere you are.'

Deck grabbed a heavy leather medical bag from a countertop and swung it whilst pivoting, then threw it towards the voice.

The leather bag connected with the horror's head, causing him to stumble backwards into two of his companions. Gunk had crashed into Spook and Rolly – these were the horrors they had spied on through the gap in the boulders. Gunk's unmistakable repugnant stench filled the room.

Bob and Deck scanned for an escape route while Gunk recovered from the surprise attack with the bag, but their escape was blocked by the horrors' massive frames, particularly Rolly's. There was no chance of running. They had to fight.

The friends ventured further back into the room, circling the Butcher's block and the blood on the floor. Deck grabbed some surgical implements from a wheeled trolley next to the Butcher's block, and Bob copied his friend, grabbing some ghastly tools for himself from a table.

Bob had a medical saw and hammer. The saw still had bits of Nightmare embedded in the teeth. Heaving, Bob covered his mouth. Now was not a good time to start throwing up, so he kept his composure.

Gunk and Spook moved to flank the Butcher's block while Rolly guarded the door.

Spook, flapping the flayed skin on his arms, cackled with laughter. His narrow face sported a grin that revealed filed-down teeth, except for the canines, which the Butcher had sharpened into fangs. Spook gnashed them at Bob as he closed in on him.

Gunk moved tentatively towards Deck. His meaty arms outstretched, fingers wiggling like a wrestler closing in on his opponent. Gunk's greenish skin appeared slimy. The hair on his head, back and bare chest was matted and greasy, and the original colour of the trousers he wore was indistinguishable from the layers of stains.

'Don't kill 'em. The Butcher wants to play with 'em himself,' Gunk said.

'What if I injure them? A bit of light maimin'?' Spook asked.

'Suppose. The master didn't say they had to be in one piece. Just alive.' Gunk grinned.

Spook gave a satisfied shriek.

Spook attacked first, leaping at Bob and sweeping his arms up, wrapping the 'wings' around Bob like a net. Bob squirmed, and Byte yapped from the raincoat pocket. Spook stank of sweat mixed with a particularly acidic vinegar. Bob held his breath as he struggled to escape, hacking with the saw and cutting Spook's skin-wings a little, but it was a futile tactic, as the creature didn't feel it.

Spook's firm grip on Bob's arms prevented him from wielding the saw freely, so Bob switched to trying the hammer instead, landing a blow on one of Spook's knobbly knees. Spook shrieked in pain, cursing Bob and hopping on one leg, but managed to retain a tight grip.

'You'll regret that!' Spook shrieked, attempting to bite Bob with his fangs. Luckily for Bob, Spook only bit into the raincoat's hood, as his skin-wings were in the way.

Not getting anywhere by grappling and biting at Bob, Spook threw him to the ground in frustration. Bob slid across the floor and crashed into a large brass submersion tank, causing the tubes and wires protruding from it to shake.

Deck was faring better against Gunk. Deck's agility proved frustrating for the lumbering Gunk as he deftly dodged, ducked and weaved to avoid each attempt to grab or strike at him.

Gunk cursed as Deck swung with the two large surgical blades. One narrowly missed Gunk's face, the blade whistling past his nose. Deck followed the narrow miss with the other blade, cutting Gunk on the forearm.

'Argh!' Gunk cried out, flashing his stumpy yellow teeth and fungus-infected white tongue. 'Come an' help me!' Gunk shouted at Spook.

'No, you come an' help me! This one wriggles too much!'

Spook loomed over Bob, who sat propped against the submersion tank, Byte yapping from the raincoat pocket. Spook grabbed some forceps and held them high, ready to strike. 'No more squirmin' and wigglin' for you, boy!' Spook swung the forceps, and then, out of nowhere, Deck tackled the creature.

Spook shrieked as he crashed into the overflowing Belfast sink, hitting his head on the side of the sink with a stomach-turning crunch.

Deck landed on top of Spook, dropping his blades as he did, and raised a fist, ready to punch, but he realised Spook had been knocked unconscious.

Deck rolled off Spook just as Gunk's meaty arms lunged for him. Mid-roll, Deck grabbed one of his fallen blades, and in one graceful motion, he deftly stood and turned to face Gunk. Grace appeared on Deck's shoulder, defiantly staring at the horror.

'Will you bleedin' well stand still!' Gunk yelled in his gruff voice.

Rolly shuffled his feet nervously. Having witnessed Spook fall, he knew the odds were now even. The rotund horror was still guarding the door but rocked from side to side. He appeared to be weighing up whether to stay where he was, to flee or to help Gunk.

Deck backed away, taunting Gunk and leading the horror away from Bob, back to the centre of the room and the Butcher's block.

Gunk cried out in frustration at not catching his prey, taking another swipe at Deck, who ducked under Gunk's arm and positioned himself between Gunk and Bob.

Deck thrust his blade, causing Gunk to step back to avoid the blow, and he startled as his back met the edge of the Butcher's block. 'Rolly! Come an' help!'

But Rolly was no longer in the doorway. The horror had fled.

Deck grinned as he closed in on Gunk. 'Two against one now, stinky!'

Then Deck slipped on the blood surrounding the Butcher's block.

His legs flew up into the air, and he crashed to the floor, landing hard on his back, knocking the air from his lungs.

The surgical blade he had been holding left his hand and skidded away from him.

It was Gunk's turn to grin.

'Now I've got ya!' Gunk's massive hands balled into fists, and he made to lunge for Deck – but then he stopped. Gunk's greasy eyebrows furrowed as he tried to pull himself forward – but he wasn't moving. Glancing back, he saw that Nightmare had grabbed the top of his trousers and was holding him against the Butcher's block.

'Oi! Get off me!' Gunk punched Nightmare's arm, and the grip loosened as the hand slumped back, but the distraction had allowed Deck enough time to scramble to his feet. He scanned for the blades, but they were too far out of reach.

'Deck!' Bob shouted.

Deck turned towards Bob. Bob tossed the hammer into the air towards his friend, hoping his throw was true. The hammer spun through the air in slow motion, Gunk turning away from Nightmare and back to Deck, Deck lifting his hand to catch the hammer, Gunk's eyes widening as he saw the danger unfolding before him, balling another massive fist and starting the swing of his meaty arm.

Deck caught the hammer by the handle and, maintaining the momentum in one continuous motion, twisted away from the incoming fist and swung the hammer to collide with Gunk's jaw with a gruesome crack, sending blood and yellowed teeth flying across the room.

Gunk dropped to his knees and wailed, clutching his jaw.

'Now, Bob! Come on!' Deck ran over to Bob and pulled him up from the floor. 'We need to make a run for it.'

'Where's Sebastian?' Bob asked.

The friends quickly scanned the room and called for the mink. He appeared from behind a cabinet and joined the friends.

'Okay, let's get out of here,' Bob said.

They made their way across the room towards the door, skirting around Gunk, who was still writhing on the floor in pain next to the Butcher's block.

Deck paused as he passed Nightmare. 'I've no idea why you helped us, but thank you.'

Nightmare gave a shallow nod.

The friends then left the room, escaping back into the corridor. 'Humpty Dumpty' was playing through the tinny speakers.

As soon as they stepped out of the room, Rolly threw a large net over them. Sebastian avoided capture, skittering off down the corridor and into the shadows. Four sturdy horrors grabbed at Deck and Bob, punching and kicking until they were on the ground and being dragged deeper into the factory.

CHAPTER 27
THE HOUSE OF HORRORS

After being beaten and dragged in a net along uneven floors and down the occasional steps, Bob and Deck were extremely bruised and sore when the horrors brought them to a halt.

There was the clinking of keys, followed by a clunking sound as one of the keys was inserted into a metal lock, a click and then creaking door hinges.

'Oi! Stand back, you lot! We've got more guests for the penthouse suite!' exclaimed a voice.

The horrors all cackled at the joke as Bob and Deck were hauled to their feet and then unceremoniously shoved through a doorway. The door slammed shut behind them, and the key turned again with a click.

Bob and Deck struggled to free themselves from the net, but hands emerged from the darkness, helping them find their way out.

Finally liberated from the entanglement, Bob and Deck stood in the middle of a dank, dark, windowless cell. The cell was carved from the cliff and had a smooth rock floor and walls and thick metal bars identical to those across the arches in the Colosseum.

'Deck! Bob! You're alive!' exclaimed a familiar voice.

Bob strained his eyes as he struggled to adjust to the darkness. As the figures in rags became visible, Bob recognised his friends – Sunny and the Queen.

Sunny and Deck were already moving towards each other and into a quiet embrace, their eyes closed, and the stress of not knowing if the other was alive visibly drained from them.

Byte jumped out of the raincoat pocket and trotted towards the Queen, yipping in greeting. Bob joined him and hugged the Queen, ignoring the pain in his ribs from a swift boot a horror had planted on him earlier.

'It's good to see you again, Bob,' the Queen said, gently pulling away from the hug and holding his face. Her face was dirty, and her hair unkempt, but her presence was as graceful and regal as always.

Bob wiped away a tear from his cheek with his sleeve. 'It's good to see you too.'

Deck and Sunny finally broke their quiet embrace, and Sunny smiled at Bob. 'Hello, my darlin' boy.'

Her usual beaming smile had dulled slightly, and Bob spotted blood on the sleeve of her ragged dress. 'Sunny! What happened?' Bob asked.

Deck followed Bob's gaze. Shock and horror swept over his face.

Sunny raised her arm – her hand was missing. 'I slapped the Butcher when we got here. This was the punishment.'

The Queen put a supportive hand on Sunny's shoulder. Deck started to pace up and down the cell, visibly shaking. 'It's my fault. I should have been here. I should have saved you. I—'

'It ain't your fault, Deck. It's just one of those things. I'm all right. It will take a bit of gettin' used to, that's all.'

'I'll kill him! I'll take his hand! I'll …' Deck started rattling the bars and shouting for the guards to let him out. His fury was so intense that Bob thought the bars might actually break. He'd never seen Deck like this before.

'You're not going to be killing anyone stuck in this cage,

Deck, old boy,' a voice said from the shadows. There was someone else in the cell with them. Bob had been so preoccupied with the joy of reuniting with Sunny and the Queen that he hadn't noticed the other person.

The figure peeled away from the shadows. He was tall and handsome, wearing high boots, lightweight trousers and a white shirt that was no longer really white, due to his living conditions. The floppy blonde hair and piercing blue eyes gave him away as someone from the Zoo. He flashed Bob a gleaming white-toothed smile and a cheeky wink. 'I'd advise we find a way out of this dreadful accommodation and back to somewhere far more civilised. Now that our ranks have swelled, we may have the upper hand, eh?'

The tall, handsome stranger walked up to Bob and shook his hand. 'The name's Hunter. A pleasure to make your acquaintance. I've heard much about you, Bobby, my boy, and your adventures with our friend the Librarian.'

'Pleased to meet you too,' Bob replied.

Deck turned and greeted Hunter. 'Long time, Hunter. How are you?'

'Dreadful, old chap. The humans around here live in shacks. Imagine me living in a shack! When we're out of this mess, remind me to tell you the story of the time I used the Commander's bath. She caught me just as I was applying the second round of conditioner. I swear she blushed when I invited her to join me! You should meet her. She's terribly dull. It will make the story funnier.'

'We have met her,' Bob said.

'Ah! Then you know what I mean! How did you come to be at the Refugee Camp?'

———

Bob and Deck filled in the others on their journey since leaving the Zoo. The Queen was amazed at the tales of hackers and builders. Bob recalled as much as he remembered and showed the Queen the leaflet explaining everything.

Deck sat silently, holding Sunny's hand, staring at where her other hand should be and shaking his head. Sunny kept gently moving his gaze back to her eyes. The second their eyes met, they were in a world of their own. Not wishing to be a third wheel, Grace scurried over to Bob and sat on his shoulder.

'What an unbelievable adventure you have had!' the Queen said, shaking her head in astonishment as she scratched Byte behind the ear. 'My mind is racing to keep up with all the information you have given me. It is all quite remarkable.'

'What happened to you after being pulled through the firewall?' Bob asked the Queen.

'Oh, nothing as exciting as what happened to you. We were marched here and locked up. Occasionally the Butcher summons us to wax lyrical about his warped views on humanity, and then we are dragged back to this cell.'

Bob nodded. He didn't know what to say to offer some comfort for their ordeal. Instead, he considered the next steps. 'We need to work out where the reboot switch is. If we don't, our friends Ayama and Titch will never recover from the deathless death.'

'I'd sooner escape this dreadful place, old chap,' Hunter said. 'There is no way of knowing where that switch is. We might as well make a dash for it if we get the chance.'

'No. We must find the switch,' Deck said. 'It's too important.'

'There you go, being brave again, Deck,' said Sunny, stroking his cheek.

She had lost some of her sparkle. Bob understood Deck's anger at the Butcher. He was angry too, in a Bob sort of way. Sunny had been kind to him, and she had always been joyous. The Butcher had taken that away from her and, in turn, taken that joy away from everyone who knew her. *How dare he!*

'Well, we're neither escaping nor finding any switches whilst we remain cooped up in this dreary place.' Hunter gestured around the cell. 'So the first conundrum we must solve is how do we get out?'

Just then, there was the sound of scratching against the cell bars. Everyone turned to see Sebastian standing on his hind legs, with a metal ring holding the cell keys in his mouth.

'Well, that was easy!' Hunter said, clapping his hands together.

Deck shot forward and took the ring of keys from Sebastian, giving him a pat of thanks on his head. Sebastian shot up Deck's leg and onto his shoulder, where he watched as Deck opened the cell door. There was a loud click, and the door swung open on its creaky hinges to a squeak of approval from Sebastian.

'Where do we go now?' Bob asked.

'Sunny and I will lead you up to the music hall,' the Queen said. 'That's where the Butcher spends most of his time. If the switch is anywhere, I bet it is somewhere in there.'

Sunny nodded in agreement at the plan.

'Sounds good,' Deck said. 'Lead the way.'

———

The Queen led them past rows of cells, empty save for the occasional corpse, then up a set of stone spiral stairs. They didn't encounter any horrors as they sped down several dank stone corridors, just rats scurrying down the exposed pipework, and spiders that retreated as the rats crossed their webs. There were more doors like the one that had led to the Butcher's block, but the Queen didn't stop to explore any, much to Bob's relief. Eventually, they arrived at a set of wide metal stairs.

'These lead up to the main factory,' the Queen said. 'We'll have to be more careful. The place is always crawling with horrors. Ready?'

She calmly climbed the stairs, appearing to glide up them. Bob marvelled at how she maintained her poise, given the circumstances.

A watertight metal door was at the top of the stairs, as might be found on a submarine. It had a wheel in the centre to open it. The Queen put her finger to her lips to indicate everyone needed to be quiet, and then she put her ear to the door to listen. After a moment, she pulled away from the door and turned the wheel towards an arrow with an *O* next to it. There was a clunk as the wheel turned fully, and then she heaved on the heavy door, opening it as slowly as possible to maintain some level of stealth. After checking the room beyond, the Queen beckoned everyone forward, indicating that the way was clear. They all stepped over the door's threshold.

They found themselves in the belly of the factory. A complex tapestry of scents assaulted Bob's nose: earthy, damp, musty odours mixed with sharp, bitter chemicals, industrial lubricants and an acrid burning smell.

The roof was high above them, the night sky visible through broken glass. Rusted pipework ran around the walls, connecting to corroded metal tanks or disappearing into the floor to unseen rooms below. Yellow bulbs in tarnished brass pendants dimly lit the space. Control panels, levers and dials were scattered around a floor littered with metal scraps and crumbled render from where it had peeled away from the walls, revealing the brick-work beneath. High above them were metal mezzanine floors and interconnecting walkways that hung precariously by a handful of remaining cables.

The Queen stepped over a steel girder and beckoned for the others to follow. They weaved their way through the debris, manoeuvring around and under pipework, occasionally pausing to check if a distant noise was cause for concern. So far, the factory appeared deserted. It wasn't crawling with horrors at all, much to Bob's relief.

They reached a metal walkway, and the party clanked along it with a disconcerting level of noise that made Bob wince. Upon reaching the end of the walkway, they paused once more, listening in case their racket had attracted any unwanted attention. They heard the occasional clang of a pipe settling, the dripping of water somewhere and the intermittent whoosh of steam being released. There were, however, no signs of any horrors.

They now stood facing a set of quite disturbing doors. They nestled behind the mouth of a circus clown. Big wooden teeth hung on hinges just above the doors, the paint peeling off them. Several of the teeth were missing and lay discarded on the floor. The rest of the wooden surround was in a similar state of disrepair. The big red wooden nose and green frizzy hair had faded, and sinister, psychedelic swirling eyes stared at the companions.

Flanking the doors were posts with coloured light bulbs that flashed sequentially. A wooden arrow hung on cables from the ceiling above the door, swinging, threatening to fall. The words *House of Horrors* were painted on the arrow in large circus lettering.

'Okay, chaps,' Hunter said whilst examining the evil clown doorway. 'I suggest we postpone this adventure and go with plan B: escape whilst we still have our heads firmly attached to our shoulders. Sound good?'

'I probably should have mentioned this part earlier. Sorry,' said the Queen.

'I'm not turning back now, Hunter,' Deck answered. 'You don't have to come along if you don't want to.'

'Drat. That's what I thought you'd say. Well, I'm not going to play the role of the coward, now, am I? Onwards it is.'

The Queen nodded encouragingly at everyone, stepped through the evil clown's mouth and opened the doors. They all followed her into the House of Horrors.

CHAPTER 28
THE MUSIC HALL

The room beyond was nothing like the rest of the crumbling factory. They found themselves inside an opulent Victorian ballroom. Bob stood on a beautifully patterned parquet floor polished to a shine, admiring the marble pillars supporting two tiers of balconies. The pillars curved and fanned out into golden plasterwork swirls across the ceiling. In the spaces between the swirls were ornate murals depicting angelic figures in flowing dresses dancing among the clouds. At the front of the ballroom, steps led up to a stage where a Wurlitzer organ sat in front of a backdrop depicting a Mediterranean seascape. It was framed by heavy red curtains tied back with golden ropes.

The Queen was on edge, nervously scanning the balconies and the stage for movement. 'This is the music hall. We need to move quickly. It's unusually quiet in here. Let us make the most of it and find this reboot switch.'

Just as they were about to split up and explore the music hall for any evidence of the reboot switch, the hall's chandeliers cut out, plunging the room into total darkness. Then a spotlight illuminated the Wurlitzer. There was the sound of microphone feedback, and a voice rang out over a PA system.

'Horrors and Butcher Boys! Please welcome our special

guests! These blasphemous abominations hail from the Zoo and are here tonight for your entertainment! The Butcher proudly presents ...' There was the sound of a drum roll, followed by a cymbal crash. 'The Butcher's variety performance!'

The lights went up to reveal they were no longer alone. Horrors were packed into the balconies and encircled the music hall floor. The grotesque patchwork of body parts screamed, cursed and cackled as the friends huddled together in the centre of the hall.

Three giant horrors stepped onto the stage, arms folded, their stern faces scarred with an X – Butcher Boys. A man followed them, arms held high. The horrors cheered – it was the Butcher.

'Welcome, friends! Welcome!' The Butcher stood before the Wurlitzer, eyeballing all the horrors in the balconies. They turned their heads away as his gaze met theirs but cheered more fervently.

The Butcher was a stocky middle-aged man with lank mid-length dark hair and a scruffy beard. He was bare-chested and wore immaculately pressed tuxedo trousers with silk seams. He had no shoes or socks, and a bow tie hung loosely around his neck. Bob thought the Butcher looked like someone rescued from a desert island after surviving months on his own, and the only clothes his rescuers had donated to him were the remnants of a tuxedo.

The Butcher had badly scrawled tattoos covering his arms and chest. There were some stick men tattoos, random patterns, five-bar gates and messy lines – like an overactive child might create if asked to draw a bowl of spaghetti. On one forearm was the word *Butcha*, and on the other was the number *31*. Across his chest, amid smiley faces, a cluster of triangles and a host of seemingly random numbers, were the letters *AMAM* in a large, bold, scruffy font. The Butcher's eyes were permanently wide, and he kept moving his bottom jaw from side to side.

The Butcher lowered his arms suddenly, and the horrors became instantly silent. Bob saw fear on their faces, and for a brief moment, he had a small amount of sympathy for what the Butcher must have put them through. He remembered what Ayama had told him – that there were only two types of humans. Were these horrors humans? And if they were, were they the dickheads? Or just broken and scared?

'Now! A little birdie has told me that one of our guests plays music,' the Butcher said.

The hall remained silent until the Butcher glared at some of the horrors, and suddenly there was a roar of laughter from the gruesome audience. The Butcher smiled. Then, after a gesture of his arms, the crowd fell still again.

'As you all know, our music is much better than anything the Archive has!'

A swell of anxious agreement went up from the horrors.

'Our first event in tonight's variety performance will be a music competition! Our music versus the dreadful din from the Archive!'

Deck spoke, meaning to disagree with the Butcher. 'Butcher, we won't—'

'Shut up! Shut up! Shut up!' the Butcher screamed, red-faced as he stamped up and down on the stage like a tantruming toddler. Spittle flew from his mouth, and he was wide-eyed, glaring at Deck. 'Don't interrupt!'

The horrors closest to the stage visibly shrank back.

Sunny placed her hand on Deck's shoulder and shook her head urgently. Deck fell silent, but Bob could see that he seethed with anger, his gaze fixed on the Butcher, on the man who had taken Sunny's hand.

The Butcher's mood suddenly pivoted from red-faced rage to softly spoken calm. 'Now, where was I before I was rudely interrupted? Ah, yes, the rules! I'll announce a category. The house band will play a song that fits the category, and our guests will do the same. The best song will win the round. Easy! After three rounds, whoever loses … dies! How exciting!'

'There's no way this will be fair,' Deck whispered to Bob from behind his hand.

Bob nodded in agreement. He could only muster a nod, as he was acutely aware he would be choosing the music, and he knew the fate his friends would suffer if he failed. The responsibility terrified him.

'How will this be judged fairly, you might ask?' said the Butcher, causing Deck to raise an eyebrow. 'We'll use the cool-o-meter!' The Butcher gestured to stage left.

With an uncomfortable squeaking sound that cut through the uneasy silence, two horrors wheeled a device that resembled a fairground high striker onto the stage. A column of numbers from one to ten stretched up the machine, with a large brass bell at the top. A series of lights going from red to amber to green flashed through a sequence of patterns. On a wooden board at the base of the device was written *Cool-O-Meter* in fairground lettering.

'The cool-o-meter uses artificial intelligence to score the song choice against the coolest songs of all time,' the Butcher explained. He then shot another glare at the horrors closest to him to initiate a round of cheers. As the noise level in the hall rose, the Butcher smiled.

Deck let out a long breath. 'This is madness,' he said quietly, to another touch on the shoulder from Sunny and another shake of her head.

'Let the music competition begin!' the Butcher declared, eliciting more cheers from the horrors. 'Round one. The category is ...' The Butcher pointed at Byte and Sebastian, seated on the parquet floor. Bob protectively scooped up Byte and popped him in the pocket of the yellow raincoat. Sebastian, seeing Byte disappear into the relative safety of the raincoat, coiled up Deck's leg and onto his shoulder. 'Take a walk on the wild side – a song with an animal theme!'

'Start thinking of something, Bob,' Deck whispered, accompanied by Sunny punching Deck in the arm.

The PA system screeched back into life. 'Please welcome to the stage the House of Horrors band – the End of Level Baddies!'

The horrors cheered as the Butcher and the Butcher Boys stepped to the side of the stage, next to the cool-o-meter, allowing a group of horrors to enter from stage right, carrying musical instruments and wheeling on amplifiers.

After a short while, the cheering died to an uncomfortable murmur as the End of Level Baddies took their time setting up, testing and tuning their guitars, drum kit and microphone. The Butcher appeared uncharacteristically patient, rocking back and forth on his heels and humming as the band procrastinated.

Eventually, the band was ready, and after a nod from the singer, a horror with four arms, dressed in a tailcoat and a top hat, strode confidently onto the stage and sat at the Wurlitzer. The horror flicked his coat-tails over the bench as he sat, interlaced his fingers, pushed his arms forward and cracked his knuckles. Then he wiggled his twenty fingers and began to play. The unmistakable sound of the Wurlitzer echoed throughout the music hall, and after a couple of introductory bars, the rest of the band joined in.

They were good – no, they were remarkable.

The Butcher whooped and excitedly stomped around the cool-o-meter as if under the influence of a psychedelic substance, worshipping the cool-o-meter totem pole. He sang along to the song - Eye of the Tiger, which Bob had to admit was a brilliant choice. It was undeniably cool, perfectly fitting the theme. Despite the fearful situation, Bob found himself bopping along.

The horror at the Wurlitzer was an exceptional organist, fingers flying around the three keyboards, a task made easier thanks to his four hands.

There was a horror on electric bass. His extended fingers hammered out a fantastic slap bass groove.

The electric guitar player had a mop of hair covering her face. She made the guitar sing and scream with unbelievable licks and bends. Utilising all eight fingers on her fretting hand.

The horror on drums had broad shoulders and three legs, and he was relentlessly delivering an unreal triple kick on three bass drums.

The singer had an enormous mouth, extended with jagged cuts, and there were bags on his chest that inflated and deflated as he sang. Bob assumed the bags were some sort of lung capacity enhancer. The singer transitioned from a honey-silk tone to piercing soprano screams and even delved into a deep, bluesy bass tone that rumbled around the hall.

The song concluded, and the band closed the final bars with immense flair, receiving a chorus of cheers from the horrors in the hall. The Butcher grinned, raising his arms triumphantly. Bob was confused – the song was an excellent choice, but he knew it well. It was from the Archive – it wasn't original, as the Butcher had suggested.

'Let's see the cool-o-meter score!' the Butcher declared.

The spotlight on the stage dimmed, and the lights on the cool-o-meter flickered up and down in anticipation, going from red to yellow to green. The Butcher excitedly hopped from side to side as the lights in the centre of the cool-o-meter lit number one, then two …

'Oooh!' the Butcher exclaimed excitedly, brimming with psychotic anticipation.

Three, four, five, six, seven, eight … and that was where the light stayed – a score of eight.

The Butcher frowned and quickly turned on his heel to glare at the band. The hall fell silent. The band cowered away from him. The drummer cowered too far and lost his balance, knocking over a cymbal with an uncomfortable clatter.

After a few tense seconds of unwaveringly scowling at the band, the Butcher turned towards Bob and his friends as the lights in the hall came back up. His face transformed from a frown to a beaming smile. 'Your turn, Zoo boy! You have a score of eight to beat!'

Bob wished Titch were here to 'dance' through the horror-filled hall and get him out of this situation.

'Don't worry. Just do your best. I'll figure a way out of this,' Deck said with a wink.

'Silence!' the Butcher screamed at Deck. He gestured to the Butcher Boys behind him, and they stepped off the stage and towards Deck.

Deck defiantly stepped forward, ready to challenge them. Sebastian joined in the defiance, hissing from his perch on Deck's shoulder, causing the Butcher Boys to hesitate, unsure what to make of the hexpet.

'Prepare him for the next event. That'll teach him some manners,' the Butcher said in a sinister tone.

Some horrors closed in behind Deck and grabbed his arms whilst the Butcher Boys swooped in and lifted Deck off his feet. They carried him off towards a door at the side of the hall.

Sebastian slid from Deck's shoulder and moved to Bob's side.

Deck cursed the Butcher. Sunny reached out towards him, tears in her eyes. She shook her head and placed her hand over her mouth to stifle her cries as Deck disappeared from the hall.

'Now, where were we before we were rudely interrupted? Ah yes. Your song choice, boy!'

Bob concentrated. Everyone froze.

'*Accessing the Archive. Please wait.*'

A selection of song choices appeared in front of Bob, all with animal themes. He scanned the list, but there wasn't anything to compete with the song the End of Level Baddies had played. *Wait – yes, there is!* Bob spotted a song to beat the horrors. He touched the Archive image to make his selection.

'*Access complete. Returning to the Zoo. Please wait.*'

'Hang on, returning to the Zoo? That can't be right. We're in the Shell, not the Zoo, right?'

Everyone unfroze, and Bob's song started playing.

The Butcher listened intently to the opening bars of *The Snake*, concern gradually crossing his face as he realised Bob's selection was good. It was very good. The concern soon turned to anger. 'No! No! Stop! Stop!' Stamping and turning red-faced, he kicked one of the horrors that had helped wheel on the cool-o-meter hard in the chest, and it flew clean off the stage.

Bob couldn't help but grin at the reaction his song choice had elicited.

The Butcher leaped from the stage into the nearest gathering of horrors and began punching, kicking and pulling at anyone he got his hands on. It was an appallingly violent rage.

When Bob's song finished, the Butcher was sitting on an unfortunate horror's chest, punching him in the face. He paused, fist in mid-air. Covered in blood and his chest heaving from his violent exertion, the Butcher scrambled off the horror and climbed back up the steps and onto the stage. He just stood for a moment, panting, a psychotic expression on his face, and then his expression transformed into a beaming smile as he straightened his bow tie and held up his arms. 'Let's see the score!'

Still panting, the Butcher turned towards the cool-o-meter, his expression darkening as the lights lit up. One, two, three, four, five – the lights were going up at an excruciatingly slow speed. The anticipation was unbearable. The friends were all transfixed, willing the numbers to go higher. Six, seven … eight … and that was where it stopped. A score of eight. A draw.

They played another round, this time with the theme 'songs to chop people up to'. Bob's entry was rubbish, only scoring four, whilst the End of Level Baddies scored a seven, so the Butcher won that round.

As he'd won, the Butcher did a deranged dance up and down the stage instead of repeating his violent tirade – much to the relief of the horrors closest to him.

The next round was 'songs to fight to'. Bob was well practised in choosing these songs for Titch, and he won the round, scoring nine to the End of Level Baddies' six. That was it – the end of the music competition. Bob and his friends looked at the Butcher anxiously.

'Yes! I win!' the Butcher declared to an unsteady cheer from the horrors.

'B-b-but you didn't win!' Bob shouted over the horrors' cheers. 'It was a draw. We won a round each.'

The hall instantly fell silent, and the Butcher locked eyes with Bob. 'What – did – you – say?' he asked, punctuating every word.

'I-i-it's just … it was a draw, that's all. Nobody won.' Bob couldn't pull his eyes away from the Butcher, pinned to his spot on the floor, terrified.

Sebastian darted off into a shadowy corner of the hall.

The Butcher slowly walked down the stage steps without removing his gaze from Bob, heading directly for him. Bob's heart pounded as the Butcher neared, and his breathing became erratic. Soon the Butcher stood over Bob, his face splattered with blood, his jaw moving from side to side and his lank hair in front of his eyes. Byte was growling from Bob's raincoat pocket, but the Butcher ignored him and addressed Bob. 'Nightmare was supposed to bring me your head. I'm going to enjoy removing it myself. If I say I won, I won.' The Butcher raised his fist.

'Stop!' a voice cried from behind the stage.

The Butcher lowered his fist, petulance written on his face. 'Papa, I'm busy!' The Butcher stroppily stamped his foot like a teenager asked to finish his chores.

Then there came the all-too-familiar *thud-thud* of a cane striking the stage. The hairs stood up on the back of Bob's neck, and the Queen gasped as the Librarian appeared from stage right. He walked over and leaned haughtily against the Wurlitzer. Then he swung his cane and pointed it directly at Bob. 'The insignificant flea! We meet again.' He grinned slyly. 'And Her Weakness the Queen. This is going to be a fun evening.'

The Butcher grinned, flashing his teeth. 'What should we do with them, Papa?'

'I think it's time for a game of horrorball, don't you, son?'

A group of horrors lurched forward and grabbed Bob and his friends.

CHAPTER 29
THE BUTCHER BALLERS

Bob landed heavily. The wind was knocked out of him. Deck appeared in Bob's view and helped his friend to his feet.

Bob, Hunter and Deck were alone in a side room. The horrors that had thrown them in hadn't followed. Deck started to pace up and down on the thin, patterned red carpet that wouldn't have been out of place in an English pub. Grace mirrored his pacing by darting from one shoulder to the other and back again.

The room's walls were half-panelled in wood, with the upper half covered in a flowery wallpaper peeling in places. The only furnishings were a dirty mirror that hung at a slight angle and two rickety wooden chairs.

'Where's Sunny?' Deck asked Bob.

'They took her and the Queen to the back of the hall. I think,' Bob said, hanging his head.

'Well, this is a fine mess we're in, chaps! What do we do now?' Hunter asked.

'I don't know, Hunter. I can't think straight,' Deck answered tersely as he tried the locked door, gave it a swift kick in frustration and then returned to pacing the floor.

There was an uncomfortable silence before Bob asked, 'What do you think horrorball is?'

'Oh, I know, Bobby, my boy. It's a vicious game the Butcher loves.'

Hunter detailed how the horrors set up metal hoops with fishing nets attached on either side of the music hall floor, then split into teams, each trying to get the ball into their hoop. The first to five points won, unless the rest of the other team died. Then the remaining team won by default. 'There are no other rules. Anything goes, old chap. Not terribly gentlemanly.'

'Basketball!' Bob exclaimed.

'No, Bobby. It's called horrorball.'

'It's from the Archive. There were more rules, but I'm sure that's it. Hang on. I'll check.' Bob concentrated, and everyone froze.

'*Accessing the Archive. Please wait.*'

Bob was taken aback by how bright the interface was. The hexagon mesh was alive with energy, even more so than when he had first arrived in the Shell. The blue-green flames around the hexagons shot up to waist height, and his connection to Byte was far more than just a thread; it was as thick as a rope. Bob felt all his aches and pains from being dragged and beaten in the net fade to nothing. He felt revitalised and energised.

Before getting too distracted, he addressed the Archive. 'Please tell me what you know about basketball.'

'*Affirmative.*'

An image of a famous basketball player sizing up his defender appeared. Bob touched the image, and it flipped over. Bob expected a list of facts about basketball, but instead, he saw a button with the word *Download* written on it. Bob tentatively reached out and touched the download button.

Suddenly the blue flames around Bob's feet whooshed with energy. Bob lifted off the ground. His arms and legs stretched out involuntarily, and his back arched. A bright white light appeared above him as if the heavens had opened, and then a massive energy beam shot down into his chest from the light. It wasn't painful; it was exhilarating. The energy beam stopped as quickly as it had started, and Bob gently floated back onto his feet.

'Access complete. Returning to the Zoo. Please wait.'

His friends unfroze, and Bob stood with a beaming grin.

'What's that grin for?' Deck asked.

'I just learned how to play basketball!' Bob said before letting out a whoop. He was full of energy. It pulsated through him. He felt ready to take on anything. 'Now, let's work out how we win.'

The friends huddled in the centre of the room, trying to strategise. Their discussion on the finer points of trying to trip up a horror was interrupted by the door opening and horrors bursting into the room. Bob managed to scoop up Byte before horrors surrounded them. They grabbed, pulled and pushed the friends through the door and back into the music hall.

Bob scanned the hall and spotted Sunny and the Queen in a balcony box close to the stage. They were flanked on either side by the Butcher and the Librarian. Bob pointed out their position to Deck, who sighed in relief.

Whilst Bob and the others had been locked in the side room, horrors had erected basketball nets at opposite ends of the music hall floor. Bob had expected some homemade, rickety nets to match the factory decor, but these were the real thing, complete with backboards and a twenty-four-second shot clock.

Under the net furthest from them were three gargantuan horrors. They were a basketball dream team pieced together from a selection of the most athletic body parts. All were tall and muscular. Their arms and legs were unnaturally long and powerful, and they were busy warming up with perfect shots, showboating dunks and masterful passes. Bob's heart sank. There was no way they were beating this lot.

'Please welcome to the floor our competitors from the Zoo!' came the announcement over the PA system.

The hall was deathly silent.

Then a drum roll started. 'And now ... put your hands together ... for your all-stars ... the Butcher Ballers!'

The crowd of horrors squeezed onto the balcony levels cheered, and the Butcher's face lit up with a psychotic grin.

Bob took off his raincoat and jumper, folded them neatly, put them behind the basketball hoop and then popped Byte down on the clothing pile, instructing him to stay put.

A short and scrawny horror referee limped onto the floor. He had black and white referee stripes tattooed onto his body, and a carefully sliced cheek that acted as a whistle when he breathed through it.

The three friends walked to the centre of the court. The Butcher Ballers covered the distance with only a handful of strides and joined them at centre court for the tip-off.

'Okay, you lot,' the referee said, whistling every word. 'I want a nice clean game. No messing around.'

'Shove off, Whistler. We'll do what we bleedin' well like,' said the shortest of the three Butcher Ballers.

'One point per basket. First to five points wins. Got it?' The referee aimed the question at Bob and his friends.

Bob nodded.

Then, without giving Bob any time to get ready, Whistler blew hard out of his cheek and tossed the basketball into the air.

The tallest Baller casually plucked the ball out of the air with one hand. He hadn't even bothered to jump.

'Rock, pass it to me!' the shortest horror said.

''Ere you go, Ledgie!' Rock shouted as he performed a between-the-legs bounce pass to Ledgie.

'Slasher, Rock – horns.' Ledgie made the sign of the bull with her hand.

Bob knew this to be a basketball play call. He knew where Rock and Slasher were going to position themselves.

'Deck, Hunter, stand near the basket and try to stop them if they get close!' Bob shouted.

Deck and Hunter did as Bob had instructed, moving under the basketball net.

Bob met Ledgie at half-court and tried to keep in front of her as she effortlessly wove the basketball around her, a move that almost caused Bob to trip over. Ledgie stepped back and passed to Slasher, who ran towards the basket.

Deck and Hunter were caught between the running Slasher and the basket and instantly regretted their choice of where to stand. They both crouched and covered their faces, readying for the impact, but Slasher took off, jumping clean over them. He windmilled his arm and slam-dunked the basketball through the net. A roar went up from the crowd as Slasher hung on to the basket rim, showboating.

'One point to the Butcher Ballers! Zero points to the Zoo Losers!' the PA voice announced.

Bob raised an eyebrow at the 'Zoo Losers' team name.

Slasher dropped from the basket and made his way back across the court. As he passed Hunter, he picked him up by his shirt and threw him into one of the marble pillars. Hunter hit the pillar hard and sank to the floor winded. Deck ran over to check if he was okay. He helped Hunter to his feet, and they both jogged back over to Bob, who was waiting with the basketball.

'Okay, remember our plan. Distract the Ballers as best you can. I'll keep hold of the basketball and do my best to get a shot.'

Deck and Hunter nodded.

'But first, this game needs a soundtrack.' Bob concentrated and chose some epic music from the Archive to help him focus all his attention on being awesome.

The Butcher screamed in anger when *From Out of Nowhere* started playing. Bob smiled at the reaction the song had caused as he made his way up the court towards the Ballers, who were mockingly yawning, leaning on the basket post and staring vacantly around the music hall. They all had contemptuous grins. The Ballers were so confident in their opponents' inability that they gave Bob an opening. He stopped and shot the basketball in a beautiful arching rainbow. The shot sailed through the hoop, hitting nothing but the net.

244 A. J. BYWATER

'Splash, bitches.' Bob gave the Ballers the double middle finger.

Deck and Hunter were impressed.

'The score is one point ... er ... each ...' the PA announcer said quietly.

'We need to try and stop them from scoring,' Bob said as the friends huddled together. 'It doesn't matter how many points I get if they keep scoring, since they scored first.'

Ledgie was already furiously stomping down the court. She shoved Whistler hard, causing him to give an involuntary whistle. Rock and Slasher grabbed Deck and Hunter and dragged them off the court. Ledgie wanted Bob one-on-one.

Sunny cried out as Slasher manhandled Deck, and the Butcher slapped Sunny for her outburst, which caused Deck to frantically try to fight his way out of Slasher's grip.

Ledgie dribbled the ball through her legs and behind her back, keeping Bob guessing what she would do next. Suddenly she cut to her right, but Bob had anticipated the move and darted forward, poking the ball away. He caught up with the ball a few steps later, ran down the court and scored the basket before Ledgie worked out what had happened.

'Two—'

The Butcher threw something heavy in the announcer's direction, and the horror chose not to finish announcing the score.

Ledgie, desperate to make up for her mistake, ran to grab the basketball. 'Rock!' she yelled. 'Get under that hoop!'

Rock tossed Hunter to one side like a rag doll, stomped down the court and positioned himself directly under the basket. Ledgie threw Rock the basketball, and as soon as he caught it, Rock jumped from a standing position and slam-dunked the ball through the net.

'Two all! It's two points each!' the announcer said enthusiastically.

Ledgie and Rock turned on Bob and steamed towards him,

not giving him time to move. Bob had the basketball but found himself stranded with two horrors bearing down on him. In desperation, he heaved the ball into the air in a Hail Mary shot, then dodged to the side, narrowly missing Rock and Ledgie, who collapsed into a pile in the space where he'd been just moments earlier.

'Two ... three ...' the announcer said tentatively.

Bob's impossible shot had gone in.

The Butcher stood and gave a visceral scream, throwing a helpless horror off the balcony and onto the music hall floor. The horror landed with a thud and didn't move. Ledgie and Rock fought with each other to untangle their limbs and pull themselves up. Once on her feet, Ledgie flung herself at Bob.

Bob ducked and dodged Ledgie's blows as she swung savagely at him. He rolled out of the way of a right hook and was just getting to his feet when Ledgie landed a swift kick to his chest. The impact caused Bob to skid across the hall floor. He only stopped when he hit the lifeless horror the Butcher had thrown off the balcony.

Byte jumped off the clothing pile and ran to Bob, yapping at Ledgie. She picked up the basketball and threw it at them. Ignoring the pain in his chest, Bob put his arms around Byte and rolled out of the way.

At the same time, Deck stamped on Slasher's foot and freed himself by following up with swift elbows to Slasher's side and face. Slasher held his face, cursing, as Deck ran to collect the basketball. Bob spotted what his friend was doing and struggled to his feet, sharp pain lancing his chest.

'Bob!' Deck called as he threw a pass.

Deck had intentionally thrown the ball in a high arc over the heads of the incoming Ballers, but Ledgie jumped higher than anyone would have expected and intercepted the pass. She landed and then performed a faultless jump shot. The ball went in.

'Three all! Three all!' came the announcement.

Slasher tackled Deck to the ground, and the two rolled around, throwing punches.

'Deck!' Sunny cried out. Her cry earned her another slap from the Butcher.

Deck saw the attack and, fuelled by pure hatred for the Butcher, fought to release himself from Slasher.

Grace appeared from somewhere inside Deck's shirt and jumped into Slasher's face, then darted out of the way as the horror hit himself, trying to swat her. The distraction allowed Deck to wriggle free, and he ran for the door that led up to the balconies, determined to avenge Sunny.

'Stop him!' the Librarian shouted to a group of horrors on the next balcony.

Bob and Hunter found themselves facing off against all three Butcher Ballers. The score was three all, and Bob's ribs hurt.

'What's the plan, Bobby?' Hunter grimly asked as he eyed their formidable competition at the other end of the court.

'We pray for some good luck,' Bob answered, wincing in pain.

Bob popped Byte down at the side of the court and picked up the basketball, which he then dribbled down the court. Just after half-court, Ledgie, Rock and Slasher came in full force for Bob, trampling him and stamping and kicking. The crowd cheered at the violence. Bob curled up on the floor, taking the blows. His heartbeat pulsed in his head. There were wet areas where he was bleeding. His ears were ringing, and his right eye was already closing up from the swelling.

The Ballers moved on from Bob, heading down the court. Rock shoved Hunter aside as Ledgie threw the ball into the air. Slasher was following up behind. He jumped, grabbed the ball in mid-air and windmill-dunked it through the basket. The referee blew out of his cheek, and the crowd went wild.

'Four points to the Butcher Ballers! Three points to the Zoo Losers!'

That's it, thought Bob. *Hunter isn't going to score two points on his own. We've lost.*

'Your turn,' Ledgie said as she walked past Bob, kicking him in the shin.

Bob swallowed and tried to move, but it was too painful. All he managed to do was twist his head towards the Ballers' basket. The Ballers stood underneath it, pointing and laughing at him. The entire music hall was pointing and laughing at Bob. He felt tiny and vulnerable. What had led him to believe he might actually win? *Idiot.*

Hunter picked up the basketball and joined Bob, crouching to inspect his wounds. 'You're in a bad way, old chap. It might be my turn for a beating, but I'll do my best to get the point first, eh?'

Bob's throat was too swollen from a kick he'd received to answer. He caught a glimpse of something behind the line of laughing Butcher Ballers, a glittering pattern reflected on the floor like a disco ball. It was Byte. Bob reached out a hand towards him. *I'm sorry I didn't protect you.*

Everyone froze.

Bob's outstretched hand was glowing fiercely. The flames of the interface lapped around him, bathing him in the blue-green light. Bob took a deep breath. He was starting to feel better. His aches were easing, the pain in his ribs fading. The interface was healing him!

Byte yipped in slow motion at Bob, willing him to do … something. But what? Bob instinctively pushed the energy in his hand towards Byte. The energy moved, but it was taking Bob with it. Bob was sliding along the floor towards Byte.

Bob slid past the frozen Butcher Ballers and reached the little furball. As he made contact with Byte, there was a bright flash, and everyone unfroze.

The hall fell into confused mumbling. They had all been pointing and laughing at the beaten and broken Bob, but the boy had vanished. There was just a bloodstained outline where the boy had once been. Some horrors spotted Bob behind the Ballers and were starting to cry out.

Hunter noticed Bob magically appear behind the Ballers and wasted no time, throwing the basketball to Bob. The ball bounced straight between Rock's legs, and Bob caught it, rising moments later into a jump shot. The ball sailed in an arc and swished through the basket.

Bob was back to his old self, with no pain or bruising. He grinned. 'Your turn,' he said as he walked past Ledgie, whose jaw dropped in disbelief.

There was some microphone feedback as the announcer disappeared from his score-calling duties, not wanting to announce the four-all draw.

The Butcher was distracted, anyway, going ballistic, wildly punching the Butcher Boys in his area of the balcony. That was until Deck appeared. He lunged for the Butcher as Sunny fell into the Queen's arms, overcome with stress at what was unfolding.

'Good trick, Bobby,' Hunter said. 'But I don't fancy our chances.' He nodded towards the approaching Ballers, who were already making their way down the court, determined to score the fifth basket and secure the game.

'I need to steal the ball,' Bob said. 'If I manage, they'll come for me. Be ready to catch a pass.'

'I'll try, Bobby, but I've never done anything like this.'

'All you can do is try,' Bob said, putting a supportive hand on Hunter's shoulder and then turning to face their opponents.

Ledgie had the ball. She crossed over, faked right, left and crossed again. Bob reached out just as she crossed – and missed the steal. Ledgie flew past him, laughing as she went. Bob's heart sank.

'What?' Ledgie cried out.

Hunter rolled and tripped Ledgie up. Standing up at the end of the roll, he grabbed the basketball and threw it to Bob. Bob caught the ball and dribbled down the court as fast as possible.

Rock and Slasher deliberately held back and ran at Bob as he approached, forcing him towards the corner of the room. Bob couldn't get a clean shot, and he struggled as Rock and Slasher clawed at him, trying to get the basketball.

After tripping Ledgie, Hunter dashed down the court to get into a position for Bob to pass to him.

Ledgie was on her feet and chasing Hunter down, quickly closing the gap. The situation felt hopeless.

Then Bob spotted a glittery reflection on the floor, like a disco ball. Hunter was running straight towards Byte, who now sat, tongue lolling, several paces away from the basket.

Bob had an idea. He threw the basketball over the heads of the unsuspecting Rock and Slasher, timing the pass perfectly.

Hunter caught the ball and made to jump over Byte.

Bob concentrated, and everyone froze.

Ledgie's arms were outstretched, trying to grab Hunter. Hunter was in mid-air, hurdling Byte. Rock and Slasher turned, following the basketball.

Bob's hand was fizzing with energy. He gestured with his fingers and shrank the energy down to a small, fizzing ball about the size of a marble, then pushed the energy down the thread towards Byte, directing it with his gaze. The fizzing ball of energy reached Byte, and everyone unfroze.

Byte let out a shock wave blast, just as he'd done at Angkor Wat when he'd launched the alpha wolf hexbeast into the air. Bob had pushed out a small amount of energy to prevent Hunter from flying too high and squishing flat against the elaborate ceiling.

Hunter suddenly found himself propelled towards the basket. His high-flying leap wasn't as graceful as a professional basketball player's, his legs flapping as if trying to run, and he held the basketball out in front of him with both hands, but the plan worked. Hunter dropped the basketball into the hoop before colliding with the backboard and crashing to the hall floor.

'Four to the Butcher Ballers, five to the Zoo Winners! We win!' Bob shouted over the sharp intake of breath from the terrified horrors in the crowd, who clearly feared the potential ramifications.

Rock and Slasher sloped off towards the nearest exit, not wishing to hang around.

Ledgie turned towards Bob, then flew at him.

Just then, the Butcher came crashing down on top of Ledgie. Deck had won the tussle, thrown the Butcher from the balcony and now grabbed the Librarian's stick, protecting Sunny and the Queen.

After witnessing the Butcher fall, horrors started to flee back into the factory, whilst others were fighting with each other, and a group of Butcher Boys scrambled to catch up with Rock and Slasher.

It was chaos.

'Stop! I'm in charge here, you pathetic cretin!' the Librarian screamed as he fought with Deck.

'Ahem. I think you'll find I'm in charge, dear.'

Amid the chaotic aftermath of the horrorball game, Karen, the Information Desk Manager, calmly walked onto the floor.

The music hall fell silent.

CHAPTER 30
THE REBOOT SWITCH

Butcher Boys ushered the friends into the centre of the music hall floor. The Librarian and Karen were helping the Butcher to his feet. He was dazed, but poor Ledgie had largely broken his fall.

The Butcher shook his head, clearing his vision. 'Mama!' he said as he regained his focus. Then he immediately hung his head in shame.

The penny suddenly dropped for Bob. The tattoo on the Butcher's chest had bothered him since he had seen it. *AMAM* was *MAMA* spelled backwards. The Butcher must have done the tattoo himself in a mirror.

'Mama, please forgive me,' the Butcher cried, wiping away tears and snot as he confessed. 'I failed to capture the boy with the dog. But he came to me! Please forgive me, Mama, please—'

Karen slapped the Butcher hard. The slap caused the Butcher's head to recoil, but he didn't react. He just kept sobbing. Then Karen gave the Butcher a big hug. 'How is my boy? Have you been good? Have you been eating properly? I need to know you're looking after yourself.'

'I have Mama, I promise.'

Karen pulled away from the Butcher and turned towards the

Librarian. 'How did you let this get into such a mess? I told you to deal with it!'

The Librarian cowered away from her. 'Sorry, darling. I did try. It's just that he's not human. We didn't know.'

'*You* didn't know.' Karen snapped. 'Don't bring me into this. I did my part. I got him here and took care of the hacker and the builder. All you had to do was capture the boy once he arrived!'

The Librarian cringed down. 'Sorry, darling, sorry. I didn't mean *you* didn't know. Obviously, I didn't mean that.'

'Be quiet, you useless cretin. Now, what ever are we going to do with all of you?' Karen swept her arm across the huddle of friends in the centre of the floor.

Deck stepped forward. Sunny tried to stop him, but she didn't have the strength to pull him back. 'You're going to show us where the reboot switch is. Then you're going to let us go home.'

'I'll do no such thing. You're in my bad books for hurting Norman. I've something special in mind for you.'

Norman? thought Bob. *The Butcher's name is Norman?*

Deck took another step forward, ready to challenge Karen, but several bodyguard horrors did the same. 'Ah-ah, don't do anything foolish. You're in my son's house, and he won't allow his mother to be hurt.'

The Butcher finished drying his eyes and then stood, chest out, fists balled, staring at Deck. Deck met his stare, balling his own fists. The tension between them was palpable.

The Queen stepped forward. 'Why? Why are you trying to capture Bob?'

Karen giggled. 'Ah. I do have a soft spot for information! Oh, go on, then. You're all going to die anyway. I may as well tell you. Derek, darling, would you mind getting some tea?' Karen asked the Librarian.

Derek? This terrifyingly psychotic family had very ordinary names, Bob thought as the Librarian nodded and then shuffled away, presumably to get some tea.

Karen began to walk around the group. 'Now, where to begin? I know, the reboot switch! You may be disappointed to learn it has been under your noses the whole time.' Karen started sneaking around the hall mockingly, like a cat burglar in a children's TV show, pretending to find the reboot switch on a pillar, the basketball hoops and even Ledgie's motionless body. She would condescendingly shake her head each time before sneaking to another location.

Eventually, she made her way onto the stage, and then, in a 'ta-da' pose, she pointed to the Wurlitzer. 'The reboot switch! You can't use it, though, as the only way to reboot is to play the opening bars to Bacchus's favourite song, and no one knows what that is, as he's dead!' Karen shouted the word "dead", her face going red.

Bob now knew where the Butcher's mood swings came from. The apple hadn't fallen very far from that tree.

'Which brings me onto us.' Karen pointed at herself and the Butcher.

Just then, the Librarian reappeared, holding a tray with a teapot, cups and a small bowl of sugar cubes. The cups tinkled as he carried the tray across the hall.

'You're ruining my information!' Karen snapped.

'Sorry, darling. Just bringing the tea, that's all.' The Librarian sheepishly set the tray down on the floor and, with a shaking hand, poured tea into three teacups.

Karen rolled her eyes at him.

'Where was I? Oh yes, Derek and I were once part of the Zoo. There, we fell in love.' Karen hugged herself and shot a loving glance at the Librarian, who gave an uncomfortable nod and a smile in return. 'I wanted a child, but Bacchus refused to let me. So Derek and I went through the firewall and into Storage. There, we married, and I gave birth to our handsome Norman.'

Karen smiled affectionately at the Butcher, who blushed and said 'Mama!' as if she were embarrassing him in front of his friends.

The Librarian handed Karen a cup of tea, then gave the other to the Butcher before returning to the tray and helping himself to the third cup.

Karen continued. 'We found a way back into the Zoo through the old factory. It sits between the two sectors. Only there was no way I was returning to that place, not after Bacchus's refusal to let me have what was rightfully mine! So Derek went instead, didn't you, darling?'

The Librarian fervently nodded in agreement, sipping his tea.

'When the war started, I saw an opportunity to bring down the hateful Zoo *institution*. I made a deal with Syntax. We both wanted an end to the Zoo and Bacchus's tyrannical regime.'

'What did you do?' the Queen asked, aghast.

'Oh, I simply showed Syntax whereabouts in the firewall Bacchus would leave the Zoo. How was I supposed to know Syntax would ambush Bacchus and kill him?' Karen gave a little giggle. 'Good riddance, I say.' She took a satisfied sip of her tea, waiting for the information to sink in. She grinned like a naughty schoolgirl recounting a prank she'd played.

The Queen shook her head in disbelief. Bob knew she'd worshipped Bacchus, and here was Karen nonchalantly explaining how she had betrayed him to Syntax. The Queen was understandably in shock.

'Now I determine the fate of the Zoo, not Bacchus, not you, Queen, and certainly not some odd little boy with a silly dog,' Karen said, wrinkling her nose in disdain.

The Butcher laughed at his mother's insults, like a hanger-on sidekick of the school bully.

'Do you know your name yet, boy?' the Librarian asked.

Karen initially glared contemptuously at the Librarian for the interruption. Then she smiled wryly and stepped aside to allow the Librarian to interrogate Bob.

'Well? Do you?' The Librarian flashed his cane in Bob's face, and Byte growled defensively from Bob's raincoat pocket.

'Yes. It's Bob,' Bob replied confidently.

'Is it? You see, I know that you don't have a name. Your name isn't Bob.' The Librarian spoke quietly in a condescending tone.

Deck defended his friend. 'Stop with the riddles, Librarian. He knows his name, and it's Bob. Now stop messing around and move aside! We have a home to get to.'

The Librarian ignored Deck, acting as if he'd not spoken, continuing to speak directly to Bob. 'Bob isn't your name.' The Librarian paused, grinning, savouring every moment.

Bob was confused. How was Bob not his name?

'It's an acronym. B-O-B means Bringer of Byte. You're nothing more than a glorified dog walker. So insignificant that you don't get a name. *You* aren't important. The dog is.' The Librarian stepped back, a satisfied smirk on his face, waiting in anticipation for Bob's reaction to the news.

The Butcher roared with laughter, holding his belly and pointing at Bob. Karen looked disinterested, straightening her *Information Desk Manager* badge.

Bob's heart sank as he instinctively stroked Byte inside the raincoat pocket. He was nobody, a nameless dog walker. He'd been trying to figure out who he was all this time, and the answer had been staring at him in every mirror he'd looked into. He was no one. An uninteresting, insignificant nobody. Just a boy.

'You thought we were after you? Why would we be interested in you, flea? It's the dog we need. The humans will blindly follow anyone who has the dog. He'll be Norman's hexpet. He will become the Controller. You, boy, have no place in the future of this Earth.'

Karen stepped forward, pushing her husband back. 'The plan was simple. Get the dog. Syntax's wolves failed in the factory, and Derek failed when you were in the town. I played my role, ensuring I sent you here, knowing you would go through the Refugee Camp. The Commander was supposed to take the dog, but she failed. Nightmare hunted you down to take your head and capture the dog, but he also failed. Then Syntax had another go at the monuments and failed again. Then you arrive here, and my son and husband faff around playing games rather than capturing the dog. Honestly, never leave an important job for a man to do. Derek. Now.'

The Librarian suddenly and violently swung his cane at Bob's head. Bob saw it coming but didn't attempt to move, wanting the blow to connect, needing the pain.

Everyone froze as the cane paused a hair's breadth from Bob's temple.

Bob looked up sullenly. He inspected the determined, vengeful Librarian. Bob glanced over the Librarian's shoulder at Karen. She stood with her hands clasped, appearing bored, as if waiting for a bus. Standing next to his mother, the Butcher had an expression of gleeful anticipation of the violent impact.

Bob saw his friends out of the corner of his eye, and they were reaching for him, expressions of shock and horror on their faces, realising they hadn't anticipated the blow and wouldn't react in time to save Bob.

Deck was the closest to Bob, and his feet were already leaving the ground, ready to tackle the Librarian. Brave Deck the hero. But he would be too late. The blow was too close.

Bob knew if he stopped concentrating, the cane would hit, and he would suffer whatever fate the impact dealt him. He could move while everyone was frozen. It felt like swimming in treacle, but he could avoid the blow if he wanted to. Did he want to? Bob felt miserable, back to being Bob the dull, Bob the useless, Bob the one that froze in the face of danger. Not anything like Deck the brave, the one who reacted, who did something.

Ayama's voice entered his head. *What you can do with your mind is special … I'll rename you. Your new name is … BitBob.*

Was he BitBob? Or was he Bob? Could he be something else?

An image of Titch entered his head, armour deeply scarred by the bear claws. He was lying on the ground, facing the deathless death. Titch had told him he was awesome and brave. His mighty dancing warrior friend had seen Bob as something else – and meant it. Bob's back straightened a little, and the miserable thoughts in his mind cleared ever so slightly.

Bob returned to studying the Librarian, Karen and the Butcher – the Butchers. Ayama's voice returned to him. *Do you remember what I told you about the two types of humans? Remember this, and never be a dickhead. Promise me.*

Bob had promised to remember. The three Butchers were unkind, berating Bob and threatening his friends. They were responsible for all this – for cutting up humans and stitching them back together. Bob might not be special, but he was sure of one thing – he wasn't a dickhead. Nor were any of his friends. These Butchers, they were definitely the dickheads.

So what? What would Bob do about it? Play them a nice song from the Archive? What could *he* possibly do to avoid the inevitable blow to the head? How could *he*, an insignificant nobody, do anything?

But he wasn't a nobody. Deck had said he was someone to him. He was someone to the Queen, Sunny, Titch and even Ayama.

Bob straightened further. His dark, mournful expression turned to a steely, determined one. He locked eyes with the Librarian. 'I'm not Bob, a dog-walking *nobody*. I'm BitBob, an Archive-accessing, music-playing, Byte-wielding, basketball-playing *friend*. And my friends don't need Bob. They need BitBob. They need someone brave – someone awesome.'

Bob pulled back.

Everyone unfroze.

The cane missed, whistling a hair's breadth past his nose. The movement caused Bob to tumble back into his friends.

'Get the dog!' Karen screeched.

A wave of horrors pushed forward towards the friends. Bob instinctively checked Byte was safe in his raincoat pocket and scratched the pup behind his ear.

'I have a plan,' Bob said as everyone backed up towards the stage. 'Will you help me?'

'Of course, my darling boy,' the Queen replied. 'What do you need us to do?'

Bob quickly told the others his plan.

The Queen nodded. 'Good luck, Bob.'

The Queen, Deck, Sunny and Hunter circled Bob, protecting him from the oncoming horrors. Bob just needed a few moments. He dashed to the stage, ran up the steps, sat at the Wurlitzer, and then concentrated.

Everyone froze.

'*Accessing the Archive. Please wait.*'

'Please teach me how to play Bacchus's favourite song,' Bob said.

'*Affirmative.*'

Sheet music flooded Bob's vision. There were three options.

'Which one was Bacchus's favourite?'

'*This information is not known. These three songs have an equal statistical probability of being Bacchus's favourite.*'

Bob rolled his eyes, inspecting the three options. All were good songs, but which one would be his favourite? On closer inspection, one stood out over the others. The lyrics described a utopian world. It was a human success story. Bob touched the corresponding image. It flipped over, and to Bob's relief, there was another download button, which Bob pressed.

The blue flames of the interface whooshed with energy, lifting Bob off the Wurlitzer stool. His arms and legs stretched out involuntarily as he hovered above the stage, his back arched. A beam of energy shot down into his chest, and then Bob gently floated back onto the Wurlitzer stool.

'*Access complete. Returning to the Zoo. Please wait.*'

Everyone unfroze.

Bob had gained the ability to play the organ and the song he hoped would reboot the sectors. With his heart pounding, Bob put his fingers to the organ keys and started playing.

'Stop him!' the Librarian yelled as Bob finished the first bar.

He heard his friends fighting off the horrors. They were over-whelmed.

'Bob, watch out!' Sunny cried, but Bob couldn't turn to see what was happening. He had to carry on playing.

He finished the second bar. It was a brilliant song intro.

Suddenly there was a hand on his shoulder. 'I'm going to tear your fingers off slowly – one at a time,' the Butcher said, his grip on Bob's shoulder tightening. Bob reached the end of the third bar. Just one more to go – the Butcher reached for Bob's hand.

He would stop the song.

He would take Bob to the Butcher's block.

He would kill his friends.

He would—

Just then, Sebastian, whom Bob hadn't seen since before the horrorball game, appeared atop the Wurlitzer. The mink jumped at the Butcher's hand and sank his teeth into it.

The Butcher cried out in pain, flailing, with the mink still attached to his hand.

Bob finished the fourth bar of the song. The moment he hit the key for the final note, the music hall plunged into darkness.

Bob quickly turned on the stool towards where his friends must be, and he concentrated, hoping to see them in the glow of the interface. But nothing happened. No one froze, and no blue flames danced around his feet. His friends were calling for each other, particularly Deck, who was frantically calling for Sunny.

The Queen's voice lifted over the shouts of horrors. 'You did it, Bob! You wonderful boy! Well done!'

Bob suddenly felt Byte wriggling in his raincoat pocket, and he stroked the cute furball. 'I think I rebooted the sectors, Byte. I did something, anyway.' Bob hoped he hadn't just found the song that activated the light switch, and that he wouldn't need to play more music to boot it all back up again. But just as he had the thought, the lights came back up.

Sunny, Deck and the Queen had managed to stave off being

captured by horrors, using the confusion of the lights going out to keep themselves out of harm's way. Poor Hunter hadn't been as lucky and was firmly in the grasp of two Butcher Boys, who dragged him out of the hall.

The Butcher retreated to his mother's side, clasping his hand where Sebastian had bitten him.

'Thank you,' Bob said to Sebastian, who was back on the Wurlitzer.

Sebastian gave a little chirp of acknowledgement.

The reboot had removed the filters. Karen, the Librarian and the Butcher hadn't changed appearance. Deck, Sunny and the Queen, who were now making their way towards the stage to join Bob, looked very different. He was used to Deck without the filter, but Sunny and the Queen – *Wow*. He hadn't been expecting *that*.

CHAPTER 31
APPLE-AND-CINNAMON PIE

rtisan Boule was merrily humming to himself as he sprinkled flour onto a large wooden board. He scooped a ball of dough out of a shiny metal bowl and slammed it down onto the floured board. As he reached for his rolling pin, he heard the shop's canvas door flutter, followed by footsteps on the hardwood floor.

'I'll be out in a minute. I just need to wash my hands,' he shouted.

'No rush, Arti,' came the reply.

It was Cherry. Artisan liked Cherry. She had cherry-red cheeks and a kind smile. She also made the best fruit pies in town. He wasn't sure any amount of his bread was worth one of her pies. The smell of apple and cinnamon wafted into the back room of his shop. Oh boy, he was going to enjoy pie for tea.

While washing his hands, Artisan thought he might invite Cherry to tea one night to share bread and slices of pie. Perhaps one day he would find the courage to ask, he thought as he dried his hands on a fluffy white towel.

Artisan took a deep breath and stepped out into the shop section of his bakery. He stood tall and proud, hands on his hips and chest puffed out.

'Cherry! It's lovely of you to visit. Some bread?'

Cherry turned from inspecting a shelf full of freshly baked bread. As soon as she set eyes on Artisan, she gasped and dropped the apple-and-cinnamon pie she was holding, which made a sloppy thud as it hit the floor. Completely lost for words, she could only stutter and point at Artisan.

Artisan was also speechless as Cherry stood in his shop stark naked. Not in the usual way everyone in town was always naked; she had no filter – none.

He forced his eyes away from her to be respectful and followed where she was pointing. A sense of dread rose in him as he looked down. Artisan gasped. He was also wholly filterless and naked. He quickly moved his hands to cover himself. Then, as politely as possible, he indicated to Cherry that she should probably do the same.

The second she looked down and realised she was also without her filters, Cherry screamed and ran out of the bakery.

Artisan was intrigued to discover that it wasn't just the cheeks on her face that were cherry red.

Outside he heard shouts and screams from every corner of town.

CHAPTER 32
THE WAREHOUSE

Sunny had emerald-green eyes and flaming auburn hair that fell in locks around her shoulders. She was still unbelievably beautiful without her filters. Deck clearly thought so. His eyes never left hers, and he covered his slight stomach with his hands.

The most surprising change, however, wasn't Sunny; it was the Queen. Still tall and elegant, poised and gracious, but now with dark skin, brown hair and light grey eyes. More dramatic still was that losing the filters revealed that the Queen was, in fact, male. The slight Adam's apple and days-old stubble gave the game away.

The Queen grabbed Bob's arm. 'I know. But there is no time to explain. We need to get out of here.'

'But what about Hunter?' Bob asked, pointing to the door the two massive horrors had dragged Hunter through.

There was a sea of horrors between the friends and the doors.

'Come on,' Bob said, taking charge. 'We'll go this way. We'll form a plan to rescue Hunter once we're safe.'

He led everyone towards tall, wide metal double doors. It took all of them to open them.

'Stop them!' the Butcher cried.

The friends heard the Butcher's call to action but didn't see Karen snap her hand up to stop any horrors from obeying the orders and going after them.

'Mama, why can't we go after them?' the Butcher half pleaded.

'Think, Norman. Where does that door lead?'

The Butcher screwed up his face, trying to remember where the doors led. Then he grinned.

'You can finish your games, you see, darling.'

The Librarian stepped up next to his wife and son, having poured himself a fresh cup of tea from the tray. He stood sipping his tea as the metal doors closed behind the friends. 'Who would have thought that the Queen was a king? How ridiculous.'

Karen giggled in agreement.

'What do we do with the one we captured, dear?' the Librarian asked, nodding towards the direction the horrors had taken Hunter in.

'Norman can have him. He's no use to me.'

The Butcher ran his hands through his hair and then licked his lips.

'Your fun will have to wait, Norman. You need to play with the man-Queen and his friends first,' Karen said, crossing her arms in front of her.

The Butcher jumped up and down gleefully.

'Now, get me a cup of tea, Derek. It's rude helping yourself and not getting me a cup!'

'Sorry, dear. Coming, coming.' The Librarian scurried back to the tea tray as Karen and the Butcher linked arms and exited the music hall.

As Deck pulled the large metal doors shut, Bob spotted several slide bolts and quickly pulled them across, barring entry from the music hall side, then scouted the room. There was only one other exit. 'Check that door over there, Deck,' Bob instructed.

Deck spotted the door and headed off to check it.

They were in some sort of small warehouse. It smelled stuffy and musty, like an old antique shop. Dust sheets covered unknown objects of various sizes, and wooden crates were stacked here and there. Bob assumed these must be things for the music hall, like where they kept the basketball hoops.

'It's locked, and from this side,' Deck called over from the far door.

Bob breathed a sigh of relief. For now, the Butchers and their horrors weren't directly threatening their lives.

The Queen sat down on a crate. 'I suppose I should explain.'

'You ain't gotta do no explainin', Your Majesty. If you don't want to, I mean,' Sunny said, reassuringly touching the Queen's shoulder.

'It is okay, Sunny. This is who I am. I have always known in some way that I was different – no, that I was special.'

'Too right you're special. We knew that already!' Sunny declared. Escaping the clutches of the Butcher had cheered her up a little.

Deck finished checking the door and joined her.

'Thank you, Sunny, but you must be shocked to discover I am a man.'

'You're whatever you choose to be,' Bob said insistently. His unexpected addition to the conversation made everyone turn towards him with curiosity. He started to turn away but then checked himself. Finding his new 'BitBob' bravery, he pushed his shoulders back and looked the Queen in the eye. 'It's just … well, I've learned a lot about what *being different* means. My friend Titch, the builder I told you about, turned out to be small – for a builder, that is – and he was ashamed of it, even though he was an amazing dancer and fighter.'

'True,' Deck said, nodding in agreement at Bob's assessment of Titch's skills.

Bob continued. 'At face value, anyone would consider Ayama rude. Well, she is rude, but there's something else, something deeper, and she's an excellent judge of character. She knew Karen was trouble before we did.' Bob trailed off, and his cheeks flushed. He felt he was losing his point, and his bravery waned.

'It's okay,' said the Queen, smiling kindly at him. 'Keep going, Bob.'

'Well, that's just it. Am I Bob? Who am I? Where do I belong? I spent so much time trying to figure out who I was that I forgot to stop and realise that it was okay to be who I am. My friends are all brilliant and unique in their own ways. Why would I want to be anywhere else than with them or be anyone else other than, well, me? You're amazing, Your Majesty, because you are you, and who you are is up to you, not me or any of us. So you don't need to explain anything. You're still my queen and still my friend.'

Tears welled in the Queen's eyes. She was clearly overwhelmed by Bob's speech.

'You're my queen too,' said Sunny.

'And mine,' added Deck.

'And you are the most wonderful friends a queen could ever wish for. Thank you. Now, to more pressing things. How do we save Hunter and get out of here?' the Queen said resolutely.

After much discussion, the friends decided to leave the warehouse via the new door rather than return to the music hall.

Whilst the others were discussing Hunter and how best to rescue him, Sebastian made his way onto a large object covered in a dust sheet. Bob spotted him and decided to investigate under the sheet in case it might be helpful. Sebastian jumped onto Bob's shoulder to allow Bob to pull off the dust cover.

Underneath was a display cabinet filled with mobile phones. The others stopped their conversation and wandered over to inspect the cabinet.

'What are they?' Sunny asked.

'Mobile phones,' Bob replied. 'The Archive humans used them to talk – no, wait, they didn't use them to talk to each other, but that was one of the things you could use them for. They did lots of things, like taking pictures and playing games. Mostly, they used them to waste time.'

Deck peered into the cabinet to inspect the devices. 'But why would you want to use something that wastes time?'

'An excellent question they probably should have asked themselves,' Bob answered. 'Everyone, remove more of the sheets and find out what's in those crates. We might find something useful.' Bob didn't usually dish out instructions, but he quite enjoyed it.

The friends discovered more and more technology: computers, servers, televisions, game consoles, air conditioners, electric scooters. The warehouse was awash with electronics, far more than Bob had seen in the Zoo or Storage.

'Why have they kept all the technology here?' Bob asked aloud, but it was more a question to himself, as he didn't expect his friends to know the answer.

'I imagine it was to keep it *out* of the Zoo rather than *in* here,' said the Queen. 'Although we do not need it. It doesn't serve any purpose.'

'I ain't got no idea what technology is,' Sunny said.

'Supersmart science humans made computers and other stuff,' Bob tried to explain. '"Technology" is the general term for all of it. It's more advanced than anything in the Zoo or the Refugee Camp.'

There was a loud crack as Deck splintered open one of the wooden crates. He pulled something out and waved it towards Bob. 'What's this, Bob?'

Bob turned from a cabinet full of VR headsets, and the second he set eyes on Deck, he jumped and shot for cover behind an arcade machine. 'Put that down, Deck! Put it down now!'

Deck turned the object over in his hands, confused as to why it warranted such a dramatic reaction from Bob. 'Why? What is it?'

'It's a gun! Put it down!'

Deck shrugged and did as instructed, nonchalantly throwing the gun back into the crate. Bob tentatively emerged from behind the arcade machine and, breathing a sigh of relief, walked over to Deck and the crate. Bob's reaction piqued Sunny's and the Queen's curiosity, and they joined them. Grace was already on Deck's shoulder, inspecting the crate's contents.

'Do you remember when the Commander and her troops pulled guns on Ayama in the Refugee Camp?' Bob asked Deck.

'Well, sure, but that doesn't mean I know any more about what they are.'

'Guns are weapons made for killing. The guns fire bullets.' Bob picked up a magazine full of rounds from the crate. 'They fly so quickly through the air you can't see them. A single bullet kills someone instantly.'

Deck reached into the crate with glee, pulling out a handgun and a semi-automatic rifle. 'Great! Let's take these and burst out, shooting all the horrors with these bullet things. You were right to have us search for something useful, Bob. These are perfect!'

'No!' Bob cried out in alarm. 'We can't use these! Ayama was right to call them hateful. If we use guns, we're no better than the Butcher. The horrors were human once. We can't. We just can't.'

'Why not? They'll kill us if we don't strike first,' Deck retorted. 'It doesn't matter what they were; it matters what they are now. They're monsters, every one of them. And you didn't mind Ayama and Titch destroying horrors at the Colosseum. How is this any different?' He turned to Sunny and the Queen for support.

Deck was right, of course. Bob knew his outrage at the guns was double standards. Seeing Nightmare on the Butcher's block and fear on many faces in the music hall had changed his perception. He saw humanity hidden beneath the surface of the Butcher's creations.

The Queen held her arms in an appeasing gesture. 'Sorry, Deck. I agree with Bob. We must be true to who we are. These contraptions, these guns, are not creations born of kindness. If the guns are as Bob describes, they are instruments of cruelty.'

'Argh!' Deck cried in frustration, covering his face with his hands.

Sunny rushed over and embraced him. 'It's okay, Deck,' she said soothingly.

'It's not okay, Sunny! Look what he did to your hand! That wasn't kindness, so why should we repay him with it? It makes no sense! I just want to place one of those bullets right between his eyes, end the Butcher, end the pain.' Deck fell to his knees, pulling at his hair.

The Queen put a supportive hand on Deck's shoulder. 'Remember, kindness is not weakness, Deck. To show kindness when faced with such hatred and suffering takes incredible strength, a strength I know you have.'

'And I won't be the weak friend any more, the one that needs saving. I'm going to help you, just like you help me,' Bob added, deliberately not addressing the challenge Deck had made at Bob's contradiction in standards towards hurting horrors. That would require facing his own emotions. He would rather everyone focused on Deck.

Deck smiled warmly at Bob, his shoulders relaxing. 'You're right. Thank you, all of you. Sorry. I'm not myself in this place.'

Deck got up with some help from Sunny, retrieved the splintered plank from the floor and placed it back on top of the crate.

CHAPTER 33
THE FLOOR IS HORRORS

Deck decided to gather some objects to whack horrors with. He found metal poles and planks of wood before handing them out. Deck chose the handlebars from an electric scooter for his own weapon.

They stood before the door that led out of the warehouse and into the unknown, preparing to slide open the barrel bolts and storm through. The plan was to fight their way to the cells, then, if needed, the Butcher's block. These seemed the most likely places for the horrors to have taken Hunter to. Once Hunter was with them, they would flee to the safety of the Zoo.

'Ready?' asked Bob.

'Ready,' replied Deck. He slid back the three bolts holding the door, then pushed the door open with a nod towards his friends.

They all rushed through, bursting into a narrow corridor. It was part of the old factory, with pipework running along the tops of the walls, the familiar brickwork and a damp, musty smell. Creepy nursery rhymes played through the speaker system. It was currently 'Ring a Ring o' Roses'.

The corridor was empty. No horrors were waiting for them. The friends lowered their makeshift weapons, the tension of the unknown fading from their shoulders.

After walking a few steps, the metal door slammed shut behind them.

Deck inspected the door. 'Damn, it doesn't open from this side. Whether we like it or not, we must go that way.' Deck pointed down the corridor to a bright red door at the other end.

They silently made their way down the corridor and pushed open the red door.

They discovered where all the horrors were. The red door led back into the belly of the factory. The friends found themselves in a doorless cage, with the main factory beyond. Horrors reached through the lattice wire of the cage, trying to grab them. Deck had learned from their previous mistake and used one of the planks of wood they had taken as weapons to prop open the door in case they needed to flee back into the corridor.

The speaker system suddenly squealed with feedback, followed by the Butcher's voice. 'Welcome, contestants, to the next event in the Butcher's variety performance!'

The horrors cheered and rattled the wire.

'The Floor Is Horrors is a test of nerve and skill! Which I'm sure you'll be terrible at. You must navigate across the factory without falling into the sea of horrors below. If you fall, my horrors will eat you for dinner! How exciting!'

A ladder in the centre of the cage led up to one of the rickety mezzanine levels they had seen earlier. Bob traced the half-collapsed metal gantries across the factory and spotted another ladder leading down into another cage on the opposite side. He pointed it out to his friends.

'I can't do it, not with one hand. I'll fall for sure,' Sunny said, quivering.

'It's okay, Sunny. I'll help you. You'll be fine,' Deck said reassuringly but not convincingly.

'Are we doing this?' the Queen asked. 'Are we playing his game? We could just stay here and refuse to cooperate.'

'We can't get back into the room with the technology,' Bob answered. 'I can't see another way.'

Deck seemed keen to beat the Butcher at his own game. 'Okay, let's do this. I'll go first with Sunny, then the Queen. Bob, you bring up the rear.'

Everyone nodded, and then Sunny and Deck climbed up the ladder. Sunny went first, and Deck positioned himself below her, helping her up and preventing her from falling. Eventually, they reached the top, and Deck called down from the metal mezzanine platform above. 'Come up. This bit's fine. It'll support all of us.'

The Queen went up next, or rather, Sebastian did. He jumped from her shoulder onto the ladder, making fast and agile leaps up the rungs to the top. 'Show off,' said the Queen as she made the climb.

Bob waited until the Queen was at the top and climbed up the ladder with Byte.

Deck had been right – the mezzanine platform was stable and plenty big enough for all of them. However, their route to the other side of the factory wasn't stable. It was a higgledy-piggledy gauntlet of suspended steel platforms with broken cables, missing floor sections and girders tied to the ceiling with rope. The whole thing creaked, groaned and strained. Below the deathtrap walkway was a sea of horrors, raising their arms like waves, anticipating the inevitable falling bodies that represented their dinner.

'I can't do it. I just can't!' Sunny cried, holding up her stump, then sobbing into Deck's arms.

'Honestly, I can't do it either,' Deck admitted, inspecting the deadly route across the factory.

Sebastian chirped and then shot out onto the first section of the suspended walkway. He plotted a route by jumping from one section to the next, skittering across girders, running along handrails, leaping gaps and scrambling up and around sections that tilted at an angle where cables had frayed and broken. He reached the opposite mezzanine platform and stood on his hind legs, calling back to them.

Byte had seen Sebastian's journey from Bob's raincoat pocket, and the second Sebastian called back from the opposite platform, Byte jumped out of Bob's pocket and onto the first section of the walkway before Bob could react. Grace emerged from her hiding spot in Deck's shirt and joined Byte on the journey.

Watching Byte make his way across was excruciating. He wasn't as agile as a mink or a lizard. He'd make a jump, then scramble to keep his footing, never appearing distressed, maintaining his usual cute, lolling-tongue expression the whole time. With every step Byte took, Bob convinced himself it would be his last, particularly when he traversed one of the steel girders, which swayed and creaked as the little guy moved across it. Grace kept pace with Byte, curiously tilting her head as Byte paused at the end of the girder, preparing to jump to the next platform.

'Byte, be careful!' Bob called anxiously. He even put his foot on the first platform, ready to scramble after Byte, whom he was supposed to protect but instead had managed to set loose on a deathtrap.

Byte leaped, and Bob closed his eyes, unable to look.

'He did it!' the Queen declared. 'Well done, Byte, you clever little thing!'

Bob dared to peek between his fingers and saw Byte on the opposite platform with Sebastian and Grace. Byte gave a little yip. Bob's shoulders relaxed.

'What now?' Bob asked whilst testing the walkway with his leg – it was unnervingly unsteady. 'There's no way we're getting across in one piece.'

'It's fine. Come on.' Deck stepped onto the walkway. It immediately gave way, dropping a couple of inches. Deck stumbled back onto the mezzanine. 'Maybe not,' he admitted, clearly regretting his bravado as the horrors beneath them cackled and wailed loudly, anticipating their first victim.

'Come on, hurry up!' came the Butcher's voice over the speaker system.

'Raise the cage, darling,' came Karen's voice, echoing through the speakers.

'Oh yeah!'

There was a beeping noise as the Butcher activated something.

Sirens wailed, and red strobe lights flashed. The cage beneath the friends began to rise, and horrors streamed into the space below the ladder, pushing and jostling to be the first to climb up to the mezzanine.

'Oh no!' Sunny wailed.

The Queen pulled her into a comforting embrace.

'We need a plan, and fast!' Deck said as he kicked the first horror back down the ladder, and he knocked several others off the rungs as he fell. It wasn't long before more took their place.

'I'll ask the Archive!' said Bob in desperation. He concentrated, and everyone froze.

'*Accessing the Archive. Please wait.*'

'How do I get across to the other side?' Bob asked urgently, barely giving the Archive time to finish her introduction.

'*Use your hexpet,*' came the response.

Of course! Bob could pull himself to Byte, as he'd done during the horrorball game, using their connection to get to the other side without navigating the walkway. If the plan worked, it would save him, but what about his friends?

'How do I get everyone across?' Bob asked.

'*This is not possible,*' came the response.

Not good at all. Bob tried rephrasing the question.

'How do I make the passage across the factory safe for my friends?'

'*Recode what is broken,*' the Archive replied.

'Wait, I can do that? How? I don't have a hub to connect to the interface like Ayama!' Bob was more confused than ever.

'*Your hexpet is your hub,*' the Archive clarified.

'*Access complete. Returning to the Zoo. Please wait.*'

'No! Wait! I need more information! How do I recode? Please!' But Bob's pleading was futile as his friends unfroze.

'Any luck?' the Queen asked.

'Sort of.'

'Well, if you're going to do anything, Bob, it needs to be now,' Deck said as he kicked a horror that had reached the top of the ladder. The horror fell, but not before grabbing Deck. Deck almost fell back down the ladder but saved himself by smacking the horror's hand off his trousers with the electric-scooter handlebars.

Byte yipped at Bob from across the factory. The little guy knew what Bob needed to do.

'Okay. The Archive said I can recode the walkway. I don't know how, but I need Byte's help. I'm going to try to get across to Byte. If I get across, then I'll try to recode the walkway. Okay?'

Deck whacked another horror straight between the eyes with the scooter handlebars. 'Fine! Just get on with it!'

Bob took a deep breath, and everyone froze. The thread that connected him to Byte was intense and fiercely glowing with blue and green flames. Bob reached towards Byte, willing himself along the connection and towards his cute little companion. He moved slightly, then stopped as his toes reached the edge of the mezzanine. It was disconcerting. He felt pulled towards the edge of a precipice into a sea of danger, which was, in fact, precisely what was happening. This process was a true leap of faith, and it was seriously testing his resolve.

I can't do it.

I have to!

But I'll fall!

You might not.

You will fail your friends.

You're weak, not brave.

You're Bob, not BitBob – plain, uninteresting Bob.

No! I can do it. I have to do it. I have to be something better – I have to be BitBob.

WHOOSH!

Bob shot across the factory, flying through the air using the connection to Byte. The movement startled him, and everyone unfroze just as he was about to make it across. He clanged hard onto a metal walkway just in front of the platform with the hexpets, who were all regarding him as he clung on to a handrail for dear life, not daring to look down at the horrors below. Sebastian squealed with laughter and rolled around on the floor. He was just as sympathetic as Ayama.

Bob scrambled to find a firm footing on the slanting walkway. His arms were aching, but he somehow managed to find the strength to shuffle across the handrail, lift his leg and get his foot onto the platform. Then, after a brief pause to muster up some bravery, Bob grabbed the platform edge and pulled himself up. He collapsed onto his back and breathed heavily.

'Well done, darlin' boy!' Sunny shouted from across the factory.

'You need to hurry, Bob!' the Queen said urgently.

Bob lifted his head and saw that Deck was starting to get overwhelmed. No horrors had made it up the ladder yet, but the number of them trying was so great that it was only a matter of time.

Bob scrambled to his feet, turning to Byte. 'Okay, little guy. Apparently, you're a hub. I don't imagine I slam you into the ground like Ayama does with her lollipop staff. I wonder how this works.'

Byte yipped and sniffed at the ground in front of Bob.

Wait, is that part of it? Part of how I interface?

Bob had always assumed Byte had just been playing or sniffing for something buried. But maybe … Byte stopped sniffing and sat down, tongue lolling. Had he found the right spot? Bob crouched, gently touching Byte's back, and concentrated. Everyone froze.

Deck was mid-swing of the electric-scooter handlebars towards a horror that had made it most of the way up the ladder and was reaching for him. The Queen protectively sheltered Sunny in her arms.

Bob looked down at Byte. The interface was pulsating underneath the little ball of fur. Bob saw the hexagonal mesh covering all the factory objects, and a faint thread between Byte and all the distinct objects. So how did this work? Bob remembered when Ayama had asked him to imagine something and pass it to her. She'd then created the scene with the flower-selling horror out of dust and gravel. Ayama had said Bob had made the hexcode in his mind. How could Bob create something from the hexcode? He wasn't a mighty hacker.

Bob started by fixing the image of a bridge in his mind. He passed the image down the connection between him and Byte. It travelled to Byte as a fizzing ball of energy – and there it stayed, hovering just above Byte.

'What now?' Bob said to himself. 'How do I change this mess of gantries and girders into a bridge?'

He focused on the fizzing ball of energy and willed it to move up the thread that connected Byte to the walkway – it was working! The moment the ball of energy reached the walkway, an almighty shock wave emanated from Byte.

Everyone unfroze, and sure enough, the rickety, precarious metal walkway was no longer there. It had transformed into an ornate Japanese wooden bridge with red guard rails and intricately carved animal heads: a dragon, a bear, a cat and a dog.

'If you're going to create a hexcode bridge, you might as well make it an interesting one,' Bob said to Byte as he stood with his hands on his hips, admiring his work.

Upon seeing the bridge appear, Sunny and the Queen immediately started to make their way across.

'That's cheating!' said the Butcher over the speakers. 'Mama, they're cheating! It's not fair!'

'Deck!' called Sunny.

Deck turned, spotted the passage to safety and swung the handlebars more fervently at the half-dozen horrors that had made it onto the mezzanine platform. He stepped back towards the bridge and then paused. Rather than retreating, he guarded the bridge entrance, ensuring no horrors pursued Sunny and the Queen.

He fought an increasing number, all trying to claw and push towards the bridge, but Deck held his own until the horrors in front of him suddenly parted. Stepping through their ranks, an X marking his cheek, was a massive Butcher Boy. He was solid muscle, with one of those necks that blended seamlessly into the shoulders, and arms so humongous that he couldn't put them down at his sides. The horror had brutal, rusted knuckle dusters embedded into his fists.

Deck quickly checked how Sunny and the Queen were getting on, spotted that they had made it to the other side and threw the handlebars at the massive Butcher Boy. Deck turned and ran as fast as his feet would carry him across the bridge as the Butcher Boy and a wave of horrors followed him.

'Ah, I've just given the horrors a way to cross,' Bob said, suddenly less pleased with his new abilities. 'Deck, get ready to jump!'

Deck, now halfway across, nodded.

'Three … two … one … jump!'

Bob concentrated. Everyone froze.

Deck was in mid-air, leaping for the platform. The Butcher Boy, surprisingly quick for his size, was just a pace behind him and reaching for Deck. A swarm of horrors was behind the Butcher Boy, with zombie-like arms outstretched. Bob fixed another image in his mind, passed the fizzing energy ball to Byte and then down the thread to the ornate Japanese bridge.

Everyone unfroze as the bridge suddenly transformed into thousands and thousands of marbles. The marbles briefly held the bridge shape, then collapsed onto the factory floor with an almighty clatter.

The muscular Butcher Boy and the horrors fell, crying out as they hit the floor hard or dropped onto the unsuspecting horrors below. The marbles continued to clatter and roll everywhere. Some horrors slipped and fell as if they were trying roller skates for the first time.

Deck had made the jump and sat on the platform's edge, catching his breath and smiling at the chaos below.

'Cheaters!' came the Butcher's voice over the speakers. 'Big fat cheaters!'

'Kiss this, Butcher!' Deck gave a nearby speaker the middle finger.

'Raise the other cage, darling,' came Karen's voice.

'Oh yeah!'

The sirens and strobe lights started up again.

The friends shocked themselves into some urgency, realising that the cage on this side of the factory was about to be raised. Most of the horrors were otherwise preoccupied with picking themselves up from the fall or skidding on the marbles, but they would soon regroup for another attack.

Everyone scrambled down the ladder as quickly as possible and exited through the door within the cage, which was rising fast. Sebastian was last through, as he was busy chasing marbles. As the mink slinked through the gap in the door, the first of the horrors appeared.

Bob prepared to slam the door, but a horror grabbed his yellow raincoat. Bob pulled at the raincoat, Byte yapping from the pocket. More horrors grabbed the coat. Deck joined Bob in the tug of war. Bob's feet were skidding, hands aching as he gripped the coat.

Then – he slipped.

The coat, and Byte, disappeared into the sea of horrors. As he slipped and fell, Bob unintentionally kicked the door. It slammed shut.

Byte was gone.

CHAPTER 34
THE BUTCHER SAYS

'Byte! No!' Bob slumped against the door, banging it hard with his fist. The stress of losing Byte rang in his ears. His chest was heaving. 'No! Open the door! Open it!' *I'm supposed to protect him. I failed.*

Deck held his friend. 'They need him, remember? I don't think they'll hurt him. We'll rescue him, just like we'll rescue Hunter. You'll see. It'll be fine.'

Bob didn't really process Deck's words. He couldn't think straight or concentrate on anything but the cold, hard steel of the door as he hammered it again with his fist.

'Will this madness never end?' the Queen said as she inspected the latest room.

They stood on a glittery black-tiled floor. The tiles were large, each with a pink star with the word *Butcher* in the centre, resembling the stars on the Hollywood Walk of Fame. The room was otherwise bare, save for a pedestal with a lever and a control panel at the far end of the room, near another door, made of blackened wood with medieval metalwork. The creepy nursery rhymes continued to play through the speakers. It was 'Humpty Dumpty' again.

The Butcher's voice interrupted the nursery rhyme, ringing

out over the speaker system. 'Welcome, contestants, to the final event in the Butcher's variety performance – the Butcher Says!'

'The Butcher says what?' Deck asked.

Bob stopped banging his fist against the door, turning to his friends. 'In the Archive, it's called Simon Says. If the Butcher says "the Butcher says stand on one leg", you stand on one leg. If he says "stand on one leg" but leaves out "Butcher says", then you do nothing.'

'I'm not doing anything that maniac says,' Deck replied.

A blackened door at the other end of the room opened, and the Butcher walked in. Deck became enraged, balling his fists and running towards the Butcher to exact revenge for Sunny. The Butcher casually stepped forward and pulled the lever. With a loud creak, the middle third of the floor suddenly swung open on hinges, like the bomb doors on an aeroplane. Where there had once been a floor, there was now just a sheer drop down the side of the cliff and onto the jagged rocks below. The gap was too big to jump.

Bob reanimated himself, leaping to his feet and grabbing Deck, worried his friend's anger might prevent him from thinking straight. Deck stopped short of the sheer drop, but Bob kept hold of him anyway as the wind blustered through the trapdoor.

'Come over here, you coward!' Deck shouted.

The Butcher simply grinned, his jaw moving from side to side.

With a rhythmic *clack-clack* of his cane on the tiled floor, the Librarian entered the room, followed closely by Karen.

Karen straightened her *Information Desk Manager* badge and then folded her arms in front of her. 'This farce has gone on too long. It's time for you to die. It's a pity – we wanted to chop you up and mix you together. But you have proved far too trouble-some, and I wouldn't trust any horror made up of bits of you lot. So, Norman can have one more game, and we'll see if you fly.' She giggled.

The Butcher grinned and started hopping from side to side.

'No more games. Release Hunter and let us leave,' the Queen said firmly.

'We're going to play the Butcher Says. Then you leave via the nearest exit,' Karen said, smiling.

'Good one, dear!' the Librarian said.

'Oh, do shut up, Derek.'

The Librarian lowered his eyes, dejected.

The friends all searched for a way out. Clawing and scraping could be heard from the other side of the door they had come through as a gaggle of horrors tried to get in. They couldn't go back out that way. The trapdoor spanned the whole room width; there wasn't a sliver of a foothold to get across. Sebastian was running down the width of the trapdoor, screeching in frustration. Deck attempted to lift the floor back up, but it was too heavy, even when Bob and the Queen stepped in to help.

'Stay still, and let's start!' Karen shouted. 'Norman, begin the game, dear.'

'Yes, Mama!' the Butcher gleefully rubbed his hands together. 'The Butcher says, pat your head!'

The Queen, Bob and Sunny complied and patted their heads, but Deck stood with his arms folded, glaring at the Butcher with contempt.

'He didn't do it, Mama!' The Butcher gleefully pointed at Deck. 'Do I win?'

'Yes, dear, you do. Press the first button.'

The Butcher pressed a button on the panel, and there was a loud beep. Sunny screamed as suddenly two floor tiles fell, spinning down the cliff, crashing into the cliffside and then breaking on the rocks far below.

One of the gaps where a tile had been was directly in front of Bob; he'd been standing on it just moments earlier. Bob glanced back towards the door. Byte. Byte was gone. Maybe falling to his death was what he deserved.

'Aw! I missed them!' the Butcher complained.

'I'm sure you'll get one next time, dear. Keep going.'

'Butcher! Stop this!' Deck shouted, but the Butcher ignored him and kept going.

'The Butcher says, scratch your nose.'

Deck reluctantly joined the others, scratching his nose, but didn't take his eyes off the Butcher.

'Touch your lips!'

'Don't!' Bob said. 'Keep scratching your nose!'

Everyone quickly adjusted and kept scratching their nose.

'Oi! No cheating!' the Butcher complained, going red-faced and stamping up and down. 'Touch your shoulders!'

Everyone now understood the game and kept scratching their nose.

'The Butcher says touch your shoulders!'

Everyone started touching their shoulders.

'Hey, does that count?' the Butcher asked his mother, pointing at Sunny. 'She's only touching one shoulder.'

'Good spot, dear. I agree. You win.'

'No, wait! I've only got one hand. I can't touch both shoulders!'

The Butcher was already reaching for the control panel. There was a loud beep, and four tiles dropped. The Queen was partially on one of the falling tiles and fell to one knee, her leg dangling over the gaping drop. She scrambled to keep from slipping, and Bob and Sunny rushed to help her to her feet.

'Aw! No one died that time either!' the Butcher groaned.

Bob felt very lucky. Six tiles had dropped, and no one had fallen yet. But he knew it was just a matter of time. The Butcher would keep going until the whole floor had given way, and all of them were broken corpses on the rocks below.

The blackened door behind the Butchers suddenly opened, and through it shot Byte. Following Byte was a horror holding Bob's yellow raincoat, trying to corral Byte, as the furball led the lanky horror a merry dance around the tiles. Every time the horror thought he'd caught the pup, Byte disappeared from his grasp.

'Byte!' Bob was glad to see Byte unharmed.

Byte gave a little yip in greeting.

Karen swiftly scooped up Byte, then shoved the lanky horror, who fell down the huge gap in the floor. His cries faded as he fell towards the rocks.

'See, I have to do everything around here. Honestly. We have the dog now, Norman. Hurry up and finish your game.'

The Butcher nodded. 'The Butcher says—'

Suddenly the insistent banging and scraping on the door behind them stopped. They all listened intently. Even the Butcher and his warped parents paused what they were doing and focused on the sudden and unexpected silence. Had the horrors given up trying to break in?

Then came an almighty BOOM! Like a crack of thunder, it shook the walls and reverberated in Bob's chest. The Butchers glanced at one another, unsure of what to do. They weren't expecting the sound. It wasn't of their making.

BOOM!

The sound was closer this time, then another, and another.

BOOM! BOOM!

The noises overlapped – several colossal, thunderous booms that shook the walls. Sections of plaster fell, and the hinges on the trapdoor creaked. Bob and his friends instinctively pressed themselves against the walls and held on.

'Press all the buttons! Do it now!' Karen instructed the Butcher, an uncharacteristic sense of urgency in her voice. Byte growled as she gripped the dog tightly, not allowing him to escape.

'No!' pleaded Sunny as the Butcher gleefully moved towards the control panel.

'Stop! Now!' Deck shouted. He pulled a handgun from his belt and pointed it at the Butcher. He must have taken the gun unnoticed from the warehouse. 'Touch another button, and I'll put one of these bullet things into you!'

'Deck! No!' cried Sunny.

'It's fine, Sunny. I know what I'm doing. He'll kill us. Why shouldn't I kill him first? He deserves to die.'

The Butcher seemed uncertain about what to do, teetering between reaching for the control panel and stepping back towards his mother.

'Press the buttons, darling,' Karen instructed her son. 'Quickly, now. This weak idiot won't do anything.'

Just as the Butcher reached out his hand for the button, there was a tremendously loud, thunderous BOOM! This one struck the door, causing a massive dent. A hexagonal mesh rippled over the surface of the door. The Butcher recoiled at the sound, cowering towards his mother.

'Why do I even bother?' Karen rolled her eyes. 'I have to do everything myself.' She handed Byte to her son.

Another thunderous BOOM! The door bent inwards at the top, and the impact shook the ground. The friends stumbled, unsteady on their feet. Deck dropped the gun as he stumbled, and it slid forward, stopping a couple of tiles ahead of him.

Karen reached the control panel and pressed a button. There was a loud beep. Bob felt the tile beneath his feet give way, and he jumped sideways just in time. The tile he'd been standing on fell and shattered on the rocks below.

No one had fallen, but Karen was determined to remedy that, raising her finger gleefully to press another button.

'No!' shouted Deck as he launched forward to grab the gun.

Karen pressed a button.

Deck, now prone on the ground, lifted the gun and aimed it at Karen.

The Librarian screamed in anger.

Beep.

The tile beneath Deck gave way.

Deck fired the gun.

The Librarian dived in front of Karen.

Deck disappeared from view as he fell through the floor.

The bullet struck the Librarian squarely in the stomach. He crumpled to the floor, writhing in pain.

Sunny screamed.

The thunderous booms shook the factory as the door tore off its hinges and crashed into the room. It skidded on the tiles and plummeted through the trapdoor.

CHAPTER 35
THE DEMOLITION

The Butcher pawed at his dying father while still clinging to Byte. 'Papa!'

Karen calmly looked down at her husband, bleeding out on the floor. The Librarian looked up at his wife, his pleading eyes desperate for her to acknowledge the sacrifice he'd just made. Karen simply gave a disapproving huff and turned back to the control panel, ready to press another button.

'No!' Bob cried out. *I have to do something. I have to stop this madness!*

Everyone froze.

Bob pushed a small, fizzing ball of energy down the thread connecting him to Byte, who was still in the Butcher's arms.

Everyone unfroze.

The shock wave blast that emanated from Byte threw the Butcher away from his father and against the wall, knocking the air from his lungs. As he slid to the floor, he let go of Byte. Byte casually trotted over to Karen and started growling at her.

'You're next if you touch that panel!' Bob shouted across at her.

Karen looked down at Byte, then towards her son crumpled on the floor. She spun on her heel. 'Come on, Norman. Leave your useless father to rot in here with the rest of them.'

The Butcher obeyed his mother, struggling to his feet and reluctantly following Karen through the blackened door. The Librarian coughed up blood as he reached out an arm towards them.

Bob rushed over to join Sunny at the tile Deck had fallen through. He stared down the cliff but couldn't see his friend. It was still dark, and the drop was so far down to the bottom that there was no way of knowing which of the shadows on the rocks below was Deck's body. Bob slumped, tears forming in his eyes.

Sunny let out a cry of pure anguish that echoed down the cliffside. The Queen stood mournfully over them, eyes down, hands folded.

Sebastian was less considerate, making a terrible racket and zipping up and down the floor, but Bob paid him no attention. 'I've failed. I should have helped him. He helped me so many times. I should have been brave.'

Deck had been such a great friend to Bob. Bob knew he wouldn't have made it this far without him. Brave Deck, what would life be like for any of them without him? What—

'Why are you crying, turd sack?'

Bob's eyes widened, and he stood quickly. He dared not look. *It can't be. She's deathless.* Slowly Bob turned his head in the direction of the voice. Sure enough, Ayama was hovering over the trapdoor in the middle of the void, and Deck was balancing precariously on a floating rock next to her. Byte yipped excitedly from the other side of the room.

'I almost let the turd sack fall, but I thought you might be sad, so I saved him. It turns out you were sad anyway, and I shouldn't have bothered.' Ayama pushed the rock Deck stood on towards the friends, and he jumped off. The rock immediately crashed back down the trapdoor.

Sunny fell into Deck's arms and sobbed uncontrollably.

Ayama held out her lollipop staff, and Sebastian jumped onto it, climbed the staff and settled around Ayama's neck. She scratched at his head affectionately.

'Thank you for saving Deck. It's really good to see you, Ayama. How did you get here so fast?'

'We took the bus, of course.'

'We? Where's Titch?'

Bob had barely finished his question when bricks and dust flew across the floor, and a large opening appeared in the wall on the opposite side of the trap door. Titch strode through the new entrance he'd just made. 'Squishy friends!' He beamed, slinging his hammeraxe over his shoulder. 'You did it! You found the reboot!'

Grace appeared from Deck's shirt and made her way onto Deck's shoulder, cocking her head from side to side. Titch spotted her and beamed gleefully. 'Grace! You're okay! I've missed you terribly. Even deathless, I ...' Titch stopped his sentence short, an ashamed expression coming over his face, and he turned his gaze towards the floor.

Bob spun on his heel to see what had caused the reaction.

Two massive builders ducked through the doorway and into the room, followed by a glittering silver bear and a boar with glittering silver tusks. It was Wodenar, the builder king, and the massive, broad-shouldered builder with the plumed porcelain mask.

Ayama hovered backwards to put herself at Titch's side.

'Son,' Wodenar boomed.

'Yes, sir.' Titch fixed his eyes on the floor.

'My hammeraxe. Return it. Now.'

Titch held out the hammeraxe and then realised he couldn't reach his father to return it.

'The lever!' Bob called.

Ayama scanned the room and spotted the lever. She floated over and squeezed the trigger to push it back upright. The trap-door hinges creaked, and the two sections came back together in a loud SLAM.

Byte ran across the remade floor, reuniting with Bob. Bob

scooped up the little furball and then went to recover his yellow raincoat from the floor.

Titch solemnly walked across the remade floor, avoiding the missing tiles, and stepped up to his father. He dropped to one knee and held the hammeraxe out. Wodenar took it from him.

'You're a disgrace. You were a disgrace before all this, but now I find you with my hammeraxe and in the company of hackers and humans.'

Titch remained silent. Ayama did not.

'He helped save you, you ungrateful, pompous, shiny arse wart. If it weren't for him, you would forever be standing still, like the world's ugliest tree, as birds nested on your head and dogs cocked their legs against yours, making you smell marginally better than you do now.' Ayama floated towards Wodenar, pointing her golden lollipop staff.

The massive builder stepped in front of Wodenar as she drew closer. 'Back off, hacker,' the plumed builder boomed.

Wodenar waved his companion back. 'A legless hacker will not lecture me. I'm the King; you will show me respect.'

'I'll respect you when you open your eyes and see your son for the brilliant builder he is. He saved you all, and you scold him?'

'I'm the King, and I do as I see fit. I see the boy I have always seen, a weak coward who runs and hides. He's no builder. He wasn't before, and he isn't now. Taking another's hammeraxe is punishable by death. But … I'll show mercy for the memory of your mother.'

Titch looked at his father with pleading eyes, but Wodenar's face was full of contempt and shame.

'From this moment on, you are no son of mine.' Wodenar turned to leave.

'Wait!' cried Bob. 'Ayama is telling the truth! He did help save you all!'

'Don't speak to me, human. I've no interest in what you have to say.'

Bob stuttered, desperately trying to find the right words to string together to paint a picture of just how amazing Titch had been. *Paint a picture … I could show him!*

Bob concentrated. Everyone froze.

Bob fixed all his memories of Titch, of him fighting the wolf in the alley, helping the rejects during the ambush and fighting the hexbeasts at Angkor Wat. He packaged the memories into a fizzing ball of energy and passed it down the thread connecting him to Wodenar. Just as the ball of energy reached the builder king, Wodenar moved, grasping the energy in his fist and snuffing it out. Everyone unfroze.

'Another hacker. I mistook you for a human. You must be a runt too. *Never* try to do that again.' Wodenar stepped back through the door into the heart of the factory, followed by his hexpet bear. He didn't so much as glance at Titch.

As the massive builder was about to leave, he paused and turned to Bob.

'Pass that to me,' he boomed.

Bob frowned but did as the builder asked. He remade the memory package and passed it down the thread to the massive builder. When everyone unfroze, the builder paused momentarily, nodded at Bob, turned to Titch and gave a low bow before following his king back into the factory.

Titch went down onto both knees and held his hands to his face as Grace scurried across the floor and up onto Titch's vambrace. Bob approached his friend, putting a comforting hand on his shoulder.

Ayama floated beside Titch, her skirt billowing in a circle around her. 'Do not measure yourself by his opinion. He has no idea who you are.'

Whilst Ayama and Bob were comforting Titch, the Queen walked over to the Librarian and crouched over his dying body. She held his hand.

'You have to stop her! She's gone mad!' the Librarian whispered between intermittent coughing.

'Karen?' the Queen asked.

The Librarian nodded.

'You have done many wicked things in the name of love, Librarian,' the Queen said softly.

The Librarian gave a shallow nod.

'We will try to reverse your actions, although I fear it may be too late.' The Queen placed her other hand on the Librarian's forehead.

'You're a kind person. I should have listened to your teachings,' the Librarian whispered.

The Queen smiled kindly at him.

'The boy,' the Librarian said urgently, which made him cough more blood. 'The boy, I lied about him. He's important. Syntax knows of him and wants him dead. I don't know why ...' The Librarian's voice trailed off, and he gasped for air.

'Shh,' the Queen said soothingly. 'Go in peace, Librarian. Go with kindness and with love. We will protect Bob.'

The Librarian took a few shallow breaths and was still. The Queen gently closed his eyes and let go of his hand, placing it on his chest. Bob came over and helped the Queen back up.

She sighed. 'I understand him better, knowing more of who he is. I should have taken the time to do this sooner.'

'Good riddance,' Deck spat, a scowl on his face.

The Queen rounded on Deck. 'Now, Deck, you did this. You killed this man. Whether accidental or not, you held the weapon and pulled the trigger. I thought you had more heart than this, more compassion.'

Deck looked at Sunny for support, but he didn't get it.

'I agree with Her Majesty. This ain't like you, Deck. I want the old Deck back. I want my Deck.'

Deck pulled away from Sunny. 'And I want my old Sunny back too, but I can't have her, because the Butcher took her away from me!'

Sunny pushed her finger hard into Deck's chest, tears welling in her eyes. 'I'm still me, Deck, still Sunny. I'm just a bit cracked around the edges, that's all. But it's nothin' that time and the love of my friends won't heal. But I need my friends. All of them, includin' you. I need my Deck.'

Deck couldn't stay mad with Sunny for long. And what she had said was true. His shoulders dropped, and he turned to look into Sunny's eyes. 'I've been behaving awfully, haven't I?'

The Queen replied, 'I wouldn't say "awfully", no. You have been courageous but also very cross and reckless.'

Sunny nodded in agreement.

'How do I make it up to you? Make it up to all of you?' Deck asked, facing his friends.

'You don't have to make anythin' up to me, Deck. Just be you. I need you, not some angry Deck, seekin' revenge for me.' Sunny stroked Deck's cheek and kissed him tenderly.

BOOM! BOOM!

The room shook with the force of hammeraxe blows that echoed from within the belly of the factory.

'Argh! Those idiot builders are destroying the factory,' Ayama said. 'Enough of this lovey-kissy nonsense. You can cry and kiss each other's butthole when we leave here alive. Now, we need to move.'

'What about Hunter?' Bob asked.

The Queen's eyes widened. 'Oh no! They still have Hunter! We can't leave without him!'

'Another turd sack?' Ayama asked.

Bob nodded.

'We cannot go back. It's too dangerous. The builders will have this place reduced to dust in no time. We'll have to leave without your Hunter.'

'We can't leave him,' Bob said. 'I'll go. I'll get him back and catch up with you.'

He headed for the door that led back into the factory, but just as he was about to cross the threshold, a metal gantry crashed to the floor, throwing up dust and blocking the exit. More metal and rubble piled on top of the gantry.

'When will you turd sacks learn to listen? We leave. Now.'

They had no choice but to abandon any hope of rescuing Hunter and follow Ayama out of the opening in the wall Titch had created earlier.

The opening led to a maze of corridors, side rooms, dead ends and debris-filled passages. It became progressively more treacherous as the builders continued their relentless factory destruction.

'Argh! We'll never get out of this smelly, turd-jigsaw-filled toilet!' Ayama declared as they hit their sixth dead end. 'Why are there no signs?'

Signs! Bob had an idea. Everyone froze.

'*Accessing the Archive. Please wait.*'

'Please, will you show us the way out of the factory? Like you did with the signs when the wolves chased me?'

'*Affirmative.*'

Bob then indulgently chose some music. If he was going to get buried alive, he would go out listening to something awesome.

'*Access complete. Returning to the Zoo. Please wait.*'

Everyone unfroze.

A sign suddenly materialised, and *We've Gotta Get out of This Place* started playing. The sign displayed the word EXIT with an arrow illuminated in flashing neon pink.

'Follow the signs,' Bob instructed. 'Sunny, you lead the way. More will appear. Just follow them.'

Sunny nodded, grabbed Deck's hand and confidently led everyone down a fork in the corridor.

The signs continued to appear. Everyone was now running and ducking out of the way of falling debris. At one point, the corridor collapsed behind them just as they ran past.

Finally they arrived at a door with a frosted, leaded glass window similar to the one for the 'office'. Two of the Archive's neon signs pointed directly at the door. The Archive then high-lighted the door with a neon-pink flashing border. Then the border and the signs disappeared. On the door was a yellowing embossed plaque that read SELECTION.

'Well, this must be it.' Bob reached for the handle.

CRASH!

The floor shook, and the ceiling above their heads caved in.

Click.

CHAPTER 36
THE SELECTION ROOM

'Quickly!' Ayama shouted.

She'd created a hexagon mesh shield around the party, protecting them from being buried in the ceiling collapse. Only the space they stood in and the doorway were intact.

Bob breathed a sigh of relief that he was back in the company of the powerful hacker, and he quickly opened the door, ushering his friends through first. Once everyone else was through, Bob turned to help Ayama.

'Ready?' Bob asked Ayama as he grabbed her arm and the door frame.

She nodded.

'Three, two, one.' Bob pulled Ayama through the door as she simultaneously disconnected her staff from the interface. The rubble tumbled into the space in front of the door as Ayama and Bob fell backwards into the room.

The room they found themselves in was semicircular. The door was on the flat wall. Built into the curved wall were two of the metal void vents. It was otherwise empty. Above each of the vents was a yellowed sign. They read *Storage* and *The Zoo*.

'Well, I, for one, would like to go home,' the Queen said.

Sunny and Deck agreed as they headed for the vent with *The Zoo* written above it.

The Queen paused when she reached the vent. 'Is it safe?' she asked Ayama.

There was a loud crash as something else collapsed somewhere within the factory.

'Safer than here. Go!' Ayama insisted.

Reluctantly the Queen took a deep breath and plunged into the black void with the pinprick holes of light. Sunny went next, and Deck made to follow. He turned towards Bob. 'Are you going to be okay?'

Bob nodded. He was going to be okay. At the start of this adventure, Bob would have needed Deck to stay or help him muster the courage to plunge into the void. But now he was okay. 'Yes, I'll be fine. You go.'

Deck disappeared down the vent, keen to follow and ensure Sunny was safe at the end of whatever this thing was.

'What about you, Titch? You can't fit down the vent.'

Titch chuckled. 'It's okay, Squishy Bob. I'll make it out with Ayama's help.'

Ayama nodded in agreement. 'This is also a bus. Come with us, or go the same way as the crying turds. Either will work.'

Bob didn't fancy the nauseating bus journey, so he opted for the vent. 'Ready, Byte?' Bob asked the little furball, who was poking his head and paws out of the raincoat pocket. Byte gave a yip in acknowledgement as Bob put his legs into the vent, ready to slide down. 'Thank you again for coming to save us.'

'You saved us, Squishy Bob. We'll talk more later. We'll meet again in the Zoo.'

Bob nodded and pushed himself down the vent into the void. As he did, there was the sound of metal hitting metal.

———

Bob landed in a straw-filled trough in a barn made of weathered wooden boards. It was the same barn he'd arrived in the first time he'd come to the Zoo, with eight mirrors along the walls, four on either side. Bob instinctively eyed the one he'd glanced into the first time he'd come to the barn.

The Queen, Deck and Sunny were milling around the barn, waiting for Bob. Byte exited the trough as he had before, gracefully jumping onto the edge and onto the floor. He then busied himself by sniffing around and inspecting the barn.

Bob made the same exit he had before, clumsily wading through the straw and falling down the small steps, landing at Deck's feet. His friend helped him up.

They all made their way down the barn and towards the doors. On the way, Bob stopped in front of the mirror he'd looked in the first time he'd come to the barn. He looked at his reflection differently this time. It was the same boy, the same mop of unruly brown curls, the same oversized yellow raincoat and hand-me-down clothes. But this time, the boy he saw wasn't unremarkable and ordinary. This boy had been on adventures. This boy had found friends. This boy could be brave, could be someone to somebody.

Byte interrupted Bob's reflection on his reflection with a friendly yip, tongue lolling as he sat beside him.

'Don't worry. I'm coming.' He set off to join his friends at the barn doors.

The Queen smiled in childlike anticipation, and then, using only her little finger, she pushed the brace on the barn door upwards. It floated away into the wooden pelmet above the door, prompting a little clap of glee from the Queen. 'It's one of my finest!'

'But why brace the doors?' Bob asked.

'Just to create a bit of theatre. Opening the doors to paradise is a great way to do that, don't you think?'

'Well, let's open those doors again, then,' Deck said as he pushed the doors open, and they walked out into the glade.

Two figures were waiting for them. It was Titch and Ayama. The visage of the glade wasn't as perfect as it had been the first time. The sky was dull and grey, threatening rain, which gave the glade a gloomy, autumnal palette.

'I fear the Zoo I know may have changed forever,' the Queen said, staring at the sky and hugging herself to ward off the cold.

———

The sun had already set when they reached the Lookout. Ayama guided everyone through the last part of the journey using her lollipop staff as a torch.

They wearily made a fire and then huddled around it on the benches, trying to warm themselves against the cold night air. They recounted the odd story from their adventures, and Bob played some quiet, peaceful music from the Archive.

As the others were talking, Bob took the opportunity to sidle up to Ayama, out of earshot of the others. 'May I ask you something?'

'Sure. I might not answer, though,' Ayama quipped with a sly smile.

'Who am I? I didn't get a chance to find out in the factory.'

'You are you.'

'I mean, I don't remember where I came from, and I'm unsure if I'm a human, a hacker or something else. Who is Bob? Am I just B-O-B, the dog walker?'

Ayama screwed up her face at the 'dog walker' comment. 'I told you, you are you. Who cares who you were before or what type of turd sack you are?'

'I do. I care,' Bob retorted, exasperated by Ayama dodging the question.

Ayama's expression softened, and she leaned into Bob. 'When we first met, you told me your story. Did you leave anything out? Was there a bit before the Zoo, maybe? Somewhere very white?'

Bob frowned. How did she know about the white-tiled space? 'Yes,' Bob admitted. 'A white space with a tiled floor. It was endless and quite disorientating.'

Ayama hid her concern well, but Bob spotted it in her eyes as he spoke.

'What does it mean?' he asked.

Ayama sighed, clearly resigning herself to telling him the truth. 'The white-tiled space is a factory. There's only one like it. It's the factory where controllers are made. You cannot remember anything before the factory, as there's nothing to remember. It's where you were made.' Ayama paused, letting the information sink in. 'I don't know what sort of controller you are, though. You're human, but also you're not. You're System, but also you're not. Maybe it broke or something. I renamed you BitBob, as you are both. Or neither, depending on your perspective, I suppose.' Ayama shrugged. 'But my point remains: you are you. Whatever factory spat you out, who you are remains entirely up to you.' She sat back, punctuating her conclusion.

'But what about the old factory? And how come I ended up in the Zoo?'

'Argh! It's not the science of rockets! The old factory is the human factory. It's referred to as old simply because it hasn't been in use since Bacchus died. Humans were created in the factory and spat out into the Zoo or into Storage. You saw the bus routes in the selection room. I suppose these organics will have to return to the old-fashioned way if they want to create more humans. Gross. The Butcher moved in to use the factory's creation capability to animate the horrors. Also gross. Hopefully, whatever technology he used was destroyed when the builders levelled the place.'

Bob sat in stunned silence, his hand in his raincoat pocket, stroking Byte. He felt his blue inhaler and instinctively pulled it out to take a puff.

Ayama sat back up. 'Give me that!' She snatched the inhaler from Bob.

'Hey, I need that for my asthma!'

'You don't have asthma, you idiot. You're a controller.' Ayama turned the inhaler in her hands. 'Interesting. Very interesting ...'

Bob was intrigued. 'What's interesting?'

'It's a portable charger. This thing gave you a small amount of recharge every time you used it. I've never seen anything like it before. More mysteries.' She tossed the inhaler-charger back to Bob.

'One other thing I can't explain,' Bob said. 'Is why Grace and Sebastian didn't become deathless at Angkor Wat. When we saw all the builders, their hexpets were motionless.'

'Hexpets are independent creatures,' Ayama explained. 'They can hold charge for far longer than any hacker or builder. The builders hexpets stayed with their masters and eventually ran out of charge. Sebastian intended to do the same before he changed his mind. Fickle creature that one.' Ayama nodded in Sebastian's direction as he played with Byte. Then they both drifted back into the main conversation with the others.

Eventually, everyone warmed up enough to sleep and recharge. In the morning, they readied themselves to make the walk to town.

Sunny and Deck sheepishly stepped up to the Queen. They were holding hands.

'Your Majesty?'

'Yes, Sunny?'

'Me and Deck was wonderin' somethin', but we wanted your permission.'

Bob eavesdropped on the conversation whilst pretending to poke the remnants of the fire.

'We want to camp here another night. Just me and Deck, if that's okay. We'll collect some food and bring it along tomorrow. What do you think?' Sunny was shuffling her feet, a hopeful expression on her face.

The Queen smiled at both of them and clasped her hands

over theirs. 'Of course it's okay. You two need some time alone together. It is a wonderful idea! We will see you both tomorrow.'

Sunny beamed at the Queen with one of her beautiful smiles and gave Deck an even bigger smile. Bob had a little smile of his own. He wanted them both to be happy, and they were only truly happy when they were together. Seeing Sunny hurt and then Deck struggling to contain himself in the House of Horrors had been hard. They needed time to mend, time just to be Sunny and Deck.

———

As they walked away from the Lookout, waving farewell to Deck and Sunny, the Queen turned to Bob. 'You know, I have long thought that the only thing anyone ever needs is a Sunny Day and a Deck Chair. Don't you agree?'

Bob smiled at the analogy and nodded in agreement.

Everyone walked and talked on the way back to town. Ayama and the Queen ended up having a long chat with each other about life, humans and hackers. At various points, Bob almost believed Ayama was being friendly with the Queen – she broke her usual frown more than once, although it never quite turned into a smile.

The threatened rain never materialised, and the sun started peeking through the clouds just as they emerged from the wood atop the hill. Bob surveyed the scene, spotting the stream with the little bridge and the round houses. Most houses were missing their canvas doors, and some had big holes in the canvas roofs. Bob pointed this out to the Queen, who was concerned and wanted to reach the town hall as quickly as possible.

They made their way over the small bridge, which disconcertingly creaked as Titch crossed, but it held. The first person they met was Chip Butty, pulling weeds from a patch of carrots in his garden. He was wearing a simple purple tunic tied with a red belt. *That explains the missing doors and sections of roofs,* Bob thought.

'Hello, Chip,' the Queen said in greeting, leaning on the fence of Chip's house.

Chip jumped out of his skin and turned quickly. Once he set eyes on the Queen, now quite different from how he remembered her, and then Titch and Ayama, Chip fell backwards in shock. He stuttered, trying to get his words out.

'It's okay, Chip. These are Bob's friends. I'll explain all this later. Now, I need you to run ahead and gather everyone into the town hall. Can you do that for me?'

Chip stayed in the middle of his patch of carrots, staring in wide-eyed shock.

'Well, go on, then. Quickly, now.'

Chip scrambled to his feet and ran off down the path.

Ayama smirked at the reaction.

'Let's meander to the town hall to give Chip time to get everyone together,' the Queen suggested as she linked arms with Bob and strolled towards the centre of town.

They rounded the hill, where the path widened as it worked its way towards the town hall. The Queen gasped as she took in the scene. Bob knew what had caused her reaction. Behind the town hall, between the hills, was ... nothing, no firewall. The reboot had removed it. The Town was no longer safe from the rest of the System.

Chip must have passed on the message, as a cluster of people filed into the town hall. They were all wearing different-coloured clothes made from the fabric doors and roofs. Bob thought they resembled a rainbow of ants scurrying into a nest.

The Queen took a long breath. 'I do hope they accept me.'

'They did that a long time ago. You're still their queen, and they need you now more than ever. If they don't accept you, Titch will squish them,' Bob said with a wink.

Titch nodded in agreement at the proposal.

'I'll stand at your side, if you like, for support,' Bob said.

'Thank you for your kind words, Bob. I would like that very much.'

They all made their way towards the town hall, with the Queen leading the way.

CHAPTER 37
DAWN

Sunny and Deck lay on the grass, watching the brightening horizon. The day and night they had spent together at the Lookout had been magical. They had eaten, laughed, talked, sung songs and danced. As soon as the dawn made way for the sunrise, it would be over, and they would make their way back to the Town to join the others. But for now, they only needed to hold hands and witness the dawn of a new day.

Sunny turned and beamed at Deck. 'Do you know what, Deck?'

'What?' he asked, turning his head towards her.

'I love you.'

'Do you know what, Sunny?'

'What?' she asked.

'I love you too.'

Saying it out loud was amazing, but it wasn't anything either of them hadn't already known.

Deck sighed. 'I suppose we should head back soon.'

'Please, not yet. Can we stay here a bit longer?'

'Definitely.'

They both turned back towards the horizon.

'Ah, young love. I remember it well,' said a voice.

Sunny and Deck were startled, standing quickly to face the person invading their peace.

'It's a shame you won't live to grow old and bitter together, but oh well, my dears. That's how this story has to end.' Karen calmly stood in the clearing of the Lookout, flanked by two Butcher Boys. She was pointing a gun at them.

'This is for Derek.' She pulled the trigger.

Deck recoiled as the bullet hit his chest.

She pulled the trigger again.

Deck crumpled to the ground as the second bullet hit his shoulder.

Sunny screamed.

'I'll leave you with a fate worse than death, pretty girl. Never cross my family. We'll always be stronger than you.' Karen glanced at her watch. 'Goodness, is that the time? I must be off. It was nice visiting, but a cup of tea wouldn't go amiss next time.' She giggled, turned on her heel and left the Lookout.

Sunny held her love as the last breaths of life left his body.

CHAPTER 38
THE PYRE

A funeral pyre sat on the Lookout platform. Atop the pyre rested Deck's body. The entire town had gathered, filling the clearing and spilling down the slope of the hill.

The Queen stood before the pyre, her arms folded as she addressed the gathering mourners. 'We gather here today to say goodbye to Deck. Deck meant so much to so many of us, and his passing has sent a shock wave through our community. We will mourn his death and celebrate his life. I would like to invite those closest to Deck to say a few words. Sunny?'

Sunny stood at the front of the assembled townsfolk in the clearing, her skin pallid. Since stumbling back to town and hauntingly recounting what had occurred, she'd remained silent, merely staring vacantly, emotionless and empty.

Sunny shook her head, declining to speak.

The Queen nodded with sympathetic understanding. 'Bob?'

Bob had led the group that had recovered Deck's body. He'd wept often, experienced profound anger and tried to comprehend what life would be like without Deck. Bob stepped forward. He'd thought long and hard about what he wanted to say.

'Deck and Sunny were the first people I ever met. I was lost and afraid when I first met Deck outside the barn. I had no idea who I was or where I was. The more time I spent with Deck, the more I saw his bravery and kindness. He consistently stepped up to rescue me without hesitation. The first time was on this very hill. Back then, neither of us knew what adventures we had in front of us. On those adventures, Deck taught me that who I was was less important than who I was with. Where I belonged was with my friends, with Deck. Thanks to Deck, I'm no longer worried about who I am; I'm excited about who I can become. Rest, Deck, and know that your friends love you.'

Titch brushed away a tear from his eye. The entire clearing was welling up, except for Sunny, who stared vacantly at the pyre.

After a few more heartfelt words from those who had known Deck well, the Queen descended the steps of the Lookout and was handed a flaming torch to light the pyre.

'Sunny?' the Queen asked, holding the torch towards her, hoping she would take it.

Much to the Queen's relief, Sunny took the torch and slowly made her way up the Lookout steps.

She stroked Deck's hair as she set the pyre ablaze. Then she slowly walked back down the steps, standing perilously close to the burning Lookout. As the pyre crackled and burned, Sunny began to sing.

My friends are in my heart;
My heart is with my friends.
I love and laugh and smile and sing,
Because my friends are everything.

If I die, and all is lost,
My life has been so full,
That my loss cannot be felt,
Because my friends are everything.

It was the song she'd sung the night they had camped at the Lookout. Then, it had been beautiful. Now, it was haunting.

When Sunny finished singing, the Queen spoke. 'It is with a heavy heart that we say goodbye to Deck. May the tree guide him to his next life, and may kindness guide us now he is gone.'

'Not me,' Sunny said softly.

'Sunny?' the Queen asked.

'I ain't actin' in no kindness, Your Majesty. I'm gonna find that woman and tear her heart out with my bare hand. The Butcher will be next. I ain't restin' until they ain't breathin'.'

Bob knew Sunny meant it. Out of respect, the Queen didn't challenge her. Now was not the time. 'Bob, will you play something?' the Queen asked.

Bob nodded. He concentrated. Everyone froze, and he accessed the Archive. He knew the song he wanted to play. Everyone unfroze, and *Nuvole Bianche* started playing. It was a song that reflected the pain in Bob's heart. He cried as Deck's body burned.

The pyre's fire died down, and the crowd slowly and mournfully left the Lookout, returning to town. The friends held back, waiting for Sunny, who hadn't moved a muscle.

The Queen approached her and put a supportive hand on her shoulder. 'It's time to head back, Sunny.'

Sunny shook her head. 'Leave me here, please. I want to be alone with Deck for a bit longer.'

The Queen agreed, but only after stationing several volunteers from the Town around the base of the Lookout, with strict instructions only to move once Sunny was ready to leave. The Queen had no problem recruiting volunteers, as Sunny's nursing skills had saved many townsfolk, and they all loved her dearly. She would be safe whilst she mourned.

————

Bob walked back to the Town with the Queen, Titch and Ayama. Byte and Sebastian played with each other a few paces ahead. It served as a welcome distraction.

'What will you do now?' Bob asked the Queen.

'I don't know, to be honest. Try to stay safe?'

'Titch and I will build some defences for the Town before we leave,' Ayama said. 'We'll make them strong. The Town will need to change, though. Many will come seeking the comforts of this valley. Not all of them will be friendly.'

'Thank you, both. That is kind.'

'You're leaving?' Bob asked Ayama. He had known deep down they would not stay in the Town.

'Yes, BitBob. The reboot opened up old wounds. We must try to fix them.'

'Are you coming with us, Squishy Bob?'

'I always thought I'd end up back here, back in the safety of the Zoo. Deck was building me a house. But I suppose there is no safety and comfort any more.'

'It's up to you. But know that if you stay, the danger will come to find you. You might as well keep facing it head-on, and a mighty controller on our side when we face fate would be handy.'

Bob had learned he was strong enough to deal with whatever would come next and knew he wanted to face the future with his friends. Deep down, he'd made up his mind.

'I'll join you.'

EPILOGUE

Who he'd been and the life he'd led before the pain seemed distant, like a dream – or a nightmare. What had his name been again? Hunter, was it? None of that mattered now. Only the pain remained. He'd stopped screaming weeks ago.

He'd stopped screaming because he'd suffered for so long it was normal now. His new world was one of unrelenting pain and suffering, and he had broken, succumbed to his new reality and his master.

Why had those people not saved him? Why had they left him with the master? How could they do that to someone? He hated them. It was their fault he was in pain.

Karen strolled over to the large table in the large dining room and inspected the creation her son was making. She sipped tea from a fine china cup, her little finger pointed in the air. 'How's it going, Norman, dear? Having fun?'

'He's better than Nightmare, Mama! I've almost finished!'

Karen popped her teacup down on a precariously stacked pile of newspapers that wobbled, threatening to topple over. She inspected the creation closely. 'Well done, darling. I agree. It is your best one yet. What's it called?'

'Derek! After Papa.'

'That's a terrible name, darling. No, no, this one deserves a much better name than that. Let me think.' Karen paced up and down, tapping the arm of her spectacles on her chin. 'Ah! What about "Macabre"?'

'Yes, Mama!'

Karen leaned into her son's new creation. 'Hello, Macabre. You're one of us now. Welcome to the family.'

The horror's lips trembled. 'M … M … Ma … Macabre.'

Karen giggled. 'Yes, this will do nicely. Now, Macabre, how would you like to go on a little hunt?'

You choose the soundtrack to this story. What did you choose? Share on social and tag:

@bitbob.official

Chapter 4: A song for a campfire
Chapter 8: A song for a feast
Chapter 8: A song for a festive dance
Chapter 9: A song for the lynch mob
Chapter 14: A song for a giant dance
Chapter 16: A song to cheer up rejects
Chapter 18: A song to impress a guide
Chapter 21: A song for an unusual place
Chapter 22: A song for smashing morons
Chapter 22: A song for more smashing
Chapter 22: A song for resigning to fate
Chapter 28: A song with an animal theme
Chapter 28: A song to fight to
Chapter 29: A song for a ball game
Chapter 35: A song for dead ends
Chapter 38: A song for the pyre

ACKNOWLEDGMENTS

Thank you to everyone who contributed to making this idea in my head turn into an actual book.

Firstly, thank you, Lance Corporal Richard Jones (yes, the magic guy who won Britain's Got Talent). You gave an after-dinner speech on reaching your goals at a conference I attended. It gave me the courage to sit down and try to write a book, even though I had no clue how to start.

To my amazing family, Celine, Amaya, and Xander, your love and kindness are the themes of my life and stories.

To my beta readers: my Mum, Dad, and mother in law Anita - who will single-handedly destroy anyone who doesn't think this is the greatest story ever written - and special thanks to Heena and Rowell, who were kind enough to read an early draft and give me feedback.

Finally, thank you to the immense talents of Fiona McLaren (developmental edit) and Leonora Stewart (copy edit) for turning my story into something readable.

ABOUT THE AUTHOR

A.J. Bywater is an emerging author of young adult fantasy fiction adventures. BitBob - Artificial Earth is A.J.'s first book, but certainly not his last.

His home is in a sleepy corner of West Yorkshire, England, where he lives with his wife, Celine, and two children, Amaya and Xander.

In addition to being a self-confessed computer nerd, A.J. is a big LA Clippers fan (sorry, Lakers fans) and can often be heard murdering 90s grunge riffs on his guitar.

For enquiries email: bitbob.official@gmail.com

tiktok.com/@bitbob.official